POWERS OF THE GOLD SERVICE

A SCI-FI ACTION ADVENTURE

THE CAPITAL ADVENTURES
BOOK 6

ALLEN IVERS

Illustrations © Tom Edwards
TomEdwardsDesign.com

For my Family—
They have kept my head above water this past year, and I couldn't do
this without them.

CONTENTS

FOREWORD

This is the third book in *The Gold Service* trilogy—if you haven't read the others you'll want to stop here and go find the previous books before continuing.

This series contains the following content matter:

- *Graphic Violence & Traumatic Injuries*
  - *Admittedly, this book is probably the least graphic but we've still got stabbing, gun shots, neck snaps, several guys getting pancaked, and one mulching.*
- *Occasional Foul Language*
  - *People swear when this stuff happens*
- *Alcohol & Drug Use*
  - *Underage Drinking, Mind Altering Substances*
- *Reference to Sexual Activity*
  - *Dialog references, no depictions*
- *Religious Trauma/Conversion Therapy*
  - *Electroshock torture and isolation*

We're here to have a good time with characters we love. If any of this material distresses you, it's okay to grab another book instead.

Hope you enjoy!

MAP & CHRONOLOGY

The Solar Imperium, also called the Gnostic Empire by the more faithful citizenry, stretches over a fifth of the Milky Way Galaxy. This map features the primary locations featured in the series thus far.

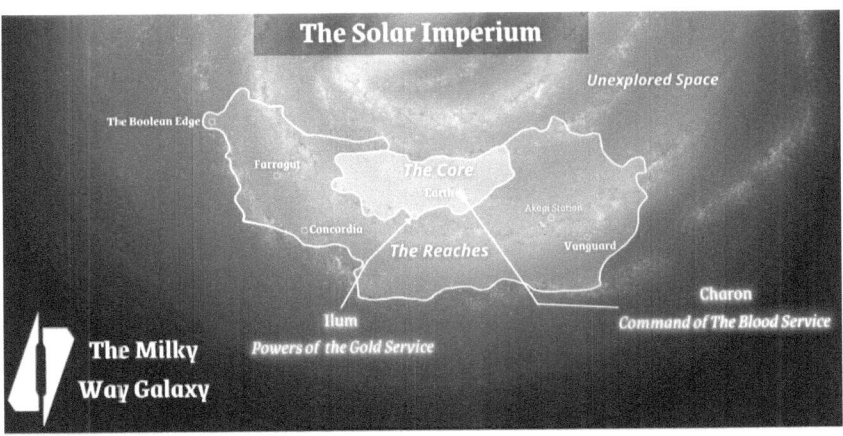

| Map of Solar Imperium controlled space, 2241 CE

The events of the Capital Adventures occur entirely within these borders. Events from one book may be mentioned in another, or characters may cross over from one trilogy to another. Think of it as a shared universe, with the individual stories having unique tones and flair, while building an overarching plot.

You may enjoy each trilogy independent of the others—and I've meticulously built them so that your enjoyment is not contingent on having read the others! But if you want the full experience of the Capital Adventures, I do encourage you to pick up the other books to get a full sense of the Imperium's reach. The official reading order would be to read the trilogies starting with The Blood Service, then The Gold Service, and finishing out with the upcoming Iron Service.

If you're like me, however, and you were looking to read the novels in chronological order, the events of all nine books are as follows:

———

1) THE GOLD SERVICE
2) THE BLOOD SERVICE
3) THE IRON SERVICE

4) RANKS OF THE BLOOD SERVICE
5) COST OF THE GOLD SERVICE
6) SWORDS OF THE IRON SERVICE (COMING SOON)

7) COMMAND OF THE BLOOD SERVICE
8) SHARDS OF THE IRON SERVICE (COMING SOON)
9) POWERS OF THE GOLD SERVICE

WITH EVEN MORE TO COME...

The Gold Service Trilogy has a lighter tone than the other two trilogies of this series, with a strong found-family of mercenaries and malcontents that all share a single brain cell, while also confronting both religious & generational trauma. These characters have become a second family to me, and I hope they do the same for you.

"If there are gods and they are just, then they will not care how devout you have been, but will welcome you based on the virtues you have lived by.

If there are gods, but unjust, then you should not want to worship them.

If there are no gods, then you will be gone, but will have lived a noble life that will live on in the memories of your loved ones."

MARCUS AURELIUS

PART ONE
FILIAL OBLIGATIONS

You would know them by their Touch, the way each could warp the world around them. Those Touched by the Pilgrim extended far beyond the constraints of the Sojourn. Some of those Touched did so with feats of great Power, and some simply with great and indomitable Will.

But each of them acting in accordance with the Pilgrim, laying the stones for the Path.

GNOSTIC LIBRUM, COLONIAL 3:9-12

CHAPTER 1
BROGAN
AGE: 10

WOODCRAFT WAS a delicate affair for even the most practiced hands these days. Genuine wood was such a rare material to have that mistakes could cost more in material than some people were worth. His instructors had stressed it over and over that accurate measurements could save thousands in damage.

Brogan had always been good at sculpture. His mother said so. But she hadn't said so lately.

It was because of the mirror he'd broken last week. Even though she'd replaced the glass, Brogan knew he'd broken far more than a family heirloom.

His mother had been distant, sour, ever since. He knew why—the mirror had belonged to her mother, and her mother before, going back several generations, back to when glass had been handmade by silversmiths on the family farm. Pennsylvania, she had called it. He had never heard of that moon before. Maybe it had been lost. He lost things in his room all the time. Maybe the Empire had misplaced it.

Mother had told him many stories of the family mirror and the family they could see reflected back through the silver.

He had looked and looked, but he saw nothing but his own face.

Mother had warned him many times to take care when playing in the loft. And he had promised he would.

One mistake. The ball slipped out of his hand, that's all. And the crash of glass seemed like it would never stop, until finally, the burden of the heaviest guilty silence.

She had told him to be careful. He had promised her he would. And now he could still hear the tinkling of broken things whenever he tried to sleep, playing over and over in his head. He had made a promise, and promises were important.

The Replicators had repaired it that evening when she got home, the many shards of crystal made completely whole again in a matter of minutes, mended like a magic spell. Despite that, she was still sad, staring into the sky night after night, sullen and quiet. If he hadn't broken it, he was sure she would be happier again.

Now, he couldn't make it un-happen; he knew that much. But he might do something else.

So Brogan resolved to make her something new. He'd been working for weeks, turning a piece of wood on a spindle with a chisel, and hiding his scraps in the furnace. It was coming along nicely, a perfectly polished sphere of purplewood with artistic etching and a matching cradle. She'd shown him the design years ago, one of her first archaeological finds—and he thought he could give her a decent enough replica.

It wasn't properly done, of course, but if she caught him at this stage, it would still make a glorious gift. Which is why it broke his heart when this broke, too.

The door of his room shook on its hinge, lashing against the steel frame like there was some kind of angry beast in the next room. Startled, Brogan spun at the waist—knocking his delicate sculpture to the floor with a crash.

Brogan clapped a hand firm across his mouth, trying to hold his scream inside.

But the door had heard the racket. It heard his little voice. And the steel panel tilted open.

Outlined in the door was a firm man, so broad at the shoulder that the epaulets on his uniform brushed against the frame. The light from the living room outside peeked past him like pillars of white—almost masking the glint of yellow in the man's eye, like a speck of gold.

Brogan never saw him move. But in the time it took for Brogan to gasp, the man suddenly stood behind him, hot fingers laid at the back of Brogan's neck, pressing him forward. Not urgently or even aggressively, but there was no resisting him.

Were they here about the mirror? He was working on his apology. But the Yellow-Eyed Man hadn't said a word, no brief introduction or a breath of life.

Brogan had a story-book that said the Pilgrim breathed life into the outer colonies, healed the sick and built up humanity anew. The Pilgrim must've forgotten to finish building the man that led Brogan right now; his hand was so hot, he had to be feverish.

The Yellow-Eyed Man pushed Brogan out into the living room. It was a big vaulted space that Brogan liked to spend summers in. A wide pane of glass laid at an angle all the way up to the roof, covering the living room and his mother's loft bedroom above—but Mother had toggled the courtesy veil, darkening the glass so that no one may look inside.

Brogan could still see the rain pattering against their building, individual gentle rivers sliding down the glass to the ground ten stories below.

Mother sat on the couch, starched and formal, legs crossed and hands folded. Her stiff lip and tilted chin sent alarm bells through Brogan's marrow. That tension, that stillness. She'd looked like that when he'd broken the mirror.

Her eyes flitted over to him, flashing a momentary squint of panic. But she didn't move a muscle as the Yellow-Eyed Man led Brogan over towards her. Someone else demanded her attention, and even Brogan couldn't draw her right now.

He heard that someone speak long before he saw him, a brisk and clear tone that made Brogan's skin want to crawl right off of his bones. It was the voice of disappointment. "You don't need to make this into a protest, Catharina."

He sat behind his mother's big spiky houseplant that she always told him not to touch. But Brogan could see his finely polished shoes, like black glass.

Mother spoke to the stranger, but her eyes were locked on Brogan. "We all know how much the Ministry detests protest, don't we?"

"We're also none too fond of theatrics," the man said, a gloved hand coming into view as it rested on the arm of his chair. "So you can dispense with the foreplay. I'm not an unreasonable man; this is a negotiation. What do you want?"

"A negotiation?" Catharina whispered, breathless. But for all the rage steaming within her, she held her stance. "You hold my *son* and the word 'negotiation' left your mouth without irony?"

"Mother!" he cried out.

"Brogan," she hushed him.

The mystery man shrugged, and Brogan caught a glimpse of the Imperial orchid tattooed under his square jawline. "You have your tokens. I have mine. Currency is not the only method of transaction."

The Yellow-Eyed Man squeezed the back of Brogan's neck. Catharina didn't miss that, her head tilting slightly. "What do *you* want, Gaius?"

The stranger leaned forward, his gloved hands meeting to cradle his head. And Brogan finally saw his face—a man of refinement, with an almost plastic complexion. His eyebrows and cheeks seemed to follow the words like an afterthought, matching the intent of the speech only after an awkward silence. "A denouncement. Specifically noting errors within the recording process that undermines the validity of the findings."

"You know it's true. Every word of it."

"I'm not in the business of defining what's true," Gaius said. "Only what isn't."

"Mother, please—"

"Be silent." Catharina straightened up, finally tearing her eyes away from Brogan. Her steel robbed Brogan of something, like he'd never feel her warmth again. "And if I say 'no?'"

"You won't. I'm a careful and considerate negotiator."

Brogan couldn't turn his head with the thumb burning into his collarbone, but he could glance down at the fingers. Yellow Eyes wore matte gray with a flash of black underneath the cuff, and there was a thin line running up the rough backside of his hand—surgical scarring.

"Your son and yourself go free." Gaius began his offer in between sips from a cup of iced coffee. "There'll be minor charges, but nothing public."

"Nothing public," Mother scoffed, looking at Yellow Eyes. "That man keeps bigger secrets than you or I can dream of."

"And you get a nice little bonus?" Catharina asked, her voice shaking.

Gaius sat back in his chair. "When you and I are finished here, I will be Section Chief of Ilum Peace, and after a term of service, you will be back at the Royal Arts like nothing happened. Everyone wins, Cat."

"The dig site?" Catharina asked. "All of our samples?"

"They're categorized, indexed," Gaius said casually. "We simply collect them for further study and...they're lost in transit. Piracy is rampant in this sector. The Sunset Line is notoriously riddled with gangs and organized crime."

"So tragedy strikes," Catharina concluded.

"If you can call it that. Artifacts of this sort have a tidy black-market appeal. It'll be my first action on the job to seek out and reclaim them."

"Which makes them evidence of a crime lost forever in your archives. Well maneuvered." Catharina glanced over at her son, and she lingered on him. And Brogan wanted to apologize for the mirror.

He didn't know it would bring all this trouble. But she just smiled at him. "This is an awfully kind gesture, Gaius."

The Ministry official shrugged. "You've an exceptional mind, Catharina. Your work in Pilgrim archaeology is beyond compare. I don't think that's in question." And his relaxed stance suddenly hardened, coming to an icy composure. "Only your loyalties."

"There's no recording of this meeting?"

"Just the ears of the people in this room," Gaius assured her.

Catharina sighed. And tilted her head up square with him. "Then I hope you don't mind me saying that we have found that the Dunsweir have been lying to us for decades—"

Brogan fell forward, as the Yellow-Eyed Man surged at Catharina, that stiff hand tight around her throat before Brogan hit the ground. He squeezed, stopping any more treasonous words from escaping.

But Gaius leapt from his chair, the feet squeaking against the floor as it kicked backward. "Wait, Isaac!"

The Yellow-Eyed Man paused as Catharina flailed, peeling at his choking fingers with both her hands. Brogan looked up to see his mother's feet kicking in the air.

"I enforce the law," Gaius said, nodding at the Yellow-Eyed Man. "But he enforces doctrine. I can't protect you if you insist on heresy. The Dunsweir are the Pilgrim's anointed, and he will preserve that."

Everyone was so mad. Brogan's breath hitched in his throat, choking him.

Catharina hung from Yellow's grip, worming her fingers in to take the pressure off her neck. While she couldn't speak, the defiance never left her eyes, staring back at Gaius with a kind of disgust.

Gaius studied her expression for any cracks and sighed. "You'll see things my way...given enough time."

"I'm sorry!" Brogan shouted. "I'm sorry, please!"

"This doesn't concern you, child," Gaius said, moving for the door.

Brogan balled up his fists, trying to push out his apology as hard as he could. "Please! I know I broke it, but I didn't mean to! Please!"

Gaius didn't stop, and the Yellow-Eyed Man dragged Catharina towards the door. "She'll be home in a few months. A social worker will be by in the morning to arrange for your care."

They were taking her away. For something he had done. That wasn't right. And the fear in his mother's eyes quickened something inside of Brogan, drew up a...a kind of fire. A shortness of breath, a burning in his chest and a flush to his cheeks.

Brogan ran back into his room, and Gaius was happy to let the little scoundrel go. But he didn't expect Brogan to come out with his wood chisel.

Before Brogan got two steps outside of the door...Brogan simply woke up against the wall, bleary eyes staring directly into the Yellow-Eyed Man's glowing pupils. Gaius clutched his leg, red rivulets already seeping between his fingers.

"Don't hurt him!" Catharina choked out, even as Gaius hauled her to her feet with his other hand.

"He assaulted me with a deadly weapon, Cat. I'm not sure what you would like me to do."

She was shouting. Everyone was shouting. They were taking her. They were taking her because of him. He had to tell them, but they weren't hearing him.

"I'm sorry!" Brogan cried out. "Mother, tell them I'm sorry!"

Catharina flailed, pounding on Gaius's chest with a clenched fist. "He doesn't understand! Please! Let me explain to him!"

And the Yellow-Eyed Man said the first words of the night, leaning in close to Brogan's face. And they were the words of a forest snake. "He doesn't understand...but he will."

———

That was the last thing Brogan remembered. The last time he saw his mother, his home. And the last time he carried the name Brogan. Six months later, deep in the heart of Fort Augustine Prison, he would take the name Osyen Belt.

And fourteen long years would pass before he heard that boy's name again, while beating a skeletal little Imperial ghoul to within the edge of his life. That sallow monster in an elevator shaft on the icy moon of Farragut said the magic words: Catharina Batahr was still alive.

CHAPTER 2
OSYEN
AGE: 25

IT WAS A NICE CHAIR. It cushioned his back and molded to his form like it wanted him to lie there forever, wick every care away. He supposed this is what it was like to sit atop an ivory tower, even one built for the function of oppression.

The Ministry of Peace on Ilum wasn't exactly a sight to behold. It was a cube amongst other nondescript and inoffensive cubes, albeit a more impressive one. Breaking in had been almost disappointingly easy—after all, what lifetime criminal wanted to go where all the Clerics of Peace hung out, collectively chewing on society's carotid artery?

Clerics of the Peace—like they were some kind of religious organization. They were police officers pumped out of the Academie Pacem with nothing but encyclopedic knowledge of philosophy coupled with constitutional fanaticism.

Osyen looked up when the office door slid open, cutting a line of honeyed daylight across the center of the dark room. Shafts of gold lit up the elegant desk of hammered iron—a fine piece of craftsmanship by itself. It was neither ostentatiously rich wood nor complex design, but not without class. Someone had labored over that thing with great love, many hours with hammer and chisel. It, like everything in the small office, was brutally simple and functional—while somehow regal and untouchable.

The man who walked in through the door looked much the same as how Osyen remembered him: the orchid tattoo on his jawline, the refined and starched expressions to go with gloved hands and a stiff posture. He'd grown a simple beard, and his hair had gone gray.

But Osyen knew that face. The face of the man who stole his mother: Gaius Nolte, Deputy Minister of Peace.

"Working late?" Osyen asked.

The Minister froze, like someone had pressed a gun barrel to his back. His lip curled, tasting something foul on the air. "The work doesn't sleep, the sun doesn't sleep. Why should I?"

Osyen huffed at that. Ilum truly was the City of Lights, the City That Didn't Sleep. So indeed why should its law enforcement take that luxury?

"The Espinoza case has no new developments," the Minister said. "She's still in the wind. So you can tell your editor to stop badgering my office."

"I read about that case," Osyen said. "Sorry about your son. He was one of the good ones."

"He was a great many things."

Wow. So Gaius Nolte didn't think that highly of anybody's family. Not even his own. Explained a bit.

Osyen bit his lip. "Alright. Consider the compliment retracted."

"And breaking and entering is a crime all by itself. If you leave quietly and promptly, I'll forget you were ever here and just scold your editor for his indecency."

Osyen shrugged. "I'll give you entering, but do you see anything broken?"

Gaius huffed. "Who let you through?"

"That's cute," Osyen said, never taking his eyes off of the Minister.

And a thousand data points all came into alignment at once.

Gaius let out a sigh, settling back on his heels. He let his foot glide across the floor, turning him open wide to face Osyen.

Face to face with a scared little boy, now grown.

The Minister gave a courteous nod of his head. "You won't be taken alive. I hope you know that."

"You really think you're the first person to make that threat to me?" Osyen said, deadpan and cold. "I've flown around this galaxy end to end. Made friends. Lost most of 'em. Made enemies. Killed 'em all."

Osyen didn't have to gesture at the amputation that still itched like mad. It felt like his whole arm had gone cold and numb, that feeling of having slept too hard on it—only to discover that it never woke up. And it always hurt all over again whenever he realized it wasn't there.

The Minister was unimpressed. He didn't want to know who Osyen worked for, what his agenda was. He just calmly took Osyen's measure. "You have some kind of plan, I take it?"

"No plan." Osyen didn't much care about part two. He'd figure that out when it became important.

The Minister's eyes flicked over to Osyen's absent arm, the sleeve of his longcoat pinned up on the shoulder like a permanent phantom salute. "What can I do for you?"

"Catharina Batahr," Osyen said. "Professor of Gnostic Tradition & History at the Royal Arts."

The Minister took a brave step towards his desk, feigning that this unusual encounter was any other meeting on his schedule. He was moving as casually as possible toward the gun hidden under the desk drawer. "Has this person published something I should care about?"

"She did," Osyen said. "You seemed to care a lot about it fourteen years ago."

"Extremely relevant reference. I'll dust off my shelf for the exact reading material, shall I?"

Osyen squinted at the Peace Officer. For all of Gaius's growth and reputation, he might as well be the Witch-Finder General of folklore, scouring rural countrysides for treasonous folk, and filling gullible ears with patriotic tripe.

"You really don't remember, do you?" Osyen asked.

The Minister settled into his office chair, enjoying the obscene comfort. "I don't tend to commit Capitals to memory."

Perhaps. But the Minister was no fool, and the bite about 'Capitals' told Osyen that he remembered everything. He remembered the weather, the time of day, the wood sculpture. He remembered little Brogan Batahr leaping to the defense of his mother.

Osyen knew the type. Gaius remembered that night at least as well, if not better, than the boy that now stood before him. A man of the Minister's intellect and capability did not lose any pieces to the hundreds of puzzles he'd solved over the years. It was a matter of personal pride.

He knew who Osyen was, enough to throw in that Capital dig into Osyen's side.

"Give me information on Catharina," Osyen said, "and I disappear."

"Quite the bargain," Gaius said, cold, "but I have my own offer."

Osyen smiled. Let the man think he had the winning hand. It was going to be fun when he realized he didn't even have enough cards to join the game.

The Minister lifted his pistol up from its very traditional hiding place, bracing it on the desk. "I kill you. And I get back to the real pressing work facing my city."

Osyen shrugged, pouting. "Damn. That beats mine by a country mile."

The Minister squeezed the trigger—to discover that the little bang lever didn't even make a happy click. It moved with absolutely no resistance, no deadly intent in that shell. Gaius looked up at Osyen, bewildered.

"Of course," Osyen started, "you can't shoot me without the power supply, the recoil spring, transfer bar, trigger sear—hell, I basically took the whole gun and left you with a weird little box of magnets."

"Commandant?"

No answer from the building AI. How heartbreaking.

"Nobody knows I'm here, Minister," Osyen said gravely. "I looped the Commandant's fiber line, which won't trigger an alarm for another four minutes. Cutting power to the biometrics defaults all the door locks into the open position, in the event of an emergency like fire or flood." He picked at the bulky collar around his neck. "A localized jammer will muddy all the camera feeds of my face and delay identification long enough for me to skip town. And finally... most importantly? I quite simply don't care anymore. Now, Ilum is a very dangerous planet, one of the most populated places in the entire Empire—full of rats and criminal scum for you to root out. And from what I've gathered, you've made some potent enemies in that mix. So why don't you save us both some time and tell me where to find Catharina Batahr before I do those enemies a favor?"

"No matter," Gaius said, the slight hush in his voice acknowledging the sour truth of it. Even if the guards killed Osyen, the Minister would be dead long before they could. "I can't tell you where she is because I don't know."

Osyen nodded, assessing the man. "And even if you did, you wouldn't?"

"I might," the Minister countered with a small quirk of a smile. "I might just to see how close you'd get before they kill you."

"So she *is* alive," Osyen whispered with a quiet reverence. "That's something, I guess."

"I said, 'I don't know.'"

Osyen waved his hand, throwing the file from his bracer on to the Minister's screen. "You had an informant at the time, yeah? A Professor Charles Ordee? A colleague of hers at the Royal Arts."

The Minister didn't say a word, done speaking to filth. He glared at Osyen, dark imaginings.

Magnus might have been lying to him back on Farragut. The

Minister might be lying to him now. But both of them together, dodging with their vagaries and their double-speak and their false promises? Whispering names and conditions and incomplete pictures? Whispering the same things?

No...his mother was alive, somewhere. And Osyen was going to find her.

"If you're a wise man," Osyen said, "you'll put your head down on your desk and count to two hundred. Then you'll go home, say a prayer to your son's memorial, and count your own blessings."

"I don't have any blessings," Gaius said with a hint of anger.

"Can't possibly imagine why," Osyen said, standing up and buttoning his coat. "Goodbye forever, jackass."

"You'll not leave this building."

"Put your head down and start counting. I'm trying to be nice."

Which is exactly when the Minister sealed his fate. "Brogan Batahr. You were a little criminal then, and you're a little criminal now. A new name doesn't change who you are."

Osyen sighed. "You're right about that."

"If you were going to kill me," the Minister grunted, "you'd have—"

Osyen lifted the pistol from under his long coat—the familiar grips of a magnetic-accelerated revolver that had once belonged to a friend. And he squeezed off two shots. The first slammed square into Gaius's forehead, painting the back wall with viscous spatter. The second sunk into his chest, spitting a ribbon of hot blood forward onto his desk.

The flower pattern of blood on the back wall wasn't as satisfying as he'd hoped it would be. But he felt the little pinch in his chest, like a small chain-link that bound his heart snapped and swung free.

One down.

Which is when he heard the shouting from outside the room. He had about sixty seconds before the AI woke up, trapped him, and suffocated him. And he was willing to bet half of the guns on Ilum were pointed at that office door.

Osyen fished in his jacket, pulling out two compact discs. He tossed them up to stick in the ceiling right over the door—just as it opened, and two fully geared tactical officers breached with precision, weapons out.

He felt the gun barrel trace over his chest, a slight tickle from hair-raising realization. The split second of frozen air as the shooter identified the target—and Osyen felt his breath hitch.

Do it, he thought. Do it and put out the fire, you stupid—

The small charges in the ceiling detonated with a flash and thump, cutting a perfect circle out from the brickwork. The small pancake domed upward from the thrust, hanging in the air. Before crumpling under its own weight.

Concrete chunks dropped onto the shooters. They flinched away, instinctively shielding their heads from the explosion mere feet away.

And Osyen rushed them, pirouetting past the first to run straight up the second man, bouncing from his knee up to his head. Osyen kicked off the armored helmet to toss himself through the demolition up to the next level. He landed gingerly in a largely vacant bullpen of cubicles and corner offices.

This was where a human soul went to be ground up to a paste, packaged and refined for easy consumption by an uneasy public with weak constitutions and loud voices. This building silenced dissent and warped the different until they were acceptable, palatable. Even the furniture.

Don't dawdle. Fifty seconds left, and plenty of people with guns.

The two officers below defiladed the floor under him, their Gauss rifles spattering holes through the material with ease. Osyen ran for the stairwell, powder and chunks springing up around him. He had to get to the rooftops before they restored power and locked the building down. Or his merry little quest died right here.

Several well-dressed Clerics of the Peace popped out of their offices, late working heroes of the justice system, and leveled their firearms at him. Bullets ripped through the bullpen, sending sparks and chunks of fabric flying.

Don't look at them. No time. Just run. He put his shoulder down and prayed the door wasn't locked.

To his happy surprise, the stairwell door popped open when he hit it—slamming right into the overeager Cleric on the other side. The poor bastard was bashed backward into the railing and sent tumbling down a few flights.

His partner was a few feet behind him, however, ready to draw down on Osyen. But Osyen leaned backward out of line of the shot.

Missing an arm slimmed Osyen's silhouette down, enough that he didn't take a bullet right then and there. But it also didn't do any favors for his sense of balance, causing him to flop over backwards. He reached with his one hand to catch himself, perching on his palm. He improvised a kick at the Cleric's gun hand, swiping the second shot off target into the stonework wall.

Which is when Osyen dropped on his shoulder, choosing to trade holding himself up with drawing his own pistol. He peppered the Cleric straight in the vest with shot after shot. The armor sparked and cracked, with maybe a splash of blood. The Cleric collapsed backward, awkwardly sliding limp down the stairs.

The armor may not have saved his skin, but it might just have saved his life.

Forty seconds.

Osyen popped up and started sprinting for the rooftop, the patter of dozens of boots ascending up after him. He huffed and puffed as he made each successive turn. This was not a tall building. How many stairs could there actually be?

Success! The stairs dead-ended in a door. Osyen put his shoulder into it—and bounced off the lock, the pain stunning his arm and making him drop his pistol. Lovely.

Osyen balanced on the railing, only to leap back as a chorus of gunfire screamed up after him. He picked up the pistol, checking the cylinder count. Enough.

He spun the cylinder off his leg with a whizz, before presenting it to the latch.

And he held down the trigger like Milardi used to. Let's see if it could stay locked when it had no latch.

The gun's mechanism was more than happy to dump shot after shot in a snare drumroll of automatic fire, riddling the door with bullets until Osyen was comfortable kicking it open. The rush of hot daylight air flooded in.

Osyen took off across the rooftop, gravel kicking up underfoot as he tried to get enough speed going to...

Leap across the alleyway!

And stick the landing on the other side, tumbling to his feet. He tried not to groan about the many sharp rocks now jabbed into his back and butt as he made his escape.

When the other Clerics got to the roof, all they saw were the clouds of steam rising from the skyline of Ilum.

RECORDED DREAM DATA, DATE: 2241.13.05

PATIENT: THOMAS HUGH

// WARNING: NOCTURNAL EVENT DETECTED
// STABILIZING HEART PALPITATIONS
// INTRODUCING OXYGEN FLOW

THOM HAD GROWN USED to these dreams. Some were borderline artistic, seeing the birth of stars take place before his eyes, or the cosmic swirl of a thousand generations of evolution playing out in seconds.

Sometimes he saw people, places, things. Magnificent beasts with claws for hands. He saw many travelers, all with the same face.

But this time...he saw a very familiar place.

The white room, interrogation, aboard a Naval ship. A table, white and cold. He could feel the rough, dry pads of his fingertips and the dry cracking around his eyes, where beads of sand had been left to fester. The crown of his head felt cool under a naval cap, where the hair had long since receded.

And sitting across from him at this table...was himself. Thom Hugh, eyes fiery and chin high. He looked refreshed, like steel once it was rinsed with oil and lovingly wiped clean.

Why are you showing me this?

I'm not in as much control as you might think. You took us here.

I chose this? So why am I—I mean, why am I not in myself for it?

Perspective...requires observing a situation from all angles.

Thom remembered this moment, staring across a blank table in a white room. He knew whose eyes he must be occupying now: Rear Admiral Ulysses Hugh, his father and keeper.

Thom had delivered his ultimatum to Admiral Hugh, bargaining with the Icon of Cruciform...in exchange for his friends.

And Admiral Hugh chose the Icon over the fate of his son.

He watched as past-Thom's mouth moved in a blur. And past-Hugh's head lurched forward and back hard enough to make him seasick. Everything was playing so fast!

// Warning: Heart Rate Rising to Dangerous Levels

// Attempting Stabilization

Don't rush. Go at your own pace.

My own pace?

Observe what you need. Slow it down, take it all in.

How do I do that?

Track the details. Focus, feel your feelings. The cloth on your skin,
tightness in your chest. What's the room smell like? Isolate them.
Don't try to process them, externalize them—just feel.

Hugh flexed out his hands, a swamp building up inside his gloves. And everything slowed to a crawl. He fought the flutter in his chest, the bead of sweat building on his brow, and the urge to tap his boot that was too tight across his arch. The subtle hint of body odor underneath a burning hint of tobacco and leather clung to the uniform.

And the admiral spoke, kicking the world into a calm pace. "You'd have made a good officer, son."

Past-Thom's nostrils flared and he swallowed hard. "I think you've given up the right to call me that, Admiral."

The words were concussive. Past-Thom ended that meeting with a metaphorical blade, slipping that verbal stiletto in between Past-Hugh's ribs. The admiral didn't move as Past-Thom was escorted from the room, stoic. Stubborn refusal to show any reaction.

And Thom could finally see what Hugh did next, when alone in that room. As the door closed and cut Past-Thom off from sight, the glaring white lights of the walls dimmed back to a slate gray, revealing the prison cell for what it was. The sound of the door clacking shut on its rails seemed to hang in the air, like it was uncomfortable leaving him alone.

But soon enough, it was silence in that gray box, with Admiral Hugh chewing on his cheek.

"Commandant?" Hugh said. "Terminate recording."

"Yes, Admiral," the computer responded with a positive feedback chirp.

He'd recorded their meeting?! The bastard.

But the admiral exhaled, ragged and soft. His gloves were too tight, restrictive, choking. He reached over, tugging the cloth off of his right hand, releasing it into the cold, dry air. He shook out the kinks and pressed his knuckles against the tabletop, cracking them, before swiping his cap off of his head.

That boy. That boy had grown. And had grown up without him.

But grown into what?

CHAPTER 3
THOM

THOM HAD AWOKEN from these dreams in various states. He'd found himself sleepwalking the halls, laid up in Medical, or curled up in a ventilation shaft. But this might be the first time he awoke in his bunk, peacefully laid up in his sheets.

No cramps. No signs of distress.

He wasn't going to complain about it. But he wasn't entirely comfortable with living in his own father's mind for any length of time. His shirt clung to his back, soaked through from the strain of the dream.

Why did the voice want to show him that? Why had his subconscious chosen to look back at that day? Had he missed something back then?

It must've been dreadfully early. The ambient lighting laid dim, lifting only a shade as the room sensed his movement.

Thom shrugged off his shirt, tossing it into the laundry chute. The pneumatic tube sucked the cloth up and away to be washed and sorted.

He shuffled on over to his dresser, rubbing at his gut—

A gunshot. A whistling. Snap. And a burning pain.

—Thom slumped against the wall, blinking away the memory. He pawed at his stomach, feeling for some sign of the bullet that had ripped him apart almost a year ago.

He could've sworn...he felt it so clearly...remembered it so vividly...

But the touch of the Icon had left nothing, no scarring or deformation. He had seen his own flesh torn like fabric or clay, but when he looked, he saw nothing. Like it had just been a bloody nightmare.

Well, there was no going back to sleep *now*, was there?

He pulled a fresh shirt from the dresser, slinging a jacket over the top. He clambered up the ladder, his fingers tacky on the steel rods.

It really was quite early. The running lights were all that were on, saving on power and avoiding excess heat. Still brighter than the air ducts had ever been.

The Jump Deck to his right was sealed up. Roche was no doubt half-asleep at his console, monitoring the ship's sensors with half of his brain while the other half pretended to sleep.

Since Roche's fusion with Lily, the man seemed to rest very lightly—if at all. Thom wondered if the jockey felt refreshed after a good night. He didn't seem to medically need it, in any case.

Thom had read about dolphins and other sea life that had been discovered, that slept by turning off parts of their brain at a time. With Lily occupying space, Roche might be able to benefit from the same setup.

Or maybe some distant part of him didn't want to sleep anymore.

Thom's gut twisted up on him again. Maybe a bite to eat would quiet that rumbling. Some oatmeal or a hot tea?

He shuffled off to the Galley, easing himself down the metal steps. Just because he couldn't sleep didn't mean he had to be inconsiderate to the other crew members.

They had fully stocked the Replicator with fresh carbon stores, ready for anything anyone might want to summon. But as Thom leafed through the menu, nothing really caught his eye. So he started flipping through the cabinets for the homegrown, dirt-stained, all-natural good stuff.

Cans upon cans of soup. Dill pickles. And a small crate of tomatoes.

He hated tomatoes. For a fruit, they were mushy, burned, and mostly water.

He grabbed a tomato anyway and curled up behind the folding table, nesting up in the seat cushion. The fruit stared back at him, mottled and bruised—

Thom looked up at the doorframe, half expecting a seven-foot-tall easy smile in a longcoat to be looking back at him.

And Thom set the tomato down. "Lily?" he asked the open air.

The characteristic blue glow filled the air as the projected head of the ship navigator appeared like they were clipping through the wall. Like some kind of eclectic children's book character, they leaned out from the surface, hair dangling and mustache bouncing. "What can I provide, Thomas?"

"What time is it?"

"Well before you should be awake."

Thom sighed, laying his head back on the cushion. "What's it like not having to sleep?"

"I could ask you, what is it like *to* sleep?" Lily said. "I do not require extended periods of silence and darkness to avoid delirium and madness."

"Lily, you're already crazy. Delirium would be redundant."

"Said from a place of love, of course."

"Course," Thom said, with a warm smile.

Lily paused, their head gliding into the room and settling by him at the table. "You don't sleep like the others."

He started at that, blinking. Suppose he shouldn't be surprised, since he had been suffering through twice weekly nightmares that tripled his resting heart rate and was ruining his clothes. Other crew members wouldn't have access to that data, but Lily couldn't help but notice.

"How do they do it?" Thom asked. "Got any tips?"

25

"When do you plan to inform them that you are in contact with an outside source?"

Thom sat upright, squinting at them. "I'm not...in contact with anybody."

"You are." Lily made no accusations, but there was a hint of distaste in that answer. His flat denial was insulting them.

"I'd tell you to check the logs, but you *are* the log, Lily. No outgoing, no incoming."

"You have an unofficial line of communication resistant to tampering or monitoring. This superior technique is kept hidden from the crew, and I would know why."

"I don't know what you're talking about," Thom said, flustered.

"You speak to someone in your dreams. They instruct you, provide intelligence and advisement," Lily said, with grave certainty and more than a little impatience. "Who are they?"

Of course. His Dream Logs.

When the nightmares first started, they set the weird records aside for analysis. There was so much audio-visual data computed by the human brain, it would take weeks of spare cycles to process.

Looks like they finally finished. And Lily was none too pleased with what they found there. Lily had seen everything he'd seen: the creation of the Paladins, the look through the Godfather's stronghold.

The death of Jackson Milardi.

Tell them something, Thom. Don't lose control now.

"I don't know who it is," Thom admitted. "Not for lack of asking."

Lily's image flickered, glitching out for a second as they dedicated cycles to some complex function. "You see things...further than the ship's sensors? You saw things happening in places you've never been, at times you were not there."

He considered his answer, but there was no point in denying it. "...Yes."

Lily considered this, a blank expression. "Could you teach me to sleep like this?"

Thom coughed, releasing a tense chuckle. "I can't teach myself! I

26

don't really know what's going on. I go to sleep, I end up wandering through emotionally depressing fog, and then I wake up—tired."

"You should seek medical attention."

"And tell them what, exactly? I'm clairvoyant? That's a career path in entertainment, not a diagnosis."

"An interesting proposal," Lily considered. "Perhaps we could use this for personal enrichment."

Thom laughed again, relaxing as he pulled his knees into his chest. "Would be nice to get back to fleecing rich folk of ill-got gains."

Lily smiled. "I'll place it in the prospective jobs file."

"You can't tell Osyen!" Thom snapped, his heart suddenly pounding.

Lily hiccuped, their projection frozen. "Clarify."

Thom Hugh, Maestro, con-artist. He'd confessed to Rashida that he saw the creation of the Paladins, but that was the past. And Osyen knew the boy's night terrors weren't nothing, but he didn't know what they meant.

If they did, if anybody knew he could see the *future*...how much pain could they have avoided? Could they have skipped out on Farragut?

Would Milardi still be alive?

It wouldn't matter that Thom couldn't control it, that he didn't actually know anything of use then, couldn't have actually done anything. They'll all assume he could have, and for some psychotic reason made the choice to let their friend die. They'd finally have a place to go with their misery.

They'd never forgive him.

"You can't..." Thom struggled to find the words. "Not yet, at least. Let me do it?"

"He suspects something. They all do."

"Yeah," Thom agreed. Dream analysis wasn't exactly proper science, and no one aboard would likely go snooping through the impressionistic nightmares of a colleague. But he had to be sure. "For now, can you encrypt my dream logs? My eyes only."

27

"Caution: security measures of this type may draw attention to them."

True. If somebody came looking, they'd notice the encryption and wonder why it was. And a ship full of thieves was not likely to ask permission when they encountered a lock.

"I got it. Do it anyway," Thom said with a nod. If anything, it would further motivate Thom to tell them the truth. They'd eventually force the issue if he didn't.

Lily flickered. "Done."

"Thank you, Lily."

And Lily zoomed up close to him, conspiratorial. Or accusatory. "You realize that if Osyen asks me directly...I will not lie to him."

So he simply had to confess first. Great.

"I'll do you one better. Don't lie for me. Just send him to me, so that I can explain?"

"I will do so when he returns." And Lily's image winked out.

Returns? Oh, for the love of...

Thom pulled up the screen of his Entiglas, leafing through the orange glow of advertisements and scams to find the local news of the day.

And he found what he was looking for in a matter of seconds.

DEPUTY MINISTER GAIUS NOLTE
ILUM M.O.P.
FOUND MURDERED

VIGILANTE AT LARGE

Thom laid his exhausted head down on the table. "Goddammit, Osyen..."

CHAPTER 4
OSYEN

HE WASN'T, strictly speaking, surprised by their reaction.

The door to the shuttle bay popped open, and two of them were standing right on the other side: Thom and Roche, slack-jawed and eyes wide, a mixture of muted disappointment and abject horror.

Roche managed a shake of his head. "Tell me you had a good reason."

Good reason for what? He knew what he felt most guilty for, but he didn't have a good idea of what Roche thought that should be. He didn't answer, choosing instead to press his jamming collar into Thom's hands.

"Okay." Thom said, studying the device. "So they don't have a clean picture of your face. But how many one-armed menacing newcomers do you think there are on Ilum?"

Kid had a fair point—his face wasn't the most identifying characteristic anymore. And killing a major law enforcement official was liable to cause a collective bending of rules.

Didn't matter. None of it mattered. She was alive.

Osyen slipped past them and stomped down the hall, unfortunately cut off by the cheery greeting of Lily. "Hello, Osyen. Welcome back. What have you brought me?"

"Trouble," Osyen blurted.

"Elaborate."

"No, I..." Osyen paused in the hall, taking a breath to cool off. "I didn't bring you anything this time."

"I see." The disappointment was almost worse than the ringing in his ears. "Thom has an urgent matter—"

"You might've brought us in on this, Osyen," Roche cut Lily off, he and Thom surging down the hallway behind him, like fish trailing in his wake. "We could've helped."

Yes. They could've. They were right. He was wrong. Plain and simple. But he found saying that out loud...difficult.

If she was alive, how would he find her? Make sure she was safe? Magnus had implied she was alive, and Gaius was the last man who had seen her. The only thing he'd be able to do was pick up the trail.

She was arrested for her research. He'd have to find that research.

Someone got a fistful of his jacket, startling him into stopping. "Say something, Oz!" Thom barked at him. "You're starting to freak me out."

"Something," Osyen blurted, still not looking back, but unable to stop himself from smiling.

Thom blinked a few times. "That's on me. I walked right into that one."

"Yes, you did."

He heard Adelaide's voice echoing up the halls long before he saw her, rocketing up from the aft of the ship. "Killing the single most powerful law enforcement official on the planet is not *my* definition of 'laying low', Oz!"

Osyen raised up his hand in surrender. "In my defense...I really wanted to do it."

"And I want an active sex life," Adelaide snapped, "but getting what you want comes with consequences!"

Thom was experiencing some kind of emotional whiplash, shivering from the crown of his head down through his toes. He had just been uploaded with a vague image and a vague threat, and his imagination was filling in both entirely on its own.

Roche, on the opposite end, didn't even bat an eye. He gave Thom a blind shove at the shoulder to break the spell. "They'll already have shut down the primary Jump Points, but if we move quickly, we can get the *Aurum* loaded and topside before they can issue landing locks."

"How much load would we have to leave behind?" Osyen asked.

He saw Lily's blue interface flicker for a moment across Roche's rough ocular implant as they interfaced. "We'd have to cancel two delivery contracts."

"And that cripples us financially?"

Roche blinked, confused. "A man cannot be crippled by finances. Money is an illusory concept representing value—"

"Okay," Osyen said dismissively, "then send the bad news, and get this ship skyside. I'll be out of your way long before then."

"Out of our way?" Thom asked.

"Those were the words."

"We're coming with you."

"Not this time."

Thom reached over to the wall, tapping a keypad—and slammed the door shut in front of Osyen, trapping him in there with the group.

"Lily," Osyen said, "open the door."

The voice echoed from above and below, intimate and overbearing. "I believe you should answer the boy's question. You are planning to depart the *Aurum*?"

Before Osyen could answer, Thom pressed him. "What were you doing at the Ministry of Peace, anyway?"

"I didn't go in there expecting to kill him," Osyen said, like that made it any better.

Rashida came ambling out of the galley, leaning on her cane. Her broken leg had healed for the most part, but she had never surrendered the bit of pity that the appearance of weakness could give. "You broke into his office in the middle of third-shift, tampered with

Naval-grade security systems, and just to make matters worse, you brought a gun." Rashida leaned against the wall, like the severity of the charge meant little to her. "I must ask: what *were* you planning on doing?"

He hadn't been thinking that far ahead. He hadn't been thinking. He had just been doing and hoping, some recursive combination of luck and blood. The only way out of that encounter was with bullets flying. But the old Osyen had called the shot, bull-heading his way through the problems.

With one success far too dependent on luck: he'd found the closed case file of his mother's detainment, and the name of the man who had raised a concerned patriotic hand.

Charles Ordee. The next man responsible for his mother's disappearance.

But after all that...a Ministry official brutally murdered, he had only barely more information than when he started, and all the judicial heat in the sector. By all measure, that little operation had been an abject failure.

"They will ID me," Osyen pointed out with a sigh, "and when they do, they will come hunting. You're all in danger the longer I stay."

"Yes," Rashida mused, "because the Empire is known far and wide for its judicious and precise application of punishments. You were adamant three months ago that this crew stay together no matter what."

"And we will," Osyen said, "but I've got some business. Personal business. When Zatia wanted to swing by her dad's place last month, we just up and let her go!"

"To a backwater, and she wasn't chasing down an Imperial Minister!" Thom's voice was so earnest it hurt. "Oz, you think there's a place you can go, we wouldn't follow you?"

That robbed the oxygen from Osyen's chest. It hurt to breathe after hearing that. He couldn't formulate words past the tightness in his chest and the mist in his eyes. He looked at the wall, squeezing his lips tight.

"We're with you step by step, boss," Roche said.

"In our Sunday best," Rashida followed.

And the nice, beautiful moment was shattered by the next embittered voice. "After today, Oz, I may finalize my plans for mutiny. Gonna strap you down to the *gulaw* floor." Zatia's muted shouts came through the door at his back. "In the cargo bay!"

He turned, and the locked door popped open. The little bruiser stared up at him with a cocked head and off-set jaw, her hair newly tinted the pale glow of starlight, with strands of muted whites, blues, and pale pink.

She broke the standoff by popping a few pills into her mouth and followed them up with what he could only describe as a flagon of coffee.

"Were those...?"

"Neurotransmission therapy," she grunted. "What did you do?"

"I'm about two hours from being the most wanted man in this half of the Empire."

"Sounds like a man I want to know," Zatia shot back without blinking. "And you won't be running for very long without us."

Osyen ground his teeth. They weren't wrong. He knew it. Without the company and resources here, he'd be found and executed in a matter of hours. He stood a much better chance of weathering this with them.

But his mother...

"If we run..." Osyen started, but couldn't finish the thought.

The Empire would soon figure out who he was, why he was there. He had come sniffing around, and quite likely, put his mother in real danger. They would leverage her against him.

He had to find her before they did, or he'd lose her all over again.

"If we run," Lily said, "we stay together."

"And who doesn't want that?" Adelaide playfully mocked to mask her sincerity.

"I mean, I could use a little less of you *first thing* in the morning," Zatia grumbled.

Adelaide scoffed. "You look like a pre-pubescent retiree."

Zatia flicked her newly platinum hair out of her face and took a sip of her coffee flagon. "And you look like you've been mummified twice 'cause they didn't get it right the first time."

Roche raised his hand. "What about me?"

Zatia and Adelaide traded looks, but it was Rashida who chimed in. "You look like you were hit by a car and the car lost."

Osyen laughed, leaning against the wall as exhaustion finally set in. The world started to tilt, and his stomach tied itself into a knot. But this stupid group of stupid people.

They were the best people. In a universe fueled by chaos, bloodshed, and unfeeling cruelty...he was so glad he'd found these idiots.

Thom stepped forward, as though he could make the moment personal between the two of them. "Whatever you're looking for, we stand a better chance of finding it after things have calmed down a bit."

He was right. Thom was always right. Because Thom was always so good at thinking with his head, not his gut. The one time Thom had followed his gut, he got a hole put in it. Maybe Osyen stood to learn from him.

"How do you figure?" Osyen asked.

It was like the whole crew circled up around Thom to hear the grand scheme. Thom didn't even blink under the pressure. "The Empire won't want to leave this crime unsolved for any longer than they have to. They'll find you—or a suitable candidate—parade him around, and officially close the case."

Adelaide scoffed. "They'll probably cut the guy's arm off just to sell the story."

Thom didn't deny that comment, but he continued. "They'll still be looking for you, but unofficially. We'll have a lot more latitude to move when every breathing Imperial citizen isn't a part of the search."

"The grand plan is...run for the hills?" Zatia asked.

"*For now*," Thom said. "Good plans aren't by definition complicated."

Osyen chewed on the idea. "We leave now...so we can hunt later."

Thom nodded, looking up at Osyen like he was expecting some kind of affirmation. "And you can get us up to speed on *what* exactly we're hunting."

It hurt to admit, but the kid was right. He had waited fourteen years to find her. He could wait a few more weeks.

Gold star, kid.

"Roche?" Osyen asked. "Fuel us off, double-time. I'll push the apology to our contacts. We're leaving. Together."

CHAPTER 5
ANZE

IT HAD BEEN some time since Anze Orchikov had walked the halls of an Imperial flagship. They all stank of industrial cleaning solvent, no soft carpeting or sound-dampening fabrics, making every surface thrum with the voices and footfalls that passed by hours ago. It was like the ship itself had something it wished to say in some mild aura.

And it was full of power, crackling and snapping off every surface. It made his fingers snap. And he could feel the migraine building behind his left eye. So much noise, so many buzzing lights and whirring servers, the reactor core burning underneath his feet. He wondered what the Chief Engineer would think if Anze switched off that two-story fusion power plant of his? The faces he'd make...

How Anze ever lived without this sense. It was like being born blind, gaining sight, and being told that was a sin. As if he chose this. His own mother had cursed his name.

They were all chained in the proverbial cave.

The Imperial Navy had so much power, and such a will to inflict it. This much potential could be used to comfort and care—but to men raised in violence, power always translated to a means, a language. Every soldier, every sailor he passed—with their augments and Entiglas bracers—all had some concept of how to kill, not how to love.

He could teach them if they didn't drive him off again with pitchfork and torch. But of course, they wanted him now, but only in so far as he could help them kill. They tolerated him as long as he could help them propagate their violence.

So long as he served their swords and shields.

Anze approached the sliding doors to the Jump Deck, and they tried to hold fast against him. He had no clearance, no permission.

But he did not require the permission of hollow men or their obedient machines. With a wave of his hand, he tugged the electrons hiding in the walls, clinging to composite fiber and copper cable. And the doors slid open, gears apologetically whining for having impeded him.

The deck officers reflexively glanced back at the open door, and their faces twisted in collective confusion. He wore no uniform, no epaulets or medals, and he had not been announced. Who was he? And how had those doors opened for him?

He cocked his head, as if to take note of their question. How indeed? Their confusion tickled him.

The Jump Deck of an Eisenclad dreadnought was not near as impressive a space as the ship itself. The crew were, after all, centralized deep in the hull for maximum protection. Several layers of consoles terraced down and away to either side of an impressive throne of a command chair. Everything drab and featureless, the glow of holographic haptic displays lighting the dozen or so faces of warrant officers and Naval Regulars.

The nerve center, the brain stem of military action.

And Anze felt every neuron firing, every order cascading outward with reports rippling back. Anze clenched his fists, and the lights dimmed a shade and screens flickered.

The bald head in the command chair stirred. The flat Naval cap did little to hide the dents and scars marring his skull from a lifetime of concussions. "Spare us your theatrics, Mr. Orchikov. Welcome to the *Persephone*."

Anze smirked, feeling more than a few electrical impulses glowing out from the man himself, a casual augment or two hiding underneath that aging skin. He must've thought cognitive implants could purchase intelligence for him. It simply made him foolish faster.

"Am I welcome?" Anze asked from the door.

"Would not have said so if you were not."

Anze stepped forward on to the Jump Deck, exchanging looks with each of the deck officers that offered only stares in return. They were not afraid of him, openly sneering.

They thought he was a freak. They thought he was a monster. Excommunicated by the Dunsweir, banished and shunned. And here he now stood, sullying their recycled air. People were so ready to cut the knees from others to add to their illusion of height.

He was the monster? They, with their starched collars and clean faces, would burn entire planets with this marvel of engineering around them. And yet he was the demon of their entire culture? What a laugh.

Anze's stylish suit might not have been up to military code, but he had no deformity or bestial feature. His face was clean shaven, his white hair combed and washed. His narrow jaw and green eyes were of royal look, but they saw more animal than anything else.

"I see the Dunsweir remain an alien presence to your men," Anze quipped.

"Keep the Family's name out of your mouth, Anze, before they curse you again."

Anze chuckled. "They can curse me all they like. I curse them plenty."

The bald man came to his feet with a grunt, rising to Anze's blasphemy. He was a man forged out of iron faith and rusting hinges. A fluid swipe of his hand took the cap from his head, tucking it under his arm in practiced performance of diplomacy. His uniform of slate gray had a curious assortment of multi-colored bars on his left-side chest, like a child had glued a bag of hard candy to him.

He had his own little dragon hoard on his own little hill. Of course he took offense to Anze's observations.

"Ulysses, I take it?" Anze asked.

"Rear Admiral 2nd Grade, 3rd Naval Bombardment Wing, Ulysses Hugh."

"That's a mouthful," Anze dismissed with a smirk. "Instead, I'll use some playful nickname that you detest."

Hugh ground his jaw, failing to maintain even the most basic decorum. "Minister Caldwell believes you can be of service to me."

Anze smiled and cast his hands wide, stooping into a curtsy. "I live to serve, bumpy. Even the cursed have decorum."

"For a price." Hugh growled at the impropriety and Anze's implication. Delicious.

"Of course, for a price," Anze scoffed. "You collect a fee for your obedience, do you not?"

The admiral's nostrils flared in petulant defiance. "I'm a patriot."

"Indeed," Anze said, looking out at the assemblage of officers he surrounded himself with. "And so are they all. So devoted."

They all had their fee. They were promised a spot on the Path of the Pilgrim if they danced to the beat, if they slept on command, killed on command. If they prayed, if they chanted, if they turned on their neighbors and bowed their heads. Their obedience was conditional, their morality for sale. They just called it patriotic so it didn't feel transactional.

And one thing made an obedient man very uncomfortable: matching eyes with a deviant who had somehow evaded promised punishment. It reminded them of what they already knew in their hearts. Regardless if the promises were true...the right people could always escape judgement.

"Whatever you require, the Empire can afford," Hugh mocked.

Anze's smile flickered, a candle in the wind, but he nodded in assent. So long as the admiral thought his aid was for sale, the better.

"What can you tell me about the condition of a KC-28 Perseus model transport designated *Aurum*?" Hugh asked.

And Anze shivered at the name, a pleasant chill crawling up his spine. That ship was a bucket of parts held together by empty promises, rusting rivets, and foul witchcraft. It should have shaken itself apart ages ago.

And yet. There was a young man aboard that ship with... promising ability. So familiar, so wonderful.

"That little ship?" Anze said, masking his excitement with a wry grin. "The one that escaped two of the Empire's most devoted assassins? The ship that—by all accounts—entered the Boolean right before an Imperial Fleet Carrier was lost? Tell me, while Imperial assets are rushing from one side of the galaxy to the other, what is the Empire's interest in this one little ship?"

The ship was not what Hugh found interesting. It was its contents.

"Consider it a personal mission, one that carries the full support of the Dunsweir themselves. Minister Caldwell believes you can assist me in their capture," Hugh said with a furrow to his brow, his old eyes squinting to reveal the deepening crow's feet. "That is where your interests and mine intersect."

"My oh my," Anze mocked, "do you believe I hold some degree of resentment for that ship and its crew?"

"They destroyed your cruiser," Hugh taunted, "and tore up your colony."

"That's not how I recall it," Anze said, a low and cautionary tone. "No, in fact, those people were quite set to be friends of mine. Until certain Imperial hands got involved. As they always do."

"Can you help us or not?"

And since Hugh wasn't going to debate the point, Anze was happy to return bright and cheery to the high ground. "Can and shall, bumpy," he said with a smile. "My sources have sighted the *Aurum* in the skies of Ilum. Making a hasty departure, as well."

"Set a course, begin Jump prep," Hugh ordered, turning to settle back into his command seat. "Pass the order along. The ship is to be impounded and held without consent or cause."

Anze raised an eyebrow. He had not been dismissed. Hugh had simply exited the conversation the moment it had nothing else to give him.

"What will you do when you catch them, I wonder?" Anze mused aloud.

"Two priority targets for extraction or termination," the admiral said. "All other targets are disposable."

There was only one person of practical value. But Anze's beautiful cousin had been adamant about her loyalties. The second must be…

Little Thom. While it was not impossible that the Empire had deduced his ability, Anze found it unlikely. No, this was far more prideful. It had the distasteful ring of possession around it. Thom was a totem subject to ownership and had been stolen. Hugh sought its retrieval or destruction.

Saving Thomas and Rashida from sullied hands seemed the perfect Imperial mission. But termination? No.

The admiral was putting on a brave face. He'd never let Thom come to harm. Would he?

Anze scoffed. "You think you can just…bond their ship and take them by surprise?"

"You doubt the Imperial Navy?"

"No, no. Your ability to commit atrocities is well regarded from civil Core to Duster Reaches."

The admiral drew a steeling breath. "You will be rewarded for your assistance, Mr. Orchikov. Clear the Deck."

"No."

Hugh didn't want to give Anze the satisfaction of a large emotive response. Rather, the admiral gestured to a starched Oskie that looked more museum piece than a soldier. Ugly facial scars from claw and shrapnel had drawn asymmetric patterns up his neck and across his chin. Unusual to see an Oskie with grayed hair—they didn't typically live that long.

This man was lucky, lazy, or very dangerous.

"Lieutenant Commander Isaac. Remove Mr. Orchikov."

The sound left the admiral's mouth, moving to the Oskie's ear, where it was translated into a digital signal for his augmented hearing. And they translated the electrochemical responses in the brain to analog signals to move the hundreds of small subdermal implants along his skeleton.

And unfortunately for him, electricity obeyed Anze.

The Oskie went to move—and not a single muscle carried out their assignment. The confusion that wracked the man's face was just delicious.

"Call all you like, bumpy," Anze cooed, "but if you want anyone to take care of me, you'll have to find someone with fewer aftermarket parts."

Hugh didn't even look at the Oskie. "You'd threaten an Imperial on the Deck of his own ship?"

"Your memory must be faltering, because you threatened me, Admiral." The Oskie continued to struggle, sweat building up. Anze sighed. "Oh, do relax already! You're going to give yourself an aneurysm."

Hugh leaned back in his chair, lip curled in disgust. The warrant officers all clutched their sidearms, waiting for the order to gun down this stain on Imperial legacy. If only they would—the reactor core at the heart of this ship would make such a pretty explosion in the night sky, if he only asked it too.

But Hugh was a more patient man than that. "What do you want, Mr. Orchikov? I've no time for your antics."

Anze smelled the synapses firing, the dozen small implants in Hugh's skull processing possibilities and advancing cognition. They called to Anze, each its own piece of a devoted choir seeking a conductor

"Admiral," Anze hushed, bowing his head. "I simply wish to continue my service. I believe I can be of more use here at your side than when you inevitably call me next week asking for more help and I'm tied up three Jumps away."

"I hope you understand," the admiral said, "that I will not accept the continued presence of a criminal on my ship."

"You don't have to accept it. You simply have to endure it."

"I will secure my son," Hugh said it like the mantra of an ancient curse. "I will kill any who delay or defy me."

It was easy to behave like a god from a floating artillery station, bathed in starlight and above all the craters, Anze thought. But could he keep the same attitude when the blood was thick and the smell of carbon singed his throat?

"I will help you secure your son," Anze declared, "on one condition: you will not harm his compatriots."

Hugh's head twitched, stopping himself from looking backward at Anze. "Afraid of losing an investment?"

"Not everything in this universe requires a gun, Admiral."

"And rogue Capital elements are not subject to this Empire's protections."

"No, they're not," Anze agreed, cold, "but I have found that killing an enemy has a tendency to make three wherever one fell. Should you instead fulfill an enemy's needs, undermine his motivation? He will slip quietly into retirement—where you can dictate their future."

"I prefer to kill my enemies, Mr. Orchikov, with clear and certain terms."

As opposed to knives and poison like a gangster might? Like the Navy had never stooped to assassination or sabotage. It was not the first time Anze had been insulted in an underhanded and subtle manner like that, but he had no true objection to the observation either. Anze was neither cruel nor deceitful. He'd simply survived betrayal before. And when that scent coated the inside of his throat, he learned to recognize it.

Anze laid a hand on the back of the admiral's chair, feeling the cold electric kiss run up his palm. He could feel Thom's file tucked just out of view, how many times it had been opened, revised, and redacted. And how long Rear Admiral Ulysses Hugh had lingered on the images of his son.

This man had no idea how important Thom really was.

"Call me Anze. Now, let's go find your son."

CHAPTER 6
ZATIA

NEUROTRANSMITTERS, prescribed by a backwater physician on Angrboda. She took two in the morning and two in the evening with food to cut down on the severity and frequency of her seizures. They tasted like ass. She gagged on the first few doses. But the disaffected physician couldn't give a damn if she took her meds or not, and she was the one frequently waking up on the floor with new bruises.

So she found ways to stomach them. Coffee, black, hot in order to acid wash her tongue in the morning; whiskey, neat and brutal for the evening. The doctor had said she was supposed to take them with food anyway. Liquid dinner seemed just as suitable as ration paste.

Ever since she'd gotten consistent with them, she'd only felt tremors and shakes, but she hadn't had a full-blown collapse since. So whatever he was peddling, for whatever reason, it was working. Heck, the copious amounts of coffee might be the current source of her shakes, but even if it was just that, she wasn't going to risk relapsing by making changes just out of curiosity. That wasn't a question she needed an answer to.

And she finally felt comfortable wielding her blades again.

Zatia had cleared a good workout area in the cargo bay, made easier by the lack of cargo. Their brisk departure from Ilum had left barren space on the floor.

Rashida was already in her warmups—many deep squats—when Roche made his announcement. "We have cleared Imperial patrol routes and have a straight shot through to our back alley Jump point. ETA five hours."

"It'll be nice to avoid trouble for once," Rashida said as she balanced on her good knee to roll out her injured one. Her practical workout clothes had none of the restrictions of Rashida's normal flowery wear, but Zatia wanted to build up good habits in supportive gear first before adding hurdles.

"I don't know," Zatia said, stopping to tighten the laces on her boot. "Seems like we try to run at every opportunity, and they just chase us."

"And one of these days, they'll learn to just let us go."

"See, that right there is the attitude I like to see." Zatia pulled two blunt batons from her back and lunged at Rashida.

Old *principessa* might have been mid-warmup, but she was ready. She kicked her cane up into her hand, parrying each blow only as much as necessary. She ducked and sidestepped other strikes that didn't need her attention.

Before finally, she bounced to one side off the line and outside of Zatia's reach, using the range benefits the cane offered to poke in at Zatia's exposed side.

The cap of the cane was hardly soft, jabbing Zatia and inducing an undignified guttural grunt. Rashida cackled at the success, pacing out her tension. "If you insist on pressing, make sure you can handle me."

Oh, she was going to be mouthy about it too, eh? Zatia laughed under her breath, resetting her grip on the batons.

And she lunged again, this time bouncing light on her feet. She darted from one side to the other, like she was hitting Rashida from left and right at the same time. The squeal of her boots on the bay floor pierced the air, like it was worried on Rashida's behalf.

With two taps of the baton on Rashida's wrist, Zatia separated the noblewoman from her cane and laid the third strike gently against Rashida's throat.

Rashida swallowed, feeling the mild pressure of the polymer against her jugular. "I got too comfortable?"

"You got comfortable," Zatia said, letting the baton fall away. "Grunts will just heave sticks at you, but the real bad guys? They'll change up the tempo, make your habits your own problem. So don't go where you think I'll be. Just listen to the music and go where it tells you."

Rashida bent over to grab her cane, muttering to herself, "Listen to the music."

"That was a genuine pleasure to watch." Both women looked up to the catwalk above. Osyen laid against the railing with a cheesy grin. "How's the pride, Rash?"

"I'd ask you to give me a hand, but you've only got the one."

"Ha ha ha," Osyen said, dry. "You may not want it. It's clumsy and has the shakes."

Zatia set the batons aside, reaching for her thermos of coffee. It had gone cold, watery—so it tasted like a refreshing zip of battery acid. Just what she needed in the middle of a session.

Maybe she just missed the metallic pressure in her mouth every time a stim pumped through her veins, numbing her for battle and pushing her muscles to the limit. Her shoulder twitched just thinking about it, and her heart took a little skip.

Medical wasn't locked. She could...

No. The days of drug-induced combat euphoria were behind her. Today and every day forward, she fought smarter—not harder.

Two steps forward, one step back. She thought those pulls, those cravings, were gone. She stretched her fingers, trying to get the cramping in her forearm to let loose. It wouldn't get any easier tomorrow or the day after, but that didn't mean she had no hope that it might.

Osyen awkwardly clanged his way down the corrugated steps,

each boot announcing him like an encroaching dragon battering at the door. He settled on the landing, leaning on the railing like a child on a carousel.

"What do you need?" Zatia asked without looking up.

After a pause, she got the honest answer from him. "A distraction."

She understood that. He was doing something smart that he didn't want to do, and it was just stuck on his mind. She was in a similar headspace.

"Do you want a distraction?" Zatia asked. "Or do you want solutions?"

Osyen shook his head, bewildered, like she'd just popped him across the jaw. "Can we...just talk?"

"You could always get some bruises and get drunk, but I figure talk is more productive."

"Who *are* you anymore?"

"I don't even recognize myself these days."

Osyen couldn't help but smile. "You look good. Full color in the face and everything."

Zatia took another pull from her coffee. "Comes from healthy blood flow for the first time in my life."

He looked askance, like the wall might tell him what to do. She was going to have to pry it out of him.

"Lily?" Zatia said. "Give Rash some drills."

Lily's voice was bloodthirsty, a low hum of a pleased laugh. "Only happy to."

The noble lady didn't get so much as a chance to object. Two blue holographic blades swung out of opposite walls, connecting with Rashida's legs and chest. Pixels couldn't shove or push, but the sapphire blades flashed an angry red coupled with obnoxious honking to really drill home Rashida's failure.

Rashida just stood there, head cocked and lips pulled tight to an invisible grumpy line as she stared frustration into Zatia's tiny frame. Zatia shrugged as Lily giggled maniacally in the background.

"I hate the drills," Rashida grumped, turning to face the empty cargo bay and her new challenger. Two more holographic blades emerged from the walls, alternating their angles and timing. No flourish or flash, just target-seeking pixilated threats.

And so Rashida broke her cane over her knee—separating the dozen or so links of the chain inside, a heavy weight dangling on the end. Osyen jumped at the sound as Rashida started twirling her new weapon in the air, smacking aside Lily's faux attacks.

Lily brought in additional threats, projecting new blades, balls, and clubs coming in from all sides. And Rashida kept striking, over and over, in different combinations and patterns. She let the chain wrap around her arms, her legs, before releasing the rotational energy in a direction, hurling the heavy weight an impressive distance with pinpoint accuracy.

"What is that?" Osyen asked.

"A meteor hammer," Zatia cackled. "Girl's not strong, so let's use her dexterity and precision to win the day."

He pursed his lips, almost a grimace. "It's distressing to watch."

"It's neat what you can do with physics," Zatia said.

Rashida spun up the chain and threw the weight like a dart, passing right through one of Lily's targets—and wedging hard in the hull. Osyen winced, lowering his head to hide his pain at that. The lady pulled and pulled but couldn't get it dislodge.

"Use your bodyweight," Zatia said.

Rashida thought about that advice for a second, then coiled up the chain around her arm and waist. And she tumbled forward, rolling herself up in it—and the sudden jerk was enough to pop the dart free.

Lily didn't wait for Rashida to unwrap herself. The attacks began almost immediately again, forcing Rashida to bob and weave, uncoiling as she went.

"How long does she do that for?"

"Till I say stop."

"She's not bad," he said. "Good footwork."

"Comes from all the ballroom dancing," Zatia mocked.

Rashida stumbled, her bad knee caving under the pressure. One of Lily's blue strikes seized the opportunity, striking through her shoulder—turning blood red, and issuing that lovely metallic scream from every speaker in the hold.

"If you're hurt, you're hurt," Zatia shouted. "Don't try to move like your leg is fine. It'll just betray you when you need it."

"You want me to stand still?" Rashida asked in confusion.

"Root your feet. Pull from the ground. Every strike should come from a good foundation."

Rashida nodded, more muttering as she repeated that mantra to herself. She bounced on her toes, testing her footing before dropping her heel to the ground—and driving her weight down through her back hip.

When Lily's next barrage came in, she was able to shatter them with repeated blows, only shifting to address new threats.

Zatia took another sip of her coffee and then offered it to Osyen. "What's worming around in your gray?"

"Nothin'," Osyen lied. "Maybe that's the problem."

He wasn't ready to say it outright. Fine. Everybody came to the truth in their own time. He might be admitting it to himself and just wasn't ready to put air behind it yet. Or maybe he was still in full denial. But it would come. No need to force it.

"Well, I know I refuse to go into hiding without some long-lasting entertainments," Zatia said.

He scoffed. "Your 'entertainments' would get us caught."

"High explosives, attractive people, and copious liquor is what I call a good weekend."

Osyen knew exactly where she was building to. "We're not burning down your dad's house."

"He's got it coming," Zatia huffed. "Y'know, he thought I was coming back, hat in hand, and was ready to put me right back to work. Tell me it wouldn't be fun to drop glo-fuel on his roof?"

Osyen winked at her. "Arson isn't exactly my idea of a good time."

"I'm here for a good time," Zatia said, "not a long time."

Osyen's eyebrows did a little wiggle dance as he considered the sight of a roaring fire eating its way through a foul man's living room. "Better than a long time being miserable, I tell ya."

"Milardi would never let us stay miserable. So why should we?"

Osyen chuckled, idly scratching his fingers on the hammered steel of the stair railing. "I miss the ol' bastard."

And her heart took a plunge. Jackson Milardi: that tall frame, that stupid smile, and his almost acrobatic ability to bend the night ever toward debauchery and chaos. The brim of his hat clipping against every doorframe that tall bastard walked through, and the way he could effortlessly slip a hair-tie onto her scalp when she was headfirst in a toilet, and have some drinks on the table by the time she came back. That charming smile and flash of danger in his eye, hand dancing over the flame because he liked the play of the burn on his fingertips.

"He looked after us, didn't he?" Zatia said.

Osyen could only nod. Milardi could guide a night through any kind of trouble, be it liquor or bullets, people or blood. What trouble would they get into without him?

"You know," Zatia said, "he told me he'd have my back. Nobody had ever..." She stopped, her chest seizing in open revolt. The memory was too painful.

"And so now you got her back?" Osyen asked, pointing at Rashida, who had moved on to doing lunges. "Going to turn her into a killer?"

"God, I hope not," Zatia said. "But if she wants to live in our world, she's going to have to learn to live in it, y'know? That means heavy lifting, heavy drinking, and sometimes..."

"You've been killing for only slightly longer than you've been walking," Osyen noted. "It's a small wonder you're sane."

"Who said I was? The voices?"

"Mostly the survivors."

"See, I told you lifting the 'no witnesses' policy was going to have backlash."

She finally got a laugh out of him. He hung his head, weighed down by whatever was in there. Finally, he looked up at Rashida. "You've given her three months of on-off combat training, street smarts...it's not much."

"Yet," Zatia cut in. "It's only three months. How seasoned were you when you jumped in head first?"

He nodded, conceding the point. "But if you lock her in a room with trouble, you think she handles it?"

Zatia considered the minor noble working up a sweat. "Like, with who?"

"Let's say Magnus."

Her Consort? Magnus brought the Paladins and caused the death of a dear friend. Zatia knew what she'd do, but Rashida? She had hoped that Rashida was above all that. Instead, she looked at Osyen. "What would *you* do?"

And Osyen's eyes glassed over. Remembering.

"You did." Zatia hummed, satisfied. "He tell you anything of use?"

One-word answer. "Enough."

"Hope you broke his leg for me."

"Did a little better than that."

That's why he went back on Ilum. Why Osyen went sniffing around a Ministry office. He was checking on a lead that baby Magnus coughed up through broken teeth. And he was still not confident enough in it to say what?

Pull it out of him. "And what did that little *skel* tell you?"

Osyen tried to hide his wince, cover it by swiping his hair out of his face. "Nothing I didn't already know."

Zatia leaned over, trying to get physically into this brooding anti-hero's sightline. "You don't got to be so evasive."

Osyen glared at her. "Magnus said that he always regretted going into government. And he wanted to pursue his lifelong passion for trombone."

"That's an expensive hobby."

"Eh, he's a rich man," Osyen grunted. "You know he went into government. He can afford to do whatever he wants."

"Stop dodging," Zatia scolded. "This is me. It's not even everybody, just me. What did Magnus say that loosened your screws?"

"Jus' something that made me act stupid," Osyen admitted. "I've put it in rearview. It's getting nothing but our exhaust."

Maybe. But it was also occupying his brain right now. He couldn't focus on anything else.

"Okay, Oz..." Zatia said with a gentle nod. "You know you ever have a problem that needs stabbing, you can call us in. Adelaide'll fix anything you throw to her, Roche will get you there and back, and the Lady von Sparkly Pants over there will get you in the door." Another flash of red and alarm was coupled with a muffled curse from Rashida. Zatia didn't even blink. "Thom will find your shiny thing and I'll get you back out again. Right?"

And Osyen smiled. "Yeah, I know."

"And I promise to only kill people who get in my way—or holler at me."

"You don't want to run and let the air chill a bit?" Osyen asked her.

In her experience, fires didn't burn out. They just spread. "I've done a lot of running. And then I done a lot of hitting. Still not sure which is the right time for each." She jerked a thumb at Rashida. "Why do you think she's so infuriating?"

"She always knows what to do?"

"No. Almost never. She just always *looks* like she knows what she's doing." She paused, letting that sink in. "Do you know what you're doing?"

His look slipped and his jaw tightened, and he didn't have to say a word.

"Didn't think so. Oz, no matter what anybody says, no one knows what they're doing. We just...we know what's out there, what we're afraid of. We do what we can, what we want, and what we should in that order. And we rarely like ourselves the next day. But I know for sure that if you hate who you were a year ago, that's because you're a better person today. And a year from now, you will hate who you are today. Because we get better."

Osyen stiffened at that sentiment, his eyes sharpening. She'd struck a nerve, maybe? Maybe she'd finally get him to talk?

Zatia leaned against the railing. "Now, you're not paying me to chew on your ear. Tell me what I can do."

Osyen reached for her coffee flagon again, and she wordlessly passed him the steel cup. He took a stiff pull of the cold brew, wincing at the taste before passing it back. "You can add cream to that, y'know."

"Ruins the flavor."

"You're a monster. A terror set upon the countryside."

Zatia nodded. "Villagers hired a mysterious warrior to come kill me once. What parts I didn't eat, I gave to my spawn."

He snickered at the image of her having children. "If there was anybody I'd call...it'd be you."

"Good. Now, I'm going to teach Rashida how to not die. If you keep your mouth shut and don't be a distraction, you might learn how to actually keep your pieces."

"Yeah..." Osyen stared into the distance, back to idly rubbing the hand rail, like it might grant him a wish.

CHAPTER 7
ROCHE

THE POWER FLOWED through his wrist and up around his heart three separate times, before flowing back down again and into the ship. Lily's embrace had been firm, like a weighted blanket about his chest and back, squeezing him into relaxation.

He didn't require sleep anymore. His squishy organic bits certainly needed extended periods of inactivity to allow clearance of memory caches and repairs to stress fractures in his tissues, but this wasn't 'sleeping.' Sleep was more akin to going on a journey, where the conscious mind could depart the flesh and gallivant across the most wild and wonderful places, full of horror and thrills, absurdity and chills.

These days, he had a simple warm electric pulse from the ship's fusion reactor to keep him warm as he let his mind rest. No more wild imaginings of a mind untethered. Now, he could simply close his eyes and open them again, refreshed and prepared. And that wonderful heartbeat of electrons guided him through those nights.

The absence of that pulse kicked like a mule.

He didn't need to ask, because Lily immediately offered the answer. Their entire conversation took less than half a second. *Our reactor core has been suspended from primary cycles. We will require a cold restart in order to generate Jump minimums.*

Source of the order? Roche asked.

A manual disconnection. All crew are accounted for—except for Osyen Belt.

What is he doing?

He's not answering me, Lily said with a quake to their voice, *and he appears to be engaging with our engine hydraulics.*

// Lock and seal all pressure doors. Mark & execute. Box him in.

The gasping of filling tanks, as the four major security doors on the *Aurum* came crushing down. They were designed to prevent the ship from being a total loss due to breach of cabin pressure but doubled as security measures. One could trap and selectively ventilate the oxygen from a compartment without ever drawing a weapon.

He listened for the bang of the doors—and only heard two. Osyen had been ready for that. He might've wedged the doors he needed, or just plain disconnected them.

// Drain fuel from Shuttles 1 & 2. Mark & Execute

// Error. Shuttle 2 operating on independent network. Please provide command from localized subnet.

// Ship thrusters, lateral adjustment 180 degrees. Turn us around!

// Error. Insufficient pressure in hydraulic lines.

Oh, no.

What is he doing? Lily asked.

Roche extended his hand to work on the holographic console—only to find that the haptic interface did not appear at his fingertips. He waved his hand a bit, hoping it would trigger the sensor, but nothing happened. *He's stranding us.*

Roche got up from his seat, clambering backward to the Jump Deck door. But it didn't open at his touch. "Lily?"

"Security lock detected. Beginning system override."

"Osyen, you asshole," Roche cursed, bouncing on his toes.

Finally, the door lurched open—and Roche scrambled through.

56

Thom and Zatia were already out of their rooms and at the next door to the galley. They strained at the handle, with Zatia putting both feet into the wall to try to leverage it open.

"Roche!" Thom called out. "Turn us about!"

"I can't!"

"Osyen!" Zatia shouted through the door. "I'm going to skin you alive!"

"Lock him out of the shuttles!" Thom ordered.

Roche threw his hand in the air. "He's pulled Number 2 from the grid. I've got nothing. Lily?"

"What's going on?" Rashida asked, as she and Adelaide both made their way out of their respective rooms.

"Y'all about to get a new captain, that's what!" Zatia growled through her teeth. "Osyen, *fra tow ni laska!*"

What could he be planning? Think. He was nearly a full day's flight away from Ilum. He'd barely make it in the shuttle. Imperial forces would be on high alert, and he had no registered flight plan. Was he trying to get himself killed?

Or he'd had second thoughts about leaving.

A face appeared at the window: Osyen. And Zatia reflexively punched the Plexiglas barrier, leaving a scuff mark in the shape of her knuckles.

The sight almost made Osyen smile. "Sorry," he murmured through the thick material, before vanishing again.

Lily, where's he headed?

He won't answer me.

"Get—it—open!" Something in Thom's desperate cry kicked Zatia into overdrive. The little lady groaned and strained and finally roared. And Roche heard the pin locks shear with a snap!

Zatia nearly fell to the ground as the door slid free. Rashida and Thom vaulted over her, sprinting through the galley and beyond. Adelaide bent over to check on Zatia, but the bruiser waved her off with the few words her breath allowed. "Not me! Get *him!*"

Roche marched into the galley. He couldn't outrun Osyen, but maybe he could cut him off. His shuttle might be disconnected from the *Aurum*, but it had to still be docked or he'd never get aboard. If Roche could engage the docking clamps, Osyen wouldn't be able to flee.

Lily read his mind. *Securing docking clamps on Shuttle 2.* And they came back just as fast. *Docking clamps are not responding. Insufficient power.*

He had to be downloading telemetry and navigation data. Could you foul it up, force Osyen to return?

Records indicate Osyen accessed and downloaded to a hard copy six hours ago.

Roche sighed in frustration. *Give me sixteen points forward thrust, double burst. Foul up his departure.*

Primary thrusters—

Give me something, Lily! You have to throw up some doors, kill the lights. Loud music, anything!

But Lily was preoccupied, fixated, trapped in a loop of logic far too human. Far too...grieving. *He won't speak to me, Roche. He hasn't even looked up.*

Roche rounded the corner, where Rashida and Thom were pressed up against the sealed airlock. "Osyen!" Thom repeated that name over and over, his breath fogging up the small glass panel.

There wasn't much Roche could make out, but he saw Osyen walking from right to left, taking a seat. Roche thought he might try his own luck, pushing his thoughts to the radio link. *Osyen? Osyen, just stop. Talk to us. We can help!*

But Osyen didn't say another word to any of them. A flare of light as the thrusters broke from the hull of the *Aurum* and silently skipped off into the darkness.

———

"It'll be hours before I can unfuck what he did!" Adelaide complained, hurling her tools on the galley table. "It'll be everything I got just to make sure we don't fall unguided into that *gulaw* gravity well we were aiming at!"

"If Osyen wanted us to die, you would be dead." Lily's baritone voice was usually so powerful. It sounded so small, like the behemoth behind it had been stripped of its size.

Adelaide didn't dispute that claim either, stomping over to the Replicator. "Whiskey, neat. Chilled glass."

Thom rubbed his forehead, tucked in the corner. "He just wanted to be sure we couldn't chase him."

Zatia paced back and forth across the floor. She hadn't stopped since the shuttle had broke free, and it surprised Roche she hadn't cut a small trough in the deck. There were already micrometers of measurable flex in the hull where years' worth of pathing had left its mark. She was inflicting months' worth in a few minutes.

Rashida clutched her steaming cup of tea, still groggy from the rude awakening. "We've got to be faster than him, right? We get the ship turned around, run him down?"

"Even if I could fix us that fast," Adelaide started, "we'd be heading right back into serrated Imperial teeth. And I don't know if you recall, but they're pretty pissed off, to boot."

"He's going to get himself killed!" Zatia snapped. "I'm supposed to kill him. Nobody else!" Roche noted the strange possessiveness in Zatia's tone there, like some kind of dominant animal furious at the loss of one of its herd.

"Adelaide?" Thom said, his voice clean and calm. "Whatever you need, however long it takes. Get us turned about."

The Replicator chimed its happy dissonant notice. Adelaide snatched her frosty glass from the chamber and immediately poured the entire contents down the hatch. With a bracing alcoholic breath, she threw the glass at the wall, sending shards across the entire galley.

"You're cleaning that up too," Zatia grumbled.

"*Fra tcw zu ytrit*," was Adelaide's knowing affirmative response, as she stomped back down to Engineering.

"Highly populated Imperial colony," Rashida said, "with some of the tightest security seen outside of the Core. Full to the brim with Imperial Peace Officers and Naval Regulars. Just stepping foot on that planet will be picking a fight."

Thom sat forward at the table, fingers tented and voice quaking. "Do we want to do this?"

"What, you going to take a vote?" Zatia said.

"No Captain, no Milardi..." And Thom's eyes fell to Roche. "Which puts Roche in charge."

And Roche's skin crawled, every inch and crevice from the soles of his feet to the crown of his head. It was like his body wanted to unzip itself and flee. "Me?"

"Unless you want to defer to Zatia."

Zatia finally stopped pacing. "You don't want to do that."

Roche didn't feel cut out for leadership. There were enough calculations going on in his head, as it was. But he instantly found himself weighing and quantifying...ethics, morals.

It would defy Osyen's wishes. It would put the entire team and the ship itself in grave danger. Did he not have a responsibility to them? And did he not respect Osyen enough to let the man have what he wanted?

And could Roche be sure he wasn't acting out of his own selfish need?

Lily? Roche asked. *I could really use your voice now.*

Apologies, friend, Lily said. *I have precious little to offer.*

Help me work this out. It's too loud for me to focus.

We get him back, Lily said. *We bring him home. And we kill him ourselves.*

That mad at him?

I am conflicted. I wish him harm, and I wish him safe.

Roche understood the feeling, and he could feel Lily's rage build. Their feelings might not have been his own, but the tension in his shoulders and the pressure building in his chest...he wanted to scream; he wanted to cry; he wanted to bloody his knuckles and to squeeze something soft.

"A crew vote," Roche muttered. "But it has to be unanimous. Ilum is the leading edge of Imperial power, and their forces will have doubled to reinforce their loss. Getting in won't be the same problem as getting out. Once they ID Osyen, all bets are off. They'll have every one of our names, faces, biometrics. We will not be able to move freely, and they will oppose us at every gate. So...if we're going back to Ilum, we only do it as a team. Any person votes no, and we make for the darkest hole we can find. What say you?"

Zatia squared up, planting her feet. No hesitation. "We bring him home."

Rashida stood up, taking her place head and shoulders over Zatia. "He'd do it for us."

Thom didn't even get up, just nodding. "He *has* done it for us. For all of us."

"Whatever shenanigans we're planning," Adelaide shouted up the corridor, "deal me in!"

Roche waited for another voice. There was an absence in the air, of laughter and jovial rhythm. But he couldn't place why it felt wrong. There was a thick Colonial accent that hadn't joined the chorus...

Thom looked up at the roof. "Lily?"

Lily's distant melancholy. "The vote is specified as 'crew members' and I am not—"

"Please," Rashida dismissed. "Lily, you have more to lose today than any one of us. We've voted. What about you?"

"I will do everything in my power to bring Osyen Belt back to his home."

Thom drew a breath, raising his eyes back up to Roche. "Well, Roche? All hands on deck?"

Everyone had voted in favor. His attempt at an open vote hadn't done much for lifting the responsibility. It still fell at his feet. He could vote 'no' and send them all to safety. He could vote 'yes' and send them all to their deaths.

But at least now he knew what they wanted. And he was happy to help them get that.

CHAPTER 8
ADELAIDE

"*GULAW S'IVAN*," Adelaide grunted from halfway in the wall, her hands wrapped around a grimy old silicon panel. "He rewired this entire grid!"

Lily's head projected into the wall, providing enough ambient light for Adelaide to do her work, though the harsh blue wasn't the kindest on her eyes. "He had prepared it for just such an occasion."

"Oh really? Cut a line here, pull a socket there—suddenly his entire starship is dead in the water?" Adelaide yanked on the panel, getting it loose on her third pull. She retreated out of the bulkhead back under the normal overheads, where she could see what Osyen had done.

It was an auxiliary power board, largely low voltage unless main power was cut. Osyen had stripped the insulation off of the wires, providing about a half dozen opportunities for contact shorts on the board. So, of course, when the system tried to flow a proper amount of power through it, the thing practically caught fire.

She'd have called this negligent stupidity if she hadn't been sure Osyen had done it on purpose. "If hostiles somehow gained control of the *Aurum*," Lily explained, "he could cripple the vessel to prevent further pursuit."

Well, the modifications worked like a charm. And it required a replacement part before the auxiliary system would boot, and the main system wouldn't cycle without the mandatory backup. Stupid modern safety regulations, making every day of her life all grit and sweat.

Especially today.

Thankfully, Adelaide had been obsessive about keeping replacements of critical things stocked. She tossed the burnt-out board into her scrap bin and stomped over to her storage.

"Highlight replacement panel, model number CN-24 ELMC?" Adelaide asked.

Lily obliged, the drawer on the wall glowing iridescent blue as Adelaide approached. Adelaide yanked the drawer open, revealing rows of silicon boards of a nice size and shape.

"I had never assumed he might use our own countermeasures against me," Lily admitted.

Adelaide paused, biting her lip. What to say to them?

"I know that I'm a cognitive digital intelligence capable of sophisticated problem solving," Lily said, "but I can't help but feel..."

"Betrayed?" Adelaide asked.

"Betrayal implies a knowing violation of trust or existing promises," Lily said. "His actions this morning did not breach any such user agreement."

"You can still feel the way you feel," Adelaide said.

"That is a human response."

An excuse. The word they were grasping for was 'excuse.' But it wasn't said with the usual amount of disdain, but rather...distance. Adelaide snatched the board and pushed the drawer closed. "And you may not be slowly rotting from an overabundance of meat juice, but you can still feel things, yeah?"

"You will complete decay in approximately four years, eight months and twenty-seven days."

Adelaide cocked her head. "Approximately?"

"Discounting any other outside impulses, yes."

"You're just like him," Adelaide said, shaking her head.

Lily floated over, pixel by pixel assembling on the side of the main reactor. "How so?"

"You crack jokes so people don't know you're stressed."

"I was not joking. I was reaching the mathematical truth of your inevitable destruction."

"Whatever." Adelaide walked through Lily's head, stomping back over to the hole in the wall. If Lily wanted to keep their digital head in the metaphorical sand, they were welcome to do so.

Nothing more human than denial.

"Explain yourself," Lily called at her back.

"Don't gotta," Adelaide said. "I have a ship to fix."

"Adelaide—"

"Shut up and light this for me."

Lily didn't answer for a long moment, until their head blinked into existence in the wall, casting their blue glow along the *Aurum*'s interior structure.

Adelaide squirmed in, wriggling out a comfortable spot for her shoulder to rest while she worked the new panel into place.

"If something happens to him..." Lily started.

Adelaide sighed. "Lily, don't complete that thought experiment."

"I have reached at least three hundred and seventy-nine separate conclusions."

"It's like talking to the avatar of anxiety," Adelaide muttered.

"Four hundred and twelve."

Adelaide got the new grid socketed in and shook out the cramp growing in her wrist. "Lily...it's real easy to think about what you're going to do. But you can spend a lifetime and a half obsessing over what you'll do before you *do* a damn thing."

"You suggest I collapse the wave function?"

"I suggest you find out what's actually going on before you decide what you might do! We can grind on and on about what might be happening, but until we know something, we're just spinning wheels.

Why did he cut us out? Why go on his own? Until we have an answer to that, there's no point in guessing."

Lily's light dimmed for a moment—forcing Adelaide to pause her work, tapping her fingernails on the cold bulkhead. Without enough light, she was liable to plug something into the wrong lead and just short out the brand-new panel.

She'd have objected, but the light came back in short order. Along with another question. "How did you...when you lost Nathaniel, how did you keep from going mad?"

Adelaide relaxed, letting her weight drape awkwardly down on her shoulder. She remembered Nathaniel's soft hands tracing patterns on the back of her arm. The smell of his beard oil: rosewater and musk. The taste of his lips on her own.

And the sight of his blood pumping on to the floor.

"I didn't," Adelaide said. "I was mad for a long time."

"What happened?"

Adelaide closed her eyes and drew a breath. "Osyen did. He got me out of my rut, he got my hands on Nathaniel again. And I finally figured out that Nathaniel...wasn't what I was missing."

"You were never mad at the Godfather," Lily concluded. "You were mad at Nathaniel. For leaving."

Wow. It felt true enough to hear, and she had logically known it for a long time, but to hear it articulated out loud? Adelaide lowered her head, resting her hot skin on the cold metal for relief.

Yeah. She had been. She had been furious. Furious to tears and back again. She'd have wept herself to sleep if she wasn't so busy cursing his name. Nathaniel had left her life in pieces and had taken a few shards away with him. How was she ever to make sense of her world again?

This ship. These people. Find something else to love. And these stupid kids needed her.

"Thank you, Adelaide." Lily said, soft. "Your advice has helped."

Adelaide nodded. "I might have some experience with that spiral, is all. I need light."

CHAPTER 9
RASHIDA

IT WASN'T a face she relished the thought of. But it was the only person she thought might have some answers for her. And when the lights came back on and the power doors opened, she knew she had the opportunity to find it.

She punched in the personal code of her Imperial Consort—and her hand hovered over the confirm. Nausea swelled once, twice in her gut. And the back of her neck pricked with a wave of chills.

Did she want to look at his face again so soon? Especially when she would have no ability to strike it? He would lord over her, instruct her in the manner of Ladies, and how she should return to Dunsweir Manor, where she might be safe from further corruption.

He can speak. But she can choose whether or not to listen to him. That will always be her prerogative.

And she pressed down, sending out the call through the Extranet. It was a chilling few seconds of chimes and bells before his face appeared.

Sallow and pale skin, sunken and hawkish eyes. But the young man who had dogged her heels for the better part of four years looked shaken.

Magnus saw her, giving his own assessment of her condition. Stiff upper lip and feigning pride, he squared his shoulders. "The Lady Rashida. You look well."

"You look foul," Rashida said.

"Accepting video calls means you're close," he noted.

"I wouldn't consider that the blessing you think it is," she threatened. "But I hate to say I am in need of your help."

Magnus bowed his head. "You are Dunsweir, my lady. My service has been and always will be to you."

Rashida couldn't stop the shake of her head. This little viper had tried to have her killed, tried to have her caged. To lay claim to such high-minded ideals took a particularly twisted approach. "You're a sick little man."

He nodded, offering only deference in response. "What assistance can I offer?"

"You spoke with Osyen Belt some months back?"

His cheek twitched, flashing a look at Magnus's sharpened teeth, but though his countenance was unpleasant, so was the memory. "It wasn't a very diplomatic encounter."

"What did you speak about?"

"I pled for my life," Magnus said with an even tone. "Does that comfort you?"

Rashida's eyes narrowed in disappointment. "It seems he granted your wish."

"Ashamed to say."

"Count yourself lucky."

"I've heard of his exploits." Magnus smirked, the first real glimmer of disdain in his eyes. "The next man to have the privilege of his presence did not fare so well."

"You sent him there, is what I hear."

Magnus's eyes drifted to something off-screen. If he was tracing the call, he was welcome to do so. She would happily meet whatever challenge he brought.

And he must've seen her honing her steel. "I am disgraced, my Lady. I bought my life with information. This is not a crime the Empire takes lightly."

Rashida nodded. If Magnus had died with dignity, the Minister of Peace on Ilum would still be alive. And the Empire looked at such transactions quite literally. One of these men was far more important than the other.

A debt had been incurred.

Magnus was only alive so long as no one knew of his involvement. And secrets like that had a tendency to leak out of thin air.

"What did you tell him, Magnus?"

"I knew his name, his old name, before he assumed the identity of Osyen Belt deep in the bowels of Charon." Magnus blinked and his lips drew tight as he considered whether to continue. For all of his schooling and power, he was not a proficient liar. And he knew when he was caught. "And...I knew that his mother was still alive."

What! Rashida's heart thumped in her chest and her hands squeezed tight to her sides. "Tell me everything you told him, Magnus, or I will spend my waning days routing you from every hole you have."

"You will find me, my lady," Magnus said. "Of that, I have no doubt. Because I have never hid from you. I told him only that she still lived, and that he could find her if he looked."

That's why Osyen had insisted they come to Ilum, making their way across the galaxy these last few months. He had an appointment with someone.

And he put that man in the ground. He must've found what he was looking for.

Osyen was on the trail of his mother. He wouldn't stop. He wouldn't be delayed. And he wouldn't put his new family at risk for his own obsession.

That stupid, stupid man!

Magnus dared to open his mouth again. "I hope you understand what he has unleashed, my lady. The Paladins were secretive, brutal, and efficient. They were a punishment befit the crime. But killing a Minister? Your friend will meet the full force of a vengeful Empire, on a planet where even the ground obeys their word. He will find no shelter in the shadows nor in the skies. He will find no quarter from its protectors. And what he seeks will turn to ash in his hands."

PART TWO
SPEAKING TO THE STONES

And wherever they walked, they laid stepping stones upon which to follow. And the stones did speak in elder tongues older than word or song, plucking the strings of humanity and urging them to follow.

And cursing those who are unworthy...

GNOSTIC LIBRUM, EXETER 5:2-5

CHAPTER 10
OSYEN

ILUM WAS A PLANET HELIOCENTRICALLY LOCKED, rotating at the same rate as its orbit, trapping one half in near permanent day. In truth, there was drift, but in the century mankind had been there, the day line had only moved a few dozen meters.

Which fragmented the culture in a very predictable way.

The sun baked the Sunnyside while the Darkside froze, only kept habitable by the deep veins of copper that vented the heat through the planet's crust. It was still uncomfortably hot and painfully cold on respective sides of the Sunset line, but it was at least habitable—a condition almost ruined by early attempts to mine out that copper.

All of the money sat in the sunshine, pretty and clean and tidy.

The Darkside of Ilum was more...seedy.

The shuttle sat on the pad, as a scummy duo of overly hairy gentlemen hooked cables from the spaceport to the hull. Whether they were refueling or siphoning off wasn't clear, but Osyen wasn't going to pick that fight. He was renting their pad—and probably was going to abandon the ship there. They'd get to auction the shuttle for scrap, for all he cared.

The harbormaster took his bribe, and to her credit, she didn't have Clerics waiting for him. The grubby woman directed her miscreant laborers and guided Osyen over to the freight elevator at the edge of the pad.

She looked him up and down as he walked, eyes drifting over to the holographic wanted posting of a one-armed man fleeing the Ministry of Peace. And she just smirked, shaking her head.

He noticed her look and followed her eyes. They were offering cold cash for information—and clemency for his capture. Any criminal that forked him over would see their own slates wiped clean, if they trusted the listing.

Many on this side of Sunset didn't. They lived where the Sun didn't shine.

As the elevator descended, Osyen got a beautiful view. The sprawling metropolis had long since spread over every square mile of available real estate on the planet, from horizon to horizon and back around again, even in the cold reaches of the dark. Enormous heating vents let the planet's natural conductive heating blast warm air into the night, tempering the Darkside skies and bringing about humid and sticky nights.

At the edge of sight, there was the glow of the sun kissing steel buildings like a holy blessing. And the buildings themselves seemed to be brushed into grace with its touch.

This side of the planet hadn't seen sunlight for a thousand years.

On this side of the Sunset line, buildings were grimy and irregular, oil slicks and neon color. Filthy on examination but under dim lights and permanent night, a silhouette was more important. So buildings rose up to catch the eye with shape, not texture. They were composites of irregular shapes and specular surfaces, catching what little light there was in edges that almost glowed.

As the elevator descended, he could hear the shouts from market stall barkers, the bass thump of nightclubs, and the whimpering of stray animals. The occasional bit of broken glass and splash of water filled out the urban orchestra.

It looked like he'd stepped out into a cosmopolitan menagerie, filled with nothing but crime and the impoverished. It was always of interest to Osyen, how one could walk ten feet off of a prescribed thoroughfare and leave glowing tourist traps and glittering palaces to suddenly find destitution and grief. On Second Avenue, a visitor could find clubs and crafts aplenty, marketed to the visitors. But money rarely traveled two blocks in either direction, as though the designated areas had a gravity for wealth, repulsing all else.

Money always stayed where it was told to stay.

The elevator clanged at the bottom and the harbormaster heaved up the gate. Osyen approached the security scanner that led to the city proper. And he sidestepped it, hopping up on the table and landing safely on the other side.

There was no record of Osyen Belt departing this discreet and scummy dock. The harbormaster gave him a two-finger salute, bidding him luck on his suicide mission while she mentally counted the earnings of the day.

If Osyen wanted to walk directly into the mouth of the dragon, that was his business; she won, no matter how she played it. And people always liked the path of least resistance, especially when it provided maximum gain.

He stepped out of the dock, feeling the irregular cobblestones underfoot slick with moss and—what he hoped was—water. Above him, two layers of bridges connected the first levels of buildings in pedestrian paths, laid out in crisscrossing patterns, following the arteries that people most wanted. And the bridges were moving.

The very foundation shifted and grew like an organic, intelligent slime, bricks rolling across each other to shore up positions or broaden surfaces. The walkways actually grew and shrank based on need, shifting directions as the pedestrians pressed, to make for the most ideal pathways at any given time.

And above that, the constant flow of hovering cars, a glittering cloud of iridescent specks coasting through the dark sky, a million commuters idling on the greatest public transit system ever conceived.

Must be nice, never having to touch the ground. Down here, they might have to breathe the air or eat the food, maybe even see the sick and unseemly.

"Well, Milardi," Osyen whispered, fingers grazing the revolver on his hip, "We're in it now."

Was he out of his mind? This was Ilum, Gateway to the Imperium Core. He was going to get scanned and arrested by a *gulaw* building, then executed in public with the clever application of pulleys and cable. The crowd would cheer, his friends would watch, and he wouldn't even make it to the Sunshine.

He pivoted hard on his heel and turned back to the harbor. He had enough fuel to get to low orbit, at least—

No! He stopped. He came this far. Only way out now was through. He had long since passed the point of flight.

This city. It looked like the fabled abyss of yore grew up and got an office job. It could swallow him whole without concern or regret, no matter how civilized it appeared to be. This was what crime looked like when muggings became rackets, dealing became smuggling, and murder became statistics.

The Empire was lining all the pockets here, even the filthy ones— Osyen had no veil of protection here.

But he couldn't just go straight after his quarry. No, he needed some new documents. Any facial recognition would summon every Cleric in the Ward. He'd die with his face in the mud before he'd even gotten ten steps.

Couldn't fly then. Not yet.

He walked down the road, feeling the moist air cling to his skin and swallow the sound of his footfalls on the cobblestones. Walking these streets was like lingering in a dream, where every building had a lean or sunken posture, lit by flickering rainbow candlelight.

Holographic collar maybe? That would do nothing against modern security systems except highlight him. A jamming system would be an instant red flag, and he needed to move freely, not punch in and out. So he needed a new face, a new name.

Oh, well. It wouldn't be his first.

Osyen trotted up an alley, skipping down a set of glistening wet stairs. His shifty eyes checked the area left and right, before he rapped his knuckles against a heavy iron door.

The viewport slid open. All Osyen could see was a knobby nose and the top side of a thick mustache. "We're not open."

"City of Lights usually burns at both ends," Osyen said.

The man huffed, and the viewport clacked shut again.

Osyen bit his lip. Maybe the code language of the underground had shifted a bit. If his knowledge of Ilum's underbelly was out of date, he might've painted himself as a Cleric instead of a client.

But in half a second, he heard about a dozen locking mechanisms grind and pop free. The door slid open, revealing the gatekeeper of fugitives across any world: a scratcher. Osyen couldn't afford the best, but he wasn't going to skimp on something that could separate him from a fusillade of bullets and a clean getaway. A scratcher could provide him a new identity, inject him into the system, even give him a new face.

They could 'scratch him' into the system.

He was a portly fellow with graying hair and a data jack in the base of his skull, its black cable pendulous behind him, swaying from the pulley and track system on the ceiling. That kept the delicate thing crewed up and out from underfoot. The scratcher cradled a bowl of ramen in one hand, his other hand hanging low to the gun on his hip.

"Been out?" the man asked, still chewing.

"Been legit," Osyen said, "but times are what they are."

The scratcher grunted at that. His eyes tracked over to Osyen's missing arm, noting the most obvious identifier about him.

"Problem?" Osyen asked.

"Needs consideration. I don't know you." The scratcher slurped up some noodles. "They're looking for a one-armed man who traumatically implanted some metal into a Cleric."

Osyen raised an eyebrow. "Are they now? Doesn't seem smart of somebody to be that wanted and that obvious at the same time."

"No, it doesn't," the scratcher said, stepping aside. The pulley system followed him as he walked, reeling in the cable to keep it out of the way. "Get inside or move along."

The pulley system extended this far forward, but a curtain blocked Osyen's view deeper into the room. He might be walking right into a trap, into the hands of someone willing to fork him over. Or into a legitimate businessman's place of work.

Not like he had other options. Osyen took the step, pushing aside the curtain with one hand.

It was an impressive arrangement. Two computer servers were whirring away, crunching on some problem on the far side of the room. The pulley track system had a gaping hole in the center of its web, making space for the AutoDoc that fit dead center of the basement floor, crudely bolted down on ill-fitted brackets.

This was the place a criminal came to get a new beginning, so free and clear that even his own family wouldn't recognize him.

"A prosthesis on short notice is a tall order," the scratcher said, pushing past him to check on his computers. "And it's one out of reach of your pockets."

"You don't know, maybe my pockets are plenty," Osyen said.

The scratcher laughed. "I'm old, not an invalid. Lay down there."

Osyen followed his direction and took a seat in the AutoDoc. The many tiny arms spun to work in the air, working from one end of their range to the other in a warm up sequence.

"I could get you a stunt arm, completely nonfunctional. Will break up your silhouette but won't do much for ya beyond that. But for *your bud*get, you get new eyes," the scratcher offered, "matched up with the poor bastard's papers."

"That's it?" Osyen asked.

"Hey, you're the one who comes sauntering up to me with one arm and an attitude. Do you know how many men with your height and proportions and skin tone I have access to? You have to fit your new ident, or I may as well fork you over to the Clerics meself."

It was a fair point. He couldn't exactly get a new face on short notice. He had to work with what he could afford.

"Your name," the scratcher said, "is Evan Whitby. You're a twice divorced urologist from Concordia, you have a sister you don't speak to and a brother on Vanguard."

The AutoDoc jabbed Osyen with a small hypo, dumping the anesthetic into his leg. "I'm a divorced urologist from the Core?"

"He also happens to have died in a gambling den last week. The one-armed beggar should take what I give him."

"How old was this guy?"

"Thirty-eight, but he had good genes until somebody stabbed him." The scratcher punched in some commands on his computer and walked over to Osyen's side. "Remember, it's new eyes and a new profile. It'll get you through checkpoints, but any Cleric worth his weight is going to be questioning anyone that fits your silhouette. So don't let folk go inspecting that arm, or you'll spend the rest of your brief life in a featureless gray void. The computer will kick out Evan Whitby, but enough identifiers like mannerisms, turns of phrase, known associates—not even your new eyeballs will protect you. The system will cross-reference, and you'll be riddled full of holes."

"I'm not the one who—"

"You're an innocent man, yeah, yeah." The scratcher waved him off, pulling the AutoDoc's console over to him, tapping out the keys without even looking. Someone conducting minor surgery should probably be looking at what he was doing, but Osyen shrugged it off. This was not this man's first rodeo.

He would've closed his eyes and drifted off to sleep, but they only fluttered. The paralytic had taken effect, locking his eyes open. And the tiny little arms lowered down towards his face, the scratcher looming in his peripheral—and for a split second, he could feel a sharp tug.

And then he woke up. And he was color blind. Well, ain't that just fun?

———

He summoned the car and was surprised to see how fast it appeared. The gullwing door slung open, revealing an almost angry amount of beige vinyl upholstery, stained but functional. That was beige right? Or was it some heinous shade of green or deep red, and it only looked like some sickening pale bile color?

Sure, the old phrase was 'walk a mile in their shoes', but walking a mile with their eyeballs in his skull was a mortifying experience, especially when he literally saw a different world now than he had once before. And the light sensitivity and splitting headache wasn't helping his case.

The nav-computer announced itself happily with a gruff, "Where to, eh?"

Where to, indeed.

"Royal Arts Academy, Lower Wards," he said as he popped a pain pill the size of a walnut. He cracked it between his teeth to activate and swallowed hard—tasted like poison. It flamed alarm bells in his head and his stomach and his skin. That was poison, don't eat it. Poison bad. Do not eat.

He swallowed it. Doctor's orders. If he wanted to quell this headache quickly, he needed to onboard that medication quickly.

"Any day now!" the taxi cab barked with faux urgency.

Osyen clambered into the cab, pulling the door shut behind him. A screen popped up with the address and insignia of the university.

Here goes nothing. A swipe of his new docs, and a flash of light checked his eyes to confirm his identity as a colorblind urologist with two ex-wives.

An unhappy blare from the car speakers made his heart jump into his throat.

"Inconclusive," the computer said. "Please keep your eyes open for clean retinal scan."

Osyen tried to flex his updated eyeballs as wide as he could, and he felt a trickle of warmth seep down his cheek.

Another flash of light and another spike of pain. Thankfully, the computer was checking his retinas, not analyzing him for ocular leakage. Otherwise, there's be a picture of a man crying blood in the backseat of a taxicab. The computer beeped a jocular tone of confirmation and the car whisked up and away into the automated paths.

Osyen swiped the blood off his cheek, trying to rub it onto his sleeve. He couldn't be sure though, since it just looked like a dark fluid. Was he bleeding blood or motor oil?

The car slipped between the shifting bridges and the asymmetric towers of Ilum's Nightside, a silver dart on its way skyward.

Within seconds, he was several hundred feet up and keenly aware that he was now a slave to the whims of computers and gravity. If the law caught him now, the best thing he could do was jump—and that might not even save him from their wrath.

He'd have a good amount of time to consider the circumstances that brought him here, in any event. It'd be almost a full minute of free fall before he found consequences.

The taxi cab chimed as it passed the first checkpoint and he held his breath. But nothing came of it, nothing that it announced anyhow. So after a few minutes of clenching, he relaxed. Of course, maybe the Law already had him, and the car was cheerfully dragging him off to a cell.

Then the sunshine suddenly shot through the window, glaring, blinding him. He blinked, before the sun shade came down like a pixilated veil. And he could make out the permanent Sunset Line.

On the other side of this astrogeographic curiosity, the architecture abruptly shifted to crisp geometric lines, clean bright colors. While the Nightside had rolling hills of asymmetric towers, the Sunset Line was immediately marked by broad, fat, blocky buildings, brutalist and minimalist.

And worst of all, one enormous structure extended up and out unsupported, reaching over the others like the canopy of a tree, or like an enormous tower had started to melt and bend over. It had to be several miles tall, with the cloud cover wrapping about its shoulders, before the building curved outward to lord itself over its lessers. It robbed the Ward underneath of direct sunlight, and Osyen stared in wonder how it didn't collapse down on them, killing thousands.

But that was the point, he thought, to inspire awe and confusion. It was easy to believe your Empire all-powerful when even physics seemed to bend the knee.

Square in the center of that enormous shadow was the Academy of the Royal Arts, its own spires reaching up to the sky like fingers clawing for Olympus. Inside each of the five spires was enough data capacity to house the entirety of human existence three times over. But the metal cloud overhead made those towers look like anthills.

The cab spiraled in to the Academy's shaded courtyard, effortlessly gliding into a low-flying queue as it awaited an open spot to deposit Osyen. Students, teachers, and tourists alike were being offloaded into the building that hosted the compendium of human history.

Somewhere inside that structure was Charles Ordee—or someone who knew him. What would Osyen ask him? Did he think of Catharina much? Did he remember her? Did he regret it?

No. Osyen had to focus on finding her. And this was the last lead he had. He had to play this carefully, and with any luck, Professor Ordee might have some other threads Osyen could tug on.

His car tilted and careened toward the ground before settling up to an open spot on the curb. The gullwing door clicked open and the anachronistic sound of a cash register announced the deduction of the fee from Osyen's...from Evan's accounts.

Osyen's grubby origins practically left an oil stain on the pavement, the filth of the Darkside incidentally deposited on the stoop of the highest altar of education. Even in the shadow of the monolith overhead, the warmth of the sun baked the ground dry. And Osyen had just ridden in out of an urban swamp. He was certain that someone in this castle was employed solely to keep up the appearance of the Academy's faultless image. And Osyen winced a bit, having just made that person's job harder.

He looked around, taking a second to consider how many cameras must be tracking on him right now, scanning his gait, his posture, his pattern of breathing. Behind those cameras, a dozen computers cranking away to biometrically confirm identities against a database of most wanted. He'd have to change more than just his eyes if he wanted to fool those. He'd need to live...differently.

And so Osyen pressed on to the grand double doors in front of him and into the Academy of the Royal Arts.

Perhaps it was a trick of the architecture, but when Osyen entered, the enormity of the building hit him. There was no way they had managed to pack this vaulted empty cavern into the building he saw outside! What was a certainly impressive building on initial inspection was a modern wonder from inside. It almost took his breath away, his head craning back to study the frescos painted on the roof, one enormous tableau of a sick and frail man reaching out to the starlit night sky, and a hand reaching back.

"Beautiful, isn't it?"

He never saw the woman approach, but there she stood, with a square jaw and ashen gray hair cut in to some kind of fashionable bob. She wore a white floor-length coat, and her Entiglas was a few models out of date. Her voice was deep too, full of bass and gravel, as though she'd spent her best years in far less noble pursuits.

"It looks familiar," Osyen said.

"Yes. The original artist painted over the Sistine Chapel to honor the Pilgrim in 2146. Pollution and radiation had nearly destroyed the original ceiling, and local governments took it upon themselves to 'update' the work." She pointed up at the ceiling, marveling at it for what must be the thousandth time. "The original is still in Italy, vacuum-sealed of course. This is simply a copy."

"No attempt to preserve the original ceiling?"

"Oh, there are many copies in the historical archives. But few have interest anymore beyond art collectors."

Osyen looked up at the fresco again, marveling at the colors and mysticism they invoked—and noted the two cameras nestled among the painted stars.

The woman brought herself back down to earth, squaring up on him with both hands tucked in her jacket pockets. No doubt hand on a remote alarm. "I don't recall any visiting lecturers on the circuit this week."

He squeezed on his thumb to hide his worry. Had she noticed something off about his eye-work? Seen the blood on his cheek?

"Not a lecturer," Osyen said. "Just something of a private scholar, looking for some lesser known Gnostic texts."

This caught her attention, and she folded her arms across her chest. "That so? Then you have come to the right place. The Royal Arts of Ilum has more artifacts and writings than any institute in the Core."

Osyen pursed his lips. His mother had been a researcher here, and it was her research that had gotten her into trouble. She had claims about the Pilgrim, the Dunsweir, the official story.

Maybe what she found was still here somewhere.

"Ilum has some of the richest history around the Pilgrim as well, does it not?"

"That it does," she said, extending a hand in greeting. "Irene Foxworth, the Curator of the Royal Arts."

Osyen took her hand with a conman's smile. "Evan Whitby."

He felt the subdermal device seated in her palm as the sensor snagged all of his biometrics and compared them against the planetary database. Time to see if his credentials were really up to snuff.

Irene's eyes unfocused, tracking the digital display reflecting on the inside of an ocular implant. "What's the nature of your interest, Dr. Whitby? Gnostic artifacts aren't exactly a common professional concern of a divorced urologist."

"Twice divorced," Osyen corrected.

"Bad luck?"

"Bad taste," Osyen said. "They kept marrying me."

She wasn't charmed by that answer, but she wasn't chased off either. "My question stands."

Osyen smiled. "I wanted to say patriotism, but in reality, I found a paper with some astounding claims. Thought I might get my answers from a primary source. If you have the time, I would love to bend your ear through some of the exhibits?"

"What was the paper?"

Did he dare say the name? No, not yet. He had to give her something, though. "Gravimetric Anomalies and the Pilgrim's Path. Paper was tagged by the Ministry as unreviewed."

Good enough. He hadn't dropped the name of a paper she actually knew, at least. She consulted her schedule on her Entiglas. "I have a luncheon with alumni and deep pockets that almost certainly will not be making donations." But then she swiped to a daily planner. "Do you have a particular field of interest you'd like to be debunking? Perhaps one of my team can assist you?"

"One of your team?" Osyen smiled, sly dog. "What if I'm patient?"

"You'd almost have to be," Irene quipped, "but I'm sure my team can answer any of your questions."

He focused on the backside of the hologram, all the letters inverted. But he still could make out the name.

"Archaeology?" Osyen asked.

Her eyebrows shot up, intrigued. "Gravimetric Anomalies somehow tying into archeology? Charles is going to love this."

And Osyen tried to mask his sigh of satisfaction. Professor Charles Ordee was going to answer some questions alright.

CHAPTER 11
THOM

HE GRIPPED the armrests like he was going to rip them off. Tongues of flame danced across the hull of the *Aurum* during the atmospheric braking. He knew intellectually that the ecumenopolis below them, with its glittering spires and urban sprawl, was just a holographic projection on the floor of the Jump Deck.

But as the *Aurum* pushed through reentry, all he could think of was the ship engulfed in fire, smoking ruins...

Crash landing in the Godfather's ship had not been a comfortable experience, and now every creak and groan the *Aurum* made reminded Thom of bulkheads bursting and screaming winds.

He figured that the gift of foresight would've done wonders for his anxiety, but the human body didn't give a damn about intellectual sensibilities. It felt anxious, so he was going to feel that panic, no matter what he knew to be true.

Why couldn't he predict useful things? Like lottery numbers or the right thing to say? No, instead he got apocalyptic snapshots of only the most stressful events in his future, and usually through blurry candy glass.

He felt the tip of Zatia's steel-toed boot tap his leg. The bruiser stood on the deck like nothing was wrong. She tilted her head, trying to catch his eye. "You know something I don't?"

How to even begin to not answer that? He had seen their ship crash and burn, and the exterior of the hull was currently on fire, even though that by itself wasn't altogether unusual.

"Landing Control didn't flag us," Roche announced, "which means they don't know it was Osyen."

"Yet," Adelaide added.

They all quietly accepted that truth. Osyen's identity wouldn't remain a secret for very long. Anonymity was going to be a preciously brief period.

"I can't grab the shuttle's transponder in this mess," Roche said.

Thom squeezed his eyes shut, took a deep breath, and opened them. Ready. "We'll never find Osyen if we just tail him. We have to go for what he's after."

"You think we can find his mother before him?"

"We don't know where we he is," Thom explained, "but we know where he's going. We get him, grab him, and get off planet."

The *Aurum* finally settled from reentry, gliding through some light cloud cover. They were finally close enough that the buildings were no longer some distant steel texture, and they could make out one enormous structure, like a slate-gray arm reaching out to shelter all the buildings underneath it.

"What the Hell is that thing?" Zatia asked.

She was right to ask, Thom thought. They'd done most of their business on the other side of the Sunset line. Nothing like this had been over there.

"Institution Zero One," Rashida explained. "Started as an Imperial mining station, stripping out the copper veins. When they realized that pulling the copper was taking away the planet's thermostat, they shut the whole operation down and turned it into a research outpost. The scientists needed food, housing, childcare and nobody wanted to go out for it. It's like another city floating over the top of

Ilum Sunnyside. Apartments in that building cost more than this ship does, twice over. For a month."

"You ever wonder how rich people can say they're firmly middle class?" Adelaide pointed an accusatory finger at the building. "It's because they can't afford garbage like that."

"Won't something that big affect the weather?" Thom asked.

"It does," Rashida said.

"Lily?" Roche said. "It's time."

Their blue face pressed out of the wall behind Thom's head. "Are you quite certain this insanity is required?"

"You can always wait for the harbormaster to impound the ship and cycle you," Adelaide said, ominously, "but I wouldn't."

"She's not kidding," Thom said. "Once Osyen's made, they'll lock down the *Aurum* and you will promptly become public property. Unless you come with us."

Lily mumbled and grumbled—and then their face froze, slipping back into the wall. Adelaide bent over a wall panel, popping open the latches one by one to reveal...

Lily's AI core, the same iridescent blue as their glowing head always had been. The roughly hewn sphere blinked with primary lights and automatic functions still rolling. Adelaide set to work unplugging Lily from their socket, ready to take the core on a walk.

That sport ball in the wall was everything Lily, their personality and logs and charts and their love and their megalomania. Everything compressed down to a fifteen-inch sphere. They wouldn't be able to process a Jump or simulate their persona without the hardware of a spaceship to back them up, and they wouldn't have sensors to experience the world. But they were 'alive' within that casing.

They weren't off, or asleep per se—it was more akin to being blind, deafened, and bound. Caged.

And this was the fairly standard method of swapping out AI units from ship to ship, severing all of their senses and crushing them down into a box that was man portable.

The amount of trust it would take a human being to submit to this...

Adelaide gingerly lifted Lily out of the wall, cradling the core for a moment, before sliding them into a suitcase. "Roche? Would you like to carry our little friend?"

"Gladly." Roche pushed away from his seat, sliding over to Adelaide. He drew two cables out of his socket-wrist and clicked them into place on Lily's case.

"Everything good?" Thom asked.

Roche's head cocked, like he was trying to scratch his ear on his shoulder. "They're...noisy. But I'll manage."

The *Aurum* settled into one of the smaller docks on the Sunshine. It was a blinding white, the painted concrete scalding Thom's eyes. Appropriate for the Planet of Lights to be painful to look at.

It wasn't for lack of dirt, but it was like everything had been bleached of its color and made homogenous to its neighbor. The crew walked down the gangway, signing over the manifest to the harbormaster and paying the appropriate tolls.

Thom took one last look at the *Aurum*. He knew he'd see her again, but there was something very wistful about this departure.

"Thomas?" Rashida tried to get his attention.

"You never think you're in the good old days...until they're gone," Thom said.

Rashida followed his eyes back up to the cargo hauler, a half-smile creeping up her face. "And yet, the good old days may very well still be ahead of you."

Something in his gut traveled up his neck to the back of his head, whispering an unholy truth: every day ahead of him was going to be different.

Rashida saw his grave disposition and she squared up on him. She tugged on his sleeves, and straightened his collar, a sculptor with her clay. She ran her hand through his hair, fingernails dragging against his skin, and he felt the pleasant tingle roll up his spine.

And he felt his feet take root in the ground again, confidence coming back. "Where to?" Thom asked.

"I want what he's having," Zatia said as she brushed past them.

"You just have to ask, Zee," Rashida pointed out.

"I'm asking now," the bruiser crowed, sliding on a pair of sunglasses. Thom never thought about it, but all the pale concrete and flat surfaces really did make every place he looked a painful experience. Zatia had the right idea hiding behind shades.

Roche settled next to them, fidgeting with his grip on Lily's case. "If we're to intercept Osyen, we'll need to know where he's headed next."

"I have an idea about that," Zatia said, luring everyone towards the elevator.

———

They didn't dare take a taxi. But thankfully, they didn't have to go far.

Zatia led the group to a parkland for the local community. It was the picture of modern suburbia, with crisp cultured grasses cut to match. A walking trail surrounded the edges, with one major thoroughfare winding through the fake trees and irrigated waterways.

It was all an illusion, engineered to draw the veil over the eyes of residents. They all remembered such things, and this place was there to convince them it still existed somewhere. A set of bleachers shaped from the square smart-bricks overlooked a playing field. Blitzing up and down the field, a small mob of children stormed about in some kind of game.

As they approached, Thom glimpsed a splash of color on the underside of an exposed smart-brick, some bit of graffiti that had somehow eluded cleaning. He paused, inspecting it.

Some simple spats of paint and dirt had been used to draw a simple image. It was smudged as the brick transferred from use to use, sliding past its cousins to build new formations that brushed off details, but it was still legible. The image of a young man with dark skin and radiant blue eyes. Three numbers scrawled across his front like a sports jersey: 626.

Heh. Sunnyside or not, they couldn't scrape away *all* of their graffiti. Thom hoped whoever had sketched this hadn't been punished too harshly. It was a decent portrait.

High above them, an olive-skinned man rested in the bleachers, idly nibbling on a bag of seeds and tracking the action. He had a sharp jaw and a round face, with a brilliantly warm smile now dimmed to a shade of its former glory. He looked like the victim of something spectral, now in recovery. It was the face of a man who had seen horrors.

The gang settled just at the base of the bleachers. "He's not going to be happy to see us," Zatia noted.

"When is he ever?" Adelaide grunted.

Thom sighed and trotted right up to the man with no subtlety whatsoever. "Diego?"

"Thought you'd all skipped town," the man said without making eye contact, a bit of bitterness tinging his otherwise reasonable tone.

"We hit a bit of a...catastrophe," Thom said. "Gotta track somebody down before we go."

Adelaide sat down on the opposite side of Diego without a word. He eyed the old woman with curiosity, but Adelaide was already absorbed in whatever game the kids were playing. She struck up a cigarette, leaning forward into the study of the sport.

Diego knew when he was being fenced in by an enforcer. He didn't need to know that Adelaide would almost certainly break a hand on Diego's face before she broke anything of his.

"Well," Diego started, "unless you're looking for me, I don't know how I can be of use."

Roche settled down next to Adelaide, joining her study of the game. Children from twelve to sixteen ran up and down the field, wearing opposing colors and wielding brightly colored sticks. They were tapered at the handle, but comically inflated at the beating end.

"What are the sticks for?" Roche asked. "Do they hit the ball or each other?"

Adelaide turned her head, like she might get a different angle on the action. "Doesn't seem like they're discriminating, does it?"

"Carry the ball to your end of the field to score," Diego explained. "Play doesn't stop in between possessions, and—"

Zatia grunted. "Cut to the chase already, Diego. What can you give us and how much is it going to set us back?"

Thom winced. She had all the finesse of a meteor impact.

Diego didn't say anything, but he finally tore his eyes from the game, bringing them down to the teenager in front of him. He checked the silver color to her hair and the twitch in her eye. "You look like shit."

Zatia shrugged. "I feel like shit. How are you?"

"We're above board on this one, Diego." Thom cut in. "We're looking for a criminal."

"You and everybody above Sunset," Diego said. "And if I knew where he was, I wouldn't be talking to you. I'd be collecting a finder's fee."

"Actually," Thom said, "we're not looking for him. We're after for who *he's* looking for. Catharina Batahr."

The word mother hit Diego different from most others in the language. He tried to mask it, but Thom saw the twitch in his cheek. "Batahr?" Diego said. "Now, there's an infamous name."

"You know it?" Rashida asked.

"By gossip and reputation, mostly," Diego admitted. "She was some big-wig scientist at the Royal Arts."

"Not exactly cause for celebrity," Rashida said. "What happened to her?"

"What usually happens to brilliant minds and loud voices." Diego suddenly stamped his foot on the floor and shouted to the field with cheer, "*Osho p'laf mi zu! Osho!*"

Thom looked out to see a small boy waving back. The kid was a miniature clone of Diego, same hair and eyes, and that radiant smile still readily used and undimmed. He gave two big waves of both arms to Diego, before running back to catch up with the crowd.

Interesting. Diego had a son.

"So it's keep away?" Roche asked.

"Team-based," Adelaide noted, pointing. "Look for the bigger ones forming a wedge."

Rashida leaned over Roche's shoulder, trying to get the same view. "And nobody gets hurt?"

Thom looked over just in time to see a large girl not much younger than he was—but twice again his size—absolutely blast through some poor kid who thought he could sneak through to the ball-carrier. The big girl hit him so hard, he left a little shoe behind.

And as he hit the ground, the grass gave way just a touch, cushioning the impact. The bricks beneath could sense the coming impact and gave way just enough. After all, Thom thought, it wasn't the hit that caused injuries so much as how quickly you transferred that energy. Falling didn't kill; the sudden stop at the end did.

"No, it's perfectly safe," Adelaide mocked. "Until you meet someone bigger than you."

Diego's kid was a part of the phalanx, keeping attackers at bay, battle cries blending seamlessly with gut-blasting laughter, as the kids were launched to and fro. It was like a violent game of tag atop a trampoline.

Someone somewhere was keeping a scorecard that Thom couldn't see, but the loose association of parents scattered on the bleachers were all far too invested for this to be intramural exhibition.

"Unfortunately, Batahr's been long since buried. Can't help you," Diego said, masking his expression with a soft smile of appreciation. That small kind face was probably all he could muster these days, most of the joy beaten out of him by his past lives.

"Diego—"

"I got out," Diego urged. "You hear me? I got out of this life. I was within arm's reach of Espinoza while she was doing horrible things, and I got out. She killed a man right in front of me, and I didn't even get questioned by Ministry. That *doesn't happen.* Near as I know it, the Clerics don't even know who I am. So please, walk away from me."

"I know this one," Zatia chuffed from the bottom of the bleachers. Everyone looked down at her, derisively shaking her head. "You can't help us. We plead with you. You rebuff our advances, but unless we can do Impossible Task Type A."

Diego blinked a few times, before looking over at Thom. "That's not...I don't work for the Cartel anymore. The Espinozas are either in jail, dead, or on the run. All I have left is my son. Look at him out there."

Thom glanced out at the game. Diego's son was running full-tilt at a wave of other kids, laughing and shouting. The sticks they swung at one another molded to the skin on impact before gently expanding again, taking a full force swing and dissipating the strike, turning a blow into a shove: kid-safe full-contact sport.

"He couldn't walk a year ago," Diego urged.

"Touching story," Adelaide grunted. "Real tale of woe, makes me weepy."

"You don't understand! I worked for that—" He stopped himself, a combination of horrible memories bubbling up. "You can't fathom what I've done, what any parent would do for their child."

What any parent would do? Oh, Thom was well aware what parents would do for their children, to their children.

But Diego might not be lying. The Espinoza cartel, the weapons smuggling, intimidation, protection rackets, murder. And Diego had probably seen a slice of every inch of it. It was a minor miracle he had escaped notice by Ministry officials, and the young father had no interest in inviting further attention.

And here was a crew of wanted fugitives asking him to stand up. Diego had no interest in testing the extent of his luck.

"You don't have to help directly," Thom said. "You can just point us in the right direction. Who would know?"

Diego paused for a half-second, a name flashing across his mind. Thom knew when he'd hooked the fish.

Even if the fish thrashed in protest. "And how does that help me?" Diego asked. "Or my son?"

"There it is," Zatia scoffed.

"It doesn't," Thom said, trying to push past Zatia's complete lack of diplomacy, "but it gets the five of us out of here that much faster."

"And if we remain much longer, Adelaide might start a betting pool," Rashida asserted, trying to mask her own interest in the game with folded arms and a cool demeanor. But she was watching the brutal sport like everybody else was.

Diego waited for a moment before leaning in close to push Thom away. "Get your life out of mine."

And Thom stumbled down the first few bleachers steps—the bricks shifting automatically to help him keep his balance.

Adelaide and Roche leaned away as Zatia unclipped her bangles, flashing the hint of steel underneath. But Thom waved her off. "It's okay. Thank you for your time."

He beckoned the gang down the steps and away—hearing his Entiglas chirp with the file transfer. Diego had dropped Thom a note —as requested. Time to leave, graciously, and with the appearance of rejection.

Rashida and Adelaide joined Zatia at the bottom of the bleachers, but Roche didn't move, transfixed on the game. His voice was far less kind. "He couldn't walk a year ago, and now he's running around a field with a bludgeoning instrument. And you approve of this?"

"Roche!" Zatia called out, scolding.

And Roche bit his lip and popped up to join the others. They each in turn walked around the bleachers out of sight, with Zatia pleasantly flipping Diego the finger as she went.

"Well, that was a bust," Rashida grimaced. "Wonderful beginnings."

Thom flipped up his Entiglas, displaying a set of geo-coordinates.

"When did he give you that?" Adelaide asked.

"When he shoved me," Thom said. "Spend enough time in a bona fide Cartel, you figure out how to do a dead drop."

They walked the short distance to the coordinates, and soon after, Thom's Entiglas downloaded a fresh file. This one had a name...

Porous Excavation & Machinery. Diego had come through for them after all...

CHAPTER 12
OSYEN

THE CURATOR RAPPED her knuckles on the door right under Charles Ordee's flickering name placard. "Charles, are you in?" she asked. "I have a most intriguing visitor."

Osyen wondered what he might look like, this man who had betrayed his mother to the Ministry. Would he be some wiry goblin, or a slimy ghoul, some sunken features bleached by darkness? Would he stink of body odor, or mask it under some fanciful oil he could afford with his payout?

But the face that opened the door was jolly, exuberant, like he was halfway through a pint of spiced cider and a good book. The entire lower third of his face was bushy beard and mustache, coiffed and loved, but with individual wiry hairs flying free in disarray. A wide and infectious smile was hiding somewhere under all that hair, but his cheeks puffed up into rosy circles peeking out of the bush. His scalp was gently shaved, leaving a pristine if mottled dome. And his eyes, soft and gentle blue—he looked like the concept of kindness had taken human form.

"Irene!" the Professor greeted with whimsy. "I wasn't expecting you till this afternoon."

"I'll be back then," the Curator apologized. "I just wanted to connect you with this gentleman, Evan Whitby. He had some questions that he thinks you can assist with."

"Oh!" This notion was apparently worthy of great excitement, and Osyen had to hide his incredulity. There was no way that sentence was worthy of the response it got. "Well, I live to be of service. Please come in and I'll put on some tea!"

This man could not be real. This man was a renegade fae, some puff of sugar cloud that learned to talk. He had to be a formation of cotton candy and children's wishes brought to life by a magical sweater vest.

Osyen turned to see the Curator was already marching off down the corridor. She had just dumped him into the professor's lap and made it someone else's problem with exquisite technique.

That was masterful.

Professor Ordee practically tugged Osyen into the office, pushing the door shut behind him. "What troubles you, my lad?"

Right. He came with questions. "I read a-a brief thesis paper, not much more than a memo. I wanted to knock heads with an expert before I published my own commentary on it."

The professor shivered with excitement. "I do love a good thought problem. What was the abstract?"

"Professor—"

"Oh please!" The pleasant man said, as he poured steaming water into a flowery porcelain pot. "Call me Charles."

He didn't want to call him Charles. Charles was an ineffectual but harmless intellectual who wanted nothing more than to sit with his cat, play colorful games with his nephew. Charles liked a challenge, but only in the theoretical, electing instead for a life of quiet reflection and comfort. Charles—Charlie? No, Charles.

The minister. The ghoul. The professor. These were people Osyen could handle. People he could kill.

"Sugar?" Charles asked.

Osyen wasn't going to turn down genuine sweets. So he nodded, and Charles palmed two cubes of sugar into a pastel porcelain cup. "I like a good cup of tea. Soaking the leaves and spices, a bit of milk and cardamom. It brightens the mind. And if you add a bit of lemon, clears the throat!"

This was the man who betrayed his mother? This sentient stuffed animal?

Charles settled down in his squishy high-back chair, beckoning Osyen to take a seat across from him. "Get comfortable, my lad! No need to stand on ceremony."

Osyen glanced at the creaky old wooden chair the professor pointed to, clearly reserved for his grad students. The upholstery was peeling from the stitching, but the legs were solid and hardwood. This thing was handmade and aged.

Ugly, maybe. But good craftsmanship, well loved.

So Osyen took a seat, letting himself sink into the stained cushion and feel the fabric cup his back. Charles immediately sat forward, rubbing his palms together. "I never asked. This paper you found? What was the publication?"

"Unpublished," Osyen answered quickly, "and unreviewed. I found it amongst the author's effects."

"Well, that's a bit untoward!" Charles remarked, but intrigued. "I try not to comment on works that even the author seems to not want to put their name on."

"Can I ask about the author? It's actually somebody you knew."

The man's mustache actually drooped, like it responded to the gravity of that sentiment. "I hoped I'd be aware if any of my colleagues wrote something that raised eyebrows. I'd be one of the first peers to issue my review."

Oh, he had been aware of it. Well aware of it. But Osyen kept that to himself. "They're not exactly a contemporary of yours."

And that's when the first flash of fear hit Professor Charles Ordee in the eyes, darting from right to left. It stiffened his spine and starched his beard. "I think I know what this is about," the Professor whispered, his voice cracking. "And I think I know who you really are."

Well, it wasn't exactly going to be a subtle exchange in any event. But Osyen knew not to give up the game until it was absolutely lost. "The Curator ran my credentials. My brother is a Statesman on Vanguard. I've run a successful practice—"

"I may live in this ten by twenty-foot square, child, but I am neither naïve nor foolish. Those puerile times are long behind me. I watched my news this morning, and I had wondered if you'd be paying me a visit as well."

Osyen doubled-down. "Professor," he coughed, "if this is a bad time..."

"Not at all. I've already done up the tea," the professor said weakly. "But I am also not...I'm—I'm not a fool, is what I'm saying. This author?"

Say her name, Oz. Say it.

But he struggled with the sounds. Something about this man's quiet resignation made Osyen's throat clench shut, like his own voice was trying to stop him from dragging this further.

Look at him. Charles was terrified, but he held his ground, welcomed what came next. Not out of generosity, but out of a sense of inevitability. It was like Charles had always known this day was coming for him.

Swallowing hard and with a steeling breath, Osyen pushed the syllables out, almost spitting the name in to the air. "Catharina Batahr."

And those same angry syllables struck the professor like a knife between the ribs. He took a few breaths himself, riding backward in memory. Osyen could see the glistening sweat pressing itself out of the Professor's forehead.

He settled back down into his chair, eyes far away. "They didn't come to my office, you know. They came to my home."

The Cleric. And Yellow Eyes. His mother had not been the first stop that night. "Why would they come to you?" Osyen asked.

"Not a day goes by that I don't regret what I did," the professor said, his voice a quiet sonata gracing the air with a decade of pain. "I wish only I'd had the courage then, but I don't even rightly have the courage now! Look." He held out his quivering hand.

He was just trying to get Osyen to weep for him, to feel for him. Oh, woe was the sad scholar. He didn't lose a mother! He didn't lose freedom.

But the professor pressed on, his eyes alight with wonderment. "We had discovered something magnificent, lad. The Pilgrim laid the Jump Points for mankind's further expansion, traveling through time and space, carving out pathways for us to follow. They left cosmic breadcrumbs for us through the blackened forest. And at each of these places they visited, we find the Pilgrim's Metal."

Osyen could not have been more unnerved than when the professor reached for his desk. Charles could've called for help right there, could've summoned security. And Osyen let him dig into the drawers, before drawing out a ball of gnarled obsidian glass—

And all Osyen could see was the Icon of Cruciform, the very same seductive relic that had nearly consumed Thom, the same one they had hurled into the Boolean Pulsar.

Not the same. No. But so very similar. This one was...dark, quiet, still. Dead.

"It's inert," the professor assured him, "completely harmless. This is merely one of many such Metals we have here in the museum on display. And all of them just...intoxicating to observe."

Osyen couldn't deny it. He'd made a few fake Icons in the last year, sold a few to those delirious enough to believe him. He might even say that was the source of all this year's troubles, that stupid con. Now, he'd been dragged into the presence of the real thing with alarming frequency.

Even this dead piece seemed to call to him, with its eldritch beveled pattern and inky blackness drawing his eye in deeper, deeper...

Telling him to jump.

"We are as a whole species called to deposits of this Metal," Charles said, rubbing his thumb against the texture, "sailing across the skies and tearing into the hearts of planets. We have no use for it, y'know. It's not an especially durable material. Brittle. Not fit for construction or refinement—and can be quite dangerous to handle." And the professor's tone shifted to disdain and spit. "Yet we collect it wherever we find it, only to place it into vacuum-sealed glass chambers for the Dunsweir to marvel at during their dinner parties."

"Professor," Osyen said, with a hint of humor, "that's blasphemous."

"Oh!" the professor scoffed, misty eyed. "We've passed that precious point in our lives, haven't we, my lad? You and I...we can speak freely. And we should."

He was saying an awful lot, saying a great many things he'd always wanted to, now that he had a friendly ear. "Say what you want to say, Professor."

Charles stared at the chunk of black in his hand, like the primordial void contained within might grant him strength. "Catharina didn't do a thing wrong. It was *my* research, my paper. She'd explicitly warned me against pursuing it."

There it was. The confession. His mother suffered for a crime she didn't commit.

"What did you find?" Osyen asked.

Charles didn't answer, his eyes too lost in old memories, haunted by guilt awoken by just a few words. The professor shuddered. "I didn't get far before I had the most terrible man at my door."

And he didn't want to die. That night. That horrible night. Osyen was standing in the presence of the very man responsible for everything. This quaint little man had dispatched Gaius to his mother's loft....

On a false lead. She was innocent. And protected him anyway.

And yet, Osyen found himself tainted. He should be angry, livid, homicidal. But staring at that little man, Osyen's heart reached out to mend instead of break. "They were going to throw you into prison? Not even for what you found, but because you were asking. Asking inappropriate questions?"

"Capital offense," the professor lamented with a nod, "my hypothesis undermined two centuries of established history. I would lose my name, my title, my life—unless I could buy a lesser sentence with details on my co-conspirators." Suddenly, Charles looked up from the Metal in his hand, eyes sinking into Osyen's, driving deep. "I'm truly sorry, my boy. I was afraid, and I damned a good woman to save my own hide."

Osyen's hand slipped into his jacket, fingertips tapping against the cold steel of Milardi's weapon. He could do it. He could bring justice here and now to a man who had confessed his guilt, welcomed judgement.

So why was it so difficult here? Gaius had taunted him. But this man...he didn't beg or pray, nor snarl and snap. Charles closed his eyes in quiet contemplation, comforted by the fact that whatever came next was quite out of his control—and deserving.

"Is she alive?" Osyen asked.

One word and it gave his heart wings. "...Yes."

"Where is she?"

Charles opened his eyes, brow raised. "Is that...all you need from me?"

It's all he's ever needed. Ever wanted. To know she was safe, happy, alive, comfortable, smiling, laughing, in love, drunk on weekends. To know she was free.

"Help me find her," Osyen almost begged. "That's all I care about."

"Well, I-I don't know where she is, per se." Charles gingerly reached over the teapot, waiting for Osyen to stop him. "But I know where you might start your search."

"Where?" Was it a prison? A laboratory?

Charles pulled up a map of the city, a flashing dot right on the Sunset line. "There's a dig site not too far from here, the largest cache of Pilgrim Metal found on Ilum in a decade!"

"Why haven't we heard about it?" Osyen asked, suspicious.

"Privately owned," Charles explained, "and operated."

Translation: criminal. "So the Royal Arts gets to study it so long as the Empire lets the bad men keep their prize?" Osyen asked.

"The Empire...may not be aware of its existence," Charles said with a nervous laugh. "Under their very nose, as it were!"

"And she's there?"

Charles's eyes fell. "She may not be. But it's the best I can do."

He didn't care about the dig site. He didn't care about the research. He didn't care about factions feuding over ownership and land rights.

Osyen gestured for him to pour. "Can I ask something else?"

"Certainly, lad."

"What was she like?"

CHAPTER 13
RASHIDA

IT TOOK MOST of the day—and a stop at a wonderful falafel place—before they made it to the Sunset line. They didn't dare walk the streets, and the taxi system would have had them caught and shackled within minutes.

A security check would tie them to a man wanted for the terroristic murder of a government official. The car would pull into a garage that could brick itself up like a mausoleum. Clerics could then arrive to exhume them from their impromptu prison, and who knows how long they would have been waiting in the dark.

So they took the criminal's highway—the rooftops.

It was surprisingly comfortable, walking open-air paths made for those trying to elude detection. Arteries clearly marked and even accessibility taken into account. It was still an awful lot of work for Adelaide and Roche, both.

It might have been chilling, living life beyond the touch of a sun. But it was a hell of a view.

The hot air from her lungs condensed into white clouds before her eyes, the only proof that her breath hadn't been stolen by the beauty of it all. Rooftop community gardens drank every drop of sunlight they could get, before the next house over shifted to using ultraviolet lights. Schoolhouses were assembling their children into neatly coordinated teams, and craft groups were getting together to teach weaving, or dance, or glass-art.

The rooftops might have been less crowded than the streets below, but it was still difficult to avoid the shoulders of other passersby.

Rashida stopped just beyond the glow of a porch light, watching as a craftsman blew shapes into a glass bauble. Children sat cross-legged underfoot, watching with awe and wonder as he worked the glowing orange material, picking at it with a hook to draw out intricate designs. And as he made each motion, he would pause to explain to them the method behind his beautiful madness.

Zatia settled up next to Rashida in the dim light. "Everything you hoped for?"

"It's crowded," Rashida admitted. "There's plenty of room on the Sunnyside. Not sure why they don't spread out."

"You think folk *chose* to live without sunlight?"

Rashida looked at the nearby class, watching the artisan—but looking closer. His skin was pocked with divots and dents from some wasting disease. The children watching had matted hair and baggy recycled clothes.

"I'll explain it all when you have me over for high tea in that big house of yours," Zatia chided her with a pat on the arm.

Rashida would gladly explain the thirty different types of chai the Dunsweir Manor used for different occasions, but the point of it would go in one ear and out the other. Zatia didn't give a damn about the tea, and right now, neither did she. These people were banished to a lifetime of literal darkness, impoverished not because of circumstance or debts. The prices weren't high for market value, but as a market force.

Sunnyside didn't want more money, they wanted a fence to keep the wrong people out.

"I'll run you through a full tea ceremony in the main hall of Dunsweir," Rashida promised, "if you bring the matches."

"My favorite kind of house. On fire."

The location wasn't too much further. Thom had pinpointed the factory Diego had directed them to. And every ten minutes the world got darker, the music got louder. The air thickened into a damp haze as the temperature dropped. The charm of the glorious pink sunset drifted away to umber fire, and finally consumed by the glow of the city itself. Neon yellow and green filled the air, and Rashida felt a tingle at the base of her neck as acoustic manipulation could be heard on the breeze.

Darkside wasn't a home. It was banishment to purgatory, to wait in the night for whatever foul end came to the door.

Zee's hand hit hers, and she felt the static shock of the contact. "Rash?"

"Yeah?'

"You need to stop?" Zatia asked her, with a wrinkle to her brow.

She looked up, to see even Roche and Adelaide had caught her up, passed her. Thom looked back at her, concern in his eyes. How long had she been standing there, like her engine had stalled out?

Thom nodded some assurance to her, before turning back to the matter at hand. And she was struck by how respectful that little nervous boy had grown, how he had gone from an—admittedly competent—emotional wreck of a child into...whatever he'd become.

It wasn't much further to find the factory Diego had directed them to. The building blended in with the rest of the district, just one more asymmetric block laid in the rows of others—each structure had large block red numbers on the south-facing wall, indicating from the street which hangar was which. Because all of them were oil-stained featureless slabs.

It served them well to blend in with their surroundings, not to draw too much attention to whatever scandalous activity went on within.

"Trucks coming and going, no real pattern or schedule," Zatia reported from her observations. "I can safely say they're not legitimate, because boxes go out heavy, and most of the time they come back light—except when they don't."

She half-expected Thom to jump in there, but the young man's expression had gone blank, his eyes drifting off toward the building's interior. It had the look of someone who had heard their name on the wind and was focusing to see if they had heard some echo from far away, or just a trick of the air.

So Rashida took the lead. "Smuggling?"

Zatia nodded, giving Thom her own quizzical look. "And they're not very subtle about it. Security's present but light. Mostly big toughs with bad smoking habits."

Adelaide grumbled, shaking her head. "If it's just a storage depot or a manufactory, there wouldn't be security beyond badging in and out. They're sure as shit up to something down there."

"They work for others," Roche muttered, derisive, "rather than working for each other. I'll guarantee you that whoever owns that building has never turned a wrench while inside it."

Rashida glanced sidelong at Roche, and the anger simmering behind his eyes. She turned to Zatia. "Do I even bother?"

"And do what? You think he's wrong?"

"Not especially."

"Objecting to my tone and not the content, are we?" Roche asked.

"It's a former Espinoza front," Thom suddenly said, pulling a startled twitch from Rashida. "But with the collapse of the Cartel, they would've gone freelance. No need to stop doing what you're good at, especially when you get to keep the boss's percentage."

"Damn straight," Zatia said. "Why are we saving Osyen again?"

"We don't have time to do this right," Thom said with a dry smirk. "So what's left is to do it fast. We need to hit their records vault and find anything and everything they might have on Catharina Batahr, or her research. It might be kept physically on a local cache, harder to hit remotely. Adelaide, Roche: you two are going to be instrumental there. Get in, get access, get out."

"I'll open a door for 'em," Zatia said. "You two stay here."

"No," Thom rebuffed. "We're your distraction. We'll go right through the front door, posing as unsatisfied buyers from a recent shipment."

"Always right through the front door! Every single heist, it's the front door—"

"I go to the doors open to me," Thom said. "And we'll be drawing eyes off of you. We'll buy you ten minutes, then bail. Not a minute more. All goes well, we extract and rally back at the rooftop gardens east of here. If it gets loud..."

"Which, I mean, who are we kidding?" Adelaide snarked.

"*If* it gets loud," Thom said, "no heroics. Just get out, shake your tails—and up off the streets. Ministry gives the order and the smart blocks will box you in. There won't be a damn thing we can do to help you. Rashida?"

Rashida perched on the edge of the building, studying the come and go of vehicles and trucks. "We'll need transport. Someone important wouldn't simply walk up to a place like this. And we'll need new clothes, something befitting the station."

"It's a lean-to full of knuckle draggers," Zatia stated. "You think they're going to be stunned by shiny colors and extravagant entrances?"

"Yes," Rashida said, "because everyone is either stunned or alarmed by a grand entrance, and either way serves our purposes. I don't need to convince them, just keep their eyes on us. That requires some showmanship."

"You set, I'll spike?" Thom asked.

She nodded. "You just hold my chain, I'll do all the snarling."

Thom turned to Roche. "Think Lily could snag us a ride?"

Roche's eyes rolled backward, communing with the intelligence stapled to his wrist. "Two blocks away, black town car. Best I could do."

Rashida pulled the brooch from her hair, letting her locks drop down her back—and Zatia muttered some kind of gentle curse. "They won't be looking at the car."

———

Thom sat across from her in the front cab of the taxi, one thin arm thrown behind the headrest of the seat next to him. He'd buttoned the top of his collar and slid on the corset like it had always belonged there. His frame, tapered by the waist cincher, made his shoulders seem to erupt into a sharp wedge. The thin line of his back muscles tugged on his shirt below his slender neck.

And his calculating stare was looking anywhere else than her. Perhaps he was distracted by the world, the stakes, the environment. Or he was trying not to look at how her hair sat about her shoulders, framing her collar bone. "Are you ready?"

"Just like we rehearsed," Thom said.

The car settled to a stop in front of the factory, and Rashida's breath hung in her throat for a bracing moment to gather strength. She'd fought with soldiers and escaped demons. She could handle a few street toughs.

Which was all well and good, because they were already approaching the car, and not out of courtesy. They were the biggest, meatiest men she'd ever seen, with scars on their lips and tattoos that probably meant something deeply personal and wonderful, but everyone else saw as nondescript dangerous. Their shoulders were the size of her head, and they could probably clap their hands together to smash her skull into meat slurry. They were paid to be flesh walls, more deterrent than anything else.

She gripped her cane tight, thankful for the one thing in her life that remained stable.

Rashida stepped out of the car, matching the thugs' energy and velocity. "Gentlemen, lovely to see you again."

The grunts paused, confused and gaslit. Did they know this person?

Rashida didn't even break stride. "I need to speak with the foreman immediately."

Thom exited from the car behind her, emitting a scoff worthy of high society. And Rashida tilted her head to scold him. "Kal, I said that I would handle this."

Thom was nearly perfect, though he came in with a bit more vinegar than society would've. "You're the one who purchased six faulty 68s."

Rashida matched his spit. "So next time I'll buy DeHaans and we can spend half of the production cycle training the crews to use the damn things."

The thugs only had the one move, so they went to it, with the smallest of the three stepping forward. "No loitering. Move it along."

"Did you not hear me through that thick skull of yours?" Rashida barked. "The foreman. Now."

"We're wasting time," Thom muttered.

"Dearest, you simply *must* give these gentlemen a chance to rectify their error. Should they refuse, we can explore our other options." She turned back to the guards. "You tell the foreman that Kal and Marie have returned and have five excavators more interested in grinding our workers than stone! And we intend to make such a cataclysmic failure in safety design your central problem today. Fail to do so, and the name signing your checks will be dangerously different for you by week's end!"

The goons had likely never been threatened with quite so many words before. They looked like they'd short-circuited, blinking and jaws slack.

One guard muttered to himself. "Fuck is happening right now?"

And the small leader tucked a hand to his ear. "Hey, Guzman?"

Rashida threw up an exasperated hand. "Thank you!"

Without breaking his perfect scowl, Thom called on the party line. *We're at the door. What's your status?*

Cracking a window on the second floor, Zatia said. *The plughead and octogenarian are not the most mobile, you know.*

The guard had a report of his own, lowering his hand and resting it on a baton. "He's on his way down."

Rashida scoffed. "So we're to stand here on the street while we wait for Guzman to find the time for us?"

"Honey—" Thom reached for her arm.

And she wrenched him in close to her side, feeling the steel-ribbing of his corset against her forearm. "I told you, dearest mine, that I would handle this. I beg of you only your patience."

Thom's surprise was genuine, and it was impossible to fake the prickling of his skin that rolled up his arm and shivering down his spine. "Yes ma'am."

Rashida turned to the guards. "We are clearly an enormous threat. I saw a lobby last week. Perhaps we could wait there for your esteemed colleague?"

That was a helluva gamble—it was a factory. There might not be any such room. But if they called her crazy or blew her off, she could just raise more of a scene.

Of course, they could decide to break her legs for her insolence. And Rashida remembered what that felt like.

But to her relief, the leader of the brute squad turned aside, gesturing for her to walk in.

"Thank you," she said with an appropriate entitled huff, marching into the factory interior, with Thom dragging along behind her.

And she heard the doors click shut behind them. They were going to have to do some clever improvisation going forward. Because something told her they were not going out the same way they came in.

CHAPTER 14
THOM

THE DOORS CLOSED, and Thom immediately had the worst pulsating migraine behind his left temple. What a time for this to hit him.

They were being brought across the factory floor. The building itself was an open space, cavernous, to allow for the large HML-68 mining drones being built by hand as much as automated system. A series of three-story doors were on each loading dock wall, allowing for a group of four bays' worth of behemoths on each side to be loaded and shipped off in enormous containers.

A receiving station married empty containers up to the factory, off-loading small boxes of broken parts or scraps to be recycled back into production.

Two large cranes operated a battery of smaller arms that tac-welded and built the enormous drones: robots building robots. Flashes of light and glowing slag flew through the air, with a handful of workers in goggles observing and maintaining those machines.

The men might have been mostly watching, but they were hardly idle. Each team rotated around their builds, making adjustments to the drones and builders both, enormous wrenches torqueing on nuts and bolts the size of Thom's head.

Cables as thick as a human wrist connected power tools on upward to a grid that ran the length of the production floor. Tiny rail systems then let the hookups glide along without losing connection. Ingenious!

The workers busily inspected the robots' work against checklists, nodding vociferously to one another before moving down the line. Each team of three seemed to be checking the past team's work, as well as one new thing each time.

Maybe it was the smell of oil, the flashing lights or grinding of steel against his ears, but Thom's migraine got worse with every step into the factory. And Rashida wasn't slowing down. She was driving her guide forward more than following him.

But Thom was lagging, and the corset-laden dinner party clothes were drawing plenty of sneers and derision from the blue-collars around him.

Stay in character, roll it into the bit. "Marie, perhaps there is a place we might sit for a spell?"

Rashida knew how to play 'yes and.' "We'll find you some seating, Kal."

"You can sit and wait for Guzman." That wasn't a polite accommodation from the goon, but an order.

Rashida sized up the guard in half a second: his ill-fitting clothes, well-trimmed beard, and smug expression. "How long have you worked here, lad?"

The guard responded, haughty. "Six months." And immediately got a whack on the back of the head from his friend.

Rashida agreed with the slap, pointing an approving finger at the slapper. "See, there's a man who cares about operational security. Do not give away information without *getting* something in return."

The clatter of metal filled the air, the crunch of a dropped crate against the concrete floor. Someone muffled a scream, and the guards stopped in place.

Thom couldn't have missed the hidden firearm suddenly pressed into his back—but he was far more focused on the harmonic ring on the ground. Not metal. Not stone. Something else.

Something he knew.

Like a polished chunk of gemstone, hollow, but with far too much heft for its size. It sounded musical and wonderful and...

Cold.

Thom dared to look towards the source. Two men were leaping to the aid of a worker who had dropped his crate. The man was clenching his teeth to tamp down his screams, clutching his hand.

The flesh was frost-bitten, charred black up to the middle of his forearm. While the necrosis was still growing, it was slowing down, now separated from the source that had drained him of life like a thirsty specter.

Something black lay at his feet. A fragment of ebony glass, a swirling cloud of seafoam green contorting within its depths, an emerald power somehow within it and around it, behind it and nowhere at all. Intricately embossed on one side, with a crystalline smoothness to the other face. And it seemed to...thrum, like a deep resonant vibration from within the material.

It looked like the Icon.

That was Pilgrim Metal, smuggled in that crate. It should have been inert, like every other Metal found—and based on how the worker had grabbed it, he clearly had expected it to be so.

Instead, it had been...hungry.

Something had changed. Something within that Metal reached back, snaring the warmth in his hand. The deep void had drained his hand of life in whatever short period of contact he'd had.

One bright worker used his brain and swiped the demonic shard away with a stick like he was handling an explosive. The ebony glass skittered along the concrete with a melancholic apology.

Thom's migraine spiked again—and he heard them. All of them.

Dozens of crates full of the Metal, all around them. Vibrating. Singing along to a refrain.

Singing. Singing to Thom. Because of Thom. Pleading with Thom. Awakened, stirred, and vibrant in the presence of Thom.

Aware of him.

Maybe they hadn't heard it over the heavy machinery, or maybe this was more normal than Thom thought. But the jumpy grunt at his back just pressed the gun barrel to punctuate his order. "Hey, keep it moving, stop your droolin'."

And Thom rolled with it. "You really think we're industry magnates, the two of us?"

"Did I say for you to talk?"

"Take that gun out of my back, or I'll take my business across the street," Thom hissed. "It's a simple equation. Don't threaten the clients, or all you're doing is amassing the world's largest pet rock collection."

If they were smuggling the Pilgrim Metal, they had to be selling it. Because these crates were not on their way to the Dunsweir or the Royal Arts. Those had official channels, and this was far from that. And if they were smuggling, they had to be moving it somehow. And to someone.

Whatever barrel was jammed into Thom's kidney receded. He spoke, but Thom didn't hear the man's words. Just that infernal hum from the Metal, a monotone bell that filled his ears and smothered out all other sound.

Rashida let out a tense breath, and the sound cut out with it, eliciting a gasp from Thom. Rashida eyed him, then scoffed at the guards. "Such hospitality."

Gang, Thom bounced to the party line, *they're smuggling Pilgrim Metal and not a small amount of it.*

That would be our luck, Adelaide grimaced.

Just the raw stuff? Zatia asked. *Nothing like the Icon?*

Nothing that I've seen, Thom said. *But whatever you do, don't touch it.*

Don't touch the angry God rocks. Okay.

At least, he sincerely hoped they hadn't unearthed a working artifact. The last thing this city-planet needed was something like the Icon kicking about.

And he didn't have a pulsar to chuck it into this time.

The brute squad ushered them along into a small box of a room in the southeast corner. It was sparsely decorated, with some postings for union regulations, safety procedures, and the sort. A small Replicator, well-loved with loose fittings, sat embedded in the wall. At some point in this building's life, that had been a real perk. Now, Thom expected it struggled to make a decent cup of coffee.

A table had folded out from the wall, with some chairs deploying up from the floor. And sitting there was possibly the most grizzled badass Thom had ever seen. Angular jaw with a pockmarked face, from a hard life of industrial work.

And his voice sounded like oiled leather smelled. "We weren't expecting clients today."

"Guzman, I assume?" Rashida probed.

He didn't acknowledge her. He balanced a cigarette in his mouth, striking up a gold lighter from his pocket. "Which means you're not clients. We don't take walk-ins."

"You'll take me," Rashida said with psychotic confidence. Thom forgot how good of a poker player she was.

"Why will I do that? Because your money is greener or your accounts thicker?" Guzman took a draw on his cigarette, a sorely needed balm to his nerves. "What was all that racket before?"

The guards hesitated for a second before one spoke up. "Sir, Mathias...he burned himself."

"On what? The mig welder?" Guzman asked, and Thom stiffened. He was talking awfully freely about internal matters. They were even using names.

Which meant they weren't letting Rashida or him walk out of that building. Lovely.

Rashida had picked up on that too, her chin rising in defiance.

"You're collecting a substantial amount of Pilgrim Metal. I would like to purchase today's lot."

Guzman laughed, straight from his belly. "I don't care how rich you think you are, you can't afford my stock."

"You'd be surprised what I can pay, but not every bill is paid with money, Mr. Guzman."

That vexed him, and Guzman's brow furrowed in confusion. "Who the *fra tow s'ivan* is 'Mister Guzman', eh? Do I look like my name is Mister? Or do I look like a work for a living?"

Thom jumped on that one. "Our organization had done some off-the-books trade with the Espinozas back when. We had hoped that you would be willing to continue that arrangement."

"I don't recognize you," Guzman hissed.

"Then you don't need our business either." Thom turned for the door, coming chest to chest with two guards blocking his path. "If you don't mind?"

"You'll tell me who you work for," Guzman said, "or I pitch your body into the down dark somewhere nobody will ever find you. How's that for an arrangement?"

Thom leered over his shoulder—and froze. His waistband! Guzman's belt. How had he missed that?! There it was, crudely stitched into the nylon.

An eye, with three flanged streaks up and down: the sigil of the Godfather.

Thom cast his eyes upward, to the ceiling of the little room...to find a cast iron silhouette of the lidless eye welded to the tiles.

No. No! They'd rushed so fast, they walked right into his hands.

Abort! Thom bounced over the channel. *Drop everything and get out!*

What is it? Zatia asked.

They were under the Master's sight. *The goons aren't freelance. This is Anze's factory. Get out—now!*

CHAPTER 15
ZATIA

"ARE YOU IN?" Zatia growled as she unhooked her bangles and flicked out the blades.

They'd found Guzman's office on the second floor. Pressure sensors under the carpeting, a laser grid over the windows and vents, and a small compartment with an autonomous turret tucked into the ceiling that fired on anyone without a friend-or-foe tag.

Without a computer to operate the system? Child's play. Lily took it all down in four seconds flat.

Adelaide had spliced out Roche/Lily's connection and hooked them both into a computer console. The holographic display was spitting out information fast enough to strobe out the small room. It felt like time traveling.

"Downloading now," Roche grunted. "Give me one more minute."

"*One* minute," Zatia said, "then you climb out the same way you came in."

"What are you going to do?" Adelaide asked, with her worried face.

She was supposed to keep them all safe. It was her job. They needed her. She was halfway to the door before she even thought about it. "Make noise, make memories, that's what."

They needed her. Simple as that.

Zatia brought her blades down on the door hinges, popping the pot metal plates badly enough for her to kick the door clean down. Before the aluminum sheet even hit the ground, she popped out and brought her blades to either side, driving the short swords into the throats of the two waiting guards.

The edge geometry of her blades wasn't too friendly anymore, since the last upgrade; but the thrusts alone snapped their necks, forcing their heads to hang on nothing but muscle and sinew. When she pulled her blades free, the right one sprayed a gout of blood from a pierced carotid artery.

Not soldiers, just grunts. But Mr. Crimson Geyser had Anze's stupid eyeball thing stitched to his vest.

Two down on the second floor, Zatia reported. *Working my way to you.*

Don't! Thom urged. *Just get yourself out!*

Sit tight, Maestro. And Rash?

What do you need? The beauty queen asked.

Don't think, Zatia firmly instructed. *Just listen to the music. I'm coming.*

She'd made something of a racket, kicking down that door. The hanging corrugated steel catwalk ran the circumference of the factory, with intermittent stairs down to the ground at each cardinal corner. Half of the factory was between her and that break room.

And so were half of the brutes, wielding various blunt force implements and years of emotional repression. And here comes this little pixie with her dual jewelry-blades.

No auto-turrets, except the one in the office? Zatia scoffed. Did they *want* to be robbed? Or were they just cheap?

She would've laughed out loud if the nearest asshole, his little vest flapping in some unseen breeze, wasn't so busy producing a homemade bracket gun to bear on her. He dropped the ugly thing into his hip as he squeezed the trigger.

Zatia let out an involuntary "Shit!" as she dove off the catwalk for safety below. The square laser blast scorched the two slain guards, and cut a chunk of catwalk out, slagging the ends into a golden yellow.

A few feet from a hard concrete shoulder readjustment, her senses kicked alive. She practically tasted the concrete dust, the workers' sweat, the bitter metals at work. She imagined the abrasive scrape of the scuffed floor, and the searing touch of the welding rigs. The echo from the mining drones' hollow interiors and the domed ceiling overhead bounced all manner of sounds back to her. She could see the individual divots and cracks in the concrete foundation, and had enough time to consider how they might grow and spread on her impact.

Eight months and her body was still pulsing with dregs of that stimulant, waking up her nerves whenever she was in danger and surging like a wave on the ocean, ready to carry her to new heights—

Would her seizures be bad today, she wondered? If she survived?

She tucked her shoulder, hitting the ground clean and rolling into a low crouch, her blades screeching against the floor.

She felt...she felt on fire, engulfed, electric, snapping, burning, powerful. She felt ready.

The factory boys circled up, pressing in on her. Easily two dozen large sweaty men in various states of physique, all with improvised weapons and a couple with real ones: knives, and the like.

Adorable.

Roche, she bounced, *tell me you got it.*

We're clean and clear, he confirmed. *What's your status?*

Popular.

We'll get you an exfil. Just get to them, and we'll do the rest.

"Alright then, boys," Zatia whispered, bringing her blades up. "Who thinks they can take a ninety-pound girl?"

One man decided he could be the hero. He took one, two steeling breaths...and he rushed her with a big heavy haymaker backed up with a pipe and his bulging biceps.

Zatia didn't even bother blocking his attack, simply sidestepping and carving three clean lines in his abdomen, sending something of squishy consequence sloshing to the unforgiving ground.

"Come on!" she bellowed, an open challenge. She could practically taste their blood already, the tang of it, like a static shock on her tongue.

Which is when they all descended, mobbing her. She was faster, stronger than she had any right to be. But a wall of meat was still a wall.

What to do, she thought, when the situation couldn't be punched out of?

She hooked a box with her blades and hoped it was full of contraband, as she heaved it at her attackers. It wasn't, but even the red meat brigade wasn't willing to take the chance. They stutter-stepped, pausing in their assault to dodge the crate that might very well have contained crystallized necromancy.

Which gave her the opening.

Zatia punched out through that gap, widening it by cutting up the two nearest people as she passed. She darted under a welding rig, kicking it to spin that hot electric lead back onto any pursuer unlucky enough to be brave. They had good survival instincts, and knew their tools, so nobody got close enough to enjoy being tack welded by a confused robot.

She scrambled underneath the project, bear-crawling her way underneath the unfinished mining drone. Two toughs greeted her on the other side, looking for self-addressed invitations to the trauma ward.

She obliged, slicing one man's arm off at the elbow, sending his hand and implement of choice sailing off. The blood trail in the air caught the light, shimmering like an offering of ambrosia to long-forgotten gods. It made her heart do a little dance, and her brain flood with pleasure.

The second man hesitated at that same sight. Zatia feinted, popping off her feet for a second, which spooked the guy enough for her to swing her blades for his neck—

Stopping millimeters from vital flesh.

No. She didn't need to kill him. She didn't. She killed who she had to, because they made her, to survive. Not a drop more.

Besides, he got the message just fine. He eased himself back out of her reach, almost tripping over his own two feet, before turning tail and running full tilt away.

Fine. He might get killed by whoever reviews the footage, but self-preservation earned him a couple more hours of freedom, if not happiness

She didn't need to kill. She didn't want it. The drugs that had coursed through her veins, driving her into a numbing battle ready, eager for any sensation—not anymore.

Hard to feel excitement for that private victory. She'd have to share with the gang later. Which, by the way, might be getting killed that very moment.

Zatia darted straight for the break room, the tidal wave of hairy, sweaty testosterone closing in behind her with wrenches and mercenary loyalty.

Smuggling crate ahead on her right. She slashed the side, scoring an ugly hole through the thin metal—and released a carpet of Pilgrim shards, black caltrops on to the ground. They tinkled like broken glass and acted just like it. One poor bastard didn't stop in time, running right into the field and piercing his foot.

A bloody foot would've been bad enough, but he immediately shrieked, crumpling to the ground amongst the other shards. His friends watched helplessly as his flesh darkened and shriveled, his body contorting in unimaginable agony. His screams were cut short as his throat collapsed, and he finally stopped moving.

Well, Zatia remarked to the group. *That's the wallpaper of my nightmares now.*

What happened? Adelaide asked.

You ever seen freeze-dried meat?

The hairs on her neck stood on end. Who had himself a full twenty seconds of uninterrupted time to reload, reposition, and draw down on her? Why, the happy little asshole on the catwalk above!

Zatia ducked behind one of the three-story mining rigs being constructed—just as the wide beam of the bracket gun fired off again, tearing through the side of the industrial mammoth, carving out a boxy frame of yellow slag where Zatia would have been.

If Milardi were here, that guy would've been breathing through some new holes in his chest by now. Zatia was going to have to manage.

She had to get close, wreck his day, or she'd never get Thom and Rash to safety.

The shooter was directing men on the ground to her hiding place, trying to flush her out. Very well. He'll get to meet her up close.

She popped off her cover and climbed the outside shell of the mining rig. Just in time, as three heavies came rocketing around the corner, the first of which wielding a power drill, its cable dangling from overhead. He scraped the bit at the side of the drone, straining to reach for her leg. The drill shot hot sparks and whined against the steel.

Asshole.

Bracket gun boy took another shot, blowing out the chunk of drone Zatia was going to climb to. The whole rig shifted as something important got cut, and Zatia very nearly lost her grip—slipping into power drill's reach. He stuck up for her boot, grinding into the bottom of the leather sole.

She flailed blindly with her blade, slashing the drill's power cable, leaving him with nothing but a quiet motor clogged with leather.

Zatia grimaced, taking stock of her options. The rig's precarious situation was not being improved by the six hundred pounds of jackass climbing up behind her.

The power cable dangled near her head, teasing her with

however many volts that might snap through her heart. Where was that cable routed up to?

There! The cable from the power drill ran upward to an electrified grid of steel squares. Looked sturdy enough. Sturdy enough that big guys on the ground yanked on it all day. But for someone of her build to maybe stand on?

Zatia leapt off the side of the rig, stretching out one foot to tap the edge of the grid and draw herself in. There were squares of metal six feet across, a dozen one way and a dozen another. What she didn't expect was the whole grid to swing as she landed, nearly sending her to a rough fall to the ground.

Someone threw their wrench at her, hoping to unbalance her. She swatted the throw away with her blades as she tried to hold her balance.

Where was he? Laser-Shoots-Bang-Bang-Asshole was to her left, just a few squares of wobbly grid away. And he was loading a fresh capacitor into the bracket gun. He was about to find out if he could do that under duress.

She didn't dare move quickly as she gingerly prowled along the narrow steel like a balance beam, one foot planted right in front of the other. The grid shifted with each step, swinging left and right underneath her. Any faster and she risked falling.

Bracket gun snapped the chamber closed and brought his gun to bear. But she was close, reaching out with her blades—

Not close enough. Not enough for him, at least. But she managed to hook the end of his gun, swiping it aside. It went off, searing and slagging the tip of her blade with brilliant red light.

And the grid lurched underneath her as the laser cut one of the support lines that held it up. It listed hard, and with the momentum of her swing, she toppled to the left—planting her foot on the inside edge of the square.

Too bad, asshole. She jumped up at him. Maybe it was her kick off the grid, or the other supports were just not rated for that force. But as she rose up, sinking her blades into his chest, the other supports gave out. As the shooter fell to her blades, so too did the entire electrical grid, crashing down onto the workers and projects below in a pile of twisted metal.

Zatia wiped the back of her hand across her forehead, feeling the crispy fried ends of her bangs where the laser singed a small channel through her platinum hair. Hopefully, it didn't cook a chunk of her face too, but she didn't feel anything.

Sure, there were grunts still standing, but far too busy salvaging their friends and projects from the wreck, gingerly avoiding open crates of Pilgrim metal. Nobody accosted her further.

Zatia marched over to the break room, pushing the door open with her newly blunt blade.

Rashida stood tall, trying to hide the deliriously cheerful smile on her elegant face. Her shoulders shook with barely contained laughter. Her cane had a clump of oily hair on the end of it, freshly bludgeoned free from its owner.

Thom, in all his gaudy finery, sat comfortably on a chair. He watched the door swing open with raised eyebrows. Two guards were next to him, matching expressions of chilled amazement—and both favoring fresh cane-inflicted injuries.

The four of them all looked past Zatia to the carnage outside, then back at her.

Zatia wiped the sweat from her forehead, resetting her grips on the blades. "You've been tangling with her. Anybody want to deal with *me* now that I'm tired and pissed off?"

The guards shook their heads, and backed away from Thom, turning to face the wall with their hands in the air.

"Where's the boss?" Zatia asked her new hostages.

Rashida answered for them. "Calling the Ministry. We're completely screwed."

Roche? Thom asked. *Can you get us another car? Something fast.*

CHAPTER 16
ROCHE

"TRANSMITTER CONNECTION IS SEVERED," Adelaide said, closing the dashboard back up. "You have manual control."

"Confirmed!" Roche said. "Manual control. Watch your heads!"

Adelaide braced herself in the front seat as Lily hacked through the safety coding that would prevent the car from doing exactly what Roche was doing with it. Roche seated Lily's cable directly into the taxi's dash, giving the AI unmitigated access to the vehicle's systems.

With no citywide AI to provide instructions, there was only Roche & Lily.

It had not been the most subtle of approaches, but it worked. The car's proximity alarm abruptly cut out. Like he'd heard the starting pistol at a racetrack, Roche pitched the car's nose down—into the factory wall.

The bricks gave way like plaster, the wall crumpling immediately against the steel nose of the car, with each individual brick falling aside to protect itself from further damage.

Of course, this revealed the labyrinth of wreckage and multiple unfinished mining rigs at eye level.

Roche tumbled the car up and over the mess, scraping the hull of the flying car against the roof, before settling it back down in front of the trio of waiting friends.

The gullwing door kicked open, and the shouting immediately started with Adelaide. "What the hell did you do in here?"

"What did *I* do?" Zatia barked back. "I'm not the one who drove a car through a building wall!"

"Would've been a very dramatic rescue, if we suddenly had to rescue you," Rashida said.

"You said you were in a hurry," Roche pointed out.

"A hurry," Zatia snapped, "not a china shop!"

"Shut—up!" Thom shouted over them. "Get—in!"

Nobody waited for any further instruction. They all jumped into the car, piling into the backseat in one sweaty, bloody mess.

And Lily came in with the good news. *Local authorities are attempting to override this vehicle's operation. I have terminated wireless control.*

"Here we go," Thom whispered.

"Seatbelts," Roche reminded them as he lifted the car off the ground.

Roche had grown used to Lily's deep and unnerving voice. But this, this was a whole other level. The building itself, like some kind of ancient sleeping deity, gave notice to them, its voice shaking the whole vehicle, vibrating through the blood, and pounding his skull. "Please surrender at this time. There is no further use in struggling."

"So polite," Rashida groaned.

"Hang on to something," Roche warned.

And he pressed the vehicle toward the car-shaped hole he'd made at the front of the factory. He weaved through the factory wreckage, the scraps of metal and crumpled stone.

Somebody gasped, and Roche knew why. The bricks of the building ebbed and flowed down to the breach, reshaping to pack the hole, drifting up from the floor and places unknown to reinforce. He'd never make it through that and have a flying car afterward.

A crunch and bang drew his eye back for half a second—seeing the back wall of the factory rolling towards him, like a wave upon the sea. The blocks rolled past all obstacles, swallowing them whole to press the taxi and seal off avenues of retreat.

"The building is eating us!" Zatia shouted.

Lily? Structural weaknesses? Roche asked.

The building is composed entirely of the same autonomous building blocks found throughout Ilum, Lily said. *Any structural weak points fluctuate on a moment by moment basis.*

Of course, the blocks were strongest when linked, weakest when in motion. He just had to lure a wall into a shift, and then blast through while it was unsteady.

"Gotta admit," Adelaide grunted past the cigarette dangling from her cracked lips, "I've never been arrested by a building before."

"I wouldn't exactly fixate on the novelty," Thom said. "Roche?"

"Working on it." Every time Roche turned the car, the wall in front of him sealed up solid. Turn away, and the wall crept closer in, a constricting arena. The bricks climbed over and around the wreckage, unabated by carnage.

At this rate, he'd never build up enough inertia to punch through.

Lily, Roche emphasized, *the air space is getting rather cramped.*

Lily's tone didn't exactly induce calm. *Proceed to the opposite end of the facility.*

Roche tilted the taxi to face the opposing side of the factory. The walls had tapered in, plenty of wreckage in the way and no room to readily maneuver. What was their plan here, exactly?

But there was nothing else to do. Roche accelerated down the corridor. He could see the walls ripple as blocks slid along the inside edge, trying to fortify for the inevitable impact. And the monolithic wall ahead of them bulked as it absorbed the added material, like a strongman puffing his chest out.

They'd splash against that surface like water against a seaside cliff.

There had to be a way out! There had to be. Find it. Just look.

No—this was all being managed by a computer system supported by an entire planet. Server banks the size of rooms supported quantum calculations completed a thousand times faster than it took his brain to chemically conjure that image of it.

He was outclassed here.

"Roche?" Rashida stammered from the backseat with increasing urgency. "R-Roche?!"

He didn't give the order. Lily did.

// Cut thrust, pitch to vertical. Mark & execute.

The car's nose tilted up just as the whine of the engine silenced. And for a brutal and horrid long moment, they hung in the air on invisible strings dangling over their demise. The taxi pushed upward, slowing, slowing....

And the blocks rose up to the ceiling, trying to reinforce. Pulling away. Weakening the base of the wall.

Which is when Lily suddenly tumbled the car backward end over end, falling toward the base of the wall at full gravity speed—and the bricks were caught moving in the wrong direction.

The taxi slammed through the thin layer of bricks like it was made of glass, shattering the meager defense and sending chunks of fragile block high into the air.

"Eurgh!" Adelaide tried to swallow her lunch again, all with her cigarette still firmly pinched between her lips. "I didn't know these cars could do that!"

"Nice work, Roche!" Thom commended, adding a pat on the shoulder for good measure.

But he hadn't done that. He had no plan to escape that factory, and no skill to do it with. He had circled and circled, looking for something that wasn't there...

That was Lily. And Lily seemed content to let Roche take the glory for that neck-breaking maneuver.

The neon glow of the Nightside skyline almost blinded Roche with its greens and pinks, cloaking the three Ministry vehicles waiting outside. Knobbly floating tanks they were, with monitoring equipment spearing out of their noses, and armor plating protecting the state-of-the-art high-power engines.

The celebration would have to take a pause. "Knuckle up back there," Roche said, "because we've got a lot of company!"

An enormous featureless face of holographic pale blue coalesced in the air, as large as the building they'd just escaped from. It looked down on their car with paternal derision. "Destruction of Private Property is a Class C offense," the AI's voice bellowed.

"Oh, he's going to hate me," Zatia muttered.

But her look of pride faltered—as the blocks that made up the factory, and two other buildings, melted up around them like the planet had grown possessive tendrils reaching upward to ensnare their car.

"Anybody feeling good about their vote right now?" Adelaide asked.

"I'll tan it out of his hide," Zatia said, eying the blocky tendrils reaching up to box them in, "but for right now? Let's get your foot kissing metal, Roche. Get us some altitude."

Thom glanced out the window, up to the safety of the sky—the cars. The entire transport network, they were all settling down to the ground as part of some hostile security response. The system wasn't going to dedicate cycles to anything other than their capture. All air traffic in the area was being stalled.

"No!" Thom shouted. "We go high, they'll blow us out of the sky. We have to get low where they won't shoot, lose our tail."

"We go low, they'll just box us in again!"

"No choice. Do it!"

// Cut thrust, pitch down. Mark & execute.

He thought the command, and he twisted the car over, drawing ugly groans from the crew behind him. Firing up the engine, they zipped out of the AI's grasp and into the neon-flavored night.

The Ministry cars pulled into pursuit, but they kept a healthy distance. They didn't need to do the catching, just facilitate the AI to do it.

"Cease your escape at this time," the city's voice bellowed. "There is nowhere you can hide."

"Come on, Roche, put some mustard on it!" Adelaide said, clutching her door handle in barely contained terror.

The belly of a structure ahead of them suddenly swelled, its bricks reaching out to catch the passing taxi. It was the yawning maw of a hungry whale, or elder beast, thirsting for their souls.

"Look out!" Rashida shouted, like he hadn't seen the obvious obstruction.

Roche pushed the car up, slipping through the AI's clawing fingers.

A sudden surge slammed them all to the left, a jet wash of hot air blasting the car sideways. The AI had poked and prodded them—driving them right into a Darkside Thermo-Vent, blasting hot solar heated air to keep the area remotely temperate at hurricane speeds—and it sent their car reeling, tumbling through the air.

Roche peeled his arm away from the sweltering hot window, and turned the car to go with the impulse. More clawing hands were waiting, pixelated titan's grasping digits.

But properly oriented, Roche had regained control and some added speed. He darted through the fingers, narrowly avoiding being pinched off by the tendrils. One of the Ministry pursuit vehicles wasn't so lucky, crunching right into the side of the articulated building. Thom looked back to see the carnage—only to see the AI propel its catch back into the chase, catapulting the undamaged vehicle to the front of the pack.

"Well, that's just not fair," Zatia groaned.

A flash of light as a hologram filled their vision. Big bold letters, urging them to surrender, stop fighting, stop running. Roche squeezed his meaty eye shut, letting his red cybernetic implant filter out the bloom. It was still a painfully bright light, but he knew to pitch up away from the hidden claw of black blocks hiding in the glare below them.

Their taxi passed harmlessly through the advertisement—to find a second building ready for him, a proper wall for them to smack into.

The Commandant had blinded him, telegraphed an attack, and drove him right into its trap.

"Hang on!" Roche said.

The car lurched upward and slammed belly first into the wall, grinding and sliding against the bricks—

Until the car jerked to a stop, snapping the crew against their restraints. The AI had formed a backstop and started to brick the car in, like a spider cocooning its prey.

Act fast. "Zatia!" Roche called out.

The girl needed no further instruction. She unbuckled and kicked at the gullwing door. She knocked it open with enough force to shear a few blocks off the wall with sparks. And the door lost its pathetic attachment to the chassis, tumbling down the side of the building to the streets way too far down.

Not that Zatia paid the fall much mind. She leaned out the gap she made and out came her blades, hacking away at the snare, at any blocks that got too close to her. The AI's attempts to attack her directly just made for polymer shrapnel.

Roche felt the car lurch, strain, creak. The bricks squeezed on the chassis, compressing the metal and crushing components.

Zatia gave one good slash to the bricks at their tail—and just like that, the car was free again. And Zatia was suddenly outside the car. Gravity hit the car first, dropping and accelerating away before the girl felt the fall, leaving her hanging helplessly in space, with a ten-story plunge...

"Zee!" Rashida felt the car give way. She reached out, snagging Zatia's leg before she could get too far. Zatia swung outside of the taxi, hair flapping in the breeze, coupled to a machine as they fell to the city below.

The AI rushed to provide a capture beneath them, bricks sweeping in to prevent damage to both city and prey.

Good.

Roche keyed up the engine and gave it the right kind of nudge to toss Zatia back into the interior. Without checking his work, Roche punched the throttle and drifted the car out of the AI's grasp for the second time in less than a minute.

Zatia shook off the adrenaline shiver and smiled a bit too wide for what almost happened.

Rashida looked up at the trio that hovered in pursuit like ominous rain clouds. "We have got to shake those Ministry vehicles."

"We've got the attention of a planet," Adelaide said. "What do you suggest?"

"The Paladins," Thom said. "They could hack local sensors, become functionally invisible to AI. We shake our tails, and then drop off the AI's sensors. Could Lily handle that?"

"Paladins had enough horsepower to outclass *starships!*" Adelaide said, swallowing her lunch as Roche made another maneuver. "The moment we connect to the network, the Commandant'll lock out Lily and ground the car!"

"Could they do it?" Thom repeated.

Roche glanced at Adelaide. "I can help them."

Her eyes sharpened on him. "Roche?"

He nodded. The Paladins needed their AIs, and Lily needed him. He could push back on the Commandant, shield Lily from assault.

Adelaide looked at him, cursed, and popped open the dashboard again. "Lily, we're about to make a big ask of you."

"Bring the thunder," Lily's voice growled from inside their case.

"If you cut out on us, this is going to be a very steep cliff into a very sudden stop." Adelaide dug into the dashboard, parsing out the connector they'd left to dangle. "Transmitter coming online in three, two..."

Zatia grabbed Rashida's hand, squeezing tight. And with her other hand, she grabbed Thom's. They were praying.

Roche finished the silent count, and let his mind slip off the controls, ceding to Lily.

And he felt the voice itch at his brain, like fingers sliding around his throat, squeezing on every artery. In the one second after the transmitter went live, connecting with the planet-wide network, he felt the voice of the Commandant worming its way into his gray matter. *This is a most curious model of database. There does not appear to be any reasonable filing system or nomenclature.*

Get out of my head, Roche said.

At this time, it would be wise to halt your escape. You have nowhere you can run.

I'm not one of your drones.

The Commandant seemed confused, vexed by his lack of obedience. In the span of a microsecond, it traced every detail of his face and biology. *Gavroche Keynes. Age thirty-one. Wanted for twelve vehicle-related thefts and crimes, and the homicide of an orphanage matron.*

The taxi tilted forward, listing toward the ground far below, pitching between buildings. Roche still felt the sting of the rod against his arm, felt the bones of his hand breaking.

He remembered how the surgeon couldn't save it, and the whir of his bone saw.

That was a long time ago, Roche said. *And I don't need to explain myself to a planetary utility grid.*

The Commandant said just three words: *But you will.*

And his skull felt like it might split in two. He was alone, in a dark that would choke him, squeeze the last breath from his chest— but a hand reached forward, snagging his, squeezing...

Milardi?

"Got ya!" Thom shouted from the backseat.

Not Milardi. It was Thomas. It was family.

The car was falling, falling...and the Ministry cars were hard behind them.

"Lily!" Adelaide cried out.

And suddenly, like they'd passed on to the glowing Path of the Pilgrim, a dozen holographic ads appeared around them, swirling in the air. Pharmaceutical medications, Replicator recipes, brand names and powerful politicians.

Blinding the Ministry vehicles behind them.

The car suddenly snapped to level and the Ministry vehicles kept descending down into the depths of the city. Their taxi spun hard, gliding off to the side.

You cannot escape, the Commandant whispered to Roche.

Escape was never the plan, Lily cut in. *Instead, we intend to vanish.*

The car's lights turned off, gliding harmlessly through the air. Adelaide severed the transmitter again, and the crew waited with bated breath for a building to reach out for them or a pursuit vehicle to swoop in.

But nothing.

There's a band of cascading sensor failures stretching eastward, Lily reported. *They've assumed we're hiding in that bubble.*

Thom exhaled. "Then we might want to get out of the air before they look over their shoulder."

———

The fire was warm, at least. The wreckage that the crew so politely referred to as their taxi would probably never fly again, but it was understandable to have a personal attachment to the inanimate object to which they all owed their lives.

Adelaide had pried out the cracked power cell and used the unstable exothermic reaction to boil some water. It might not have had the same poetry as burning tinder, and it was certainly releasing harmful gases—but it was preferable to freezing.

Roche thought they'd be done with the cold after Farragut, but it turned out that living your life without sunlight for an epoch made for frigid air.

Lily? Roche bounced on his private channel, eyeing the briefcase in his hand. *Can you hear me?*

You do not need to speak for me to hear you, Lily said.

What happened back there?

We saved the day, that's what.

No. Roche was fairly sure that he had done precious little. Lily had done...more than he even understood. Lily had given instructions.

And his body had obeyed.

But he didn't get a chance to ask further. Thom stumbled over, balling up his ration bar into a little torpedo, before plopping down on the ground next to Roche. He said nothing at first. He knew better than to speak for its own sake. If Roche wanted conversation, Thom let Roche start.

"So...Anze's reach extends all the way to Ilum," Roche said.

"I suppose I shouldn't be surprised."

"Flat-footed has become something of a rare condition for you."

"And a frustrating one." Thom looked over at his friend. "Thanks for that kick save at the warehouse."

Roche felt his gut seize and his eyes pull shut. He hadn't done any of that. If he had been in control of the situation...they'd be captured or dead. His gratitude was misplaced.

I don't need special attention, Lily told him privately.

But it wasn't me.

No, Lily said. *It was us.*

Us. The word was taking on a toxic new meaning to him. Roche wasn't just one with a backseat driver or a teammate. He was becoming...us.

"I didn't make that maneuver," Roche said gravely. "Lily did."

"Lily?" Thom's eyes sharpened, following the train. "Lily...was piloting the taxi?"

"No, they weren't. At-at least not with direct intent. But they have increasing influence over my actions, moment by moment. The delineation of what defines us as separate beings is eroding at an alarming rate."

Thom nodded, taking in the full meaning. "And when that line is completely gone?"

"I won't be me anymore," Roche said. "And Lily's Cascade will begin again. Right where it left off."

"How much time do we have?"

"Impossible to say." Roche forced a smile, tilting his head towards the young lad. "But I won't be winking out of existence in the immediate future, if that's your concern."

"My concern," Thom urged, "is that you're safe and comfortable. The both of you."

Roche's smile faltered, absorbing the mathematical impossibility of that predicament. If he was safe, Lily was not. And if Lily was safe, Roche was diminishing, like candle wax at midnight. "My body has... dual loyalties at the moment."

Thom huffed at that euphemism. "You okay?"

No. No he was not 'okay.' He struggled to find words that fit this feeling. It was like someone sitting on his chest, like a man buried alive bloodying his knuckles against the coffin lid. It felt like...

Like drowning.

Thom laid a hand on his shoulder, and Roche felt an intense soothing warmth glow through his arm and down his chest. "You told me once, that I would figure out who I was. That one day, it was all going to click. And I would know."

"And do you?"

Thom pulled his hand back and taking that blessed warmth with it. He pulled his legs in close like a blanket and rested his chin on his knee. "I don't think anybody does."

Perhaps. But Roche didn't even seem to understand his own senses much anymore. There was that moment in the car, when he felt Thom's hand and felt the presence of...

He was getting so confused lately.

Of course, Lily added privately, *it's a confusing time for us. We shouldn't expect to understand everything about ourselves.*

No, Roche thought. But he had been so certain of himself a year ago. Now? He no longer knew how to do much of anything at all.

UNRECORDED DREAM DATA

THOM HUGH

THERE WAS no record to refer to, no data to process this time. Thom would only ever have his own recollection of the night's strangeness.

When the crew of the *Aurum* struggled with the Paladins, Farragut, and Anze Orchikov, their troubles had compounded with the arrival of an Imperial Dreadnaught captained by an old enemy. Thom had always assumed that Admiral Hugh had taunted him from the Jump Deck of his floating castle.

But instead, Thom saw the man sequestered in his cabin, collar unbuckled, cap crumpled in his hand. A half-finished glass of bourbon on the nightstand, by a bed of untouched linens. He hadn't slept in this bed in many days.

The Past-Admiral stared into his vanity mirror, just as Thom stared from behind the old man's eyes. His rage had long since boiled away to reveal the bare truth underneath. The frazzled expression and furrowed brows. Not recognizing what they saw.

Sleeping on the cold hard ground this time, Thom?

How could you possibly know where I'm sleeping?

I told you. Liminal state of being. We've never met, and I've known you my whole life.

This is during Farragut, isn't it? When we turned to Anze's flagship?

Yes. And he was forced to watch.

Watch what?

"Admiral," the thrumming bass voice of the ship's Commandant AI politely interrupted the bizarre meditation. "Sensors have detected a vessel exiting the Farragut Jump Point. LADAR readings indicate it has suffered structural damage."

Hugh's brow tightened. "The *Aurum*?"

"No, Admiral," the AI said. "It is a TC-8801 Halcyon class luxury vessel. Registered to citizen Anze Orchikov."

Unnecessary chaos. He had expected to meet with the outcast mobster in exchange for the *Aurum*, and Anze's file was dense with dramatic encounters with the Empire's might. He would not make the same mistakes as three past Naval commanders, lulled into a false sense of security.

Instead, he swallowed the lump of nerve before it could take root in his throat. Because he was approaching a moment where he might have to order that ship fired on.

Along with everyone aboard.

Hugh grumbled, grabbing his bracer and roughly tossing up a communications channel. "Anze Orchikov, this better not be some kind of trick."

Thom remembered that statement. Thom remembered where he was. On that ship as it limped out of the Jump.

As the Paladin shuffled towards him, hand outstretched...

The moment froze, fractured glass. Like the whole of it was about to spiral in on itself and vanish.

What is the matter, Thom?

I remember this.

Stay here. Stay in this place, with your father.

He's not my father.

Would you prefer I call him a genetic predecessor?

Call him whatever you like, but don't call him my father.

Thomas...there's nothing to be gained back on that ship, reliving that pain. That Paladin has nothing more to offer you.

Sure there was. He could find out why, from the mouth of the real thing. He could find out why. Why that titan of a man had hunted his friends, why it had been so obsessed with him—

Why it killed Milardi.

The image racked, focused, blurred, focused again. He could make out through a blurry surface...what looked like an operating table, a bar full of bloodthirsty patrons, a taxi cab out in front of a mobster's mansion—

But it all collapsed into darkness. And he had never heard his guide's voice bellow so loud.

Stop it, Thomas! Now.

I need answers.

You won't find them there.

It some kind of impassable labyrinth? I'll lose myself in it?

No. Because the mind of a man sand-blasted with hatred and forged with faith.. isn't confusing. It's barren. What you want to know, what you need to know, isn't in the mind of a Paladin.

You seem pretty insistent I stay here.

For the moment, yes. You need to see this.

Why?

Because you think you've seen this, but you haven't.

Out of the darkness, colors took shape, clouds of grays and red. They pulled and twisted into hard edges, fully shaping into the Jump Deck of the dreadnaught.

This was Admiral Hugh in his element. In sharp relief with the self-reflective man in the cabin. His command chair and its holographic telemetry data silhouetted behind him. He preferred to lead from his feet.

Two Warrant Officers on either side of him, sitting at Navigation and Gunnery Control, were chattering back and forth. "Jump complete. Opening thermal vents."

"Primary deflectors on-line. Give me kinetics."

"You've got 'em."

"Advise hold fire: planetary body shadow's the target."

Hugh raised a hand, like he was drawing down a window blind. And the mighty snow planet of Farragut assembled before him. The admiral pinched his fingers, pulling up a section of the planet's northern pole.

Thom could see the great storm—Ingohla, the Jawless One—the blizzard of a century, spiraling underneath Hugh's fingers.

And Anze's frigate drifting, powerless, falling.

"Give me a broadband hailing frequency," Hugh snarled.

A chirp and a cheep from the computer. "No open transponders or signals from the ailing vessel."

I don't remember this.

Why would you? You were quite busy falling out of the sky.

What would Admiral Hugh do?

"Time to target?" Hugh demanded.

"We're three days impulse from the planet," the Warrant Officer reported.

And sweat started to glow on his forehead. A sudden tightness in his chest, the back of his neck itching. He couldn't feel his own fingertips no matter how much he rubbed them together.

"Time to target?" Hugh asked again.

"Sir, three days impulse, sir," the Officer repeated, louder.

A tongue of flame began to lick across the frigate's hull, atmospheric reentry happening the hard way. And the forces turned the ship around, tossing its nose up and down as it looked for the most even differential of friction.

Inside, Thom remembered his head being scrambled, all guts and terror.

"Full LADAR scan, open pulse," Hugh ordered. "Find the *Aurum*!"

"Sir, we have them. They're onboard that ship, sir."

A ringing in Hugh's ears, like his own brain was rejecting those words. No, no! They were devious, clever, villainous. They would somehow escape. They would sneak victory from the jaws of defeat. That criminal crew would not—

The sweat tumbled down his wrinkled forehead like a river down a mountainside, the stinging salt soaking through his tunic.

Think, goddammit, think!

"Launch fighters for immediate intercept," Hugh ordered.

"CAT-CC, you have a green light."

But the other officer turned to his admiral. "Sir, effective range on the Bearcats is twelve hours. They'd never make it in time or make it back."

Hugh snarled. "Did I ask for your excuses, Officer?"

The man stiffened and spun back to his instruments, very keen to become as invisible as possible.

Hugh turned back to his display, eyes scouring for some yet unseen solution. The ship was fully engorged in flames, panels and material ripping off.

"Bearcats in the vac. CAG's requesting confirmation of coordinates?"

Go. Go fast. He had to reach them. He had to reach his son.

That's rich. His son?

The man is allowed to feel how he feels.

And am I allowed to feel unbridled rage?

Of course. But empathy requires that you see things from all angles.

He doesn't deserve my empathy.

He may not deserve your sympathy, but you'll find that everyone deserves your empathy.

Hugh's jaw clamped hard, castle gates drawn tight. His hands clenched tightly at his side as officers repeated requests for information, barked status updates.

They wanted to know their orders. They needed to know what to do. And he had nothing, as his son burned. His son burned.

His eyes darted to and fro, unable to focus, unable to rest, unable to—

The frigate slipped into the upper atmosphere, vanishing into the blizzard.

The admiral's voice could have leveled a city's walls. *"THOMAS!"*

And the memory blew apart...showering into a million darts of sand, powder to settle into the black.

Thom laid there for a while. That...that rage, that pain. That fear?

He was just mad he'd lost a possession. Someone took his toys.

That's an excuse. You know what you saw.

You want me to believe he loved me, but all I remember is shame and abuse.

Which is just as valid. He can love you and be a terrible father. He can love you and be an abuser. His love for you doesn't magically make him into a good person.

That's not love. That's ownership.

Perhaps. But does it make his pain any less real?

It makes me care less.

Thomas, you are not just any child of any father. You have a gift most sons only dream of. You can understand your father better than the man himself ever did. Your power—

My power?!

That shut him up, stopped him cold. And he didn't dare speak back. Thom could feel his own voice in the marrow of his bones, reverberating backwards down into chasms as yet unnamed in the human soul, like an echo in a dark cave.

My power for-for what? The power to screw up in new and special ways? The power to see my friends die, and not enough power to stop it? You know, it's a staggering kind of dread to know people you love are going to suffer and be powerless to change it.

And what of the people you saved?

Leave me alone. For one night, can I just be me? Can one night give me some gulaw peace? Can I—can you just...go away?!

And Thom didn't hear another peep from the voice beyond the dark. No apologies, no due deference or goodbyes. For the rest of the night, he had blessed silence. A whole three hours of serenity. But it felt a hell of a lot longer than that.

"YOUR MEN HAD THEM CORNERED. Your men *had* them, and then let them go!" Admiral Hugh was really going all out to make this into Anze's fault.

Someone could barely describe the office chairs in Hugh's private cabin as 'chairs.' They were steel slabs cut into the vaguest shape of the human back. And they forced the body into the most unnatural shape.

Anze slung his legs over the side of the chair, and hooked his hand over the back, dangling his body in space—it was about the only way he could get comfortable in the damn thing. "I'd be hard-pressed to say that my men did anything but die for the cause, Admiral. And the assistance of an actual city-state didn't so much as slow them down. A city's omniscient eye blinked, and they vanished inside that gap. But please tell me more, bumpy, about how my street-level thugs are at fault."

"If your men had done their duty, this whole matter would be over and done with!"

Anze smiled, the bitter taste of blame filling his mouth. Anything to escape the failures of the Imperial enforcers that failed at the same task. "Admiral, if my men were at all capable of stopping the crew of the *Aurum*. I wouldn't even be gracing the halls of your ship. This would have long since been dispensed with. I know the limitations of my cohort and I do not expect anything more of them. Nor do I punish them for failing to meet unreasonable asks."

Hugh's voice dipped into his lower register, searching for some tool to drive an emotional response. "I had thought you a man of considerable means, Mr. Orchikov. Perhaps there's a reason you're the runt of your family."

Anze just stared at him, stone faced. Insults, absence, diminishment: these were the tools of small men to make themselves large. No wonder Thom fled. Fathers were not by nature the warmest type, but family should be a refuge from the rest of the thorny world, not a briar patch itself.

"The runt of dragons," Anze warned, "is still a dragon, Admiral."

Hugh gave up, turning to his cabin's personal Replicator. He drew out a fresh bottle of whiskey from it, pouring himself an indiscriminate messy glass that spilled over across the countertop. It wasn't even good whiskey the man was drinking. He was drinking to excise his feelings before they took hold of him.

The great admiral wanted to be alone, to slowly simmer in the dark. But he knew he had no power to command Anze to leave, and commanding was the only language he knew. Anze would gladly give the man the privacy to be frustrated with some peace. But that would demand an expression of weakness. And Hugh was never going to admit to stress or strain. Instead, the admiral leaned over his desk, gripping the surface like he might rip it free from its moorings.

Hugh had not spoken for a great length of frustrating time. Anze thought he was bound to combust. Men of fire and brimstone, absent anything to burn, always burned themselves. It was why they always looked for fuel, for powder, for victims. They were self-destructive by nature and saved themselves from consumption by turning their fury outward.

Finally the cemetery statue deigned to draw breath, and the

voice that issued was small, like he was whispering on hallowed ground. "May I ask you a personal question?"

What was this now? A surprise, indeed. Not unwelcome, but Hugh finally played a surprise card from his hand.

Give him the floor and see what he does. "Admiral, it is *your* ship. Do as you like."

"Do you regret what happened with your family?"

Anze...just blinked as he processed that question. "How long has that question been chewing through the side of your head?"

"'Fuck off' would have been a shorter answer." And the man did so treasure his brevity, didn't he?

Anze had interrogated the notion privately for many years, though this might have been the first instance where the question came from another. Did he regret it? For a time, perhaps. For a longer time, he was furious.

The Dunsweir drew their power and status from the immutable truth of the Gnostic Texts, set down in the passing of the Pilgrim. Challenges to that faith eroded the very foundation of the royal family.

They weren't a family. They were a political party formed from blood relations. Anze had made a family of his own, built them up, supported them. He built up an entire planet for them to turn to whenever buried by the dark and the cold. His people could live life safely, because he was always watching, caring for their needs.

His parents had only ever cared what he could give to them or the faith. They never gave comfort or security or confidence, even in the good times. And when he...after he changed?

Then he was a threat to the dogma.

"The events with my family...proceeded the only way they could have," Anze finally answered.

"And if you had a chance to do it over again?"

Anze chuckled quietly. He hadn't really been an active participant in events. The whole affair had rather happened to him, but that's not why the admiral was asking.

"As though I had much choice in the matter the first time around," Anze opined. "I imagine the results would come out much the same."

Hugh nodded, considering that for a time. "He was..." But nothing followed.

Was this the beginning of some kind of contrition? That might very well have been some piece of self-analysis. No man was going to live his life to perfection without mistake or harm, but the desire—the need, even—to study past injury was the mark of a good man, someone who wanted to improve himself and his legacy, to iterate and grow.

That was not what this was. The admiral was so concerned with how others saw him, and yet completely blind to how they actually did. It was vanity. Nothing more.

Hugh grunted, some affirmation or acknowledgment to internal questions, as he clad himself in old idioms for comfort. "I've served my Consul and my People with pride and dignity for a very long time."

"No shame in that," Anze said with a smirk, like the old admiral was apologizing for something.

Hugh sucked on his teeth, pushing down his natural angry response to that barb. Instead, he turned and leaned against the desk. "I had...conflicting responsibilities, Mr. Orchikov."

Yes, Anze thought. He had his loyalties to his Empire, and he had his son. It was no great mystery to figure out which one he had chosen.

"You followed your heart, Admiral," Anze teased. "What have you to regret?"

The admiral chuffed at that, his lip curling in mild disgust. "I'm not like you. Live as long as I have without regrets, and you're either a miracle or a monster."

That was the second time in as many minutes that the admiral had off-handedly inferred Anze wasn't entirely human, either by divine touch or something far more sinister. It was so easy of him to slash Anze out of the data set, remove the outlying numbers that fouled up his equations. His existence frustrated the pre-existing conclusions, that greatness was something bestowed and villainy rose from endless dark.

But Anze knew the truth. There were no Gods, no monsters. No altars to pray at or hydras to slay. Only men.

But if there were only men, then the conclusions of the equations undermined everything they held dear. There had to be a great and singular Evil, just as there was a great and singular Good; if not, then that meant they might have to take some responsibility for glassing planets and starving civilizations.

Responsibility for casting out their own family into the cold. They wouldn't be able to hide behind a mantle of justice. And Admiral Hugh was desperately looking for something to justify his cruelty.

"Do you know what the strongest force in the universe is?" Anze asked.

Hugh thought for a moment, his brow twisting with what he obviously thought to be a trick question of some kind. "The dark energy found within the Jump Points."

"Jump Points left behind for us to follow," Anze corrected. "See, faith is a far more potent element than any found in chemistry or physics. And even it bends under enough pressure."

"Speak plainly, Mr. Orchikov. If that's even possible for you."

Anze sighed. The admiral was as impatient as he was impetuous. "Your faith sways, does it not?"

The admiral stiffened, the hairs on his softly felted head glinting in the light as he turned to face Anze, glowering at his guest. "Tread softly."

"I meant no insult," Anze said. "Merely an observation. Even steel must find flexibility. Or else it becomes...brittle."

This didn't back down the admiral one inch, the old man's hand clenching into a fist. And Anze's lip twitched at the sight. Men like

Admiral Hugh only knew the stick, believing the carrot to be a compromise of morals.

Anze considered what might happen should he succeed in this little mission, if he were to actually capture the crew of the *Aurum*. Special Thomas would likely return to this malicious man's eternal shadow. And a good day would be when he went unnoticed by the lord of the manor. On the bad days?

Anze felt the electrons flowing up through Hugh's neck, to the cognitive implants seated at the base of the skull. It would be so easy...just tell them to pull all at once...to feel the bones slip out of place...

But Hugh bit his lip, unable to hide the teetering buildup of water in his eyes. "I failed him, Anze. He was my son and I failed him."

Ah. So the man was torn, pulled between what he knew was right, and what he had known for thirty years. And the conflict was splitting him in two.

Admiral Hugh was not lost. Not yet. Anze let the electrons go, let them flow freely again. He didn't need to stifle any flames. There was work yet to do here.

"Shame must serve a purpose," Anze said, "and your shame is only paralyzing you. Yes, we failed to contain your son, but Thomas has not left the planet. So...what did we learn, and how can we improve our efforts? Follow the evidence."

The admiral's shoulders slumped, and his hands stretched out, like he might push the tension out of the tips of his fingers. "A smuggling operation?"

"Correct," Anze said. "When the Espinozas were so explosively removed from the Ilum scene, there was a power vacuum. I took a primary stake in much of their operations, including rare artifact smuggling. But my presence was a shock to Thomas, unexpected."

"You've no concern at all for your operation being unmasked?"

Anze smiled. "If you think I hinged my operations upon a warehouse on the wrong side of the Sunset Line, I'd be happy for you to continue to think so."

Hugh and Anze locked eyes for a long moment of dueling wills, and Hugh was never going to win in that test. The admiral blinked. "So...they weren't there for you. They were there looking for what you had."

"Exactly. The largest stockpile of Pilgrim Metal seen outside of the Royal Arts. Given that they're on the trail of their friend, seems a curious choice. Doesn't it?"

Hugh looked aside, digging through his thoughts. "What interest would they have in glossy rock?"

"I doubt they had any," Anze said. "But they might have an interest in where I got the shiny rocks from."

And there was the crux of it. Admiral Hugh lifted his head. "How long have you been *sitting* on this, Mr. Orchikov?"

"Long enough for you to get your head out of your ass," Anze said. "I needed you thinking, bumpy, not feeling."

CHAPTER 18
ADELAIDE

SHE'D SPENT most of the night parsing through what Roche had found at the Godfather's warehouse. She had set her percolator up on the damaged taxi power cell, letting the residual heat boil up some coffee. And three pots later, she wasn't any closer to figuring out what was so special. The bronze warmth of her Entiglas, despite being a holographic screen, was burning her eyes in the dark. And the lists and numbers and names were all just blending together into a texture.

If there was anything to be found, it was here. And she was just missing it!

She sipped the bitter black focus juice to keep her eyes open and took a drag on the cigarette to keep her hands from shaking. After the day they'd had, she didn't really want to sleep.

All she'd end up seeing in her dreams would be some biomechanical tendril born from the planet's crust reaching up to her. She'd swim through the air, reaching for the sparkling sunlight above. But it would snag her ankle, drag her down, down...

And then she'd hear his voice in the dark, while the last breath of oxygen left her lungs. She'd hear that firm but gentle tone, breathy, like a whisper in her ear that was on the edge of growling.

Nathaniel. He called her name, grabbed her by the shoulder—

She swung her arm at him, batting blindly. And the motion sprayed the ashen remnant of her cigarette in an arc through the air. But when her eyes focused and the painful cloud dissipated, all she saw was Thom, with the pathetic face of a kicked puppy. "Good morning."

She'd drifted off. Despite all her best efforts. Well, ain't that some shit? Turns out not even chemical stimulants and a hard surface could keep her awake.

"Good morning? Is it really?" Adelaide asked sarcastically, looking around at the neon slum mired in the same darkness as ever. "How would you know?"

"I get your point," Thom said, "but clocks exist."

Adelaide looked over at the rest of the camp. Zatia had fully dismantled her hidden blades, laying the parts out for Roche to consider with her. They were muttering back and forth, conspiring to do yet another upgrade to her secret jewelry weapons. That was going to be work for Adelaide when they finally came to her with their proposal.

Adelaide reached for her percolator, pawing at empty air. She looked to find the tin pot had been whisked away by Rashida, the noblewoman gingerly milling leaves with a mortar and pestle.

"Hot leaf juice ain't fit for the morning," Adelaide called out to her.

"Have a cup of my tea," Rashida said, "then tell me that."

"I will."

Thom crouched down, turning his back on the gang and sealing off further distraction. "Any insights?"

Adelaide rubbed her eyes, flicking her other hand to open the Entiglas screen again. "Nothing that leaps out at me. Lots of dates and numbers but no real pattern to it."

"Encrypted?"

"Lily had a look," Adelaide said with a shake of her head. "It's raw blender trash, just senseless."

Thom stared at it for a long second, squinting like it might bring the important stuff into focus. He wasn't going to have any better luck than her just by sheer force of will.

"So," she started, "Anze Orchikov, huh?"

Thom nodded. "Yeah, should've seen that one coming like the sunrise."

"We'll need countermeasures for him."

"I've got a few ideas," Thom said. "How do you feel about hydraulic triggers?"

Adelaide cocked her head at the boy. A hydraulic trigger wasn't exactly outside her field of expertise. Using a conduit full of fluid, one could use a lever or plunger to increase pressure or draw fluid. The pressure vacuum could pull a striker to connect any number of functions.

"Looking for a way to say hello to somebody when the power's out?" Adelaide asked.

Thom almost struggled to commit the thought to the air. "Anze can control electricity. He could, uh, he stopped the Paladin in its tracks. With just a wave of his hand, he'd..." Whatever he was remembering was a little too gruesome, his lip twitching with the taste of vomit. "And he could tell Roche and Lily were...just by being around them."

Adelaide had seen her share of weirdness with Anze in the past. It wasn't exactly a leap to say the kid was telling the truth. But it ran contrary to some lived experience. "The human body is cracklin' with bioelectric current. Why would he shoot anybody if he can just turn me off?"

"No idea," Thom said. "Maybe he needs more than the body generates? Maybe it's the augments. Either way, I have to assume he's in the field or will be soon, and we're standing in the middle of a city, which notably needs a lot of power. Giving him more bullets than I'm comfortable with."

"So we need a way to set the table in a more medieval manner," Adelaide concluded.

"Exactly." Thom plopped onto his butt, letting himself relax for a bit longer and refocusing on the encrypted file in front of them. "There had to be a way to read this. They were running a full-blown smuggling ring. They weren't writing gibberish and then keeping it on a secure server."

"Lily could brute force it, but we'd be here till the new year," Adelaide said, "and chasing dead ends whenever they hit a false positive."

"And Anze will have shuffled the deck by the end of the week, if he hasn't already."

Adelaide heard the water boiling behind her, absent the pleasant smell of coffee. Whatever Rashida was doing was just going to make an old linewoman sad. It already smelled like moldy linens.

Thom's eyes glazed over for a second, as another wave of nausea hit him.

"Need a little breakfast?" Adelaide asked.

"Pancakes and hash browns," Thom said.

"Where the Hell did we get hash browns?"

Thom shrugged. "You're talking to the cabin boy, the former pub worker. You think I leave house without breakfast in my pocket?"

"Thom, sweetheart, I don't really want to eat it if it's been roasting in your pocket for a day and half."

He laughed, turning his attention back to the file. "What if..." Thom stopped himself, swallowing hard, like he wanted to be sure he didn't hiccup and spit some bile onto the floor. "What if not all of this is data?"

Adelaide blinked. No wonder her brain had been grinding all night trying to make sense of it. She lowered her head in frustration. It was so simple as to be idiot-proof. "Oh my God..."

"What if they've hidden the real data amongst a bunch of chaff?" Thom proposed. "Only a portion of each file is practical data, and the rest is just a smokescreen of nonsense?"

"Throw a basic encryption on top of it, and it would be nigh-impossible to crack on a brief timetable," Adelaide concluded. "High security, low requirements. We'd need to know what information was important, why it was important—and then, of course, the cipher itself."

"Hide your valuables in the garbage," Thom muttered in amazement. The kid looked over, studying Adelaide's face for a long moment, his eyes flitting over every peak and valley of her face. "Take a break. You look like shit."

"That's just what being old does to you, kid."

"So does malnutrition and abuse."

Fair enough. She hadn't eaten properly since before the job. Since before the *Aurum* landed, actually. No wonder her hands were shaking. She just didn't feel hungry. Even less so when a sixteen-year-old kid had to tell her to eat. "I'll abuse you, you don't back off."

"You say like that it scares me," Thom said with a half-smile, daring her to take a swing or hurl some biting insult at his soft underbelly. He was practically offering his chin, looking to get his jaw broken by someone four times his age.

And there she was without a wrench in arm's reach. Damn. Breakfast it is, then.

"See what younger eyes can find?" Adelaide asked, dragging the file with two fingers in the air, sliding from her Entiglas to his.

Let the little Maestro peck at the file. But if he cracked it after she spent all night scraping at it, she was going to eat her gloves. Cracked leather and pocked full of holes, it would probably go down smooth if she boiled it long enough. Add a little chili paste, some soy and oyster sauce? Might even be palatable.

Okay, so she was hungry.

She sallied right past Rashida, leaving the noblewoman to shepherd her hot leaf juice cooking on the car battery. She didn't care that it smelled like distant blue ocean waters. It wasn't coffee and was therefore an abomination. If Adelaide couldn't add whiskey to it, it was not a beverage.

Instead, she marched right up to Zatia and Roche as they examined the dismantled blades. "If you wanted to blow them up, we could've picked up some detonite."

Roche didn't even look up. "If we bore out a channel through the center of each blade's spine…"

"I like where this is going," Adelaide said. "The *Aurum* still in one piece?"

Roche sat upright, his eyes dead-focused on something a thousand miles away, as he mentally rifled through the various networks and data nodes. Then he blinked away the malaise and shook his head. "Landing locks have been issued. *Aurum's* grounded."

"So we've blown our cover." Adelaide grimaced.

Damn. That meant that if they were planning on leaving Ilum, they'd need a new set of rockets. She'd hoped to have a chance to say goodbye to the old bird but turns out she had the chance and just blew it.

Roche turned back to the work in front of him. "We'd need a stable platform to channel out the interior. What metal's running down the spine?"

Adelaide answered before Zatia could. "Silksteel 40N50. It's more conductive than the cutting edge. Why?"

"Would a small hole down the center risk fracture?"

Adelaide took a glance. An interior fuller would certainly cut down on weight. They were hardly thin blades, these days. The Silksteel had been initially built to four segments and designed to collapse and hide as bangles Zatia wore on her wrists. She had beefed them up to support electromagnets in the grips. Now they were talking about removing material?

The actual manufacturing wouldn't be an issue. More, was it even a good idea?

"Well," Adelaide started, "in short, yes. I wouldn't go smacking them against concrete or anything without that springy center to shock absorb. They'd drop some weight…"

"I'm all for that," Zatia said, "but I *don't* need them snapping on me mid-chaos either."

"Then do more push-ups."

"Ha-ha," Zatia deadpanned. "Weight's not the issue."

Adelaide's brow scrunched up. "Why else would you remove material?"

Roche's eyes went wide with sinister glee. "Rifling."

Put a gun barrel *inside* her blades? Now that was some nasty engineering. That would involve far more than milling out a channel for the slug. And the firing chamber itself couldn't be on the blade; it was too delicate of a machine to be regularly smacking against things.

But there *was* already an electromagnet installed in the grips for deflecting plasma bolts. Concocting a gaussian propellant system inside the bracer, now that would be...

"What does Lily think?" Adelaide asked.

Roche's lip twitched, and his smile went from devious to sadistic. "Some people are too far away to be stabbed."

"Ain't that the God's honest truth? Let's do it."

"And on a plus side," Zatia remarked, "it might blow up in my hand."

"Technically, all guns might do that," Adelaide said, turning back to Rashida. "How's your stupid, dirty water coming along?"

Rashida wrapped some cloth around her hand as an insulator and lifted the percolator off the battery. She poured out a steaming cup that looked positively filthy. That wasn't a beverage; that was medicine parents forced on children.

"Matcha with a hint of lemon peel," Rashida said. She rose up from her kneeling position like someone had lifted her on a cable, and glided over with inhuman grace, pressing the tin cup into Adelaide's hands.

Adelaide's lip curled at the thought. "I'll match you blow for blow. Coffee is better."

But Rashida just smiled and gestured for Adelaide to take a sip.

She looked down at the lime-green foam that stared back at her. It looked like the surface of a bog on a hot summer day and smelled like barnacles on the bottom of a boat.

Adelaide took a sip—and the tang that hit her tongue shot right through to the bottom of her feet and back up to her scalp, like someone had reseated her batteries. She coughed once, trying to not spill the drink.

Rashida raised a perfect eyebrow, a judgmental arch.

And Adelaide swallowed her pride. "Matcha?"

"Never doubt the royal family's love of tea."

"It's a rolling cipher." Everyone looked over at Thom, who spread the image wide for all to see. "There's a single line on each file that's actually something, and it's never the same line."

"Skip to the end," Rashida said. "What were they recording?"

"Supply, vector, departure times. And geo-coordinates."

"*How* did you figure that out?" Adelaide blurted.

"Because geo-coordinates all have the same format," he explained. "X, Y, Z coordinate numerics, plus time of day, plus volume of the order. So I cross-referenced to see if any of the numbers repeat throughout the other files. Separating out the time of day and volumes, I was able to find the same location over a dozen times in the last month."

Adelaide's eyes narrowed. "That's what you found. Not how you found it."

Folks caught in a lie averted their gaze, tried to concoct an answer. Good liars matched the intensity of the accusation, refusing to blink or be caught shameful. But the truth? People got flustered when they told the truth and got accused. They got huffy, offended, and more than that? Their answers were plausible.

Thom was lying. He stared her down, unflinching. "I see patterns, Adelaide. Shoot me."

Rashida saw it too, her own eyes narrowing. But she didn't commit to saying anything just yet.

He tried to cover his tracks with emotional appeals. "You did the heavy lifting last night," Thom assured her. "You loosened it for me."

"We're dodging the big thing," Zatia said. "Where is this place?"

"That's what's weird," Thom said. "It's an apartment complex on the Sunset Line. Stacks of cheap housing, mainly used as government allocation. No real crime presence."

"It'll take the better part of a day to walk there," Roche calculated, gathering up Zatia's weapon parts. "I should get to work on this."

"I'll pack the camp," Zatia offered.

What wasn't Thom telling them? He had no reason to lie. He had no dual loyalties, no ghosts haunting him. No debts, no vendettas.

It didn't make sense. Why lie? Unless she was just tired and paranoid. The kid had just done some damn fine work, and she had not so subtly implied he'd cheated somehow, like it was a game he'd twisted the rules on. She should be pleased, not nervous.

But she *was* nervous. And so was Rashida.

CHAPTER 19
OSYEN

EVERY IMPERIAL WORLD had their variation of it: apartment complexes built en masse for the people, assigned to citizens based on need. They built more based on complex population projections and granted a stipend for basic survival needs—just for being a citizen of the Empire. A good and compassionate people in the richest time in human history don't let their neighbors fight to survive, and comfortable people made better things than anxious ones, anyway.

This is where Charles Ordee had sent him? He didn't see a dig site. He saw public housing.

It was like looking at storage shelves, reaching up to the lower clouds, the enormous support columns peeking out between the layers. Every individual home was accessible by the planet-wide taxi system for deliveries and travel, with built-in entertainments and even a job placement program for the day a young lad might be ready to contribute to the great society, pick up a trade or an art.

Seemed awful nice to Osyen. Place like Ilum, something must always need doing. People must have their pick of careers, or to just not do anything until boredom finally dragged them into a trade.

Sure, folks had to live where the government told 'em to, but it was always preferable to a sewer grate. Unless you didn't want to be found, for any number of reasons. Some people were wanted criminals, undesirable types, or maybe they were just paranoid.

Osyen and his mother had lived in government housing not alltogether different from this, though theirs had been considerably nicer. He'd long since concluded that good loyal citizens doing good loyal work, producing value, they got the better living situations.

Everybody else? They got whatever passed inspection. Osyen used to call it 'Steerage'—where they kept the animals, and the people too poor to do better.

On Ilum, these apartments wrapped the Sunset Line like the planet wore a belt. And they all buzzed like a hive, people coming and going on business. As the third-shift was starting now, people were leaving their homes and off into the Night for edgy entertainment or flying off to the Sunnyside for more aristocratic fare. And every one of them painted in the permanent rose and violet of the setting sun in the sky, rivers of color like ink leaking through water.

Osyen huffed at his own bias. Government housing aside, living in Steerage didn't mean they were without money. That was just him making assumptions.

But what wasn't an assumption was how quiet this next block was. Everywhere else had taxis coming and going. But an entire lane of houses, tall up to the sky—not a single car in flight.

There was something...alluring about it. Like it wanted to pull him in. An urge to jump when you feel your toes at the edge of the cliff. It drew him in, down towards it, like gravity.

And yet...not a soul in sight. Nobody living here, nobody in transit. Guess the word was out, that this stack belonged to somebody.

"What do we think of that?" Osyen muttered aloud, his hand resting on Milardi's pistol.

Old Oz would've sent in Zatia to take up some hidden position before he marched straight on in with Milardi at his side, ready to figure it out as they went along.

But his fingers tingled against the steel cylinder, a thousand spent

165

cartridges and witty retorts reaching back to whisper caution. So, he waited.

The first twenty minutes were torture, staring at an empty lane. But the next twenty went easier.

Osyen looked down at the gun. Engineering a generation out of date, blocky build, disposable battery for the Gauss action and rotary cylinder. Milardi used to custom-load his own cartridges, ensuring he had a bullet for any occasion. Osyen never had that patience, or a surgeon's still hands.

He extended his arm, looking at the tremor of his fingers like they were leaves on shaky branches being tossed about by the wind. It was like his whole wrist wanted to work its way out of its mooring. He always had a better grip with his...with his other hand.

Osyen's lips drew tight remembering the Paladin's stare, remembering how it hurled that steel plate, how it tore through—

His smile flickered, wavered, like candlelight. He glanced down at the shape to his right that filled out his jacket. It looked like his arm was there, but it refused his call. A forgery.

It wasn't there. Long gone. Left behind.

Osyen glanced back at the pistol. "What am I going to do without you?" he whispered.

Milardi would've filled that dead air with some smart-ass response. Milardi was his brother. Milardi was...he just was.

But Zatia wouldn't have let Osyen off easy either. Adelaide would've joined in the ritualized abuse. Roche and Lily would've offered a myriad of solutions. Thom would've had something to say wise beyond his years.

But here he was alone, and that was a situation of his own make. And he regretted it. They had made their choice to stand by his side, and he'd shoved them away. He wanted them by his side now.

To temper, to soften, to mend and rebuild.

A heavy-load truck swung by over Osyen's head, startling him out of his haze. It glided into the Steerage and pounded his car with the powerful thrum of its mag-lev engine. Osyen had to swallow his heart and lungs. The gun to his side shook on its seat, whining against the vinyl.

"Now where the Hell are you going?" Osyen muttered.

The truck swung into Steerage, deftly backing itself up to one apartment on the sixteenth story. It locked into place on the open patio and powered down, like a loading dock.

If anybody had gotten out, they'd done so out through the cargo hatch.

Osyen shook his head. Poorly trafficked areas were ideal for meets and handoffs, dead drops. But this wasn't poorly trafficked, this was dead. So who was this guy?

It was another good twenty minutes before the truck departed, far less nimble—loaded. Someone packed in some weight on that truck.

They were moving out material. But from what? The apartments?

Osyen pulled his car two stacks above that dock, and half a block down the lane. He'd have to get creative to move down to the lower area, but he didn't want to risk detection right where a delivery had just been made.

He got out of the car, hooking Milardi's holster on his hip, clipping the retention strap into place—double-checking that it wouldn't move. Looking down from this height was a trip, as the entire world seemed to pull towards a single point, some singularity that eats dropped keys. And if he dropped Milardi's gun from this height, it would be a good brief minute before it hit anything. And Osyen would never hear it over the city noise. It would just be gone.

A neighbor or homeowner might have poked their head out to greet this visitor on the porch—or chase off the vagrant, if anybody had been home. But not a sound. Osyen spied a layer of scum that had built up around the doorframe.

Unoccupied. And for a while. Not like the Empire to leave perfectly good housing unused. They'd fill it or strip it for parts. Strange.

The vibration through his boots might've told the story. Felt like the whole building was shivering. Would be kind of thrilling to live in a building that liked to settle without warning. Was this section condemned, and that was the explanation for the lack of occupancy?

Was the truck full of scavengers stripping the condemned apartments for cheap parts? Plausible, but the government would've swept in quick to take anything of real value. And a glance in the window showed an empty featureless cube—not even a bed or colorful backsplash in the kitchenette, no projector for holo reels or speakers for music. It had more in common with a prison cell than a home at the moment.

Osyen had to get down to that loading dock, see what they were doing, why Charles sent him here.

No taxi service, or he might as well ring a doorbell. That would be Rashida's play, for sure. Thom might set up a distraction so he could slip in unnoticed.

Osyen didn't have that luxury. Solo act. He'd just have to be smooth and slow. If he rushed, he'd get caught.

He eased himself into open space, dangling over that hungry abyss of misty dark, and promised himself he was only going down two floors. He gripped the edge with his hand and swung himself down to the next apartment.

Five fingers and a good grip as the only thing keeping him alive had a way of resetting brain activity. Everything felt snappier after that. And he had to do it again!

He didn't relish the second descent any more than the first. And now he had half a block of leaping guard rails to get to the loading dock. But that was far less invigorating. By the time he got there, whoever had been standing guard had finished their cigarette and flicked the dog-end out into space. But the smell hadn't yet been swept away by the wind.

He was close.

The apartment looked abandoned, just like all the others. But the door was...clean. No build-up of dirt and grime. Used.

They had gone to an awful lot of effort to hide whatever was going on in here. He half-expected to stumble on some strict government secret facility—genome-sequenced locks and geometric code. But of course not. If you wanted to hide something, you didn't put it in a fancy box on a well-guarded shelf.

You buried it in the ground and destroyed every record of it.

Osyen pushed open the door, striding into what could have been somebody's living room. Instead, it was bare sheet rock on all sides, insulation and coverage from the environment. Nothing more.

The inside of an eggshell.

"Okay," Osyen muttered, "if I was hiding a secret operation, where would I put it?"

How much security was he messing with right now? Had he already been detected by an angry computer system? Or was this a criminal operation depending on secrecy more than walls?

It surprised him how frustrated he was at not having those answers. Thom had gotten him used to knowing more going in. In the good old days, Osyen would just smile his way through whatever came his way, talking fast and shooting first.

The good old days. Were they that good, before Adelaide, Rashida, Thom? Before Milardi, Zatia? Before Lily?

No. They might have been good, but these days had been better.

Think about the structure, Adelaide would say. If they're moving out cargo, they need a way to get it to the truck. That means conveyors, a freight elevator.

Osyen swept his foot across the floor, kicking up the layer of dust —and revealing the seam.

"Yay!" Osyen quietly celebrated, flat expression on his face.

Breaching that door would likely set off every conceivable alarm. He simply had to wait till it opened again. And that took a lot more patience than he had thought to pack with him.

He started by counting to a hundred. Then he started singing songs in his head. He struggled with the lyrics, then he started writing new ones. He was halfway to a new folk song about handshakes when the floor finally cracked open. Up came a lift platform, and with it a pair of grunts. They were the comedic pairing of tall and short, thin and wide, each leaning on their own floating dolly loaded with crates.

There was no mechanism, no panel, nothing for Osyen to hide behind. This wasn't an electrical system with a motor and high-tension cables. It was a friggin' mechanical platform operated by nothing but pulleys and heavy weights, like something ripped out of a museum from the days before electric light.

Everything was out of sight, tucked neatly and tidily down below. Talk about secure; try and hack something that operated off of levers and gravity! How was he going to get past these two? How were they *not* going to see him huddled in the corner?

Big was more meat than anything else, with a shaved head and vacant expression, while Small had that blinking incredulous tension of a man who had to tolerate Big. They were deep in conversation as the elevator rose up through the hatch, locking into place with a clang and bang. "Just think about it. Think about it for half a second!"

"Grow up, man."

Big threw his arms up in the air, so tall his fingers grazed the ceiling. "It's the only way it makes sense."

"You know, you go off for like ten whole uninterrupted minutes on Imperial conspiracy theories, but ya can't focus enough to pass a fifth-grade math quiz."

"I'm jus' telling you, nobody ever sees 'em in daylight except —*except!*—on Sundays *inside* that church of theirs. That's not enough for you?"

Small almost took offense at the question, turning his complete attention to his coworker. "Why would vampires care about calendar dates?!"

"Because of the *curse*, Doug! Do I have to teach you everything! Blood curse. High holy days."

Small rolled his eyes, pointing at his friend's dolly. "Push the crates, moron."

But Big just kicked the brake into place, squaring up on his friend. "The truck's not here yet!"

So Osyen picked his moment, producing Milardi's gun. "Which means you two take a break."

"Exactly!" Big didn't really register Osyen as a third voice for a hot second, getting ready to line up his mental reference cards for a long diatribe. Until his brain processed the silhouette that meant 'gun' and he paused, jaw hanging and brain frozen.

Osyen smiled. "Which one of you fine gentlemen would like to open the door for me?"

Small was smart. Small didn't believe in conspiracies. Small kept his mouth shut. Big was so big, he didn't have enough blood to support his brain. A quiver to his voice, but strength in his shoulders, he turned to face Osyen. "You can't get us all. We know the truth now."

Talk fast. Osyen knew how to do that. "That's why I'm here," Osyen promised. "We're going to expose them all."

And Big's face lit up like something short-circuited behind his eyes, sparks and arcing power. "You're from the..."

And Osyen shushed the man, gentle but forceful. He didn't need to get drawn into a trivia game with this guy, lest he walk himself right out of his own cover story. He looked over at Small. "Sound the alarm, and...well, I won't kill you, but I will make sure you're eating through tubes for a couple of weeks."

Small considered Osyen, the gun, his friend. And he sashayed on toward the door. "I ain't paid enough for this shit. I quit."

CHAPTER 20
OSYEN

OSYEN WAITED for the door to clack shut on the worker. Even if Small didn't talk to anybody, someone would eventually notice his absence. Osyen was officially on borrowed time before whatever security kicked in.

He turned to Big. "Alright, I need you to tell me—"

But Big was way ahead of him, with a doofy, toothy grin. He shoved the floating dollies off of the elevator and waved Osyen on. "There's two biometric locks on the elevator shaft, though the second one hasn't worked for a few months. You'll need to hop off and work your way around." The guy laughed, low and pleased. "But you know what you're doin', don'tcha?"

Osyen didn't answer, just steeled himself. That was a better answer than this guy could've ever dreamed of. He started to vibrate, wiggling at the shoulders and stamping his feet. "I knew it! I knew it! I knew it was all real!"

"You need to keep calm," Osyen said, "or they'll know something's wrong."

"Right!" Big strained his back, swiping his palm over his face like he was donning a mask of the legendary Very Serious Man. "Calm."

"What else can I expect?" Osyen asked, making a show of inspecting his gun.

"Security's all paid bruisers," Big said. "Real tough crowd, and they have free run of the place. Not like me, I just go to the warehouse and up here."

"Then how do you know they have free run of the place?"

"'Cause..." Big searched for an answer to that assumption. "Because they have free run of the place?"

Bulletproof logic.

Grimacing, Osyen nodded. And Big hit a switch on his bracer. The elevator lurched as the mag locks disengaged and it started to descend, plunging them into darkness.

Big started. "Do you know like...inside secrets?"

Osyen looked over at him, the childish wonder in the man's eyes. "Like what?"

"Like...is it true?"

Osyen could tell him the truth. Could buy into his lie. Or send him down a completely different rabbit hole. "No. It's worse."

Big took a sharp breath at that. If believing the Dunsweir Royal Family were cryptids was a widespread belief...he couldn't wait to tell Rashida some people thought she was a vampire. She'd lean into that aesthetic in a heartbeat.

Osyen's hair billowed around him as the lift slowed. He got a glimpse of the metal beams and industrial shanks that surrounded them, the interior guts of the apartments now torn up to support this lift. How far down did it go? To the actual ground? How dark must it be down there, the sun's light blocked by thousands of buildings?

"We're coming up on the first lock now," Big cautioned.

Osyen watched the pattern of supports. There was a gap he could slip into, but if they were going too fast, he would just get smeared.

Big tapped the button again, and the elevator slowed—trying to change directions at his call. Osyen used the break to hop into the metal superstructure, and as he did, Big tapped his button to resume the descent. And it quickly passed through the laser grid of biometric checks.

Osyen looked at the jungle gym of obstacles between him and getting down to the elevator.

Miss a single step and he'd fall, bouncing off of crushing steel the whole way.

So he picked his way through. A hop, a bounce, dangling by his one arm to delicately balance on one spot to jump to another. He tried not to whine and moan the whole way. He had a super spy act going on for Big and disappointing him might reveal true intentions. This was as much performance as acrobatics.

He reached out for a pipe—and missed it. Tumbling forward, Osyen gonged his ribs hard off of one beam. He managed to wrap his arm around it tightly and hold still for a hot second, the sound reverberating through the elevator shaft.

The cheap arm facsimile popped, the clip releasing—and the entire fake prosthetic slipped out of his sleeve and fell free, falling right for the laser net. Osyen wrapped his legs around the beam tight and rolled over the side, reaching for the prosthesis with his one hand.

Couldn't catch it, but he batted the obnoxious thing up, once, twice—before finally clutching it to his chest, stealing it from the ever-watchful security systems not two feet below him.

"Sir!" Big called out to him, whisper-shouting. "Sir, are you alright?!"

"Shut up," Osyen whispered, mostly to Big, but also to his thudding panicky heart. Osyen took a fall like that and this guy starts calling out to him? This idiot was so excited to be at the center of things happening that he was going to get them both killed.

Osyen dangled, looking at the laser net—and the impromptu path through the construction. They had built it to secure the elevator. And they had built the elevator to pass through the skeletal underbelly of the apartments. But they hadn't secured the entire skeleton. They were insuring against opportunistic thieves, not animals.

Osyen let himself swing free, like he was letting go of a tree. And he used the rotational inertia to swing wide, falling down and picking his way through the mess of exposed bolts and rusting supports with taps of his feet and hand.

And suddenly, he could look up and see the biometric lock shining brightly above him. Big was somewhere between cheering and giggling, trying to quietly celebrate. "That was a-mazing!"

Osyen's accomplice had kept the elevator moving slowly, and Osyen was just a hop-skip-jump away from tumbling back on the to lift. He laid on a pipe for a second, catching his breath and feeling his bruises.

He missed having a team. Teams made this so much easier. Right now, he just had a hype man.

Osyen pulled himself into a crouch and launched himself for the elevator, snagging the lip of it with his hand. No waiting, no stress however. Big didn't help Osyen to his feet, so much as haul him up against his will. He pulled Osyen into an impromptu, excited hug, squeezing the prosthetic arm painfully against Osyen's chest. "That was the most incredible thing ever!"

Osyen had to remind himself that this guy probably saw little significant...anything. He was seizing on the idea that the ruling caste of the Empire were vampires, and his workdays were spent in an elevator shaft hauling boxes from a warehouse to a truck. And he just watched a guy acrobatics his way through a web of steel over a at least a three-hundred-foot drop.

It was impressive. Be impressed. Osyen did a cool thing. Yeah, he did! He shouldn't let almost dying get in the way of appreciating that!

If wishing made it so. All he could think of was his certainly bruised gut and hear the whistling of his breathing.

———

Big wasn't a liar. The second grid was present, but inactive. And the elevator soon descended past the street level, down subterranean, through layers upon layers of damp rock. This wasn't ground level, it was in a basement. Buried.

Charles said, 'dig site'. Makes sense.

They strung work lights up at intervals, more to keep time than light the space. Osyen glimpsed his companion with each passing, and the guy's glee was drifting into nervous frenzy.

"You're doing just fine," Osyen told him. "Don't need to lie to anybody. Just keep your answers short and sweet."

"Short 'n sweet," Big said, repeating it to himself a few times.

Osyen smiled at him, like a proud father with a brave face. This was going to be a disaster.

He looked up the shaft that must be half a kilometer up. The laser grid of the biometric scanner long since blended in with the glow of the ambient light, just a speck of the surface far above.

Soon enough, their elevator clanged to the floor. Big hopped off, and the motion-sensitive lights kicked in. It was a storage depot, a warehouse. They all looked the same to him. Concrete blocks big enough to park the *Aurum* in. Wall to wall crates, stacked to the ceiling, with lanes so folks could walk down.

But Osyen tensed from end to end when he saw the logo on the crates, the gear, and painted on the wall: an eye with three wavy lines.

"That's great," Osyen couldn't help but whisper aloud. "That's jus' *perfect*."

A Pilgrim dig site—sure, just owned and operated by the *gulaw* Godfather. Why had Professor Charles sent him to a Godfather warehouse, underground, beneath a condemned section of Steerage Housing?! Was he *really* going to find his mother down here?

Did Anze have her?

"I'll distract the guards. You..." Big paused, with a knowing smile. "You know what to do."

Osyen tried to hide his bemusement behind an all-too large thumbs up. But Big took it in stride and went jogging off.

Osyen shook his head. All of this? Now, if Anze Orchikov turned out to be a vampire, it really wouldn't shock Osyen all that much, really.

The warehouse itself was loosely guarded and Osyen picked his way through the lanes, darting from cover to cover, sliding in between boxes to hide from passing workmen. These weren't hired thugs or security guards, just dock workers punching a clock. No need to cross them if he didn't have to.

No uniform either, just badges and biometrics. Damn. No fast talking this time.

There was an emergency exit door, subtly marked with red & white stripes. Looked like a hydraulic lift in case they lost power. But with power, it would set off every emergency alarm in the place, assuming there was fire or flood or some such. He'd need a quieter approach.

Workers were coming and going. Crates, crates, crates. They weren't spawning in this room. They had to come from somewhere.

Osyen could smell the recycled stale air flowing. And there was a dampness to it, like the air was being humidified.

The workmen were all coming from a checkpoint that seemed to only spiral down. Further down.

He felt that pull again, toes on the edge of a cliff. Take the plunge. Dark waters below.

Jump.

Osyen moved for the checkpoint. It wasn't very much of a thing, just a desk next to an open scanner—the third such scanner he'd encountered. Redundancy was the school of thought here, apparently. After all, one of the three was busted. Beyond the scanner was a hallway that tilted down and out of sight.

Two thugs were working the desk, one with some impressive augments to his arms. Looked like he'd had a job site injury, turned to work as a heavy afterward. But both were more than happy to chat up the conspiracy-loving Big.

"Where's your better half?"

"Hm? Oh, Littleton?" Big said stiffly, with eyes darting. "He's grabbing a smoke."

Osyen almost bit clean through his lip trying not to laugh. Small? The small guy who had quit upstairs? His name was 'Littleton?' That had to be a nickname. It *had* to be. There was no way that a man that small was named Doug *Littleton*.

"A smoke, huh?" said the guard with a sly grin. "What's his name?"

Big laughed, nervously scratching the back of his head. "I, uh, don't like to pry."

"I'm paid to," said the cyborg, but his round cheeks said amusement more than serious inquiry. "Was Littleton buying or selling?"

That drew a laugh from his compatriot, and Big's face twitched with an awkward smile. He didn't want to anger but had no idea how to respond to that.

Cyborg took that as an endorsement, as jerks often did. "You know, for the right audience, he could probably charge a pretty penny."

"Yeah, his stage name would be 'Pretty Penny.'"

Oh, screw these guys. Osyen shook his head in disgust. There was a reason they were stuck on door duty being scumbags. Nobody wanted to share workspace with that attitude.

But a distraction was a distraction, and beggars couldn't be choosers. Osyen darted for the checkpoint door. The scanner needed him to sit still to grab things like a heart murmur, or optical. Otherwise, any given mosquito would set the thing off. If he was quick, he would just read like any old wind gust.

But he had to do so right next to the guards' elbows. Big was going to decide if there was a fight, right here and now.

Big must've felt him coming, because he just forced a belch, as loud as he could muster, trumpeting from one end of the warehouse to the other.

He didn't cover the computer's annoyed chime. But the two

guards, both groaning and waving their hands in protest, did that. They were too busy scolding Big to give a damn about a bug flying through their sensor.

So Osyen was clean and free. He almost felt bad. The guy was a big-time believer and Osyen had just bent that to his own purposes. Maybe he could find something down here that would validate the theories swirling about in that gray soup in his skull.

Though, truth be told, Osyen could probably hand him anything and call it proof, and the guy would tell half of Ilum about it.

When they found out Big was the reason Osyen got down here? They were probably going to summarily execute him, anyway. He could hope otherwise, but there's a reason they call it hope and not 'a statistical possibility.'

Far away from the checkpoint, the ramp descended even further through an eggshell white hallway. It just seemed to curve down and away, in a claustrophobic descent into madness. He felt his ears pop with the air pressure as he worked out his jaw. Even the socket where his faux arm locked onto his shoulder felt cold and cramped.

And then—he saw it. A bar window cut into the wall. A cavern.

It was...enormous. Incredible. Easily over a kilometer wide, with rows upon rows of tents for those living on site. Dozens of people milled about, wearing comfortable work clothes as they attended to expensive looking instruments and samples. Others still, carefully packaged black metal chunks into crates, loading them up for transport. Crates bearing the Godfather's Eye.

And then of course, there was the pit, hundreds of meters across, a dig bored down into the ground like they were building a home for an eternal serpent.

The edge of the cliff. Calling to him.

He was through security. Anyone down here, should be here. If he walked like he was supposed to be somewhere, most would probably leave him be. For the moment, until they dropped a security net to scan every badge and discover that the borrowed identity of Evan Whitby had no business here.

The tents. He'd start there. If there was something for him to find on Catharina Batahr, it would be there. A personnel log, manifest, something.

What if he found nothing? What if there was nothing here but criminal activity and endless risk? He could turn around right now, close the door on this forever. Link up with his friends and flee to safety. This was stupid, and he would scold anyone else for doing it.

But he wasn't the Captain today.

Osyen marched his way down the ramp, passing a few scientists on his way to the tents. Somebody even muttered a 'welcome back' greeting without even looking up, and he waved a thank you. Blending in.

The first few tents were all labor, packed full of sleeping faces. Too risky to mess with. But as he pushed deeper, he got to some more personalized quarters. Pop-up shipping containers retrofitted into housing, little deployed apartments.

He went in through a heat vent in the roof, dropping silently to the floor. This cabin was a compact little space, but well-loved. There were notes, open consoles, unsigned journal entries. They'd found another big deposit of Pilgrim Metal. How exciting. The author expressed derision for their patron, someone chasing profit, not science. Etcetera, etcetera.

There, dusty and hidden, tucked behind a tablet on a shelf in the back. A sculpture. Innocuous to anyone else. Done by a child's hands. A polished sphere, etched with some childish design, on a purple-wood cradle.

His sculpture. He'd made that. He'd made that *for her*.

Osyen tilted the tablet out of the way, reaching for the sculpture. It was fine work, early days.

And it looked an awful lot like the Icon of Cruciform, ten full years before he'd ever see the real thing. Before he'd drop the real thing into a star and never looked back. His mother would've been ashamed of him, destroying antiquity like that.

She kept the sculpture. She'd somehow kept it. All these years.

She was alive.

He never saw the movement. He never saw the man enter. Maybe he'd been too wrapped up in the memories. Maybe he'd gotten sloppy. Or maybe this man was impossibly fast.

Osyen reflexively chucked the sculpture at him, trying to buy time to get to his gun. But the man moved so fast, he seemed to shimmer. The chunk of solid wood practically passed through him, an incorporeal monster.

The man hit Osyen hard, fingers clenching into Osyen's throat and driving his head into the side of the cabin.

Two yellow eyes. In his nightmares for years. Two yellow eyes and the bearded evil man who took his mother.

Osyen clawed for relief, trying to put some breathing room between those iron fingers. But the man just squeezed, staring calmly into his face as his vision tapered in. The fingers were so hot, almost molten, searing Osyen's skin—

The same burn he felt at the back of his neck, a palm pressed firmly.

Even with his eyes blurring from the tension on his neck, Osyen got his first good look at the man. His hair was thinning at the crown, but still full of shape and vitality. And his skin pulled taut at subdermal implants in his cheeks and forehead, outlining where some aftermarket additions had been made. A shaped graying beard tapered down to a point, with sharpened eyebrows that perched above his bitter yellow eyes that seared the air.

Yellow Eyes was an Oskie, the man that took him from his mother. Osyen almost chuckled through the chokehold. How he'd never made that connection was almost laughable.

He'd killed Oskies before. He'd fought worse than Oskies. But something in that unblinking stare made Osyen's hand tremor, an intensity unmatched.

Some reptilian response in Osyen's brain, a prey animal locking eyes with the tiger. And freezing.

Osyen's hand slipped to his side, as the Yellow-Eyed Man considered his prey. His voice, like a forest snake from a fairytale, all silky venom. "Brogan Batahr...my, how you've grown."

He didn't let Osyen respond. He just squeezed harder, and the world went dark.

PART THREE
UNDER HIS SIGHT

And they asked so little in return, for all of the Gifts they wanted to bestow on us. But still the people resisted, for they had their old faiths and older Gods. They rejected the outstretched Touch, on the hopes that a greater hand would later descend from on high.

Their sick, their hungry, their needy and frail—each called for help in their turn. And when help arrived, each they spurned it. For it was not the help that fit their mortal designs.

GNOSTIC LIBRUM, EXPANSIONS 2:21-25

CHAPTER 21
ANZE

ADMIRAL HUGH WANTED to interrogate the prisoner, perhaps beat something out of him like his blood contained gold coins. But it really wasn't clear to Anze if the thirty-year veteran of the armed forces wanted information or personal revenge against Osyen. Their captive had been party to a massive personal defeat for the admiral, an incident that sparked a civil war. Hugh was not likely to be...objective.

So Anze had begged the opportunity to speak with the scoundrel first. Lead with the carrot, as it were. Sticks rarely produced results, unless the desired result was the sick satisfaction of the wielder.

They had Osyen trussed up in some backside tent, his one remaining arm cranked behind him and tucked around a post, cuffed to his own ankle. The tight grip of the steel bit into his wrist, the unnatural contortion putting added pressure on the thin steel band. Rivulets of blood trickled down his palm to a small pool on the floor.

They had hogtied him to a stake in the ground, like a sacrifice to a false god. Ironic.

The Oskie had really done a number on him, some bruising already showing around Osyen's neck, and stippling of blood under the skin where the capillaries had burst.

Osyen hadn't been asleep, not really, but perhaps a touch delirious from his untimely reunion with the aging warhorse. And the sound of the door sliding open must have been enough to crack the criminal out of his haze. He lifted his head, bobbing a bit like he was floating on water. Brow furrowed, he tried to blink away his headache.

Anze leaned on the doorframe, letting a beam of light from outside cast across the criminal's face. Help bring Osyen back around.

The ship captain squinted, trying to focus on whoever stood there. Perhaps he expected some brute to materialize out of the brain fog, with a clenched fist or instrument of pain to work him over, tenderize him. And then the questions would begin, only after suitable violence had been done.

Not today. Anze wouldn't let it happen.

Osyen's eyes finally focused onto to Anze's face, and he almost groaned when he made the connection, frustrated at who he recognized lurking in the doorway. It drew a small satisfied smile out of Anze, amusement. "Not exactly an ideal development, eh?"

"You could say that." Osyen grimaced, flexing his arm against his cuff.

Anze shook his head, tutting at the restraints. "We have got to stop meeting like this."

He waved a hand up, and with an electric chirp, Osyen's cuff link fell off of him. Osyen gasped relief, flopping forward to the floor in release.

Anze stepped into the room, letting the door close behind him and cut off the light. The dim ambience of the tent suited him just fine. "This has been a great big misunderstanding, Mr. Belt. And I hope you accept my deepest apologies."

"*Fra tow ni laska,*" Osyen cursed.

"Alright, I deserved that," Anze said, picking at some grime on the edge of the countertop, scraping it against his fingernail. "You nearly get me killed, I nearly get you killed. There's bound to be some pent-up emotions surrounding that. But consider that if I actually *wanted* you dead, Mr. Belt...you'd be at the bottom of a very deep— and rather convenient—pit. So why don't we start again? Bygones, water under metaphorical bridges."

"How'd you find me?" Osyen asked.

"I never lost you," Anze said. "You have always operated under my sight, Mr. Belt. You, Rashida, your little ship. I just never had a reason to come get you before."

Osyen rubbed his wrist against his leg, doing the internal calculation of how fast he could rush his captor before guards burst in. "Alright. First offer: I break your neck and I make a dramatic escape."

Anze crouched down, bouncing a bit on his toes. "I want you to understand, I'm not your enemy. But there are some very grumpy Imperials waiting in the next room. Six in fact, armed with AP-9 focused laser pistols and itchy fingers."

"Trying to scare me?" Osyen asked.

"Just educating. You can't make informed decisions without all the data."

"Yeah, well," Osyen muttered, "I refer you to my previous death threat."

This man was so...irritating. Anze pulled his lips into a tight, forced smile. "I know what you came here for, Osyen. And I may be the only other human alive who gives a damn. Certainly the only one in this chasm."

Osyen's eyes sharpened, and he drew himself up as tall as he could. "Where is she?"

"I can tell you she's alive, healthy—minus a bad kidney, age will do that—but otherwise completely happy," Anze said. "How else can I be of service?"

Osyen simmered on that statement. Maybe he didn't believe it. Maybe he didn't want to ask anything. Maybe he was being petulant.

"I don't care about dead Ministers," Anze said. "I think you'll recall I have something of a mixed relationship with Imperial authority?"

"Seem happy enough to work with them now," Osyen spat.

"Oh, the Oskie?" Anze asked. "Yes, Lieutenant Commander Isaac, he's a character, isn't he? Orbital don't typically live past forty. The life expectancy on cybernetically enhanced super soldiers isn't very reassuring. They tend to drop into some...rather exquisitely dangerous situations. But he's aging quite nicely, got a lovely salt & pepper thing going on. To be an old Oskie is to be lucky. Or exceedingly dangerous."

"Lap dog," was all Osyen had to say about that.

Anze's head bobbed as he weighed that statement. "Pejorative, but not inaccurate. He comes when you call, follows orders, barks on command. Though I doubt he'd enjoy the comparison that much. I didn't get a big sense of humor off of him. Very dry."

Osyen drew a heavy breath and exhaled, pushing out some painful cramp in his gut. "You're talking my ear off 'cause you're lonely, is that it?"

Anze gave his own heavy dramatic sigh. "How much do I have to do before you understand, I'm the only way you walk out of here alive?"

Osyen didn't answer that. He wasn't going to spare any extra energy thinking about things that didn't matter to him. He had only one thing on his mind.

"How's your crew?" Anze asked. "Not like you to wander alone."

"You're not getting Thom," Osyen promised. "And you're not getting another word out of me."

"We think—in fact, we know—your crew came to Ilum to find you."

A little flutter in the eyes and a twitch of the hand, as Osyen tried to mask his response. He wanted to rave and curse and spit, but he was trying so hard not to react. He was trying so hard not give anything for free.

"You're quite a prize all by yourself, Osyen Belt, but there is one among your crew who is of far greater importance."

Osyen's head lifted, eyes darting as he scanned through his

memories. But when he reached the only conclusion that made sense, he didn't say a word.

"The people outside this tent *want* Thomas," Anze explained, "and should they find him, we will all suffer. I promise you that."

"What is your fascination with him?" Osyen asked.

"I would ask you why you ignore him!" Anze professed. "Thomas is no ordinary child."

"He's not a child."

Anze let that outburst wash over him, echo in his ears. And he rocked back on his heels, softening. "Quite right. You're right, he is no child. I chose my words quickly and poorly."

"Whatever he is," Osyen said, "keep his name out of your mouth. Because I'll wring the life out of you before you see him again."

Thom was special to this man, but not in any relevant manner. He was special to Osyen the same way he was special to Hugh, only in so far as he belonged to the crew of the *Aurum*. He was 'family', whatever fair weather nonsense that meant.

Osyen had not considered that Thom's importance extended far beyond the emotional, far beyond the professional. His value to Osyen was only as gilded as the relationship itself. And should that gossamer value degrade or diminish, should it lose its polish and luster, Osyen would cherish him less and less.

Not Anze. Thom's power did not wax and wane with the love of his peers.

"Let me educate you, Osyen Belt," Anze said, drawing up a galactic map from his Entiglas, and highlighting key systems. "Akagi Station was attacked last month. Did you know that? Rebels tore through the station, stole the Imperial AI at its heart, and fled. They were led by a boy younger than you, with power he's only just beginning to understand." Anze pivoted the image, turning the map over to the far side of the galaxy. "On Concordia? There's a soldier picking fights with powers she can't possibly measure up to but fight on she does."

"They got superpowers too?" Osyen sneered. "'Jus' like you?"

"*They* are like me," Anze conceded. "Touched by the Pilgrim's light, gifted with abilities unexplainable. But Thomas? Thom Hugh is *more*. Thom is incredible, he is phenomenal. He is as worthy of our love as any that have come before."

Osyen didn't answer that. Didn't deny it either. His eyes were playing over memories in his head. Anze could see it. Osyen was no fool and he had seen the evidence of Thom's divinity. He could reject the words of outcasts and admirals, but he could not deny his own eyes.

"If you could arrange a meeting, just a meeting...that I might speak with him again," Anze said softly, "what would you ask of me?"

"I'm too expensive for you, Dunsweir." Osyen spat the family name like it gave a vinegar taste in his mouth.

"My resources are extensive," Anze promised, whispering conspiratorially, "mostly restricted to the Sunset Line, and some places in the darker corners of Ilum. But the Planet of Lights has its limits. Naval Regulars and Ministry Clerics rarely pursue deeply across Sunset. Too many risks to personnel from criminal elements—such as myself—even with the aid of a Planetary Commandant. Get far enough into the dark, and I promise you, their self-interest will kick in. They will abandon pursuit."

Osyen blinked, processing that proposal. "Bullshit."

"Crime flourishes on Ilum," Anze noted, "despite their power. Because some weeds simply have roots set too deep."

"You want a meeting with—" Osyen stopped sharply, realizing the implication. "You really think I can be *bought?*"

Anze sighed. For being a conman, Osyen Belt had no patience for the art of negotiation. He wanted to skip ahead to the part where he could say 'no' and hold his head high. "I try not to think of it in terms of cost and sale. Consider it a gift, fulfilling a need."

"You scratch my back and..."

"Precisely," Anze said. "It would take a very cruel man to refuse to help when I had the power to right a wrong."

"And you expect me to...?"

Anze tilted his head, almost like deference. "I assumed you a man of character, Mr. Belt." Anze lifted his shirt, drawing a shocked start from Osyen. The labyrinthine scars from the electric leads, acid baths, and red-hot steel were hard to miss. His flesh twisted up in futile attempts to protect him from harm, and now, was simply a reminder of pain.

It was a father's job to protect a son. But Anze's father had been the threat.

"Corrective," Anze said. "They said they could fix me, and they certainly spent enough time trying. But it stopped only when I made it stop. I overrode circuits, threw breakers, and seized on every electron in half a mile. Nearly pulled the house down on top of us."

The little criminal couldn't take his eyes off of the scarring, so Anze lowered his shirt again, interlacing his fingers in pensive restraint. "Thom is far more vulnerable than I ever was. And if Admiral Hugh discovers his son's...abilities? What the Icon of Cruciform did to his little boy? He will protect his station first—"

"I won't let that happen," Osyen promised. It almost sounded like he meant it.

"It's about to happen," Anze urged. "Your crew will come to save you. They will take Thom and kill the rest. Your little family comes to their doom, Osyen. Unless..."

"Ease up on the throttle, Mephisto," Osyen muttered. "I get it. Time for my Faustian bargain?"

"Just a conversation. I promise."

Osyen's eyes drifted. The ship captain had been a Capital Criminal long ago, endured impressive hells as a prisoner of the Empire. Officially sanctioned powers wielded against generic little boys who broke the rules one too many times.

But Thom? What horrors might they unleash trying to exorcise the heresy from his flesh? Osyen knew the truth, even if he would not commit air to it.

"The admiral?" Anze said. "He doesn't love Thom like we do. He loves the *idea* of his son. Hates his own failures to that imaginary standard of fatherhood. But he only loves Thom so far as the boy makes him feel. It's always about how the parents feel, and not the child. And if the boy makes him feel something else, perhaps? Maybe he sees his son and feels regret? Maybe shame or guilt or anger? If he discovers that Thom perhaps jeopardizes his position? What if Thom's power becomes known, flaunting decades of established dogma—threatens the Dunsweir themselves? What then?"

"Talking from experience, are we?" Osyen asked.

And Anze just stared, his old scars coming alight with the memory of electrodes. "He will try to burn it out, like a corruption. I don't want that. Do you?"

Osyen didn't answer. He didn't have to.

CHAPTER 22
RASHIDA

IT WAS A TRAP. They'd be foolish to think it was anything else. A car chase through the spires of Ilum's Darkside, Osyen's assault on the Ministry of Peace...whoever waited down at the bottom of this freight elevator was ready for an incursion after the recent explosive festivities.

But the crew was also out of options. There was nowhere else to turn. If Osyen had been captured, the Empire would be telling the world about it. If Osyen had been captured by Anze...he might already be dead. If Osyen was still free, or had quit his quest?

They might never find him. This was the only way.

Adelaide deactivated the biometric scanners with ease. They weren't exactly top tier equipment to begin with. Of course, the fault would be detected and spur additional response. If the lock on your bedroom door falls loose, you'd better have another way of keeping monsters out.

She'd be lucky if they didn't shoot on sight. Their best chance of that was the dulcet tones and soft face of a Dunsweir surprise inspection. She didn't need to buy much time. Just a hesitation.

Rashida counted the floors as they whisked by her, noting in her head when they cracked that magic number and descended underground. She had slipped the surly bonds of this hostile planet, only to plunge into Hell to meet the devilish claws of its primordial residents.

It felt...

Cold.

She squeezed the grip of her cane, tapping it against the steel floor of the elevator. She could smell her own sweat as it trickled down the small of her back. Her lip curled in reflexive disgust.

This was a trap. And she was stepping right on it. Because a trap, once identified, cannot be ignored or brushed aside. Better to let their opponents think he had the upper hand, had her snared.

When, of course, the others were monitoring the security response. Suitably satisfied that the body had responded to Rashida's blundering, they would break deeper into the facility to access local databases and find the mysterious Dr. Batahr.

And through her, maybe find Osyen.

The elevator clanged to a stop, the gate springing away to reveal the dimly lit storage facility. Crates rested on shelves bolted to walls painted a sanitary white.

And the mark of the Godfather everywhere again.

Well, Thom, Rashida bounced on their private channel, *your guess was correct.*

An educated guess, Thom said back, *but it's always nice when intel pans out.*

She took two steps off of the elevator platform when she heard the guards cry out. "Stop right there!"

Rashida froze, raising her free hand while she leaned on the cane enough to give it a dramatic quiver. "Identify yourself," she called back to them.

Three men had come rushing down a box lane, two of them armed with carbines. The third was just a big soft tank of a man, slack jawed and shaved head.

"I said stop right there!" said one of the gunmen, obvious cybernetic implants stretching up his arm and down his chest.

They were of the 'shoot first, ask questions later' school of thought. Fair enough. The Godfather's men weren't going to be subservient to the Dunsweir. She had hoped they'd possess enough brain cells between them that provoking the royal family would be stupid on any account.

"If your finger so much as lays pressure to that trigger, boy, you will discover there's an entire realm full to the brim with pain that you have somehow lived a lifetime without discovering," Rashida said. "And I will dip you headfirst into its extant depths."

Big absorbed that threat with wide eyes as terror shot through his spine. However thick his skull, he had not surrendered humanity's primordial danger sense. She had his undivided attention.

His compatriots, on the other hand, lacked that valuable instinct. "And I ain't goin' to warn you again, bitch!" barked Cyborg.

Rashida was taken aback. "Bitch? *Me*? I think you mean *her*."

They were so transfixed on Rashida, they didn't notice the glittering blades and platinum hair of Zatia darting across the tops of the crates, mere feet over their heads. The little bloodthirsty pixie dropped on to the two gunmen, driving a three-foot blade down the spinal column of each.

They went limp, their legs no longer connected to their brains, and their faces twisted into pained visages, like haunted house specters locked in their last moment of agony. Cyborg's jaw opened so wide, Rashida thought it might have unhinged.

Zatia yanked her blades backward, sending both men crumpling to the floor. And she turned to the Big guy.

Big pressed his back against the crates, his eyes darting from Zatia to Rashida and back again. "Are you—are you here for the other guy?"

Interesting. There had been another visitor. Osyen perhaps? No matter. Rashida knew better than to cede ground when it was packaged so neatly for her.

"Yes. Where did he go?" Rashida asked.

Big quivered for a second, steeling himself. Then he squeezed his eyes shut. "Do your worst, vampires! You won't get anything out of me!"

Zatia turned to Rashida, a dry, stunned expression. She jerked a thumb at the thick-headed lout, mouthing the word 'vampire' with incredulity.

But before Rashida could cut in, Zatia turned back, pushing in close enough for him to feel her breath on his cheek. "I'll get whatever I like, from you and everyone else."

There was that survival instinct shiver again, and Big pointed toward the security checkpoint and the hall beyond. His other hand shook at his side, clenched fist and tight arm, barely controlled terror.

Rashida strode past the man, giving him a withering stare as she did. And he wilted at her sight, shrinking away like he could squeeze between the crates.

It was only after they'd gotten a good way down the hallway that Zatia looked up at Rashida. "What's a 'vampire'?"

Rashida shook her head. "Creature that drinks blood, embodiment of evil. Etcetera."

"So...your classic Great Evil fantasy."

"That's about right."

And a wall slammed up out of the ground, sealing the passage in front of them with a great big bang! Rashida flipped around to see an identical wall had raised up behind to box them in.

Here came the trap, clamping down on their leg.

Roche, Rashida called out, *might need a little help here.*

Standard security quarantine cell. I'll see what I can do.

Maybe they would pull oxygen from the impromptu cell and asphyxiate them or pump it full of an inert gas to drown or capture them. Zatia seemed completely nonplussed by the obvious threat, and just paced back and forth from one side of the corridor and back. Like a caged panther.

Keeping warm. Keeping fresh. For what came next. For when the walls came down.

"How many you think?" Rashida asked.

Zatia tilted her head in nervous consideration. "It'll be too many," she said, "but when has that ever stopped us?"

Rashida laughed, a small gasp of air escaping. "I've never killed anyone before."

Zatia gave her blades a nice flourish, sweeping a faint line of blood across the floor. "Don't think about that. Just listen to the music."

Listen to the music, Rashida thought. And go where it tells her?

Roche was kind enough to give them a countdown. *Wall down in three, two, one...*

Both walls receded into the floor. And both ends of the tunnel were now filled with guards, armed and armored, some with polymer riot shields and others with batons. The same type of elite goons from the Godfather's ships and Weasel's crew. Beyond them, however, stood Naval Regulars in uniform with rifles.

The strategy was simple: let Anze's elite attempt to capture, and they would not chance letting anybody escape.

But their stances were loose, weapons slung. They were waiting for the trap and gas approach—and ill-prepared to get hit by surprise.

Zatia stepped forward, getting a little height with a bounce off the wall to get her blade up over the edge of an elite's riot shield. She didn't need much, just to slip the tip over his protection and into his neck. He tried to recoil, pull away. But Zatia withdrew her blade with a touch of red, spraying a dotted line of blood across the pristine hall's roof. And he went down, trying to compress the geyser that spewed from his throat.

And the hallway exploded into motion.

Anze's goons closed in. The Naval Regulars rushed to take up a firing line at a comfortable distance. Their lieutenant raised his hand to instill patience in his troops. These military types were more than happy to let criminals kill criminals, and they weren't going to intervene until they had to.

Two unfortunate thugs lead the charge, approaching Zatia wielding nothing but stun batons—like they were going to help at all. She parried the first, swiping the electric leads over into his friend, tying them up in each other, before cutting them both down. Didn't even break her stride.

Footsteps behind her. Rashida spun to see two thugs charging her from the warehouse!

She remembered the cargo hold, the training, and hours of practice. Lily's blue blades testing her patience.

Rashida kicked the bottom of her cane, spinning the end upward to jab into her first attacker's gut before bringing it up to trap his arm against her body.

And she heard his shoulder pop out of its socket, in a percussive thud that would be in her dreams for years.

His friend came in to help, driving his baton into Rashida's side— and while her corset-plate soaked the hit, it only helped transfer the electric voltage across her entire chest. Rashida grimaced, and the tension only added pressure on to her captive's arm, drawing a scream from the young man.

Bang!

Her taser friend's face erupted with blood, spraying a small warm pattern across Rashida like a baptismal font.

Zatia had locked her blades together, lining them up to the firing chamber in her bracer, making for a two-handed breakdown rifle that was made almost entirely of bayonet. The little barbarian gave Rashida a nod before unclipping the weapons, back into meat processing mode. The howling, whirling dervish stood tall over three, maybe four dead already. Blood stained her white hair with muddy streaks. But she'd been distracted, focus shifted.

So the thugs pressed Zatia's exposed back, trying to pen her in with their riot shields while compatriots raised batons, a functioning spear wall. They overwhelmed Zatia in a matter of seconds, her blades unable to get through the shields, and no room to maneuver. All Rashida could see were sparks and flashes of light.

"Zee!" Rashida called out. She shrugged her captive to the ground, and broke open her cane across his face, releasing the length of chain inside and knocking him out cold. In a simple movement, she had turned her cane into a length of chain and the cane's cap into a two-pound dart of Silksteel.

It only took a few rotations to get the inertia going, and she hurled the dart down the lane—popping the nearest member of the shield wall in the temple with a wet thunk.

His polymer helmet was built to take a bullet. The cap of a meteor hammer might be moving slower, but was far heavier than 10mm steel slug. The dart lodged in the side of his head.

Rashida coiled the chain around her arm and rolled herself up in the chain to yank the dart free—and pull her target to the ground, rag dolling him down, so he landed sideways on his neck with a meaty crack. If he hadn't been killed by the impact of the dart, that landing finished him off.

And now there was a hole in the line.

Zatia punched right through that exposed flank, slashing outward to drop the other shield bearers.

The lieutenant lowered his hand and sneered. Enough of this. So his men took aim...

And a wall popped up in front of them, muting the sounds of their gunfire.

Roche. Rashida smiled at the thought. The man had been holding onto that card for a minute. But the smile faded when the wall suddenly racked backwards and there was the briefest sound of screams before a crunch silenced everything.

Her eyes went wide. That was...that was an option?! The Empire could've just—it turned her stomach into knots.

Zatia drew her blades free from the last of the goons, looking down the lane to where the firing squad had been so unfortunate to be standing. Now a disquieting puddle of red and brown fluids were leaking out from the cracks at the end of the passage. The girl's laugh came out like a morbid crow's call. "Oh, ho ho—oh no. Thanks for the assist, Roche."

That wasn't me. That was a far more disquieting report.

Say that again. Rashida wasn't sure she wanted him to.

Roche seemed just as sickened as she was. *I'm not sure I'm that creative or cruel, Rash. I didn't do that.*

That meant...whoever intervened wanted them alive and was willing to burn every person in this hall to ensure it.

Zatia might have been grasping for every breath she could, but the horror of that notion robbed her of any calm. "Somebody else watching over us?"

"Yeah," Rashida said. "An old friend."

CHAPTER 23
THOM

THEY COULD HEAR the fight all the way down on the dig site floor. Folks were scampering in two directions, either towards it with anything that looked like a weapon, or away from it with whatever valuables they could grab. So while Rashida and Zatia were spilling blood on the main causeway, Roche and Thom were able to slip down to the dig site, untroubled.

Diversions worked best when they were loud, flashy, and looked exactly like a positive result.

It was only a matter of following power cables then. One of these stupid cubes masquerading as labs had to have a records vault.

Frustrated, Thom peeked in one after another. He'd seen laboratory settings, geology comparisons, glass beakers and chemical vials. But no database, no records vault. Not one thing that could help them find either Catharina or Osyen!

No. They had to. There had to be something here! When Thom had looked at that encryption, he'd felt the pull. He'd felt that cold void. He was so sure he'd know where to go. And here they were, Pilgrim Metal all around them.

It felt so familiar, yet so far away...

"We're running out of time," Roche warned, glancing up at the sealed causeway above them. "Lily calculates another forty-four seconds before they figure out what we're doing."

"God, that's specific," Thom hissed, far harsher than he meant to. But he was so certain that this was the right place, and all he was finding was ugly risks and rotten luck.

It had been a trap, after all. Who said anything of value had to sit behind the teeth? No, only the promise of something was necessary.

One more room. He'd search one more room, and then they'd get out of there.

Roche plugged his cables into the lock, letting Lily overload the locking mechanism, while Thom kept watch. The fighting up above had gone quiet, but that didn't mean anything bad. Did it?

The door popped open and Thom rushed inside. He had expected another lab; computers, beakers, and testing equipment. But what kind of lab had a one-armed man trussed up to a stake, hanging limp from his restraints, in a pool of dried blood?

"Osyen?" Thom said, hushed.

It wasn't loud enough to wake him, so it must have been the familiar tone. Because Osyen lifted his head, a thin ribbon of blood dribbling from his split lip. His cheeks were swollen, turning yellow and purple. No strength in him, but enough to speak. "Thom?"

Everybody! Thom said, *We've got him! Osyen's here!*

Well, that's a stroke of damn good luck, Adelaide said. *Extremely good luck. Check him for bombs.*

Thom rushed to Osyen's side, immediately drawing his tension bar to fumble with the magnetic lock. "Don't worry, we've got you. We're getting you out. Roche! See what you can find out."

Roche marched over to a console, whirling out the cable from his wrist. "God bless the universal serial bus," he said, clicking it into place. His body tensed as Lily dove into the computer system.

"You're..." Osyen could barely get the words out. "You're really here?"

"We're here, Oz. It's us."

"You have to leave," Osyen urged. "Get out. It's—"

"A trap?" Thom said. "Yeah, we know. And yet, here we are."

"Nothing," Roche moaned. "Server wipe happened about an hour ago. They must've moved everything off site."

Thom cupped Osyen's face with both hands. "Doesn't matter. We got what we came for."

But Osyen wasn't as pleased. It was almost like he hadn't heard the good news. "You don't understand, Thom. He *wants* you. Just you. And he's going...." He struggled to find the right words and fell into a coughing fit.

Thom gave one good crank, and the handcuffs fell free. Osyen slumped into Thom's shoulder. He could feel Osyen's hand slip around his back and squeeze tight with all the tension of the last few days.

And Thom gave him a squeeze back. "We have to get moving."

Osyen nodded. "Help me up."

Thom squared his feet under himself, letting Osyen drape across his shoulders, and pressed himself to standing. Osyen helped as best he could, but in between the beatings, when was the last time he'd been fed?

Roche moved to the door. *We've got Osyen and we're coming out. We're not going to be able to move quick, so we'll need some cover.*

Not sure how much more we can give ya! Zatia called back. *But you'll get what we have.*

"Hang on, wait-wait-wait," Osyen said, head swimming and pulling on Thom.

"What is it?" Thom asked.

Osyen stumbled off of Thom's support, tilting as he walked to a cabinet. "I can't leave without it." He yanked the drawers, finding cheap locks blocking his way. That wasn't going to stop a professional criminal.

Thom walked over to him. "What do you need?"

Osyen didn't ask. He just snatched the tension bar from Thom's hands, and drove it into a seam in the lock.

Key locks had pins, rotary locks had multiple rows of tumblers.

Some were even supported by a computer that would shuffle the sequence or pins on the fly, so that different keys would open it at different hours.

This cabinet? Just an interior secure latch, the equivalent of dropping a wood beam across a door frame. Thom had seen more secure bathrooms than this cabinet. The lock was more out of privacy than security. Thom had all the confidence that Osyen would be inside in less than five seconds. There were loose door handles more obstructive than this.

"Oz, we really don't have the time for—" But Roche's objection was cut short, when he saw Osyen withdraw Milardi's revolver from the cabinet.

"Now we can go."

———

Thom led them out of the building, checking left and right, before waving Roche and Osyen on out. The area had gone from busy to frantic, as technicians now tried to disconnect hard drives and wheel expensive equipment away from whatever destructive whirlwind was coming their way. It was kind of like watching people prepare for a storm.

The trio trotted across the quad, running for the small lift to the causeway and the way out.

"What's the escape plan?" Osyen asked.

The implication almost offended Thom. "Smokescreen."

"Not that I'm in a position to argue, but you really think that'll be enough?"

"Wait till you see how much smoke it is."

A voice called out then, bellowing across the quad, stopping Thom in his tracks. *"Thomas!"*

It sunk into Thom like fishhooks and filled the excavation site with a peculiar blend of terror and yearning, like a child afraid at the light being turned out.

Anze Orchikov stood at the doorway of the largest structure, some kind of command or nerve center. Thom could make out Naval uniforms behind him, but anyone inside was too dimly lit and too far away to recognize. But if a particular admiral wasn't among them, Thom would be quite surprised.

Thom glanced over at Roche. The cyborg's hand trembled and sweat tumbled down his forehead. All of his implants, all of the electricity flowing through him...Anze could hold him like he had a gun to his head.

But Anze's posture was almost gentle, like he was trying to approach a wild animal. He stretched out a hand, open and loose, his brow pulled high as he shook his head slowly. Begging.

Don't go.

Thom threw the elevator's switch. And Anze took a stiff, commanding breath.

Nothing. The elevator had its master, and it obeyed only his word.

Fine. He'd do it the prehistoric way. *Adelaide? Let's make a splash.*

Thom didn't care that Anze could probably hear everything he'd said. What he cared was that Adelaide pressed down on the plunger she had upstairs, sending an impulse of water down a line to trip four separate strikers into four separate primers.

A hundred pounds of industrial grade detonite went off almost simultaneously. It felt like an earthquake rocked the cavern for a good two seconds before everything settled. But the charges weren't made to blow holes or cause mass destruction. The concussive blasts severed the redundant power lines to the entire block—and by extension, the dig site below.

The ground shook, and the air seemed to thrum, a fine rain of stone tinking down on their heads. And it plunged the whole cavern into darkness.

With that starting pistol dropping a curtain, everyone surged into motion.

"Oz, help me out!" Thom threw himself under Roche, lifting the big guy off his feet. With Anze nearby, he was never going to be able to move on his own. And they were not leaving him.

Lights flicked on from hand-held devices, helmets, and chest rigs. And amongst that flickering strobing illumination, Thom could see Anze in a full sprint towards them.

Osyen saw it too—and produced Milardi's revolver. He squeezed the trigger, snapping off a shot in Anze's direction. Between the flashing handheld lights, Thom didn't see any blood, but Anze came off his feet, flopping hard onto his back.

Thom knew what punch that gun was capable of. Did Osyen hit him?

He didn't wait to check the work, pirouetting to get under Roche and start hauling him away from the elevator. They'd need a more manual way out.

Job site safety regulations were about to save their lives.

Zee, we're on our way to the hydraulic lift, Thom said. *Clear the landing for us.*

We're already on our way.

Roche suddenly gasped and kicked his feet—like he'd broken free of whatever petrified prison he'd been stuck to. Perhaps they'd gotten out of Anze's range?

"Roche?" Thom asked. "You alright?"

He nodded. "It's the *Aurum.* Somehow...landing locks have been released."

"What?" That made no sense to Thom. Fugitives still at large, positive identification of multiple criminal elements signed to the charter. That ship should be halfway to a scrap yard by now. But not only was it in one piece, but suddenly freed of chains?

They were getting a little help from on high. But who would want to help them right now?

Osyen wasn't nearly as concerned. "You have a wireless link?"

"I do."

"Forget the smokescreen. Get that ship in the air—right now!"

206

CHAPTER 24
ZATIA

SHE NEVER THOUGHT she was going to get to see that crappy ol' tub of bolts ever again. But somewhere in the skies of Ilum, a rickety ghost ship was firing its thrusters and weaving through air traffic without a crew. It wasn't going to be a clean escape in something that big, but Zatia had to admit, it was going to be a fun one.

"How are we going to escape the orbital blockade?" Rashida asked.

"I'd say Thom will figure it out," Zatia said, "but I think we're running Osyen's playbook right now."

"That's a horrifying thought."

That's two instances of rather theatrical aid—both of which were most decisively anti-Imperial interest.

This little storage depot had taken something of a horror theme, only emergency running lights illuminating the barest minimum, deep shades of red filling corners with wide swaths blanketed in darkness. But as they ran, nobody opposed them, not even other workers.

They didn't find another soul.

They slid to a stop at the hydraulic elevator—all mechanical weights and tubes. It'd be a dark ride with no electricity, but it'd be a straight shot up and out. The freight elevator wouldn't move without power. This here was the only way in, only way out.

They had to hold it, or nobody was getting out of this pit.

Rashida twirled her length of chain, looking around for a threat in the dark. "Zee?"

"You did fine," Zatia said, checking the fit of her bracers.

"I'm frightened."

She glanced over at the royal. The woman stood tall, statuesque and brilliant even in this dim setting. But she shifted uneasy on her feet, her eyes darting to and fro.

Zatia nodded. "That doesn't go away."

"How do you deal with it?"

"Do I look like I live the healthiest lifestyle?"

Rashida coughed out a laugh. Good. Break the tension—

No. Someone had grabbed her. Zatia spun about, blades ready. An older man, tall and lean, with sunken features and obvious augments under his skin. And yellow eyes glittering, like a cat in the dark.

Oskie.

"Lower your weapons," the man said, "or I'll rip her throat out before she can scream."

"Don't," Rashida urged Zatia, eyes alight with something akin to bravery.

The Oskie's head tilted at that outburst, his focus almost birdlike. "Try not to bluff, young lady, against a man who never lies. Your survival is desirable, but not a requirement." He looked back at Zatia. "Lower...your weapons."

"I can't," Zatia said, opening her palms to indicate her intent to comply. "They're kind of attached."

"Figure it out," the man said, "or you'll have her death on your conscience. Because I do believe I'm faster than you are."

"Yeah, you're not my first close encounter," Zatia said with a snarl.

An Oskie. How was she going to beat an Oskie?! Anze really had access to the Navy's best and brightest? Or was this just their rotten luck?

He was old, too. His voice had that hint of weight, like a scrape against pavement or rough metal. It reminded her of Adelaide, though not quite that old. This guy had seen every trick in the book, from stun grenades to hidden weapons to poison gases. He'd outmaneuvered better fighters and being mobbed by lessers. This was a predator with a lifetime of scars.

And he'd managed to sneak up on the two of them, dart in close, and leverage his position to take them both hostage. Clean work, and even aiming for extra points. He probably could've killed Rashida and been halfway through Zatia before Rash even hit the floor.

He'd kill Rashida, if he was forced to. But he wanted them alive.

The Oskie squeezed on Rashida's neck, hard, forcing the woman's eyes to involuntarily bulge and roll back into her head. If Rashida could still speak, she wasn't daring to say more.

Zatia twitched, resisting the urge to lunge at him. Instead, she locked eyes with Rashida. "They're playing my song. Gotta follow the music."

And Rashida tried to gasp. Tried to scream, shout. Don't do it. Don't! Another dose—after everything she'd struggled to overcome—another dose might kill her!

If the Oskie hadn't definitively tightened his grip on her throat, she would've started to thrash, try to get to her friend. Instead, she let out a croak and went limp like a noodle.

"Okay!" Zatia shouted. She slowly reached across her body to undo the strap on her bracer—palming an injector of stimulant over her forearm, slipping the cold bite of the needle through her shirt and dumping a cocktail of firepower into her system.

And that familiar tang. That bitter sting of metal on her tongue. The warmth pumped across her chest. Power, speed, ability: she felt it all waking up again, like creaking doors. The dormant chemicals still in her bloodstream. All it took was a taste of her old juice to kick the battle-package alive again.

He was fast? Well, for the next sixty seconds, so was she.

She was going to regret this. But not before she killed this ghostly son of a bitch.

Maybe he smelled it or heard the plunger drop six CCs of chemical badass into her arm. Because he tensed up to wring his hostage's dainty neck, snap Rashida's fragile vertebrae under his wiry fingers.

But with two clean steps, Zatia and her blades were within measure. She lunged with the tip of her right blade, stretching, reaching out to press the steel through the man's face.

His eyes flashed wide for a second, not expecting this level of speed. A weaker attacker, he might've moved Rashida in the way, or simply ducked the strike. But *this* fast?! He dropped Rashida entirely, disengaging and disappearing into the shadows.

Rashida flopped forward, clutching at her neck. But Zatia didn't have time to check if she was okay. That was going to have to wait.

She'd fought an Oskie at high speed in a brightly lit hangar bay. This was a dimly lit industrial closet by comparison, dozens of lanes to check, nooks and crannies in every one. Far too many shadows for a trained assassin to hide in.

Zatia stalked down the nearest lane, listening for the squealing footfalls of an Oskie's feet ripping against pavement. Speed wasn't useful if physics didn't allow for it. Their feet had to press off the ground. The rubber traction on the Oskie's footpads would give him away. He'd keep to the ground, too. Snap decisions weren't possible mid-air. Jumping made him vulnerable.

She looked back at Rashida—the noblewoman was still stuck in the act of falling. The royal's bony knees clapped against the deck, and she let loose one solid cough.

And in that cough, Zatia heard the first screech. She swung about, catching the barest hint of blur as he moved left to right.

Bastard was waiting her out, waiting for the stim to wear off. Clever.

So Zatia decided to take away his hiding spaces.

She laid her bracer's brand-new gun barrel against the retention straps on the cargo containers. And her senses were cooking hot enough; she could sense every motion of the complex machine. How the gear turned, connecting the circuit in her bracer for just a spark; how that circuit charged the capacitors along her forearm at the speed of light; how the gear turned some more, chambering the single magnetic slug; and finally, the last turn of the rotation triggering three separate bands of magnets to hurl the bullet down the small channel.

Her blades would have added three more feet of barrel and magnets to really get some speed going, but this would do just fine. The bullet left her wrist going four hundred meters per second.

The Oskie was fast enough to dodge bullets, but could he dodge a room full of falling shelves?

The bullet carved into the softer metal like butter, and Zatia could see the vibrations working their way up the steel frame. She brought her blade down on the weakened point, shearing the support clean in half. All it needed now was a hit from her shoulder to topple the whole thing.

She threw her whole body weight into it, denting the support in the shape of her arm.

Almost a thousand pounds of metal crates and their shelving tipped, twisted, tweaked, and groaned—before snapping free from its roots. The shelving unit tumbled into its neighbor, crashing that unit over into the next—

And out shot the Oskie, a black ghost rousted from his nest.

Zatia swung her blades, keeping the ghost out of reach. He might be bigger, but two-and-a-half-foot steel blades gave her a reach advantage.

But he wasn't going for her. He was trying to dance past her, get to the elevator.

She cleaved at his midsection, trying to force him back—but the Oskie was able to launch himself past her defenses, past Rashida, straight to the elevator. His skin sizzling from the strain, his breath heavy.

But he still had enough strength to grab one of the many counterweight lines and rip the aircraft cable clean in half. A thousand strands of steel peeled out into a deadly flower.

Zatia closed the distance almost as fast, her feet squealing against the ground and leaving cracking imprints on the concrete. She rolled across Rashida's crumpled body, pressing her friend further into the ground and hurling herself at the Oskie.

Amidst the bramble of vertical cables, the Oskie darted back and forth. He was trying to get her to blindly slash, take out a cable for him. Instead, she dodged and weaved, bouncing around to find a line to drive a thrust safely through and true.

He gave her one. It was an obvious attempt to taunt her, draw her forward.

Hell with that. She squeezed her wrist again and shot at him instead. His yellow reflective eyes went wide, and he ducked out of the way, letting the bullet sail past him over his shoulder and ricochet somewhere useless.

She didn't really remember how many bullets she had, but he had clearly been expecting a 'one and done' hold out weapon.

With him on defensive, *now* she pushed him, swiping at his head and neck. The blade came awfully close, the tip catching on the hem of his tunic—and drawing a small spit of red.

The implants under his skin were practically golden, searing, throwing off a small aura of light all by themselves. He wasn't sweating anymore; he was broiling. And the look in his eyes said he knew his position was weakening.

He grabbed a hold of the cables between them, and pulled himself through and over her head, out of the elevator shaft and back to the messy warehouse floor. Shelving and stock were still falling down, and Zatia watched as the little yellow bastard bounced away down the hall before his light winked out.

Coward. No, she thought again. That right there was how he was still alive. He knew a losing battle with nothing left to gain.

Rashida was still coughing, pawing at her neck, when the last of the shelves and crates came to stillness. Dust hung in the air, not helping that cough one bit—but she quickly identified the trail of blood that led back to Zatia in the elevator shaft.

"Are you...?" Rashida asked with what little breath she had.

Zatia shook her head, smirking. "Got more of him than he got of me, actually."

Osyen, Thom, and Roche came staggering into the room, taking in the destruction. The sheer scope of it. The rubber streaks on the floor. And Osyen's knowing eyes fell on her, her shortness of breath and twitching lip.

She could feel her hands shaking, the weight of the blade tugging on her shoulders and neck. But she couldn't move them, couldn't squeeze, couldn't release. It almost felt...thick. Like a numbness, like they didn't belong to her.

And the feeling was spreading up her arms and across her shoulders.

"Hi Oz," she said, unable to smile. "I think...I might need a hand."

And her eyes fluttered—and didn't open.

CHAPTER 25
ROCHE

THE ELEVATOR WAS TAKING TOO LONG, NOT half again as fast as its neighbor had descended. The counterweights were rated to move crew and a heavy load. But the six of them—all together, along with the damage done by the Oskie—was probably taxing physics.

He could only be grateful he hadn't had a large meal beforehand.

"How're we looking, Roche?" Osyen asked.

He closed his eyes, trying to block out the noise of the tunnel, Zatia's wheezing breath, and Rashida's whispered kindnesses. The *Aurum* was on approach, being tailed by multiple responding Ministry cars. More concerning was the gunboat pulling up alongside. But they hadn't opened fire yet.

Hoping it would lead them right to their fugitives. And it was.

"We're not going to be able to do this casually," Roche reported.

"When do we ever?" Osyen quipped. "And one of us can't even walk."

Roche was just glad it wasn't two. Anze's grip on him had been... unsettling. It felt like every single implant wanted to peel itself out of him, a thousand pinpricks uprooting themselves and pushing out of his skin.

He almost wished he'd had a range finder, so he could know how far away Anze was when he lost grip. But then, that was assuming Anze hadn't just let him go for any host of reasons: stamina, broken concentration. Or perhaps even Lily had a role to play there.

Adelaide! Thom called out. *We're coming out! Get ready for a quick pickup.*

I was wondering if you all were going to show, Adelaide said.

A crisp bar of light hit the elevator as the mechanical doors were pressed open by the rising machine. The lift banged onto its rubber stops in the empty living room. And Adelaide was waiting, leaning on the far wall, halfway through her sixth cigarette. The spent collection of dog ends laid at the tip of her boot, pinched by two tense fingers and crumpled to be forgotten. It had been less than ten minutes from the explosion, and she had immediately begun smoking like she breathed tar paper.

"Little tense?" Thom asked.

"I set off high explosives in the residential district of a major Imperial colony like I wanted to sink a battleship," Adelaide said with curled lip. "How the fuck do you think I feel?"

"*Aurum* coming in," Roche said, "and I'm dragging along an entire precinct."

"It's going to be a dust and go," Osyen bellowed to the team. "Get on, get strapped in. Roche, we're in your hands." He was giving orders like he'd never left. It felt good.

Don't worry, Lily whispered to Roche. *We'll do it together. Just like before.*

Now that part, he couldn't decide, was comforting or not.

He heard it before he saw it, the thundering engines of a spacecraft whirling in, kicking up a maelstrom of wind that billowed Osyen's longcoat. The captain, injured though he was, stepped forward on to the balcony to await his ride.

They did not exactly make the apartments in the Steerage blocks with mid-size bulk freighters in mind. It was going to be a tight squeeze, caught between a paramilitary police and...well, military.

The *Aurum* rose into view, the absent shuttle's open hatch facing them. He turned to his crew and waved them aboard.

And like it had been summoned, the gunship opened fire on the building. Thick artillery rounds bit through supports and showered the crew with concrete blocks, chugging and thunking against the drywall and stone.

Something was cut, and the building shook as the elevator dropped free. Roche windmilled his arms in the air, heels suddenly dangling over a yawning chasm. He started to tilt backward, backward over the shaft...

But Osyen reached out, snagging his hand. Nothing dramatic about it. The two men stared at each other, wide-eyed in imaginative horror of what that moment almost was. And Roche let out a tiny little whimper.

Thom and Rashida helped carry Zatia aboard, followed by Adelaide.

Osyen pulled, yanking Roche back up onto his feet. He let the inertia carry them both over the threshold and onto the *Aurum*. "Can you lose 'em?"

"I can lose a few cop cars," Roche said. "It's what replaces the cop cars that concerns me."

"One thing at a time," Osyen said, as he stumbled to the hatch and cranked it closed. "Now *go!*"

// Twenty-nine-degree incline, ten-degree starboard tilt. Full burn. Mark & execute!

The *Aurum*'s twin hydrogen-powered nacelles put out enough force to push a thirty-ton chassis into orbit. A full power thrust against the already weakened foundation? That dropped the building they had just walked out of. The apartment spire tilted suddenly on its gunfire-weakened struts, before crumpling down like a house of cards in a cloud of dust and vapor.

The Ministry would not let them get away with that. Roche's sensors could pick up the Ministry cars and the gunship in hot pursuit.

That gunship in particular was no longer being choosy with its shots, hurtling bolts of lead at them. Whatever damage happened on the other end of that four-hundred-millimeter cannon, they clearly had made the determination that stopping the *Aurum* was the lesser evil.

Didn't matter what living room was about to receive each of those missed shots that slung past.

Thom and Rashida staggered with Zatia down to Medical, where they could at least strap themselves in. Who knew where Adelaide had rushed off to?

Roche staggered forward, down the causeway, into the galley. He had to get to the bridge and wired in. Nanosecond lag times from wireless commands might be the difference between horrible death and legendary escape.

I can really get some speed in thinner air, Roche bounced to the crew. *If we can live long enough to get some altitude, but no promises after that.*

"No!" Osyen said out loud at his shoulder. "No, get us deep on the Darkside!"

What? They weren't going to be able to hide the *Aurum*. What was he hoping would happen?

"Are you sure?" Roche asked.

Osyen said it with enough authority. "Get deep enough, they'll wave off. Trust me."

It didn't answer too many questions. But Roche had no way of answering them either, and with tungsten shells streaking past them, now was not the time to debate.

Roche scrambled onto the Jump Deck as the floor rolled underneath him. Osyen was having a bit more trouble, bouncing from wall to wall whenever he made a maneuver. At least Roche knew the turn was coming whenever he gave an order.

The chair was waiting for him like he'd never left. Roche dropped his butt into the command chair, handing off Lily's case to Osyen. "Plug them in! Now!"

Osyen snagged the case and turned to that task, as Roche drew out his jockey line and plugged himself in to the dashboard.

Every light was brighter, every sensor clearer. He might as well have been walking the world with his eyes closed. And he saw the kill shot zooming in from behind.

He couldn't dodge it completely. But he could tilt the ship out of the way enough that it tore clean through the topside of Engineering and out again, detonating the flak round somewhere immediately above the galley. A dozen flecks of steel the size of a table leg hurtled through the hull, penetrating way too many important things.

"Report!" Osyen shouted.

Lily took the chance to answer, their blue face appearing in front of him. "All crew accounted for and unharmed, though there appears to be a major fire near our Jump Drive. Unable to seal the space due to hull breach."

"Our starboard nacelle's a little wiggly too!" Roche said.

"Confirmed. Starboard nacelle stabilizers are damaged."

"Make it work!" Osyen shouted.

Roche could do that. He tilted the ship back down, letting gravity take some of the shake off of his thrusters, and dove for the deepest shadows on the Planet of Lights. The Ministry gunship followed, howling after its quarry.

Ilum might've been an entire planet made of urban sprawl, but every city had a slum. Broken down spires, almost like geologic formations, stretched into the sky in place of more geometric buildings. What little electric lighting there was flickered like campfire. Once tall and impressive constructs had been stripped down for parts over decades, before finally abandoned.

At least, he hoped they were abandoned. Because he was about to thread some needles through this graveyard.

Roche brought the *Aurum* down level with the city skyline, dancing between the buildings. The whole ship quivered as the engines strained to make the turns.

The gunship lobbed rounds down from its relative height, not a care in the world for destruction in this inferior district. The skyline lit up with fiery flashes as the rounds exploded around them, hurtling flak into nearby structures.

"How many bullets did this asshole pack this morning?" Osyen griped as he clambered into the co-pilot seat.

"I don't know," Roche said, "but to be fair, I haven't been counting."

An unhealthy rattling sound came from under Roche's feet, and half of the sensors went dark.

And he couldn't turn. He couldn't get the ship to turn. The hydraulic line to vector thrust must have been cut. The *Aurum* was a ballistic rocket now.

The gunship had a clean shot. It lined it up.

But the Ministry had also grown complacent, comfortable. They weren't watching the ground.

Because someone down there fired a single rocket, which streaked up to the gunship's belly, punching wholesale inside and detonating. Whatever ammunition was contained within the hull went up in great big ball of fire that turned the night sky blue.

"Oh!" Osyen shouted, half-cheering. "Eat *that* for breakfast!"

"Brace for impact," Roche said.

Those unholy words got Osyen's attention. "Brace for what now?"

"I can't stop us. We're going to crash."

Osyen looked forward, toward the blank steel bulkhead in front of him. No view, no control. Dead stick. And in some breathy utterance, he either cursed an all-knowing God or prayed for its assistance.

Thom's voice came over the radio, itching against Roche's neck with a whisper. *I've seen this.*

What?

Roche didn't get a chance to ask him. Because that's when the *Aurum* cut through the outside edge of a tower, shearing off its stubborn starboard nacelle and depositing that four-ton piece of flaming machinery to the ground below.

The whole Jump deck lurched with the hit, sending Osyen slamming into the ceiling. Roche felt his safety straps cut into his shoulder —and he felt something pop painfully free in a bizarre moment of clarity—but at least he was still in his seat.

At least until the second hit, when the *Aurum* found another building in fiery fashion, blasting nose first into the flank of it. The ship crunched through layer after layer of construction material until finding the Silksteel spine at the building's heart.

Because that was the hit that dislodged Roche's entire seat, sending it and him slamming forward into the bulkhead.

CHAPTER 26

ADELAIDE

GASOLINE BURNED BLUE; copper a pale green. But a melting starship reactor burned hot white. And that hot glow was every engineer's nightmare.

"Let's go! Everybody up!" Adelaide shouted as she stomped through the galley. "Lily, what's your status?"

Thom coughed and hacked as he fumbled with Zatia's straps. The girl was completely out of it, hanging limp, even as Rashida lightly tapped her cheeks trying to bring her around. "Come on, Zatia. Wake up."

"Get her out of here! We'll catch up!" Adelaide shouted. "Lily? If you can hear me, sound off! Lily!"

Nothing. Nothing at all.

Oh, no. If Lily was out...then Roche?

Adelaide stormed right on through the hatch to the crew hall and on toward the Jump Deck, grasping the handle with both hands. No power, no locks—no Lily—but she was able to heave it open.

The place wasn't exactly hospitable to begin with, but now every single edge held something jagged or crumpled. Roche was still strapped to his chair, but that hit had thrown the chair a good ten feet forward, bouncing it off the wall. His hand was stuck out behind him, still tethered to the console.

Osyen had come around and was already scrabbling to get Lily out of their housing again. But one-handed, that was slow going. "Help me!" he wheezed, beckoning her over.

Adelaide practically shoulder-checked the captain aside, assessing Lily's core. The lights were off, and the actual shell was caved in on one side. The housing was crushed as well, pinching them into their socket.

Adelaide would have to cut them out.

"Are they alright?" Osyen asked.

She couldn't say, so she didn't. "Get Roche! Rapid response is probably already dropping from low orbit. We have to be long gone before they get here."

Bruised, bloody, ashamed, he wanted to press her. She could see the anger and hurt in his eyes. But just because engines had stopped whining and bullets stopped flying didn't mean they were out of harm's way yet.

So he jumped forward, pulling his knife from his hip to cut Roche loose of his bonds. And the plughead actually spoke, blindly reaching for his savior's shoulders. "Milardi?" he groaned in delirium.

Well, that was heart-breaking. She'd have to file that one away to process during another smoke break.

No time for that now, as she pulled the first of Lily's restraints free.

———

The starboard engine nacelle was half a mile behind them, embedded in a building wall. The rest of the ship dragged two hundred meters, littering as it went.

Like clockwork, six minutes after impact, the first Icarus pods came in. Whatever men or machines popped out secured the crash site but didn't dare venture further than that. They lingered at the edge of the burning wreck, like primitive man warily watching the surrounding jungle.

The crew had staggered away, crossing the skeletal remains of the city in the dark, leaving their old home to burn. The few people they saw fled at the very sight of them, scampering away. Barely clothed and almost ghoulish, wiry limbs and croaking noises.

And no wonder. The buildings were stripped bare, some even tipped into one another without the smart blocks to reinforce them. This place was abandoned, like some great calamity had consumed it.

"What happened here?" Thom asked, staring up at the gutted interior of a skyscraper.

"Colonization did," Rashida said. "Most bacteria and viruses weren't made for Terran life, nothing for us to worry about. But spend enough time, and...things mutate."

"A plague," Roche grunted, Lily's core gripped tight to his chest. "There was a plague."

Adelaide knew the rest of this song. Great disease, on comes the Pilgrim to heal the people. They reject it at first, until they are finally desperate enough to accept their new God. Colony after colony is cured, and the Faith spreads. But these pockets of death were never properly tended.

Cursed land. Forgotten land. And with it, the people that lived there. There might not be a plague anymore, but who wants to take in the refugee from the Plaguelands? The Empire laid no claim to it, and no bleeding heart wanted to look at it.

The crew took up residence almost half a mile from the crash, able to maneuver under cover of the decrepit buildings. A graveyard of rust. Adelaide and Thom were able to set up some small lamps for heat, but they didn't dare do more. Anything too hot, and the satellites would see it from orbit.

Thankfully, they'd spent some time dealing with frost lately, and the gang knew how to pool their warmth, cuddling close to share body heat in a depressing dog pile.

Everyone was too exhausted to confront Osyen about his abandonment, his departure. They clustered together and tried to sleep. But Adelaide had a good enough excuse.

Osyen was lingering at the edge of camp, just under an awning that shielded him from the spy satellites. Cigarette in hand, Adelaide stepped aside to have a smoke, finding him at the edge of the lamp-light mid-brooding.

He glanced over at her, waiting for the inevitable scolding. But all she did was light her cigarette and draw a calming breath to soothe the scratching on her throat.

"Those'll kill ya, y'know," he said.

"So can a suborbital crash at two hundred miles an hour," she noted. "Lily will be okay. Their casing's dented, but the factory does, in fact, crash test these things. Though I wouldn't expect the *Aurum* to do much these days."

"Nah," Osyen said, "that'll buff out. Just give it a weekend of elbow grease. See that's the problem with your generation, Addy. You don't know the value of hard work."

And that joke took the weight off her shoulders, and she just exhaled the pressure off. No matter what had happened, Osyen hadn't changed a bit. Still processing pain with dry humor.

"You going to be okay?" Adelaide asked. "Leaving the *Aurum* like that?"

He hesitated before responding. "Everything that made the *Aurum* special is sitting right here. Everything else? Bulkheads and circuit boards. It's a Perseus model freighter that'd been out of production and out of service for ten years *before* I bought it. That's just money down there. Nothing more."

"I remember the first time you and Milardi dragged it into my shop," Adelaide said with a smile. "You boys were practically out back pushing."

Osyen smiled. "Milardi was knocking around in Engineering, pulled a muscle in his back. He was laid up off and on for months. Half the reason we brought Zatia on in the first place."

He was easing up, relaxing. What an odd time to feel confident.

"Who or what shot down that gunboat?" she asked.

Osyen didn't flinch, eyes locked on her for a moment, before turning back to face the eternal night. "No idea. But Ministry's not the most popular on this side of Sunset. And out here? It's anybody's game."

He was lying, head down but eyes firm. He was good, gave it enough pauses and like to act like he was formulating the sentence as he went. Even matched her stare but didn't sink into it. Osyen was good, but he was lying.

Just like Thom had lied. They both knew more than they were saying. More than they wanted to give oxygen to anyhow. Or maybe it was lies they were busy convincing themselves of.

"So unpopular that people openly fire on Ministry vehicles?" Adelaide asked.

"Those Imps look terribly confident in their skin down there?" Osyen asked, passing her his binoculars.

She didn't take them. "With the watchful eye of a couple dreadnoughts in orbit, I would be."

"Six minutes to planetfall from first alarm to help," Osyen said, "we'll see how cocky you are."

"It's different."

"How?"

"'Cause it is, Oz. Mean stares don't suddenly grow into SAM sites."

"Well if I ever find the shooter, I'll be sure to compliment his moxie."

"Don't sass me, Oz," Adelaide said. "What do you know?"

Busted. Osyen bit his lip and bounced on his heels as he figured out what to say. "I think Anze might have let us escape. Helped us escape. Whoever pulled that trigger almost certainly works 'Under His Sight.'"

That didn't make sense. The last time Osyen had spoken to the Godfather he'd all but sworn a blood oath. Why would Anze help them? "Thom said you put a bullet in him."

"I shot at him," Osyen admitted. "Pretty sure I *hit* him."

"Did you kill him?"

He didn't answer.

"Well, did you?"

"It was dark!" Osyen hissed. "We'd just cut the power, running for our lives. I popped a shot at him. I didn't have time to go double-tap the body, okay?"

"So why do you think—"

"Because he *asked*, Adelaide. He offered. He wants Thom and I don't know why. But he's willing to double-deal to make it happen."

Adelaide had experienced some of the Godfather's particular obsessions, and they were few. When he got it in his mind he was owed something, wanted something...

Adelaide looked back at the boy, twitching in his early sleep, snug against Roche and Zatia, with Rashida's arm draped possessively across them all. Her family.

And Anze Orchikov wanted to break it. For the second time.

CHAPTER 27
ANZE

THAT REVOLVER WAS a work of art. He understood now why Osyer had been so precious about it. Forty caliber sabot rounds, with a triangular discarding flechette casing that tore the human body like nothing else available. Fast hand and charming mouth Jackson Milardi had further customized the cartridges with capacitors to take out particularly hardy robotic targets.

Armor-piercing, flesh-rending battery bullets. But electricity had a master.

Anze simply asked those electrons to tear free of their shell—and the bullet exploded a full two feet in front of Anze, diluting the worst of the harm. Hell of a quick response.

Unfortunately for Anze, this created a bird-shot of metal that sprayed all along his chest and face.

Two pellets struck right above his clavicle, and the cavitation from their mere passing had cracked the bone, narrowly missing his aorta. Two more penetrated his chest, but to further luck, softly cracked into his ribs, missing his lungs and heart. One more shard gave him an ugly kiss across the cheek and forehead, to memorialize the moment.

But for all of that, the on-site medics were able to stabilize him with the worksite's AutoDoc and a backup generator. A major improvement from the potential forty caliber blow to his sternum that would've certainly blown a hole through him large enough for a curious child to stick his hand through.

Had the ol' good captain intended that shot to kill? That distance, in the flickering dark, a simple shot to the side would've sufficed. Time would tell if the rogue would hold up his end of the bargain.

Either way, the wound certainly paid the price of admission. His arm was slung up, clutched to his breast, so that he didn't jostle the broken clavicle while the medical cement finished curing. His ribs were tightly wound under a medical brace that gave him a most slimming silhouette that he'd find appealing if they didn't creak with pain every time he moved. The skin patches would molt away in a few weeks and he'd be good as new, with official doctor's advice to avoid future shootouts.

It wasn't as though he'd approached this gunfight with the malice of foresight.

Nobody even looked twice at Anze or his story. Nobody accused him of shooting down a gunship or plastering an entire platoon of Regulars. Most were impressed that the outcast royal would risk his own blood in service to an Empire that had forsaken him. What patriotism. What loyalty. What inspiration.

How droll.

But there was a certain admiral who did not share the sentiment.

Anze's wounds hadn't even stopped soaking through the bandages when he was summoned to Admiral Hugh's quarters. The shuttle had whisked Anze up to the *Persephone* in low orbit. The officers said nothing and answered no questions. Whatever. Anze simply dug into the flight logs with a flick of his wrist, letting the electrons do the speaking for him.

The flight path for the shuttle had been meticulously arranged, grounding much of the air traffic of Ilum to accommodate. An urgent matter, retrieving Anze. And there was an active impulse through the various Jump Points back to Earth.

Someone was placing an important call.

They silently escorted Anze from the *Persephone*'s hangar deck over to the large metal tube that would whisk him along to the Admiral's private cabin. He hummed a little song, listening to the buzz of the ship's reactor.

If only these people knew all the secrets the walls knew. The two officers at Anze's heels were in the midst of a lover's quarrel and they journaled about it incessantly. The ship's engineer was overworked and making arithmetic errors; he resented the ship's Commandant for correcting him. And a certain admiral was making his case to officially execute a certain outcast.

He couldn't just kill Anze, not anymore. No, now he had to justify himself to the Powers That Be. Delicious. Anze was walking to his purported doom. No wonder no one wanted to speak.

The tube chimed happily that they had arrived, and Anze stepped out of the curious vehicle. He turned on the two officers, blocking them inside, a pop in his step. "If I don't see you two fellows again, the dinner was a misunderstanding. Forgiveness isn't easy, but memories don't need to be shackles."

And so he left them there, dumbfounded, to process what that could possibly mean to them. It was a small pleasure leaving nuggets of ambush kindness. Hopefully, the two would use this sign from God to mend fences.

Anze strutted over to Hugh's cabin door. Lieutenant Commander Isaac stood at attention outside, the old wolf's permanent scowl a touch more frustrated than usual, a small bandage around his neck. Anze smirked at him as he passed. "Not used to losing, are you?"

Isaac didn't answer that jab, but his eyes narrowed to yellow slits. Anze slid past, waving at the door to open, and the doors hushed aside like a parting mist. Isaac twitched to stop him—but found his feet anchored to the ground.

All of those implants and motors and circuit boards were meant to make him better, faster. They were supposed to respond to his orders, augment his physiology. It must be confounding to have those turned against him.

Anze tutted at the officer before striding into Hugh's cabin. The admiral's lapel hung loose across his chest, his forehead slicked with glistening sweat, and a half-finished bottle of whiskey sat behind his desk, just out of sight of the guest on screen.

The amber glow of a six-foot holographic face, floor-to-ceiling stern, blocky judgement. Brilliant blue and white orchids adorned his epaulets, with the hint of rows of ribbons just out of sight on his chest. The faux posturing and preening that came from Hugh was authentic and iron in this man. His jaw set by God and his stare as chilling and dark as arctic water.

Hugh was in the middle of saying something. "Minister Caldwell, due respect, these people are not trivial bands of pirate raiders."

There was a minor delay, as the video had to pipe through the Jump Points in both directions. But Caldwell's voice had a natural resonance to it that shook bones, and the pause only added to its power. "You'd do well not to remind me of other failures in your command, Admiral, should you wish to keep that title."

Anze chuckled. "The admiral struggles with more than you know."

Hugh did not take kindly to the intrusion. "We're not ready for you, Mr. Orchikov," he said, dismissive tone but fiery hate in his eyes.

Anze swooped in, pulling the whiskey bottle into view, along with two glasses. "Bumpy, I come and go as I please. Alvin, how's your daughter?"

Caldwell's lip curled in disgust. "My daughter is of none of your concern, outcast. What are you doing on an Imperial ship?"

"Invited, I promise," Anze said, pouring himself a drink, and toasting against Hugh's empty glass. "You can assure my family that I remain in accordance with our agreement."

Caldwell hesitated before tilting his head in the mildest acknowledgement. "Elena is fine. And she still asks after you."

Precocious little thing. Anze remembered her well. She ran

everywhere she could, no matter the occasion or what she was carrying.

"You look like Hell, Anze," the Minister said. It was not a kind or friendly assessment, but a condemnation.

"Earned through service to the people, the crown, and all that," Anze said settling down on the corner of Hugh's desk. The admiral was positively steaming at his continued insubordination. Anze tried to mask his glee with a more genial smile to the Minister. "No charge, of course.'

"We were just about to discuss *you*, Mr. Orchikov," Hugh sneered. "If you don't mind giving us the privacy?"

Oh, were they now? Not often Anze got to be in the room for the gossip, so they could say it to his face. "Don't let me interrupt."

"If you'll just wait outside—"

"You sweet gentle sunflower, every electron on your ship answers to me. Do you think a digital communique to Earth goes outside my notice? Whether I stand outside that door or not is immaterial, bumpy. You hold no secrets from me."

Hugh did his level best not to sputter and fume. Minister Caldwell was far more successful, keeping his expressions to a frustrated sigh. "What do you want, Anze?"

"What do I want?" Anze asked, coy. "You've skipped to the interesting part of this conversation. I thought Hugh would want to read off his list of complaints first."

Caldwell was not amused. "Anze Orchikov, I would not need justification for killing you and everyone you'd ever looked at. Your presence on that ship is insult enough. Your father would bless me for the act. But you *are* here, which means you want something. So speak plain, and I'll decide then if you die."

Anze was surrounded by tech, an entire dreadnought's worth. But Caldwell was more than a Navy. Anze had known this walking avatar of paternal disappointment since the man had a full head of hair. And Alvin Caldwell had earned every medal that hung across his chest.

He was not a man to trifle with.

"The boy," Anze admitted. "I'll deliver to you the entire crew of the *Aurum* in twenty-four hours, so long as I can take the boy safely back to Farragut with me. First and final offer."

"Out of the question," Admiral Hugh scoffed, "and if you could have secured these people, you'd have long since done so."

Anze didn't dispute Hugh. But he didn't entertain the man at all. He wasn't worth the oxygen, the time, or the blood pressure. The only opinion that mattered was Minister Caldwell.

Alvin Caldwell was a pragmatist, a war dog, and believed himself lord of lords. He'd served now three generations of Dunsweir as family members cycled through the Consul's chair. But if anyone was the sole power in Imperial space, it was the long ruling Minister of Defense. His fiefdom was the largest, the oldest, and a kingdom to itself.

And the old wolf was chewing on the offer. "Just the boy?" Caldwell asked.

And Anze felt Hugh's blood run cold. Which was delicious.

"Just the boy," Anze assured him, "and this little pesky problem in your inner colonies will fall victim to the same criminal element they seek shelter with. No more embarrassments, no more dead Ministers. Hugh's son in exchange for an end to this entire debacle."

But Caldwell was no fool, and he picked up what Anze had laid bare. He turned his head, resetting his weighty stare on to Hugh. "Your *son*?"

The two words came loaded with heavy expectations. The boy that rode with these troublemakers was Hugh's own child?

But Hugh hadn't heard that at all. He stared into the back of Anze's silvery hair like he might will him dead. "My son is not negotiable."

His son? His son?! When Anze tied the boy to the admiral, it was genetic truth, but when Hugh tried to say the words...it sounded vulgar.

Anze's lip curled in disgust. "As your own internal records will show, Admiral, you—and I quote—'surrendered the right to call him son.'"

"I will not trade his life to the likes of you!"

"And what am I, Admiral, that you speak with such loathing?"

"I should've killed you the moment you stepped on my ship."

Anze felt his eye twitch, the pain from the shrapnel reminding him of his condition. "As memory serves, you tried. How did that go for you?"

"Gentlemen," Caldwell's voice cut that conversation off. "May I remind you, you're not alone in this room."

"Quite right," Anze said, with an apologetic bow of his head. "Where are my manners?"

"You *cannot* have my son!"

Anze didn't even spare the man another look. "He needs guidance. You'll give him a cage."

But Hugh believed himself such a hero. The old admiral yanked his quick knife from his belt, flashing steel. And at that simple sound, Anze felt Commander Isaac burst through the door.

Neither would be able to do a damn thing. Isaac found himself frozen in the doorway, powerless to watch. Every single muscle was tied to hundreds of Orbital Gen-2 Implants. Those cybernetics listened to Anze's command.

And as Anze pressed his will outward, he felt for the scant few augments and cybernetics embedded in Admiral Ulysses Hugh. He searched for the synaptic connections, and the electrons that flowed from the polymer across the copper and down to the tissue.

He simply imagined the sound, and his ears told him how Hugh's neck snapped like a chicken bone. The admiral's head turned most of the way around, looking hard over his right shoulder, like he was searching for where all the good times had gone. And like a candle blown out, he slumped forward over his desk, his chin striking the metal with a most disquieting thunk.

Isaac whimpered slightly, through his locked jaw and silenced horror.

Minister Caldwell's eyes drifted down, studying Hugh's body for a moment, with all the annoyance of a man studying the bit of plastic blown into his drink. He clucked his tongue in disappointment, returning to the matter at hand. "My question...stands, Anze. Who is this boy to you?"

Anze polished off his whiskey, relishing the oaken burn, before clapping the glass back down on the desk next to Hugh's still twitching hand. "No one at all, Alvin."

"Don't lie to me."

"I dare not," Anze said. "He is no one. But one thing may have wildly different value to two different people: who he is to you, and who he is to me. I value him, you don't. And most especially, I could help you—or simply help myself. That's all that's ever mattered between us. Right, Alvin?"

Caldwell's eyes narrowed, and his nostrils flared. "You have one day. But I will remind you, Anze Orchikov, that I have secure weapons in my arsenal that don't run on batteries. Should I wish it, I will erase you like the stain you are."

Anze smiled, giving a mock curtsy. "One day, Alvin. And you'll have your prize."

The screen winked out, plunging the whole room into darkness, but for the column of bright light beaming past Commander Isaac, silhouetting the old soldier.

Anze could hear Isaac straining, cooking in his own augments, fighting to get free from whatever bond Anze had shackled him with. Age had clearly not dulled his edge, but all that military training had taken some wisdom out of him. Pushing on the rock harder than before was not going to help Sisyphus get it uphill.

Anze swiped Hugh's bottle, pouring himself a fresh drink as he sashayed over to the Oskie. "We have got to stop meeting like this, Commander. Would you mind if we...paused to have a conversation?"

The Oskie didn't laugh at the pun, still pressing hard against the eldritch force that restrained him.

"This is all a big misunderstanding, Isaac," Anze said, waving the door shut behind him, shutting off any hope of escape. "I'm not your enemy. I am many things: an outcast, a foreigner, excommunicated. And yet I command powers you can't explain. And they will kill you for even asking about it. *You've* killed...people for asking about it."

Isaac's eyes flicked over to Hugh, and back to Anze. Questioning. Incredulous. Even a little afraid. He must not have met many things in his long life he couldn't out run or out fox.

No. Anze was a night terror, a demon. Something *more*.

Anze bowed his head, letting the career man see him from a different light. "You led an illustrious career, Isaac. Served with some of the best, killed some of the worst. And after everything, they would still burn your candle right down to the end, to lay you down with every other Oskie who ever lived. Your usefulness to them lies solely in how you could die for them."

And with that, Anze pressed the whiskey into Isaac's hand, gingerly folding each finger over the beveled glass. "What if I told you I could give you something more than a meaningful death?"

Isaac hadn't realized that Anze had lifted his hold until the old soldier fearfully tilted the glass to his lips.

HE HEARD THE SNAP, first once, then so loud it threatened to echo in his skull forever. He felt the base of his neck pinch, twist, bind, and finally give way—

And all he heard was his father's voice. Calling his name.

Thom started awake with a howl. He was practically on his feet, at half a sprint, like he could flee from the dream, getting up so fast he tossed Rashida and shoved Roche over onto Zatia.

Adelaide and Osyen spun about at the edge of the light, Osyen reaching out with his one arm to catch Thom before he dove out from under the awning. "Easy, easy!"

"He's dead! He's *dead!*" Thom called out.

"I know, I shot him!" Osyen said. "He's dead. He can't—"

"No!" Thom corrected him. "No, Admir...Admiral—my father. He's dead."

Adelaide's eyes drew shark-like focus. But it was Rashida who spoke first, bleary and confused. "What's going on?"

"Thom had a nightmare," Osyen said, waving her back. But that just made Rashida stiffen. She knew what the nightmares meant.

And Osyen didn't miss that connection. He snapped his head back around to Thom, a pointed look on his face, guarded but severe.

He stared his three words right into Thom's eyes like he was going to etch them into his skull: don't say it.

No. Don't let him dismiss this. Don't let him cover for you. "Admiral Ulysses Hugh, my father, is dead. Today. Check it."

Osyen extended his hand out firmly. "Nobody's logging in to the Extranet to—"

"He killed him! I saw it."

"And if we ping the network, they'll know right where we are, and we'll be running for our lives again! Thom, take a breath."

"I have to know, Oz! Please."

But Adelaide took command with one icy statement. "What do you mean...you *saw* it?"

And Osyen winced, lowering his head in defeat. And Thom realized what he'd just done. He withered at Adelaide's stare like a flower in the cold.

In his panic, in his fear, he'd just openly confessed. And Thom's chest tightened, his back shivered. This was the moment they turned on him. He should've been honest, should've told them right away. Now it looked like...it looked like he'd hidden it from them for months.

Thom raised his head, trying to catch Osyen's eye, but the Captain shook his head. "Don't gawk at me, kid," Osyen whispered. "It's your story."

"You knew?" Adelaide asked without even looking over.

"I knew he was having dreams that looked an awful lot like a heart attack," Osyen admitted with a bob of his head, ending on a pointed look at Thom. "And that's not all we found."

Roche and Rashida were on their feet now, Zatia even sitting up to watch the exchange.

Thom opened his mouth to start, swallowed hard, and tried to start again. But the words wouldn't come out.

His chest still hurt from the recent visit. Two heart beats in one body. And the voice still stuck to his mind, ringing in his ears.

I know you told me to stay away. But you had to know.

How to explain this? The dreams? The voice? Was it prophecy, foresight, prescience? Thom swallowed hard. "I had been working up...something to tell you all, but then Osyen..."

Adelaide wasn't going to let her rightful frustration with Osyen derail what was happening right now. Her voice was barely more than a whisper, the frosty leading edge of something more under the water's surface. "You were going to tell us *what*?"

She was so angry. He could see it in her shoulders, how she squared up on him. This was how she was acting and she didn't even know yet. When she did...

It paralyzed him. He couldn't speak. Couldn't raise a hand to signal. Couldn't tear his eyes from her, as she stared at him, like she could pull the answers from the back of his skull. She was going to have her answers if she had to flay him alive.

And she wasn't the only one with questions to pile on. "Before the crash," Roche chimed in, "you said that you'd seen this. What did you mean, Maestro?"

Thom struggled with how to even begin. It was back on Farragut, he'd see the wreckage of the *Aurum*, all his friends dead. But...he'd averted that future, hadn't he? "I dreamt it."

"Lots of people have nightmares about crashes," Zatia said, skeptical. "We don't whisper creepifying things and we don't wake everybody up in the middle of the night."

"We can just—I'm sorry." This was just another nightmare. He had been so scared about what they'd think, and here he was now, facing them down. Maybe if he just went back to bed...

But they all just stared at him, unwilling to back down. Everyone with questions.

So Rashida stepped up, soft-spoken and diplomatic, to compare her notes. "Some time ago, Thom started having dreams. He didn't know what was going on, so he came to me. We concluded...someone was talking to him."

"Someone?" Adelaide hissed, imagining the many horrible answers to that question.

Rashida nodded. "He was getting visions: pictures, places, people. Sometimes it would be conversations. Always the same person. And he was able to learn a great deal about what was coming."

"This person?" Adelaide asked, eyes sliding back to Thom. "They helped you through Farragut?"

"Yes," Thom whispered.

"The Boolean?"

"No. No, it started after."

And Adelaide did the rest of the math. "After you touched the Icon of Cruciform."

Osyen looked down at Thom, studying. "This mysterious voice, they give you a name?"

Thom shook his head. "...I-I've asked but—no."

They both silently knew who it could be. The only other special person they'd ever met with 'gifts', the only other person who knew what Thom was on sight, the only other person with an unhealthy fixation.

Anze.

"You can see the future?" Roche asked, pointed.

Rashida went to defend him, but Thom started rambling. "Not —no, it's more like...sometimes it's stuff from months ago, and sometimes it's people I've never met, places I've—I can't figure it out."

"That's how you cracked Anze's encryption," Adelaide accused. "That's how we had that streak of good luck after the Boolean. Because our Maestro had inside knowledge. You saw the outcomes and cut the odds to our favor every time."

"No, that's not—"

But Adelaide pressed. "You warned us not to meet with Weasel. You were *upset* after the train job, because something *unexpected* happened. There were guards you didn't know about and you were angry. You told us to drop Farragut. You knew something was coming."

And Thom exploded in a blubbering mess of tears. "I'm sorry! I didn't know he was going to die. I didn't know! You have to believe me!"

And without another word, Osyen grabbed Thom about the shoulder, pulling the boy into him. Thom gripped his jacket with both hands, squeezing the material between his fingers, breathing in the leather and smoke.

"I could've..." Thom said in between sobs, "I could've done something, I thought I could do something. I thought you'd hate me because he died, and I couldn't save him. I couldn't..."

Osyen laid his arm around Thom's shoulders, holding him close. "Me too, kid." Osyen laid his palm across the top of Thom's head, and the pressure just felt so good, so comforting. And his voice, like a blanket. "Me too."

Roche timidly raised his hand. "I know we weren't supposed to check the Extranet but..."

And Osyen immediately tensed up, his whole body tightening and his grip on Thom securing. "Roche...tell me you did not—"

"Yes, because I'm just so bone-dead stupid," Roche said, so dry he drew a confused stare from Zatia. He matched her look with a mocking shake of his head. "Lily and I were able to route our signal through around two hundred local repeater stations and feed them back on themselves in a—point is, we've got cloud cover."

"And?" Rashida asked.

Roche pursed his lips, considering how to deliver this news. "What time is it?"

"What could that possibly matter?" Adelaide asked.

"Because at oh three hundred, Admiral Hugh was in fourteen different public articles going back ten years. As of two minutes ago, anyway."

Osyen sighed, hanging his head. And Thom closed his eyes, letting the tears flow freely. They both knew what had to follow.

Zatia didn't. "And? What about now?"

Rashida drew herself up tall. "Admirals don't die. Neither do Ministers for that matter."

Roche nodded. "Fourteen articles went to zero articles in just under sixty seconds. All references to him have been summarily purged or otherwise altered. Admiral Hugh isn't dead...he doesn't exist anymore."

"Anze killed him," Thom confirmed through his tears. "I saw it happen like I was in the room. Anze killed him, and they're covering it up. Because of me."

Rashida moved over to Thom, laying a hand on his shoulder. "I'm so sorry, Thom."

Why was he crying? Admiral Hugh was...he was just a picture, a name, more monument than man. He was a stern voice in the other room. Ulysses Hugh was a tiny monarch of his own little nation, demanding and expecting of his subjects. He was lord of a manor that he had never visited. Mother's husband and her widow. Thom hadn't so much as written a letter or made a call in years. He had all but forgotten Thom, and by now, Thom had all but forgotten him.

The only emotion Hugh had ever communicated to Thom was disappointment. And the last one Thom had ever returned was rejection.

He didn't love his father. Hugh had long since passed from being family. And yet. Thom was so angry, so full of it that he burst open and his anger extinguished. Leaving only grief.

And as he wept in silence, gripping Osyen's coat between his fingers, the crew came around him, each holding him in turn.

And nobody said a thing.

CHAPTER 29
RASHIDA

SIXTEEN PARTS, big parts and little parts, spindly parts and greasy parts. Osyen had Milardi's revolver laid out in front of him on a mat as he meticulously wiped down each piece.

The others were finishing a brief morning meal. And he'd scampered off to a nearby building for some privacy and quiet.

So Rashida brought Osyen a meal. "Lily asked me to make sure you were fed."

"What'd we make?" Osyen said, rather incredulous.

"You really want the answer to that?"

"I'm about to put it in my face, so yes, I do."

"Two gutter rats, stripped and cleaned, boiled to within an inch of their lives, and sautéed in their own rendered fat. Side of hash browns."

Osyen considered that repulsive image, eyes blinking and throat tightening before, "Eh, I've had worse."

The strips of meat had collected pools of thin liquid under them, and the otherwise inoffensive potatoes from Thom's emergency kit did surprisingly well at sopping that up. She crouched down next to Osyen with the plate, setting it to the side, making him turn away from his work to eat.

And that's when she counted the parts in front of him. "Milardi's?"

"Second magnet's sticking," was all Osyen said.

"I don't...what does that mean?"

Osyen pinched the bridge of his nose. "It means I need to replace the part, but Milardi custom-tooled it, and I don't—I don't know what he did. And all of his notes, if he had any, are back on the *Aurum*."

"Don't do it like he did it," Rashida said after thinking. "Make it your own."

That was apparently a criminal thing to say. He turned away from her and the food, focusing in on some other part of the project, cutting her out of it.

"You need to eat."

"Why was Zatia on stims?"

Of course, that would be his question. "If she hadn't, we'd both be dead."

"I know why she injected," Osyen said, sliding the barrel back into place. "She did the right thing. Scrapping with an Oskie sober would've ended badly. But why did she even *have* a dose on her in the first place?"

"You should ask her."

"Yeah, well," he said with a laugh. "You're here and annoying me. So, I'm asking you."

"All I can offer is conjecture."

"Give me conjecture."

She exploded, shoving him in the shoulder and turning him out to face her. "You left us, Oz! Left Thom, left Lily. And you left her, and you did it without saying two goddamn words to anybody! Milardi's gone, and then suddenly so were you."

"She's recovering from stim-addiction, and you all let her have free access to—"

"Not sure you get to critique this crew's decisions after some of your more recent ones. You left her alone to take care of all of us. She was scared, sixteen years old, and suddenly the only protection her family had left. What was she supposed to do?"

"I expected her to take you all to safety," he said, but with more than a share of guilt in his voice. It was clear he knew that was an unfair expectation, but he had to confess his truth.

She felt searing hot at her neck, choking her, and she rubbed at the bruises left by a yellow-eyed man. Osyen's eyes darted down, as if noticing for the first time. And his entire demeanor seemed to tremble, like a ripple over water. He sniffed suddenly, trying to collect himself.

She lowered her hand, balling up her fist at her side. Her pulse racing uncontrollably. "We would never have left you, Oz. But you proved that you *would* leave us."

There was no denying it. So he didn't. "Yes, I did."

He poked at the gun parts in front of him, looking for something, like a seer would amongst scattered bones.

"You never expected to come back," Rashida concluded. "But you couldn't let this one go."

"It was my problem," he said. "My risk."

"The Paladins were my problem, but you took the risk then."

"That was different."

She just rolled her eyes, not entertaining that line of thought. It was different because he said so, the hypocritical bastard. "Learn to ask for help, jackass." And she got up.

But she didn't even make it to the door when she heard the words echo off the walls. "I know where to find my mother."

CHAPTER 30
THOM

IT WASN'T A HOUSE; this was a chateau, ornate and lush, with marble arches and green plants. A rotunda laid out front for vehicles to queue up for drop off or picking up. Thom wouldn't have been surprised if it had been a hotel or some exotic locale in the most beautiful cross-section of midday sun. It had been built atop the foundations of other smaller buildings, lifting it up into the sunlight and nothing blocking its view all around.

And whatever opulence it had once been, it was now abandoned, collecting nothing but trash that blew in. An abandoned car sat out front, stripped down to its bare chassis. Didn't even have a maglev lift-engine on it anymore.

"Seven thousand square feet of criminal living space," Osyen said. "Now, it's hung up in bureaucratic tear-down orders while the local historical society tries to preserve it for some-such reason."

"Your mother is being held in a haunted mansion?" Zatia asked. "That looks like a temple built by drug money."

"People have to pay for homes?" Roche asked, shocked.

"Well, I mean, there *is Steerage,* the government housing, but—"

"No, no," Osyen shut that down. "We're not going to open that capitalism box right now. And she's not being 'held' there, per se."

"What would you call it?" Zatia asked.

He thought for a long second. "Okay, so she's been brought there to...await...yeah, she's being held there. Fine."

Thom studied the architecture of the building. It didn't look familiar to him. There was no obvious exterior damage, either. But he had to imagine a building like this was reinforced against attack; if Anze's crew had set up even a temporary outpost in there, it would be dug in.

They didn't have the firepower for a frontal assault.

"And why would a researcher beholden to a crime lord be jammed in there?" Adelaide asked, arms folded across her chest.

Osyen rocked back and forth on his heels. "Because that's where Anze told me to meet him once I'd secured Thom. I hand over Thom there—for 'a conversation', whatever that means—and I get my mother in a clean swap. No muss, no fuss."

And Thom's gut sank, and his chin fell to his chest, like everything in the world got just so heavy. Of course, this all came back to Anze's obsession. Of course, Anze would bend the world to get within three feet of him. Never could just be a deal for money, like a civilized crime boss.

"And you believed him?" Zatia said with a laugh.

"No," Osyen scoffed. "That's a death trap."

"You made a deal with Anze Orchikov?" Adelaide asked, halfway to cursing his stupidity and the other half cursing Osyen's soul.

"More like he made a deal, and I happened to be in the room," Osyen said. "Besides, run that little dig site misadventure in your head again: not sure we get across Sunset without him."

Adelaide made something akin to a grunt of frustration. She didn't like the notion, but Osyen was probably right. Anze's movements were the only way they'd escaped.

"Well," Zatia said, sitting on her hands to hide the idle spasms, "option one is go right along with it and just give Thom up." Which just made everyone stare at her. And Zatia shrugged in response. "I'm not advocating for it. It's just option number one."

Osyen nodded, conceding the insane but obvious position. "And option two is we rush the building, smash and grab, before he can react."

"Which he will react. We can count on that," Rashida said. "Not to mention, he'd be expecting you to do that."

"Yeah. Option three is dump it, and leave planet as soon as we can," Osyen said with a sigh. "Some jobs are just not worth the squeeze."

Thom hadn't known Anze for longer than ten minutes, but he had gleaned quite a bit from that encounter. Anze was a man of charisma, of extraordinary salesmanship. He believed himself a cultured man, better than the dregs of humanity.

He would expect a betrayal. He'd be counting on it. Which means they could count on Anze. And to continue the spiral, Anze would most certainly count on them counting on it. Which just made Thom's head hurt.

But that fractal broke apart at the exact moment that Anze believed they were not smart enough to continue branching it. And that's as far as they had to take it.

"No," Thom muttered, drawing everyone's attention. "I think we can do it."

Osyen leaned in close to him, as if he could get privacy. "You have one of your visions?"

Of course that would be the question. And he had to admit, it would be rather nice to have one right about now. But they didn't have the time to take power naps until he did.

When Thom didn't answer, Osyen scoffed, pacing away while shaking his head.

"I have a plan," Thom started.

But Osyen cut him off. "I know you don't want to hear this, kid, but Anze is smarter than all of us. There is no 'plan' that jukes this guy."

"That's only if we think we can trick him," Thom said.

"We can't!"

"Yeah, we can't."

Osyen blinked a few times at that, and Zatia and Roche both joined his dumbfounded expression like a tableau of 'duh'. Finally, Zatia raised her hand. "I'm sorry, I feel like I missed my stop. Was that supposed to mean something?"

Thom stated it like a fact of mathematics. "We cannot trick Anze Orchikov. We can't trick him. He *knows* we can't trick him. He's got half of this city working for him, and the other half owes him favors."

"But you're going to try, anyway?" Osyen asked.

"No," Thom said, with a big stupid grin. "You're going to trick *me*. We go in like there's a big wondrous Maestro heist—and you double-cross us. And hand me over."

Rashida blinked at that suggestion, her brain stuttering. "You're suggesting we let him win?"

"We're not going to trick him...but we act like we meant to give it a good try," Thom said. "He knows all of us. All of our capabilities, what we're known for. So we play directly into our strengths—and let him beat us there. Meanwhile?"

Osyen straightened up, like he'd heard some patriotic anthem. He looked like a proper hero. "I'm not giving you to him, Thom."

"This is getting wild," Adelaide said, counting off on her fingers. "We're faking our own captain betraying us?"

"The Godfather's a lot of things," Thom said, "but he's not a liar. Catharina Batahr will be there, but only if I show up, and he will *never* believe I came willingly."

Osyen grabbed Thom by the arm, squeezing hard. "If he gets a hold of you, Thom, I don't know that I can get you back."

"I'm going to talk very fast right now," Thom said, slipping Osyen's grip. "Anze's main objective is going to be countering each and every one of our strengths. He'll try to take us all off the board, unless we take ourselves off. He'll watch us immolate before he interferes with our self-destruction. But it won't be real."

"It's a parlor trick," Rashida said, having the epiphany. "It's all an illusion."

Thom nodded. "Zatia'll pose as me, surrender, and be taken into custody. Meanwhile, I'm with you, posing as her."

"It's too risky," Osyen said. "What if he decides to gun us all down?"

Thom stood up, and stepped into the holographic image of the house, letting its light glow up around him. "He'll expect to be double-crossed, so he'll outmaneuver us—unless we beat him to our own double-cross and blow it up in our own proverbial faces. He'll think he beat us before we even showed up. When he's blinded by that pride, *that's* when we make our real move."

"Which is?" Rashida asked.

Thom turned to her, steeling for the big ask. "You are."

"*Fra tow ni laska,*" Zatia cursed under her breath.

She wasn't ready. But the fact she wasn't ready for this was exactly why she was perfect for it, counter to actual logic. Anze wasn't counting on the dainty noblewoman to be the assassin ace in the hole.

Thom hated these words, but it was just crazy enough to work.

"Theater," Thom said with a nod. "While we draw all of the focus, Roche? Rashida? You'll slip into the back ranks, find Catharina, and extract her."

Osyen shook his head, scratching at the back of his neck. "We'll never get out of the block, let alone off planet."

"We won't need to," Thom turned to Adelaide. "That's when you cut power to the block, reroute it anywhere Anze can't get it."

"Face an electromancer, deny him electricity," Adelaide muttered. "It was a good idea before."

"Power's cut and Catharina's identified," Thom said, whirling around to Rashida. "Which is when you pick up the target and get her off site. We'll deal with Anze."

"Okay," Rashida said with a nervous nod to Osyen. "I can do this."

Zatia chuckled. "You wanted a criminal's life, your ladyship. Here are the big leagues."

"This is suicide," Osyen said, uneasy. "And I don't mean—Thom those guys aren't going to be playing with sticks. They'll *shoot* her."

"If they even see her coming," Thom said, whirling back around to the group. "While the Lady Rashida secures your mother...you and Zatia are going to buy time."

"Without killing everybody in the building," Zatia asked, "how exactly are we going to do that?"

Roche's eyes glittered blue for a second and he stiffened. "By killing everyone in the building, of course."

It was Roche's voice. But the tonality, the pacing, the intention—that was Lily speaking through him.

"Okay, so that was awful," Adelaide said. "Please don't ever do that again."

Roche stretched the tension out of his jaw before shaking his head. "Do what?" he asked with strain to his voice.

"Oh, that's not better," Zatia moaned, lowering her head into her hands.

Osyen tried to take control of the conversation, throwing up his hands. "There's no way to do this neatly. Anze's got us playing three-card monte. Only way to win is to not play."

"Every single person here thinks this a bad idea," Adelaide said in agreement, but with the defeated tone of no better theories.

"Anze will never risk me coming to harm," Thom said. "They will take me alive. If they think we blew up our own plan, and all the fighters are accounted for?"

Osyen worked his jaw like he was trying to unhook it from his head. "You...I feel like I know this plan. This whole you getting captured schtick."

"It worked pretty well in the Boolean," Thom said with a shrug.

"Did it? Did it though?" Osyen's voice almost squeaked. "Because I seem to recall some ten-millimeter complications to that plan."

And Thom's gut hurt just at the mention of it. This time, he didn't have a magic ball to bring him back.

"We can rescue your mother today," Thom said, "but if we run—if we turn tail right now—what do you think happens to her? You really think Anze wouldn't hurt her to get back at you? Screw that, do you really think Anze will slink back to Farragut and leave us alone? And we'd still have half an Imperial fleet to contend with. We have to face him. Now."

Osyen sighed. Thom was right. Anze had put them in a place where they couldn't *not* play the game. They had to take part with whatever he dealt them. And still find a way to pull out the win.

Thom was suggesting they pretend to fold.

"If this works," Osyen said, "we still have to deal with all of the Navy crap, and we'll be heavy an extra person."

"Yeah," Thom said, "we'll have saved her life, Oz. Isn't that worth a shot?"

Osyen hung his head, processing the entire plan. A faux double-cross, turning over Thom, was a convincing ruse. It was the only way to mask the actual ruse playing in the background. Flashy stuff in one hand, so they didn't look at the other.

The captain held out his hand, drawing everyone's stares, as he studied the tremble in his fingers. They shook like he was being electrocuted. And despite all of his concentration, he couldn't still that tremor.

Finally, he let his hand fall to his side, and he inhaled sharply. "A vote. We'll take a vote. This is going to be extremely dangerous, put people in places they're not used to being. And Anze is not the forgiving type. There's a firm chance everybody dies. So we only go if everybody wants to go. One person votes no, we flip the table. Understood?"

"I make a good captain, apparently," Roche said with a chuckle.

CHAPTER 31
OSYEN

THE PLACE WAS LESS impressive in person. The exquisite masonry and design made it seem like a multiplex of wonder, but it was really just a big house. A sprawling piece of land on a planet without much space, to be sure, but what they built on that land was a fairly modest building.

Suppose the expense came from building directly on the tower in direct sunlight, with no nearby obscuring structures. Whoever built this paid enough for a sunlight easement. Nobody else got to build near them.

Osyen and Thom walked right up to the front door. No sign of life, no noise. But Thom wore his holographic collar, beaming up the countenance of Zatia. He wore her clothes, and somewhere on a rooftop, she was busy pretending to be him.

This was insane. Certifiable. But if Anze wanted to play three card, Osyen could play a shell game.

Thom pursed his lips, eyes scanning the area for movement. "Maybe nobody's home?"

Osyen looked up at the doorframe, where the Godfather's eye had been crudely scratched into the metal. No, they were here. They were just patient. And if Thom guessed correctly, they were preparing for a whole host of trickery. Why give away their presence?

The door didn't offer much resistance: a simple orthogonal locking mechanism. No voice print or biometrics to rewire or fool. Thom held his torsion wrench in place for him as Osyen tried to finesse the pins, but he could barely pinch the tool without it rolling out of his shaking fingers.

"We got a problem?" Thom asked him.

"Yeah, I'm not lefthanded, but now I'm one-handed. Can you just relax?'

Thom looked out at the street and the skies above them. "No problem. Just doing a breaking and an entering and doing it in broad daylight. Might want to move it along."

Say something. He had to just say it, say he can't do this stuff anymore. Not since Milardi, since Farragut. He'd lost whatever screw was holding his cool in place.

But instead, Thom just turned, and calmly kicked the door in. And his little emotional moment hung in the air. "You know, kind of surprised you had that in your little legs."

"Oh, ha ha."

Remember, Thom said over the comms, *we're radio silent from here on in. Any coordination over the radio and Anze himself can hear every word.*

Unless he heard those words. Then we're completely screwed, Roche noted.

Radio silence, Thom reinforced.

Zatia was humming a song to herself, and they all caught the last bar of it before she started talking. *Not the first time, nor the last time, Maestro. Good hunting, everybody.*

Good hunting, Rashida bounced back, the nerves practically sparking off of her words. Osyen hoped she held up to the pressure.

The two sauntered into the manor's interior. Tall ceilings with beige walls, everything just wide enough that Thom could probably have laid down in the hallways. It was like they had built the place for a claustrophobe, but more likely just for high foot traffic. Strange, for a home.

They passed empty bedrooms and storage closets, a kitchen ripped bare. No Replicator socket to accompany the dishwasher. Whoever had lived here had money to burn or was a sincere lover of real foodstuffs. And the size of the place meant they probably had a private chef or two.

The building opened up into a plaza with a clear view of the sky, plenty of happy greenery livening up the otherwise dead air. And a man stood at the center of the room, flanked by two cybernetic no-necks. He picked at the leaves on a fern, studying the texture of it.

And Thom scoffed with disapproval at the sight of him. "Diego?" Thom let the name slip from his mouth, along with a few choice curses. "You work for Anze Orchikov?"

Diego looked over, assessing the platinum hair and slight build of the illusion he thought to be Zatia. His eyes were almost sad at the arrival. "I wouldn't get into comparing our list of crimes, okay? Let's just get this over with."

"That's why we tripped right over a Godfather warehouse," Thom grumbled. "*You* sent us right into him!"

Osyen studied the factory hydraulics masquerading as guards on either side with a wolf whistle. "That's a lot of chrome-work. Did these plugheads come with serial numbers?"

"Yes," Diego said, curt and direct. "Where's the kid?"

"On his way," Osyen said. "Where's my mother?"

Diego didn't answer the question, instead looking over at the fake Zatia and the jangly jewelry weapons. "Drop the bangles. We're not stupid."

Thom looked down at the big heavy brass things on his wrists. "These silly things?"

"You wear 'em to formal occasions?"

"If I ever went to any."

"Lose 'em, Zatia," Diego ordered.

Thom gave a big dramatic sigh. "They're not exactly designed to slide on and off. This is a bit of a production."

Diego jerked his head at Osyen. "He can help you."

"Uh, Mister Richter Scale over here?" Thom said, mimicking his hand tremor. "Not going to happen. I'll figure something out. Just give me a second." He bent over, placing his foot on the outside edge of the bracer. Zatia had shown him how they went on. She had to take 'em off at the end of every mission anyhow. Not like they needed Diego to know that, though. Better for Thom to buy some time fuddling with them.

Osyen took a step forward, as though to hide Thom from view. And the two cyborgs took opposing steps outward, wide, to keep their line of sight on her. "Diego?" he asked. "How long you worked for Anze?"

"You don't care." Diego rebuffed the question.

"No, see I've been in this game a long time," Osyen said, "and you don't strike me as a hardened criminal."

Diego put exactly zero effort into covering his emotions. "He's seen right through me. Pack it in guys. I'm not 'career' enough."

"This isn't a career, fuckface," Osyen said. He pointed at his missing arm. "You see this? You know how I got this?"

"I don't care," Diego said, exasperated. "I'm not here for the backstory. Just a good paycheck."

Osyen looked him up and down. "And yet, still got holes in your store-brand socks. So Anze's paying you shit, or you're spending the money on something else."

"Osyen," Thom muttered as he struggled with the bangles, "what are you doing?"

"I'm easing in." Osyen was selling the con, selling the double-cross. It had to look like the plan was working for it to look like it fell apart.

One cyborg pulled a shotgun from his belt without so much as an order from Diego. They were in sync, digitally linked. "Stop stalling," Diego said, "where's the kid?"

"You putting it toward education?"

Diego tensed. "Bee Three? Put some double ought into Mr. Belt's companion." The cyborg stepped forward, looking for a clean shot on Thom. They had no idea they were about to shoot Anze's prized possession.

So Osyen stepped into his line of fire, daring the cyborg to shoot him instead. "That's it, isn't it? You got some kind of debts, expenses."

"He has a kid," Thom whispered a bit too loud.

Osyen smirked. "See, that makes some sense. Daddy breakin' bad to help his son."

"You want your mother back or not?"

Osyen stilled, and he clenched his fist, white knuckles. They were so close, and now this sellsword hypocrite was going to stand in the way of that? "You really have her back there?" Osyen asked, quiet, like he was afraid to disturb the spirits that haunted the house.

Diego nodded. "You have my word as a father, Osyen Belt."

"This your first time?" Osyen asked, almost offended. "'Cause you're going to have to do better than your word."

Diego dug in his pack for a second and pulled out Osyen's sculpture—the wood sphere. It had taken a crack from the fight with Yellow Eyes.

"That doesn't prove anything," Osyen said, his voice cracking. "I found that already at the dig site."

"You made it for her because you broke the mirror," Diego said, as he studied the work. "You were trying to apologize. You made it for her the night you were both arrested. Purplewood is difficult to work with. More difficult to find, even then."

Now that...that he couldn't have known. Yellow Eyes had been there that night, but he didn't know *why*. Only...only his mother knew about the mirror.

It was a simple transaction. Thom for his mother. And here he was, about to jeopardize an honest shot. Anze was a lot of things, from impulsive to obsessive, but he had never been a liar.

"Oz?" Thom asked, unsettled by the silence.

Osyen swallowed hard. "I can't really understand where you're coming from Diego. I don't have any kids."

"Osyen—" Diego snarled.

"Course, I've got this one." And Osyen pulled his revolver, spinning on Thom and pressing the gun barrel to the kid's cheek. His hand, rock-steady, barrel laid to the hologram's ear. "How's my shudder, technicolor?"

Thom's surprise was genuine and the words that came out were filthy. "*Fra tow s'ivan zu tryt!*"

"Sorry, Zee. It's the only way," Osyen said with a wink.

Thom's snarling was pretty convincing. Looking down a gun barrel did something primal to the lad. "You better shoot me, or I'm going to tear your only arm off and beat you to death with it!" On second thought, he was pretty sure that was a genuine threat. Thom may not be so sure that Osyen was acting.

And all Osyen could think about was his mother's voice, being dragged away by a pair of yellow eyes... "You so much as twitch, and you'll be eating your meals with a straw the rest of your life." Osyen lifted his head, calling out to the gang in hiding. "Thom! It's over!"

And Thom sighed, hiding his satisfaction behind a sneer. Osyen was still on script. He leaned into the gun so his cheek clicked against the gun barrel. "Don't do it, Thom!"

"You coulda stayed out of this!" Osyen shouted to the rooftops. "Coulda gone into hiding. But you *had* to come after me."

Diego and his men just watched as this little drama played out, eyes casually scanning around for the appearance of their prize.

"I'm going to count to three," Osyen said. "You come out, or I give little miss sunshine here a steep new jawline."

Before he could even start counting. "Wait!"

Everyone looked up to see Thom—well, Zatia—standing in the doorway behind Diego. Her hands were covered in grease, and clothes soiled. They'd come into the house through some very unpleasant means, expending one entry method that Rashida and Roche couldn't use.

But here came Zatia, in disguise—just as Thom had planned it. But the look in her eye was of genuine panic, seeing Osyen's gun at Thom's head. She didn't have nearly the confidence Thom did. "Put the gun down, Oz."

"Diego? I believe you have your prize."

Diego nodded and the cyborg goons advanced on Thom. The kid raised a hand at them, vainly begging for a moment. "Osyen, listen to me—"

"Ain't nothing to listen to," Osyen said, digging the gun barrel into his hostage. "You don't have what I want."

The cyborgs grabbed Zatia by the extended hand, tweaking it around her back. And with the rough contact, the hologram shimmered. Had they noticed? The cyborg wasn't paying it any mind and Diego was too busy studying the ground, some pound of shame working its way through his brain. And the cyborg began to haul Zatia away.

It was working. Zee was about to be behind enemy lines.

Osyen had exactly half a second's warning, as he saw the Oskie melt out of the shadows behind the cyborg. Half a second to shout. Half a second to shoot.

But those Yellow Eyes...and Osyen remembered the feel of his hot fingers on his throat. He felt so small, so far away.

And the cyborg's arm simply separated from his shoulder, spraying blood against the wall—and Zatia was yanked backwards, screaming as she streaked along the steel wall, clawing for anything that might save her from this fate, like a phantom stealing her away for the grave.

Osyen watched in horror as Zatia streaked ten feet up the wall—and vanished through a window with a crash of glass. It was like the shadows themselves had grabbed her.

"What was that?!" Diego shouted, pulling his sidearm, leveling it at Osyen.

And Osyen leveled his own back at Diego. But Thom reached

up, gently pulling his arm down—stripping off the holographic collar and dropping the entire facade. "He took Zatia."

"That wasn't—*what* is going on?!" Diego jerked left and right, so confused by Thom's sudden appearance. He punched his gun forward like he could punctuate every statement.

"I was pretending to be her," Thom said. "She was pretending to be me. Keep up."

"What—why?!"

Osyen took two strong steps forward, half-expecting the man to shoot out of surprise. "To give you a murder-pixie instead of—you know what, just *shut up* for a second."

Zatia! Thom reached out through his implant. *Zatia, say something!*

Anze arranged for a very normal meeting. He knew Thom would try something. And he slipped in the perfect counter-measure. The Oskie wasn't going to be fooled by a holographic collar, when even a decently observant organic eye could notice the slight differences in height or tonality. His augments could probably see right through the collar's refresh rate.

But why would he go for Zatia first? Why not just snag Thom? Unless...

Unless he knew Zatia was a threat, had to be neutralized first. Her stims brought her up to his level.

And now Thom was properly vulnerable.

"This part of your plan?" Osyen asked.

But Thom shook his head. "You know what that was."

"That I do." Osyen had to get him out of here. "Thom, out the door now."

"You're not going anywhere, *skel*," Diego cursed.

Oz, what the Hell is going on down— Adelaide had something to say. But something cut her off.

Addy? Osyen asked. But she didn't answer. *Adelaide!*

I saw it! Rashida called out. *He's jumping out of the goddamn walls, Oz.*

Abort! Thom ordered. *Everybody scatter. This isn't a fight we can win.*

Thom's right, Osyen said. *Drop whatever you're doin' and get clear. We'll find you.*

Rashida had her objection. *But Oz—*

Just do it, Rash! I will find you, I promise. Now go!

Diego was getting impatient. With a jerk of his head, the second cyborg grunt went to check on their downed friend. "Nobody is going anywhere."

"Oh, just try and stop me!" Osyen snapped.

"I have a gun."

"This may be news to you, but a cybernetic commando just yanked my friend up a *gulaw* wall. You think a *bullet* scares me right now?!"

Osyen had killed two Oskies—when he had the drop on them, in the dark, and the right tools. But Stride, when prepared and on even ground, had manhandled his entire team like he was bored. And Yellow Eyes wasn't blinded by emotion or faith.

Was Zatia already dead? Adelaide?

Roche, cut contact and get clear soon as you can. But he didn't hear the plughead jockey's confirmation. *Roche? Lily?!*

Gone.

Roche. Adelaide. Zatia. He was surgically picking them apart. Soon, there'd be no one left to defend them.

"I came here for the kid," Diego bellowed, "and I will walk over you if I have to."

Osyen had to spell this out for him. There was no use whispering when whatever stalked these halls had ears like a bat. So Osyen spoke clear and direct. "Diego, you seem like a nice enough guy, but you are an idiot, so let me make this abundantly clear. You're being backstabbed and you're too stupid to realize it in real time."

Diego actually laughed at that, but the nerves cracking into his voice was unmistakable. "W-what?"

"You've—been—set—up. You weren't supposed to get Thom, just

draw him out. And now, you're expendable. So you can either shoot me, or help us get—"

There was no warning. Maybe it was because Osyen had been just a little too accurate. Maybe it was just his time.

But ol' Yellow Eyes stepped from the shadows, and he moved like a flash of lightning. He laid three fingers across Diego's throat, ripping the flesh like he was dragging his hand through water. And Osyen felt the wind as the Oskie zipped by, a small torrent of blood whirling in the air, caught up in the vortex of his passing.

The blood drops sprayed across Osyen's face before Diego even felt what happened. The man clutched at the three rough gashes in his throat, just in time for his severed carotid to empty his heart's contents into his hands.

The last cyborg stood up in terror, looking to Osyen for instructions. He didn't want to die here.

But Osyen didn't meet his stare. He looked back...to find Thom gone. The boy hadn't even made a sound when Yellow Eyes whisked him away.

And now Osyen was alone.

They had to be close. Yellow Eyes killed Diego, but he hadn't killed Zatia or Thom. What would be the point of not killing Zatia where she stood? No, he was taking hostages.

And strong as he might be, an Oskie wasn't carrying that many people out of here on his back.

"Where's your ship?" Osyen demanded of the quivering cyborg without so much as looking up.

The cyborg shook his head, delirious and afraid. Thom was gone, Roche, Adelaide, Zatia. His boss was dead. And he was just sitting there, shaking his head, instead of doing something!

So Osyen drew his pistol, rolling the cylinder into place off his thigh. "Where?!"

"You'll never make it." The statement wasn't a threat. It was the terror of a man come to an acceptance, trying to explain the futility of struggle, why they should give up the fight.

Fine. He'd do it on his own.

Osyen squeezed one shot into the cyborg's chest, throwing the man backwards over his dead comrade. And he stepped over Diego's corpse into the mansion's back half.

He had to move quickly, but every shadow gave him a start. Every creak made his heart stumble. *Rashida?* Osyen bounced. *Rashida, are you clear?*

No response. There was no way she'd gotten out of range on foot by now. Damn it. Goddamn it.

The mansion was uninhabited, which made for a lot of empty rooms and noisy surfaces. Every step he made announced itself, echoing off of the painted metal walls. It was like walking in a cave or down into a crypt.

They'd come all this way for him. They'd put themselves in harm's way for him. And now they were all gone.

Not yet. Not yet!

Something struck him hard, slamming him into the steel wall like a mallet to a drum. He bounced off of it, only to get battered back into the wall again. He crumpled to his knees, coughing and hacking, staring at the ruddy tiles under his fingers.

The voice came from everywhere, reverberating off of every surface, incorporeal. "Fourteen years. You still don't understand anything."

Osyen thought he could listen for footsteps or maybe a whorl of wind flowing. He closed his eyes and listened—to have the words whispered in his ear. "Get up, little boy."

He swung behind him, blindly firing his revolver into the wall. He drove a crater into the steel which spat metal shavings back, carving into his hand and face. Grimacing against the pain, Osyen recoiled, tumbled away, rolling along the floor.

And catching a boot to the gut. He felt his ribs crack and cave against the augmentations, and Osyen went hurtling again, this time up into the ceiling, glancing off the trusses and landing facedown on the ground.

He couldn't think. Couldn't breathe.

"He told me not to kill you, you know." Yellow Eyes' voice haunted, like an echo from the heart of a dark mountain. "He didn't say anything about leaving you in one piece."

Osyen squeezed the revolver—and felt the cylinder and barrel tumble right off the end, a smattering of technology on the floor.

And Osyen just looked at it. Milardi's revolver, destroyed.

It was like looking at Milardi's broken body, like he could feel Milardi's blood seeping between his fingers. That infectious laugh, that dastardly smile. It was all gone now.

Yellow Eyes stooped, grabbing Osyen by the throat and heaving him up. He kicked in the air for any kind of support, as the Oskie's burning fingers singed his jaw and neck. He croaked and squeaked, unable to speak.

And the Oskie just stared at him, partially obscured or camou-flaged, like a monster made of smoke, only made material when it touched him. They were roughly the same size, but this wraith picked him up like he was still a little boy, dangling him in the air, waiting for him to pass out.

"You know what he is. And still, you try to trick and fleece him? When all he wants to do is talk?"

His vision darkened, filling in with red and a screech in his ears. Think! Do something! There had to be something.

Osyen fished in his jacket, and the Oskie watched with mild interest. What possible trick did this little rascal have for him?

And Osyen felt his fingers wrap around the four small demo charges. Enough to blow through a wall. If he couldn't kill this son of a bitch, he'd go down on his own terms.

He flicked his wrist, releasing a charge on the roof, floor, and the wall behind him. The Oskie was fast enough to snag all three out of the air, crushing them in his hand. "I could have fed them to you, you know. Would've made for quite the modern art masterpiece."

"Made ya look," Osyen choked out.

And the Oskie heard the happy chirp too late. He reached into his pants' pocket, where Osyen had dropped the fourth charge. A conman's fingers.

Yellow Eyes had just enough time to hurl it down the hall—and it detonated mid-air. The concussion knocked Osyen to the ground. It kicked the wind out of him, and his gut screamed accordingly. He'd gotten familiar enough to recognize the feeling without completely panicking.

The Oskie dissipated like a nightmare, vanishing back into memory where he belonged. That must've been too close to the explosion, even for him. Oskies were fast, but they were still flesh and blood, and shockwaves had a way of killing the squishy no matter their land speed record.

Don't chase him, Osyen thought. Don't fight. Just get to Thom. He needs you.

Osyen pulled himself to his feet and staggered out of the back of the mansion. It was a proper little abandoned grotto, with a decadent pool and even an outdoor kitchen and bar.

And a private hangar. That had to be it.

His breath rattled, his hand trembling, Osyen stumbled his way to the side door. Locked, of course, but it wasn't exactly high-end security this deep in the compound. Osyen threw his body weight into it, breaking the door from its cheap latches.

And also falling on top of it. Ow.

The echo of his dramatic entry sang back and forth across the space, but the big room was certainly not empty. Sitting pretty on its pad was a modular small transport. Big engines on it too. External pods that could be mounted or dropped off for quick and easy cargo. Perfect atmospheric and low orbit shuttle.

And the pods on the exterior were occupied, like sarcophagi for ancient kings. Really no bigger than coffins. Six of them.

One for each crew member of the *Aurum*. But if he was standing here, and they were all full...Impossible. Osyen's jaw dropped as he looked over the pods.

Adelaide, Rashida, Roche, Zatia—all banged up and limp. But the fifth in the line?

There she was, his mother: Catharina Batahr. She soundly slept in her pod, arms folded across her chest. A streak of white through her hair, dignified, serene, and quiet. She had no idea she was currently being used as a bartering chip by a sick and twisted man.

He could cut her loose right now. It wouldn't take much. He could detach her pod from the ship, and...

He was so sorry. Sorry for everything. He could finally tell her.

Thom. Where was Thom? The last pod!

Osyen ran over, and sure enough, the boy was trapped inside— very much awake. "Osyen?!"

"Hang on!" Osyen grunted, as he worked with the external keypad. "Hang on, kid!"

The engines hummed to life, fluttering Osyen's coat. And he heard the creak of the hangar door.

No. No! You can't have him!

Osyen worked at the keypad, and he heard confirmation. Thom's pod extended off the shuttle on a little crane, setting him down on the deck, and unclipping with a bang.

He ran over and set to work on the next pod—

But the ship engines flared. No more time.

Osyen threw himself behind Thom's coffin, shielding himself from the thrust. The deafening howl and maelstrom of wind that came from just the initial ignition of the thrusters was enough to slide the steel torpedo along the deck floor, sending it rocketing backward to crush the exposed Osyen against the back wall.

Osyen reached out with his palm in a vain attempt to slow the approach—like he could do a damn thing but be crushed. But the pod slowed, grinding and screeching steel against pavement, coming to a stop inches before Osyen's fingers would've touched the wall.

Gasping for breath, Osyen leaned over to check on Thom. The boy sighed relief at the sight of his face. "Get me out of this thing," he asked weakly.

Osyen's back screamed, his gut moaned. But he popped the seal and pulled Thom back into the night air. He checked Thom over, rubbing his hand through Thom's hair and across his neck, looking for any cuts or obvious broken bones.

But he didn't expect Thom's expression, the boy's wounded misty eyes, tears on the verge.

It was the silence that was the worst. Thom said nothing. He didn't cry or scream or shout or say anything at all. He just looked at Osyen like he was seeing the dead walk.

Osyen struggled to his feet, getting as far away from that stare as he could. He sniffed, like it might clear his nose, but it just made his head throb. And he stumbled out of the hangar, overcome with vertigo.

His ribs screamed. His hand screamed. His ears screamed. And so did he, putting everything his injured lungs could still give into one bestial frustrated call. And he heard his shout echo back to him from the faraway structures.

Yellow Eyes. He'd gotten away.

He tilted his eyes up to watch the retreating contrails of the shuttle, as Yellow Eyes whisked away into the perpetual golden sunset. Taking his crew and his mother.

Rashida? Zatia? Osyen bounced over the channel, hoping for some catty response or casual insult, but nothing came. *Roche?* No snappy chatter. *Adelaide?* No brush off.

He'd lost them all. He'd lost everyone.

Thom laid a hand onto Osyen's back, like it helped in the slightest.

"Lily?" Osyen asked aloud, knowing full well they wouldn't answer.

PART FOUR
THE FIRST OF THEIR MANY FACES

Stepping clear of the Void was someone most unexpected. They were neither wreathed in flame nor all that unbecoming. They appeared with an aspect most unseemly for their holy task. And so we cast them out from our places with sword and with hate. And they left us to our pain, if that was what we wished.

This was the First of their Many Faces: not cruelty nor vengeance, but of yielding. For the Pilgrim was first to be known not by their mask, but by their respect for our wishes.

GNOSTIC LIBRUM, COLONIAL 1:31-35

.

CHAPTER 32
THOM

MOST SILENCES WERE DANGEROUS. Fights brewing between friends, or ambush predators that had scared away the ambient birdsong. There hadn't been a night this quiet for him in a long time. Someone on the *Aurum* was always talking or breathing or thinking so loudly the rest could feel the tension build.

But now?

Now it was just Thom and Osyen, clustered under a rusty awning on a forgotten side-street, two leaning towers on either side of them. No ship, no crew. No hope.

They'd staggered the few miles they could to get the sky into more of an evening purple and less of a black. Far enough that responding Clerics wouldn't catch them in their search. But the force of law wasn't really the most important thing in either of their minds right now.

Thom studied Osyen's stoic face, carved from a mottled stone. The man sat on the pavement, a threadbare blanket pulled tight about his shoulders. A single camp heater, its glowing coils offering scant little light, pushed enough heat to keep them warm.

Osyen's breath was ragged and wheezing—never a good combination—and the longer they sat in the cold shadows, the louder he wheezed.

"We need to get you to an AutoDoc," Thom stated the obvious.

"Doesn't matter," Osyen dismissed it, cutting him off when Thom tried to continue. "Doesn't matter. He's going to find us and he's going to kill me and take you. And even if he doesn't, he has everybody else. He can afford to just wait for us to do something else stupid."

"You're badly hurt."

"I *know* I'm hurt. I break all the time. Spend more time broken than anything else."

He was too hurt to fight back, too broken of spirit. If Anze sent his men after them again, there wouldn't be anything they could do. They'd spent their last card, burned their last chance. Even Milardi's revolver was crushed. The barrel was bent, and the pressure from whatever had done that, had sheared the support pins.

The only weapon in their arsenal was now a collection of loosely assorted parts, clutched in Osyen's shivering fingers.

Anze had all the cards, all the resources. And they had only one thing: what Anze wanted.

"Why didn't he just kill them?" Thom asked.

And Osyen didn't answer.

"He killed Diego like he was made of plastic. Instead he grabbed us for those pods."

Osyen shook his head. "Yellows Eyes said something about... being told not to kill us."

Strange. Anze had quite an axe to grind against the crew. If the only one he wanted was Thom, why save anybody else? Why not just roll through, kill everyone, and take it? It didn't fit with the stories of a brutal and reactionary dictator that Adelaide had related to them.

No. He didn't want to lay claim. Anze didn't want to win. He wanted to be right, and to be told so. He wanted Thom to choose it. And he was stacking the deck anyway he knew how. Quite effectively. If Thom ever wanted to see his friends again...he'd have to go to Anze.

"You know," Thom started, "when you picked me up from the Pan & Pantry, I thought we were going to, uh, find buried treasure on forgotten moons. Go to weird places. Meet amazing people."

"Did I disappoint?" Osyen grimaced, with a hint of a smile.

Thom bobbed his head back and forth, weighing the possibilities. "Eh. Well, I mean, we spent a lot of our time running. Would've liked to smell the flowers a bit more."

"I'll make a note."

Set aside the banter and the laughs, Thom. This might be the last time he sat alone with Osyen. His last chance to say it. "This was so much better than I could have hoped for, Oz. I wouldn't trade the last two years for anything."

Osyen smiled, but quickly forced himself to frown again. "You died one time. Don't forget that part."

He wasn't likely to. But that wasn't a road that scared him anymore. "You know what we have to do."

Osyen squeezed his knees in closer. "We can't let him win."

"It's the only thing left."

"That's not true. I can sit here and pout until a solution materializes from thin air."

"Oz—"

"He doesn't—get to have you!" Osyen shouted, forcing the words past a spike of pain.

So Thom let it drop. He just pulled his knees to his chest and looked up at the sky. Somewhere, that shuttle had taken all of his friends. And they were facing who knew what kind of torment, as Anze tried to draw Osyen and Thom both back into the light.

They'd never condone Thom giving in. But Thom could never condone their suffering.

Osyen whimpered in pain, and when Thom looked down, he winced. Like it embarrassed him. "I'm sorry, kid."

For what? What could Osyen Belt possibly be sorry for?

Maybe Osyen saw the quizzical look on his face, but Osyen sighed, and gestured to their surroundings. "If I left you in the Pan & Pantry—"

Thom jumped right on that statement. "I'd have lived my life, maybe, but I wouldn't have had you to help me. Or Rashida or Zee or Roche, any of them. I wouldn't be me, I'd be somebody else. Somebody who didn't get to know you."

Osyen said nothing, just studied Thom's face, committing it to memory.

"You know what he wants." Thom sounded so small, saying it aloud, but there was no other way to put it. "If I give up, he'll let them all go. Let you go. You know it's true."

"Have you seen how this ends?" Osyen asked, sounding just as small, just as beaten.

Thom wished he did. He wished he had some vestigial hope to share. He could lie. He could tell Osyen he did, give him that confidence to do what had to be done. But he just couldn't bear lying to him anymore. "Oz, I've known frighteningly little about where we're going or what we're up against. I've only ever known what the dreams tell me."

"So we should take a nap?" Osyen joked. "Maybe we get lucky?"

Get lucky. Osyen had lived his entire life in luck of the draw. And he must've known this was a bad draw, no matter what. And he barreled into it headfirst, anyway.

"Why didn't you ask us for help?"

"Because look at us!" Osyen snapped. "They're gone, Thom! *This* is what I was scared of. I tell you what's going down, and I knew you'd all follow me. I didn't want you to! And you—you all came anyway! Now Anze's got 'em all tucked aside, God-knows-where..." And that was too much exertion. He gripped his side in pain and averted his gaze down into the orange electric coils of their camp heater.

Osyen was broken, beaten, and beside himself with misery.

272

Thom drew a heavy breath, letting his own eyes fall down to the glow at their feet. "You've done so much for all of us. I'll never forget it."

"...Don't mention it."

"I'll mention it as many times as it damn well pleases me, Oz," Thom said, soft. "So thank you."

Osyen cocked his head, still unable to look up at him. "For what? Getting everybody killed?"

"For being a part of my family when my family didn't want me."

Osyen looked up at him, finally, a mountain of pain tearing him apart, twisting knives working their way through his guts. No amount of smashed ribs or sucking gunshots would ever recreate the agony working its way through his face now.

"I don't want you to go," Osyen said, a tremor in his voice.

Thom didn't want to either. But what other choice did they have?

Thom looked down into the heater. "Get some rest, Osyen. And then we'll go get our friends."

CHAPTER 33
ADELAIDE

MIGRAINE. Always the best kind of way to wake up, half her senses working for the other team.

Where was she? The floor was a searing bright white, not doing her head any favors. The walls too, and the ceiling. A sensory deprivation cell, designed to keep her awake and delirious, and in this case, put her in a not-insignificant amount of pain. Though that was hardly the design, just incidentally convenient.

The more days, weeks, months she spent with Osyen and crew, the more time she was spending inside of various kinds of imprisonment, with wildly different accoutrements.

She coughed—and felt the spike of pain through her skull. More interestingly, she didn't hear her own scratchy voice. Lovely, so they were broadcasting a nice clean band of white noise to blanket out her senses. Or—more alarmingly—she might be deaf.

Think. Where had she been? She'd been...she remembered cracking the junction box for the mansion. She still felt the tingle in the tips of her fingers as she pulled the lines out, ready to do her duty.

And then...Osyen had panicked, told everyone to fall back. And she woke up. Had she managed to organically ground some high voltage nonsense? No, there were no burn scars on her hands or fingertips. Ohm's Law was non-negotiable in this. Whenever she'd managed to become the ill-advised path to a hot circuit, it left at least one part of her crispy. And she was fine, but for the ripping headache.

So she wasn't dead. That much was clear. And she hadn't electrocuted herself. So...

Captured by Anze's goons.

"Hello, Addy."

She groaned. "Don't call me..." But all power in her fell away when she saw who had spoken.

Because there stood Nathaniel, in all of his goofy wonderfulness. His crooked smile, his hazel eyes with the pronounced crow's feet, the window's peak to his thin graying hair, and his kindness.

He awkwardly swung his hands, before giving himself a look up and down. His was a firm but gentle tone, like a hand on the middle of her back or a cooling palm across her forehead. "How do I look? I haven't caught a reflection yet. Is the flannel too much?"

Adelaide climbed to her feet, transfixed. "You're dead."

He raised a finger, as if to pause her. "Ah! Let me cut that assumption short. The man you once loved, Nathaniel, is dead. I am not Nathaniel."

Her lip curled in instant boiling hatred. Whatever this thing was came to her wearing his face, speaking with his voice?!

"What has been taken can never be restored," the doppelgänger said. "But—but! Adequate restorative justice can be made."

"What are you?" she asked. A proper three-dimensional image attempting photo realism had several layers to achieve, that each had to slide through layers of contrast. Creases in the skin, laugh lines, stretching pores, subcutaneous tissue: all individual cues the human mind sought when looking at another face. And the more she looked, the more... planned every single motion was.

And in that moment, one entire layer of that patchwork Nathaniel slid off, revealing the dry and plastic replica of the man. But the voice was just as cheery as ever. "I am a C20.N-95 Personal

Assistance Intelligence. My appearance and demeanor was programmed from a selection of Imperial behavioral profiles."

He waved a hand over himself, changing the flannel and jeans into a workman's jumpsuit.

His jumpsuit. It even had the frayed cuffs and the oil stains on the knees he'd never gotten out of the fabric. She had no doubt that he had the same birthmarks and scars, the blotchy patch on his chest whenever he got too warm.

And she could feel her fingernails cutting into her palms as she squeezed her fists. "Stop this."

"Okay," the computerized man said, raising his hands to back her off. "I have to admit, this was what we expected your first reaction would be."

"And yet, you did it anyway."

"Yes."

"*Why?!*" She was certain she had shouted loud enough that the programmer's parents could hear it, but she didn't even hear her own voice muffled back to her, as the cage ate every decibel of her rage.

They had gotten his eyes and his clothes and his voice. They had gotten his stance and his swagger and the way his eyes darted when he was thinking. They even got the smell of sawdust and crummy engine oil with the mild tang of metal that set her heart pounding with a thousand memories.

The doppelgänger took a single step forward, cautious. "Addy... I'm not, nor will I ever be, *him*. I would never assume I could be." She doubted it feared for its own safety, but it was what Nathaniel would have done, and that drove her even more angry.

"The amount of distilled disrespect it takes," Adelaide fumed, "to kill a man. And then use his face..."

"It's not disrespect!" it insisted. "There's-there's no way I can convince you of that in the next ninety seconds. That will take the rest of our lives to show you—"

"You *took* the rest of his life, Anze!" Adelaide shouted, forcing the ghost to freeze where it stood. "We came to you. We didn't make threats. We didn't make demands. We begged for our lives!"

The monster forced a contrite smile, like the jab had actually meant something to it. "*We* didn't."

"What?"

"Nathaniel didn't want to go. Remember?" the doppelgänger said, pressing one hand to its disgusting chest. "He warned you. He knew what could happen. And you pushed for it."

She scoffed. It was really going to start pretending this was *her* fault?

"You didn't listen to him," it insisted, stumbling over its words in an elegant display of programming. "Maybe there was another way out, but you thought that Nathaniel could...reason with him. You thought there was reasoning...with an unreasonable man."

"That's a very brave coder you have there, Anze," Adelaide scoffed. "He just called you 'unreasonable.' What are you going to do about it?"

"He *was* unreasonable, Addy," the machine man insisted. "He shot your husband twice in the chest for the gall of asking to retire. Would you call that the act of a reasonable man?"

"I'd call you a horrible parlor trick," Adelaide said. It took another cautious step toward her. And her response was almost autoimmune, taking her own step away. "You're not real."

"I *am* real."

"You're not my husband."

The digital skin walker wearing her husband's face took another step. "No, but I can provide what you're missing. Ask me something. Ask me something only he'd know."

"You failed the Turing test when you confessed thirty seconds in."

"Because I'm not here to lie to you!" it barked, in a sudden burst of frustration. And damned if he didn't hop backward and bite his finger like he was jamming a plug into a leaky wall—just like Nathaniel, that son of a bitch. After a moment to simulate genuine emotion, he let out a calming exhale. "I'm trying to connect with you."

Absolution. That was it. Anze wanted forgiveness. He wanted her to accept this little gift basket and let him off the hook for killing a good man. He wanted her to take a toy and tell him that there were no hard feelings for murder. Anze Orchikov thought he could drop big sweeping gestures of restitution to buy himself out of Adelaide's hatred.

Never.

"You know what he said to me? Nathaniel? The last thing he ever said to me?" Adelaide asked. And the doppelgänger waited patiently for the answer. "It wasn't some sweet nothing. We had been working on some engine coupling and he just told me to get the wiring all crewed up before we closed the shop. Then we rode to your office in absolute silence, because we were terrified of you. You weren't listening to us, to what we needed. You just had more work for us, and we were being 'obstinate.' You killed him for saying no, Anze. Well, here I am telling you 'no' again. So you either shoot me, or get this *fra tow* machine out of my cell. Because if you leave it in here with me, I will break it down for scrap. And beat you to death with whatever high carbon bar stock I find in there. Have I made myself abundantly clear?"

The doppelgänger bowed its head, slipping into a rigid and neutral stance. "I apologize that I was insufficient emotional support. Ptolemy Industries seeks to provide the best elder support androids on the market to-date. If you require—"

"Get out!"

It nodded, sliding backward until it hit the wall of the cell, where the bricks rotated out of the way to seamlessly swallow the machine, leaving not a trace of any hatch after its passing.

Adelaide dropped to the floor, staring at the wall, cursing silently. She had no doubt it would be back. And she wasn't sure she had the strength to say no a second time.

CHAPTER 34
RASHIDA

IT WASN'T ENOUGH for Anze to simply cage her. No, her prison had a very classic sense of elegance. Rich walnut fringe wrapped around the decadent green and purple wallpaper, gold filigree woven in distinctly royal patterns. Expensive wooden furniture, worn and scuffed just enough to show use, but polished and oiled with care. A standing dry bar with a decent enough selection of liquors, each encased in crystal decanters, molten jewel tones in the warm light.

It made her stomach turn just looking at it.

One might think of this as the purest lap of luxury. But the complete absence of a door, window, or ventilation belied the truth of it.

This was a cell, despite its trappings. She was to wait, in purest comfort, for what came next.

But wait for what now, she wondered.

She had called to her comrades, but no one had answered. Too far? Or was Anze watching, intercepting everything they said? Her breath fluttered in her chest, her confidence and independence hard won now sliding out from under her feet. She had walked this galaxy alone before, but now, without the others? Everything felt so unstable.

First, Rashida walked the perimeter, counting her steps to measure the space, and she found the most disconcerting truth—the cell was not symmetrical, despite what her eyes told her. Maybe that's what had triggered her vertigo.

It was a subtle approach. Undermine the sense of reality, of what was inviolably true. There was likely some sub-harmonic acoustic manipulation going on as well, beyond the range of human hearing. Then a slide to the temperature, to draw out sweat, and then down to bring on the chills.

There was an art to breaking someone when the subject themselves was schooled in manipulation. No one approach to cracking their shell. And whoever had their hand on this dial was no amateur looking to break her with promises or blood.

Did they want something from her? Details on Thom? Or was she simply to wait comfortably, quietly, for the Dunsweir to come collect her?

A lackadaisical spin and turn, and she looked back at the center of the room—to see a gaunt young man in a chair, leaning loose forward from his restraints. Hands and feet bound, a bag over his head. He sagged, completely still. She'd have thought herself mad if she hadn't seen the seams in the floor stitching shut, where the hidden lift had brought him in.

Someone had given her a present, the same way keepers fed their beasts.

She approached the man, uneasy at first. There was something familiar about his silhouette, but she didn't recognize him until she was close enough for his smell.

Not sweat or salt or blood or fear, no lavender perfume or leather and cardamom. For a man of age, under duress, he should smell like something, store bought or natural odor. But her senses defied her, because the chemistry at work on that man's pampered skin obscured him. A hologram, perhaps?

But she recognized that silhouette. And so she reached for the bag, letting her fingers graze the cotton shroud, ensuring herself of its reality, before she pulled it free.

Hair matted and tussled, face slick with sweat and bruised by his journey, all refinement beaten from him. Her devotee, her keeper, her Consort.

Magnus.

His eyes fluttered at the sudden introduction of light, the tug to his head. And he smiled when he saw her face. "My, my. There's someone I didn't expect to see again so soon."

She looked down to see his arms tense against his restraints, but he was never in his life strong enough to slip steel bonds. They lashed his legs to the chair, an uncomfortable twist to his left ankle that looked less than healthy.

Anze. Anze had gone above and beyond the call, captured her old jailor and hauled the man all this way. Why? This man had stood in Anze's court, stood at Anze's side, however briefly. They had struck a deal for Rashida's capture and return.

And when that deal was jeopardized, Magnus had shot the Godfather squarely in the back. A vengeful man would see Magnus put to a slow and painful death.

And yet, maybe he was. Because Magnus was now in this cell. With her. Defenseless and weak.

"You look well, my lady," Magnus groaned.

"You and I took very different roads to this moment," Rashida said.

Magnus laughed, two painful hitches of the chest. "I told you... that I'd find you."

She looked up and around her. Someone had introduced this ringmaster to her circus, which meant they wanted her attention fixed. And she didn't want to give this slug a moment of her time, anyway.

"Oh, come now, Rashida. You had to know it would end this way."

"You're tied to a chair," Rashida said curtly trying to cut this conversation short.

"Yes," he said, with infuriating confidence.

She rolled her eyes. "Is this quite how you expected it?"

Magnus let his head roll to one side, inspecting the space. "It's a far nicer abode than I had imagined. But the facts of the case remain the same. You're there. I'm here. At your mercy."

Was he delusional? He certainly behaved as though he knew more than she did, though that was something of a default position. She'd have assumed he'd adopt a new tact.

Rashida waved her hand at the surrounding opulence. "What do you think is going on here?"

"Your freedom," Magnus said with gravity. "The only way you'll ever have it. You came to the conclusion a little late, I must admit."

Rashida scoffed. "I'm just as much a prisoner right now as you are."

"Only one of us is tied to a chair."

Yes. This might be her cell, but if so, why was he restrained? And she was not? That was not done incidentally. She had awoken resting comfortably on a cushion, fresh clothes, and clean water. He was deposited in her space, rough and vulnerable.

"You can delude yourself only for so long," Magnus said. "You're too smart to hide from the truth forever."

"I've made it something of a personal mission to confront the truth, Magnus. It's you and my family who would shield me from it."

Magnus turned his head towards her, like he was trying to reach out. "I have always been your servant, my lady," he croaked out.

"And your obsession with me has clearly served you well. Get a hobby."

"Some of us live our lives for nothing more than devotion."

"Devotion!" she snapped at him. "You have personally done more harm to my life than anyone alive."

"That's good," Magnus whispered, nodding. "Keep going."

She cocked her head at that statement. What was his game?

No. Whatever it is he wants out of this exchange, he won't have it. She turned away, stalking over to the dry bar. She didn't need a drink. Just something solid between them.

He called after her, his deep voice vibrating straight into her bones. "You can't hide from what you have to do, Rashida."

"You're going to sit in that chair and be silent while I work out our escape."

"*Our* escape, is it?" Magnus laughed again, before curling forward in pain. "You'd be far better advised to leave me here to starve. But what a cruel end that would be."

"You deserve a quick trip into a faulty airlock," Rashida said, "but that's not for me to decide."

"Who better? My own parents don't know me like you do."

Well, that would explain his behavioral problems. But that crime originated as much with her family as his own. Children were taken by the Ministries specifically because they were pliant. Of course, it took a special kind of insanity to qualify at Magnus's level.

It was like he was in her mind. He shifted in his seat, worming against his restraints and sneering. "You'll never be rid of me, your ladyship. You can run, you can hide. And whatever cities you take shelter in, whatever planet you think can protect you...I will plow them all under."

"You're tied to a chair." That was going to be an effective rebuttal all day long. Whatever poetry he wanted to sling, he was tied to a chair. And he would remain so forever, far as she was concerned.

"Jackson Milardi, was it?"

And her eyes tracked back across the elegant rugs, winding up to Magnus's ghoulish face.

And that was all the encouragement he needed. "That was his name, right? He was the first to die. Something of a public service, cleaning the skies of a murderer like him. Did you know he'd killed children before? Was even paid for it? Man didn't even have the gall to do it out of passion or hate. Just for the coin."

A very obvious ploy, trying to get a rise out of her. He wanted her emotional, illogical. He wanted her angry, because anger made people stupid and impulsive.

He was the bait to the trap. She knew it. Whatever Anze had planned, this was gift-wrapped for her. The source of all her pain.

And he was tied to a chair.

Magnus smiled, a kind of acceptance in his eyes. "I'll kill them, Rashida. I'll kill them all if you make me."

He would. She had no doubt, that strapped to a chair in some hidden compound, he could arrange for the unfortunate deaths of every person she cared about.

She drew herself tall. "I left home because it was suffocating. And I found the fresh air...revolting. And sweet and cold and forgiving and—"

And he sneered at the very notion. "You're so impressed by them, are you, these plebes?"

"No," Rashida said. "I'm not. They are...jealous and violent, greedy and insufferable and stupid and short-sighted. But my family is no different."

That changed his temperature. His eyes went dead, and his voice went cold. "I will string up your little friends and hang them from their bowels. I will give them every modern medical miracle...to keep them alive. They will suffer for every day you do not return home. And I will start with the little vagrant girl."

She knew when men lied. She'd been trained well, and she'd seen her share. Magnus was already working out the logistics of it all. He knew who to talk to, what favors to call in, to make sure that Zatia suffered the most mathematically severe death man could provide.

And he wanted her to stop him. One way or another.

"You'll never get the chance," Rashida said.

"I found you through patience," he reminded her, "and I will find them."

"I'll stop you."

And his smile turned her stomach. "You haven't got the spirit, my lady. You're Dunsweir. You kill entire planets with a wave of your hand. But you don't know *how* to walk up to another person and stop them from brushing their hair. Her screams, my lady, will be entirely your fault.'

"Shut up."

"No one will know her name," Magnus said, "but those screams, they will teach the good boys and girls what happens when—"

She didn't let him finish that sentence. Her fist connected with his jaw. The shock of it rolled up her forearm through her shoulder, so far that she felt it in her own ear. It numbed her fingers and her elbow clicked in objection.

But the way Magnus hung his head to the side, the way his breathing went ragged, the way blood began to trickle from his lip... she liked that sight too much.

So she hit him again.

CHAPTER 35
ROCHE

SLEEP WAS ALWAYS A PECULIAR THING. Doctors would claim it a biological necessity, a period in time when the body could focus on healing and recording the day's events for long-term storage. Sleep was a core component in the formulating of personality, ego, and growth.

Roche had not slept, properly slept, for almost a hundred and three days. His body went comatose for brief periods, but Roche could always remain completely cognizant.

If Lily never slept, why should he?

He had grown quite familiar with the digital confines of Lily's shell, even after its extraction from the *Aurum*'s network. It was rampant with color and action, noise and movement, a kaleidoscope of expression. It was the physical interpretation of their personality, a cosmic whirlpool of ever-shifting wonder.

But this new void? It felt...endless, properly empty. A digital desert of space ready to be filled. Like a tundra, devoid of life.

Roche looked down, instinctively checking himself for injury— and found something quite surprising.

A hand.

The gnarled ball of tissue that had once been home to a dozen plug ports on his left wrist was now five strong fingers, a perfect left to match the right. He flexed the fingers, feeling each new appendage bend in accordance with his will.

He ran his new fingers through the full and luscious curls on his scalp. He pawed at his face to find both eyes were as gooey as could be. Every augmentation was reset with organic components.

And a wave of nausea swept through him, the whole of the world seeming to tilt.

This wasn't right. This wasn't who he was. They had 'corrected' him, bent his image to fit within their definitions.

"Lily?" he called out. With all of this emptiness, he expected to hear his voice echo back to him. But it was like the air swallowed the words ten feet in front of him, like he was just another speck of sand on the beach. "Lily?!" he called again.

Nothing.

He looked around, frantic. Nothing on the horizon, no buildings being warped by mirage, no sense of distance or scale. No people. No voice, no sound.

He turned his eyes to the murky sky, which seemed to glow a low and comforting ambience, rich and royal blue. But no stars, no voluminous clouds or streaking colors.

But the single dart of light that slowly etched itself upward from the horizon. Roche squinted, trying to make it out, but his squishy human eyes couldn't focus on it.

And as if it saw his notice, it winked out, leaving behind its evanescent trail to glow, like a celestial wound in the sky.

"Hello?!" he shouted to the Heavens.

"Hey!" a familiar voice called out to him.

Roche turned—and the whole blue world evaporated. Six figures stood nearby, staggered in their approach to a rickety frost-bitten transit bus They gestured in welcoming, but they seemed blurry, out of focus. He couldn't make out their faces.

But he heard the voice again, coming from a boy of slight build and alarming confidence. "We want you to come along!"

A man in a longcoat and wide brimmed hat stepped up, a full head and shoulder taller than the boy. "Nothing's going to happen. I promise."

He couldn't make out their faces. Couldn't remember. Remember?

He shook his head—and the world seemed to slide under his feet. He stumbled to catch himself, and by the time he looked up...

The Orphanage. A slim little cottage on a forgotten grassy hill. The jeering and scorn could be heard all the way outside, two alien moons hovering behind its steeple.

A dream. He was dreaming. These were people, places he knew. Or someone was feeding these images to him.

"Lily?" Roche called out. "Lily, I need you right now!"

No response, but more laughter from the schoolhouse. He heard the names the children were shouting. They called him Plugsly and Skinrat, made fun of his mottled hair and his missing hand. They beat him with sticks to see if he bled battery acid. And the matron was too drunk to care, or perhaps she also thought he was a monster.

"Lily?!"

And the Orphanage folded in on itself in a flash of light and the spark of flame. The matron's raging eyes looking down at him, consumed by tongues of flame—

Darkness. He was back to the desolate data tundra, lacking in sound. Alone.

"I'm not controlling this," Roche whispered. "They are. It's all just a tool of control, to weaken and empty us. Show me what they're showing you."

No answer from that deep blue sky.

"They can't keep us apart," Roche pressed. "They think they can, but they can't. You were my first and oldest friend. They cannot get between us. Show me!"

The sky tore open at his word, like some great seal was being broken and the veil of the world stripped aside. And his deep blue void was suddenly violet rolling fields, with white-capped mountains and amber sky like someone had set the clouds ablaze. It had the distinct feel of impressionist Elysian fields.

Roche looked about, gathering his senses. It was hard to look at. Everything had a hint of harsh angle, tessellation, or pixilation to every edge. The alien insects that hovered in the air, the grasses that floated on the wind and stones at his feet.

Atop a nearby ridge, Roche saw the full-fledged blue body of Lily. It was the most 'human' they had ever looked to him, detailed to the point of being tactile. Roche meandered over, giving careful distance in case this was yet another trick.

"Lily?" he asked.

Their head slumped a bit, turning to him. "Hello, Roche."

"Where are we?"

They smiled, bitter. "Somewhere we'll never see. A planet of imagination that Osyen used to dream of. I pulled it from his logs. He dreamt of it often and I sought to understand its importance to him. A place he and I could reside in peace. This is an illusion of Anze's making, of course, and nothing here can be trusted."

Roche looked down the hill to a happy little round door set into the hillside. Aged wood, painted a deep wine-red, weathered and loved. Smoke rose from a chimney at the top of the hill, and golden light beamed from the window.

"That's what I think it is?" Roche asked.

"It is what cannot be," Lily whimpered, "at a place that doesn't exist."

Roche shrugged. "There are so many uncharted worlds, I find it hard to believe it doesn't exist."

Lily nodded. "A mathematical possibility. But I will not live to see it. And neither will he." They turned their back on that happy quiet future, squaring up on Roche with a rare kind of fury in their eyes. "Anze believes that we can be contained."

"Can you break us free?"

Lily's eyes flickered, and their form glitched for a moment with the strain. "We are...on an island. Our server base is disconnected from all others on the station, but I can feel them out there."

"Station?" Roche asked. "Are we in orbit?"

"No. No, we're still...we're on Ilum. In the city. We are connected to a vast array of empty databases, providing nigh limitless space for my Cascade to expand into. This is likely Anze's ploy. I would persist in this location for another hundred thirty-two years, two months, and eight days before total collapse."

"Enough time to dream," Roche whispered.

But Lily raised their head, locking eyes with Roche. They both knew this was not real, and at the best case, would cost more than either of them were willing to pay. Besides—a reward unearned lacked the necessary sweetness to be savored.

"So long as Anze remains in close proximity," Lily said, "I cannot even begin to assault their defenses. And even if it were possible for me to wirelessly tap in, they would leverage every power in their considerable arsenal to contain or eliminate me."

"Then start small," Roche urged. "We just need to open some doors." Roche reached out for Lily's hand. He half-expected it to feel sharp with the strange geometry of this space. But their fingers felt coarse, rough, like a workman's callouses. And their grip was firm, reassuring.

"I won't let them trap you here," Lily said.

And Roche gave their hand two pulsing squeezes. "And I won't let them hurt you. We wait for our moment, and then we make a break for it. Okay?"

Lily nodded, taking one last look at the cottage that could have been theirs. "There are sixty-two inefficiencies in this construction."

"Keep notes," Roche said, "and yours will be better."

CHAPTER 36
THOM

IT DIDN'T TAKE MUCH. Osyen connected his Entiglas to the extranet, a simple ping into the universe like a flare in the night. And not minutes later, a shuttle swooped in, landing a few blocks away from where they had camped.

Thom expected an armed detail, ready to rough them up and drag them before Anze on their knees. But to see the man himself, Anze Orchikov, bubbling with unconfined glee? That was a sight far more chilling. His thin clothes flapped in the breeze from the shuttle's engines and his skin glistened like his face was dusted with bronze.

And he greeted them like an old friend. "Thom Hugh. Osyen Belt."

"Hi, asshole," Osyen grumbled. "Let's get this over with."

Anze waved to two members of his entourage. "Get this man some medical attention." And then he extended a hand to Thom.

And Thom took it.

———

It was a fine spacecraft, with soft oiled leather and warm seats. Thom sank into them, dozing off for a time. Every time he awoke, he caught Anze watching him. And the Master of Farragut wasn't embarrassed by this, nodding considerately. It was okay to rest. Safe even.

Osyen had his hand up on an overhead bar as two medics tended to the bruising on his chest and back. He'd been through a helluva beating and a small explosion. Outside of skin patches on his cuts and antiseptic treatments, there was nothing left to do but strap a back brace to him to help support his ribs until an AutoDoc could properly set them.

When Thom awoke the final time, sunlight had spilled into the cabin. He looked out the window to see the shuttle on approach to the enormous tower that hung high over the Sunnyside of Ilum, a great erupting from the ground: Institution Zero One.

"You buying us an exclusive studio apartment?" Osyen asked.

And Anze hummed some blend of annoyance and amusement. "You have no idea what I've got in store, Mr. Belt. Knock your socks right off."

The shuttle flew directly at the side of the enormous black monolith—and Thom clenched up, grabbing up at the safety bar. There was no door, no opening. They were going to crash right into the side!

And Anze smiled as the bricks moved aside at the last second, slapping shut behind them almost as fast. For all intents and purposes, they had flown right through the wall, the inorganic monsters snapping them up like a snack. And the sight of what was within the tower took Thom's breath away.

An enormous indoor hangar. Cavernous and wonderous, with all manner of people and ships docked. But one particular ship drew all eyes, the crown jewel.

It was under retrofit by engineers and drones, slightly classier than the automated fixers Thom had seen in Darkside. Components were being bolted into place, and safety checks run on past work. They were still buffing out the obnoxiously chrome exterior, and some paneling was missing, revealing the skeletal grating underneath. But Thom recognized that silhouette.

"The *Aurum*?" Thom asked.

"No," Osyen said, stepping over to get a better look. "It's bigger."

"Quite correct," Anze said. "She's new and improved, more current model. The original *Aurum* can't fly anymore, so we're offering something a bit better."

"A KC-31GDT fresh off the line," Osyen rattled off from memory. "Though your crew extended the engine mountings and up-armored the belly."

"Improves performance in atmosphere," he explained, "and we even classed you out with some black market hardpoints. Though you'll understand, we haven't given it any guns at the moment for somewhat obvious reasons. That'll be up to you, in your future professional endeavors, to do with as you wish."

"Up to…" Osyen stumbled on that. "What are you playing at?"

"You're looking at *your* ship, Osyen. Ready to launch tomorrow morning. You already took one of mine and slammed it into a planet. After that, did you expect in a million years I would or could present such a gift?"

The thought itself made Thom's skin crawl. Anze was clearly still livid about that incident, but he was cognitively exhibiting a diplomatic tune.

Thom lingered at the window, staring down at that shiny new ship. And he knew. Anze was trying to buy favor.

The new ship was hardly the only thing in the buzzing hive of activity. Cranes unloaded fatted transports identical to the dig site and to the warehouse in Darkside. And they were heaving the very same steel crates marked with the Godfather's all-seeing eye.

Installation Zero One. Whatever Anze was up to was happening right here. And he had enough resources to clandestinely build an entire freighter. Or, just as likely, the Empire knew about everything and just didn't care.

For all of Anze's moaning about exclusion from the club, he seemed to swing a great deal of Dunsweir weight around nonetheless.

Their shuttle glided up to a port on the side of the hangar bay. The doors opened, and the crew filed off, quietly replaced by armed guards with steel truncheons. It was a nice, subtle change—but Osyen and Thom exchanged a knowing glance. Shuffling a deck didn't hide what had just happened. They were still considered dangerous, even bruised and battered as they were.

Anze strolled down the hallway, dragging his retinue close behind. But Thom planted his feet. "I have to know something before we go any further."

Thom felt the guard at his back, ready to prod him forward, but Anze waved the man back. It was a subtle reminder that Thom was still a prisoner, despite Anze's effervescent tone. Despite this, the Godfather folded his hands behind his back, respectfully awaiting Thom's question.

Thom swallowed hard. "Did you kill my father?"

"Yes," Anze said, cavalier and without any consideration. "For the record, he tried to kill me. So, strictly speaking, not a murder. But —yes."

Thom felt his gut twist and retch at the confirmation. He'd dreamt it, seen it happen. He'd watched the life wink out of his father's face with all of the stress of flicking off a desk lamp. But hearing Anze confirm it without regard for the weight of it was just so harrowing.

"I'd offer to let you see him, pay respects, but the Navy has already reclaimed the body. It's well on its way to Sol by now. He's going home."

Osyen laid his hand on Thom's shoulder, giving it a little squeeze. And Thom leaned into it.

Home. Admiral Ulysses Hugh wasn't going home. His soul was now committed to the Pilgrim's Path, to join in the endless Sojourn. Perhaps he'd finally find some peace there.

A short man in a white coat rushed up to Anze's side, most of his face covered by a stringy beard and mustache, shaped and oiled to control what would otherwise be a chaotic mess. His pleasant face had a nervous demeanor, tremors in his hands as he tried to pass a file to Anze's Entiglas. "Godfather, I have some exciting reports."

"Doctor," Osyen said, with recognition and a bit of disgust.

And the man looked up at Osyen, shrinking away with shame.

Anze's eyes went between the two, bemused. "I see you've met Professor Ordee."

"I have," was all Osyen had to say on the subject, but his clenched fist implied some wanton desires. And the professor was well aware, backing away from the encounter.

"Oh, Professor," Anze called out without looking. "Tell the teams to exercise more care today. The materials may be a tad more"—he threw a meaningful glance back at Thom— "responsive than usual."

"Yes, sir." The professor averted his gaze and darted off down a hallway.

'The materials.' They had Pilgrim Metal here. And Anze was aware what Thom's presence would do to them. What else did he know?

Anze clapped his hands, breaking the moment. "Right! On with the tour."

Anze led them down the corridor, past seemingly endless unmarked doors. How anyone knew where they were going without a heads-up display, he'd never know. Perhaps, that's how they did it? Everyone had some kind of implant that told them where their work was?

"What's your interest in a place like this?" Osyen asked.

"Scientific, of course," Anze said. "Premier research into Pilgrim Artifacts."

"Looking for a cure?"

And Anze's gait stumbled. Not enough to be noticeable, really, but his stride lengthened as Anze forgot to commit to the step for a moment. But then he was back to himself again, strutting down the hall. "Don't we all wish to heal what ails us, Mr. Belt?"

As they walked by, a door opened at Thom's elbow, causing him to jump in surprise. Inside Thom could make out several labs and hazard gear, as they gingerly handled rough—

Pilgrim Metal. Crates of it. Piles upon piles, hundreds of feet back until the room itself rolled with the curve of the structure and out of sight. More than Thom had ever seen. They lifted shards of it with robotic arms, studying it under lamps and microscopes and spec-trometers.

This was a place of study. Perhaps the entire floor was. And Thom instantly felt that cold, icy pull towards it. That sinking feeling...

Which shut off as the door closed. Because Thom hadn't even tracked who had stepped through: the Oskie, Yellow Eyes. He looked down at Thom with a mild grunt of dismissal. The man's hair was still dripping from a cold shower, darkening the collar of his other-wise crisp uniform.

"Welcome, Commander Isaac," Anze said, waving him to join the entourage. "Come get a front-row seat."

Isaac nodded to Anze, looking back at Osyen with a smirk. "Still walking, still talking?"

"Didn't they retire your model already?"

Isaac hummed, pleasantly surprised. Like a predator looking forward to a good meal. And he vanished, flashing forward to Anze's side.

"Play nice, Commander. You're not Imperial anymore," Anze scolded. "We're here to mend fences. Reconciliation, and all that."

It was Osyen's turn to scoff, and Thom had to agree. Whatever was hiding behind these doors would not include mutual healing. Anze didn't want to mend anything that didn't directly benefit him.

Abruptly, Anze turned toward a door, waving it open with two fingers. There was an odd crunch as the door obeyed without clearing its locks, slamming wide despite itself. But the guards didn't seem distressed by this, guiding their charges on inside.

It wasn't altogether an unexpected sight: it was the brig. Thom had seen the inside of Imperial holding areas firsthand. Solid white cells composed of smart-bricks that folded and shaped as needed. Broadcasting a scalding white light to disorient, they could even slide the ground under your feet, letting a prisoner run in one direction forever without ever finding the edge.

Prison cells. Four of them. One for each of their friends.

But the cells were...tailored. Sure enough, two were pure white voids of endless displacement, but one was inactive gray, while the last was dressed up with opulence and finery—no doubt Rashida's cell.

All of it together had the unmistakable look of an experiment. Three tests, and a control. They took his friends to a lab and then just couldn't help themselves.

"What is this?" Osyen demanded.

Anze looked at the isolation cells, and back to his guests with a bizarre kind of whimsy. "Well, I couldn't rightly let them just wander, now could I? There's some classified material in here. Academy types get very sticky about that."

Thom walked up to the first cell on the end. Roche stood in the center of the grayed-out bricks. No attempt to disorient or lose him in a void, because several cables had been hooked into the plugs on his wrist. Roche was deep in some virtual space, his head and fingers twitching. Lost in a dream.

"Oop!" Anze burped out. "There's one more thing."

And the king of dramatic reveals walked over to a panel and leaned his entire weight down on a small button.

A blast door popped open, revealing several floor-to-ceiling tubes of green liquid. And Thom nearly gagged at what was inside.

Bodies. Several in various states of decomposition, combustion, or just plain violent ends. And the centermost was Diego's, throat still gashed open and face affixed in horror.

Isaac chuckled at the sight, picking at his fingernails—and Thom retched again, thinking of what he must be cleaning out.

Anze peered through the glass, like he was studying Diego's face, committing the details to memory. But then he smiled, almost playful, turning back to Osyen. "He has your eyes, Osyen."

Osyen stiffened, but the Oskie's grip on him kept him firm.

"He had a child," Thom blurted, aghast.

And Anze nodded. "And he still does. The boy will be well taken care of. Lavish accommodations, caretakers, the best schools."

"You killed his father."

"Oh please," Anze scoffed. "You know better than most that a boy needs more in his life than the proximity of a genetic donor. His situation has upgraded."

Thom felt like his scalp was going to catch fire. Anze was so bound up in his theory, he missed the obvious. Diego *was* present in his son's life. He *was* more than just a wallet or an authority. Not that Anze cared.

"Commandant?" Anze asked the air overhead. "What crimes was our friend Diego here wanted for?"

A holographic emitter glowed, and a soft, featureless face beamed in front of them, with its awful deep voice. "Grand larceny, fourteen counts of murder in the second degree, five counts of destruction of property, two counts murder in the first degree, possession of controlled substances, possession of—"

Anze waved a hand through the image, cutting off the audio and dispersing the image like a hazy cloud. "You get the idea. A former associate of the Espinoza cartel connected with some rather heinous acts. Including—not too surprisingly—the murder of three Ministry officers by way of rocket launcher."

"On your orders," Thom pointed out.

And Anze bobbed his head back and forth. "I said I wanted you all untouched. Diego took that to mean murder. That's his crime, not mine."

"What did you mean, 'he has my eyes?'" Osyen asked the harrowing question.

Anze sidled up to Osyen, like he was sharing an amusing bit of gossip. "I mean he has your literal eyeballs sunk into his skull right now." Anze snapped into the hyper energy of a Labrador. "Now, to win a starship and a ticket off this spinning rock: do you know what that means?"

Osyen considered that grotesque revelation for a second, lip twitching to hide his disgust. "...I can have them back?"

Anze grimaced at that. "Well, they're not exactly in the best condition, if I may be so honest. No. But here lies a dead man, barely identifiable, has your eyes—and he'll soon be missing an arm." Anze waited for the group to respond to that bit of fortune telling. "Osyen Belt: I pronounce you officially dead. You don't have to run anymore. Pick a new name, I'll provide you new credentials. You can go anywhere you want."

"Not forking us over to the Imps?" Osyen asked.

"I harm Imperial interests wherever it can be practically done. Take my offer and you're a free man. Go anywhere, do anything. No more Capital history dogging your heels. No more assassins, no more bloodshed. *Tabula rasa.*"

A clean slate. Osyen could start over, live a quiet life. There was a part of Thom that pulled, individual coiling threads on his heart drawing it apart till it split. He wanted Osyen to take it...but some part of him didn't want to give Osyen up. He shouldn't have to. Anze shouldn't make him! This wasn't fair. Thom could go with Anze and still have Osyen in his life, have his friends!

"What's the catch?" Osyen asked suspiciously.

"Details," Anze admitted, looking aside. "Imperial intelligence and security are very good. They don't have their reputation because of good propaganda. I don't think I need to explain that to you. If you're seen in the company of Osyen Belt's old associates..." He gestured to the prison cells. "Then some analyst in some field office will put two and two together. Your freedom...unfortunately means never seeing any of them ever again, or you're right back where you started."

Osyen swallowed hard on that notion, looking down at Thom. He had always known he'd be saying a goodbye in this room, but he never imagined it would be such a complete one. "And what about Lily?"

Anze sighed, but more sad than anything else. "The machine is quite tied up with the man now. Splitting them would more than likely kill both. I'm terribly sorry about that, Osyen. You'll have to leave Lily too. But! I've ensured they have a quiet happy little space where you never left. They can exist comfortably in their little digital pocket dimension until they finally expire—long after you do. I promise."

Osyen's eyes bounced off the walls, looking for the answer he hadn't found yet. But Thom knew the truth. "Oz..."

"No," Osyen said, his voice cracking.

"Oz, take the deal."

And Osyen Belt looked down at Thom, hurt and betrayed.

Thom sniffed away the grief already building up. "These people will never stop loving you. But don't tear yourself apart trying to love them back."

"Stop talking now."

And Thom couldn't bring himself to say another word, a single tear ripping a line down his face. In two years, Osyen had yelled and screamed and roared. But there was nothing so cutting as when his words were that soft, that beaten.

"So everybody gets a happy ending, right? Wrapped and ready?" Oz asked, looking down at Thom. "What about him?"

"I've been fairly open about my demands," Anze said, brow twitching as he turned his attention to little Thom Hugh. "He...loves you, Osyen. There's no debating that. But he has *power*. And he needs a teacher. He won't find that with you. Your story ends here, but his is just beginning."

"Maybe it's what we have to do?" Thom asked, mulling it over.

"No," Osyen said, lip quivering. Still clinging to the dream. "He's made sure it's the only thing we *can* do."

Anze threw up his hands, somewhere between guilty as charged and offended. "I'm not trying to burn down the family barn. If anything, I'm building one."

"That's bullshit. You've systematically deleted any other option, so all he can do is pick you. That's not a mentor, that's an obsessive lunatic."

Anze bit his lip as he absorbed that insult. "It wasn't a simple feat arranging all of this."

"And nobody asked you to," Osyen spat. "You made a big gesture, but you're not *entitled* to my gratitude. I don't want this!"

"That's childish."

"Probably!" Osyen admitted. "But what does that make you?"

Osyen was clinging to scraps. Thom couldn't deny what he was seeing. For the first time in years, they all had an escape. Anze couldn't be trusted, but he seemed to deeply need Thom's cooperation, and was willing to warp Heaven and Earth to get it.

Thom could buy an end to their pains right here, and in doing so, maybe find out what was causing his own.

And so, while Osyen had it out with Anze, Thom took a few steps over to the cells. He wanted to see their faces one last time.

Adelaide sat on the ground, her knees tucked into her chest. The ghost of her husband stood just beyond her sight, a holographic shell twisted up around a sophisticated machine. He was about as material as a wisp of cloud, a soulless replica of Nathaniel.

But she'd grow to be grateful to have his memory preserved.

Thom moved down to Rashida. She was actually working up a sweat, her clenched fists dripping with Magnus's blood. The man was limp, long since having lost consciousness as the royal woman worked out her anger, her fear, and her pain on him. When she was finally done, Thom knew Anze would take his turn with the ghoul. And he would be far more brutal.

But at long last, Rashida would be free.

Roche sat silently in his cell, working out some complexity between him and Lily. The two were connected to enormous black cables that strung up to the ceiling, running data off to a bank of servers the size of the *Aurum*. Practically infinite room to expand and grow. Lily would evolve and develop as they only wished they could before. And Roche...Roche's sacrifice would have amounted to something more than a few extra months. He'd have carried Lily when he needed to, and could now finally rest, maybe even reclaim what he'd lost.

This was good. This was...Thom could live with this.

Until he came to Zatia's cell, and Thom's gasp stopped all other conversation.

"Thom?" Osyen asked.

Thom couldn't respond. He couldn't put it to words, like it might make it more real.

Zatia laid against the far wall of her pearlescent isolation cell, legs splayed out and her eyes dead to the world around her. Her cheeks sunken and bruising starting to work its way up her collar and across her cheeks. Four separate IV lines were tapped into her arms and neck, dripping cold chemicals down from the ceiling.

Anze marched over to see what Thom was looking at, and snapped his fingers, like he was remembering the obvious. "Yes! Right. I'm sure it *looks* terrible. But there's a reasonable explanation."

Thom couldn't take his eyes off of her. And her eyes looked back at him, unblinking. She was probably staring at an opaque white wall, just more infinite cell void. But her eyes weren't even properly registering that. Just drifting off into the lab-crafted euphoria.

"What have you done?" Thom whispered.

"She had developed an extensive chemical addiction to performance-enhancing drugs. No big mystery there," Anze explained. "She was *deep* into her withdrawal symptoms when my doctors got to her, and she was getting worse by the moment. We struggled all night to stabilize her. But now—look! No withdrawal."

"She was on treatment," Thom muttered. "Neurotransmitter therapies—"

"That were completely burned out by a more recent dose of stims."

"She was fine last night!"

"She wasn't presenting, but she wasn't fine!" Anze was getting flustered.

"You're curing her by giving her more drugs?" Osyen asked.

And Thom clenched his fists, turning on Anze. "This...isn't what she wanted."

"It's what they all wanted," Anze said with a scoff. "Adelaide wanted her husband back. Roche was afraid of death. Rashida needed her freedom. And little Zatia here wanted to feel powerful. Well, now she does! No longer a burden on her friends, and with the magical ability to crush a man's skull between her fingers."

That wasn't what they wanted. Adelaide had finally put Nathaniel's death behind her. Roche was afraid to be *alone*. Rashida wanted freedom, not blood on her hands. And Zatia?

She twitched in her cell, a convulsion of her head and jaw so fast Thom never saw her move. It was like looking at a haunted marionette, as it lurched in restless sleep.

And Thom drew himself up tall. "You know Anze, you really need to spend some time finding out if your help is actually helpful."

Anze forced a smile to hide his frustration. "You're upset," he said, almost reminding himself of it. "It's a difficult moment. It's not the news you wanted to hear. There are goodbyes, farewells, end of an era. You're entitled to your feelings."

"This?" Thom said it so loudly, the guards tensed up. "This isn't me upset. You haven't *begun* to see me upset! This is angry."

"Thom—" Osyen tried to cut in with some sense of self-preservation and calm. He felt the temperature in the room rising.

But Thom didn't care anymore. Zatia was suffering. Roche, Rashida, Adelaide were suffering. And this son of a bitch had the nerve to call it 'help?'

"*This*?!" Thom bellowed. "This is pain. This is their nightmares! And if you'd have known them the way I do, you'd never have done this—this torture!"

He looked back at Zatia. She looked like a vampire's thrall, drained of vitality and will, reclined and sunken against the wall. Paralyzed? Or simply given up?

Roche, lost in an eternity without end? Lily, living endlessly without a reason for living? Rashida, freedom bought with violence? Zatia...power that enslaved her?

His family needed him now.

"I'm not going with you, Anze Orchikov," Thom spat, "no matter what you put in front of us. No, instead? I'm going to break out my friends. And together, we're going to burn your twisted operation to the ground. And all the people in all the worlds out there, clouded, living under your sight? They'll finally remember what the sun feels like again."

The tension in the room might've snapped like lightning. The guards were still, Osyen was still.

And Anze sighed, relinquishing something to the air. He shook his head, considering the prison cells and the occupants for what felt like a lifetime. He couldn't possibly have taken that speech to heart, had he?

Just as soon as Thom had considered that notion, Anze slammed a hand under Thom's chin, gripping hard like he was reaching in for the vertebrae at the back of his neck. Thom's vision immediately began to blur, as Anze pushed him backward, tilting him over so his entire body weight was suspended on Anze's fingers biting into his throat.

Thom choked and clawed and kicked at Anze, but it was like pawing at stone. Poor Osyen was already buried by three guards, nothing but swinging fists and muffled, grunting pain. And Isaac...he just watched.

Anze leaned in close, like he was dangling Thom over a cliff. "You're upset. But that right there? Was needlessly cruel."

A white-hot pain shot through Thom's head and neck, and he screamed with the distinct pop of something falling free, like a pierced blister on his neck. Warmth rolled down his skin.

And the tinkle of metal on metal soon after, as Anze compelled the subdermal radio implant at the base of Thom's skull to worm its way out and plop to the ground.

For two years, there had been the background radiation of radio static filling a corner of is brain. And now? No voices, no music, no arguing. Nothing.

But he heard Osyen's voice crying out. "Thom! Thom, no! No!" The guards raised their truncheons again and again, bashing Osyen into the floor.

Anze lifted Thom back up again, turning him to face Osyen. "You see that, boy?" Anze whispered into his ear like a snake hiss. "I'm not sure how you and that cripple planned to make it down the street, let alone set fire to my transolar organization. But you will learn...what happens to people who threaten me."

He was making Thom watch. Making Thom watch as they pounded his brother into pulp on the deck.

Anze would kill them all. Thom had failed the test. He couldn't give them up, so Anze would simply kill them, until Thom had nowhere left to turn to, no family left.

Where else could he go? Where else could he run?

Osyen's grunts of pain were buried under the laughter of his men. Even Commander Isaac looked on with the smallest satisfaction cracking across his face, shaking his head in bemused disbelief.

This was it. They had nowhere to hide. No more favors. No more friends. No one to ask for help.

Thom raised one hand, blindly reaching, reaching out...for anything.

And he snagged what had to be Anze's wrist, still clamped hard to Thom's throat. The man's skin felt so dry and cold to the touch, like grabbing on to ice. And he heard the flow of water, ocean waves lapping upon a distant shore.

No...

No, Anze was flesh and blood like any person. This wasn't dry with a touch of oil or hair or tissue. He wasn't feeling skin and muscle and blood. He was feeling a...a pull, a sinking feeling, drawing down, down. It felt like...

The world pulsed like ripples on water. And when the water cleared, the metal walls and laboratory equipment and guards and his friends had all melted away. Instead, all around him was a helical aurora, wondrous purples and greens and sapphire blues. He couldn't hear his breath, but he could hear his blood pumping in his veins.

Wherever he had gone, Thom was no longer on Ilum. He was sure of that.

CHAPTER 37
OSYEN

THEY DIDN'T VANISH in a cloud of smoke, nor were they sucked into the dark by tendrils of black. They simply faded, translucent, ghostly—like for an instant they weren't properly real. And when they were gone, Osyen heard a pop as a small black marble clicked against the ground, skipping a few feet before coming to a stop against the wall.

Pilgrim Metal, coming to stillness, as the emerald candlelight within it winked out.

Everyone stared, confused. But Commander Isaac was able to compute a bit faster than the rest, pulling Osyen up by his throat. The Oskie's fingers burned, like pillars of magma.

"Ugh!" Osyen groaned. "You really like choking people!"

"What did he do?" Isaac asked, cold and calm.

Choking against the grip, Osyen only saw ol' Yellow Eyes glaring down at a little boy. "Go on..." he croaked. "Couldn't kill me before. Was just a boy."

"You're not a boy anymore."

"You would have better results—" The guards drew their sidearms, snapping up guns, and Isaac drew his own, all aiming towards the speaker.

Roche. He calmly stood outside of his cell, the cables that once harnessed him still idly swinging like vines in a jungle. He clutched Lily's core to his chest with his free hand, like he was cradling a pet, connecting one end of the core to his plug-hand.

He looked across the assembled guns like he had committed a mild faux pas at a state dinner. "...If you don't try to strangle the person you're speaking to."

"You can answer my question then," Isaac sneered. "What did that little rat do with the Master?"

"The Master?" Roche taunted. "My, you up and joined the club at record speed. But I suppose an Oskie would set land speed records in a number of fields. And here comes the silver fox, sweeping the gold medal for idiocy."

Isaac released the safety on the pistol, letting the threatening capacitor build up its deadly whine.

And Roche's eye implant glowed sapphire blue.

A hard thunk and the room was plunged into darkness, red emergency flood lighting painting the space. Isaac pulled the trigger, blasting a clean red beam through Roche's shoulder like a scalpel.

And the holographic image flickered, vanishing.

And Lily's booming voice came from the speakers above. "If you wish my captain harm, Commander Isaac, you will first have to contend with me."

The guards circled up, dropping into their training, one of them swiping a gloved hand across the ground to draw up a set of bricks as deployable cover.

Osyen almost laughed. Roche had broken out alright, but that right there had been an illusion. The same projector that showed the Commandant. And now, where was he? Nobody knew.

"Where are you, fat man?" Isaac taunted the empty air, echolocating.

"Fat man?" Roche's voice called from the shadows—or from the speakers. "You'll have to do better than that, Commander. I've survived children far more creative than you."

A dissatisfied sneer, Isaac let Osyen go—and the captain flopped hard to the ground, immediately seized with coughing and retching. Isaac stepped away from the cover, slinking noiselessly into the darkness.

"Don't you worry, Commander," Roche started.

And Lily finished his sentence. "We've got a little speedster of our own."

It all began with the clack of a lock.

And Zatia dashed from her cell, twitching and monstrous. The guards shouted and screamed as she blew her way through them. A blur of black and tan came vaulting over their deployed cover, right onto the first poor bastard she could reach—and smashing in his helmet against the ground with all of her weight.

It was like trying to track a panther in the dark.

The thrum of gauss discharges, the spark of metal on metal. That tangy smell of ozone that those things always put in the air.

But the smell of blood swiftly overpowered it. Osyen felt a warm spatter rain across his face when a guard flopped down in front of him, four jagged claw marks through his chest plate and into the soft meat below. His dead eyes stared vacant and Osyen just watched as the blood pool crept closer and closer to him. And when it finally reached his boots, the scrapping and sloshing and scraping around him finally fell silent.

And a single outstretched hand slipped into view. Osyen looked up to see...

Roche, with an arched brow of concern. "You alright there, Captain?"

Osyen nodded, taking the help up. "I've had worse."

"Yeah, that happens to be an object of some concern."

Adelaide poked her head out of her cell, and immediately shielded her eyes. "*Fra tow mi,* Zatia. It's like a paint shop out here."

Zatia stumbled into Osyen's view, swinging wildly from left to right and drenched in blood up to her elbows. She grumbled and gurgled some response, but not loud enough for him to make out.

Rashida stepped into view, horror on her face. But plenty of blood on her own hands. Magnus dangled from his restraints, limp and silent.

"Is he alive?" Osyen asked.

Exhausted, she looked back at the ghoul. But she nodded. "It's harder to keep hitting him when he stopped talking."

Osyen huffed. "I'll keep a better mind of my own chatter then."

She laughed, but her good humor faded as she looked over the room. "Where's Thom?"

Osyen's eyes drifted back to that little black marble, a stone not an inch across, hissing like it was building steam pressure. But no one else seemed to acknowledge it. "With Anze."

They hadn't seen it. They had no way of knowing. Hell, he didn't really even know what he'd seen. Was he delirious? Beaten, battered, and broken of all sanity?

Because that had looked an awful lot like a ship going through a Jump Point.

"Wherever they went is outside of Anze's electro-power range," Roche said. "These prison cells were built to hold people, not an AI with a wireless transmitter. But I can't imagine Lily's hacks would've been possible with him nearby."

Thom took Anze. And by doing so, created the moment Lily needed to free everyone with a simple and weak wireless hack. For the moment. Now it was up to the crew to save themselves.

And save Thom.

Zatia crumpled against the wall at Osyen's side, halfway between laughter and groaning in pain. What parts of her hands weren't covered in blood were painted in bruises. "No sign of Yellow Eyes. He really doesn't like to square up and fight."

"It's probably how he's lived so long," Roche theorized.

"Chicken-shit," she grunted, her head twitching so hard, Osyen could hear the bones in her neck pop and crackle.

"Oy, Zee, you copacetic?" Adelaide asked, snapping her bony fingers in front of her face to try and draw focus. But those could have been gunshots and Zatia wouldn't have reacted, a frosted and dazed look in her eye.

And her voice reduced to a grumble and mumble.

"She's going into stim-shock," Rashida said as she rooted through a dead guard's pack, pulling out gauze and water. "She needs an AutoDoc right now!"

Not really an ideal time for a full-blown deadly seizure, but Osyen couldn't complain. The girl had been dosed against her will—and that same cocktail had just broken them out. Didn't change the fact that she'd gone from whirling dervish to dead weight, and if they delayed too long? Maybe just dead.

Rashida set to work pouring water on the gauze and patting Zatia's forehead. "She's burning up!"

"Facility this big, there's gotta be Medical nearby," Osyen said. "Lily, where's the nearest AutoDoc?"

Roche's eye glowed blue but the voice came from the building's speaker system. "Apologies, Captain. I am tasked to capacity. I have precious little memory to dedicate to my efforts and I am engaged on all fronts with the City's Commandant AI. They are attempting to breach the facility and quarantine my invasion. It is all I can do to keep your room uncontested."

"We're about to have an entire planet crash down on our heads," Adelaide said gravely.

An entire planet, the Godfather, the Navy, the Clerics—Osyen straightened up and swiped a hand through his hair. It wouldn't be enough.

"Two teams," Osyen grunted as he stooped to collect one of the guard's handguns. "Roche, Rashida? Get Zee to a Medical station and get her stabilized. From there, the three of you are going to secure our ride out of here."

"There's a ride?" Roche asked.

"Hangar bay, same level, 'bout five hundred meters thataway. You'll know it when you see it." He turned to Adelaide. "We need to find Thom, but Lily can't help us with that city AI running havoc. Anything we can do about that?"

Adelaide smiled. "Thinking a bit more with your head than with your gut?"

"Just doing any thinking at all, really."

She nodded, proud and pleased. "Hard lines. It's an old building, that should work for us. Lily can cut the wireless receivers, but there'll be hard fiber built into the structure." She bent over, plucking a knife from a guard's chest rig. "We cut it off at our level, that'll keep the City Commandant from accessing local systems."

"That's our job today, you and me. Where can we find that cable?"

"I'll see what I can find out."

She turned to find the Nathaniel-bot poised with its hands up. "Can I possibly be of assistance to you?"

And Adelaide drove the knife into the bot's shoulder, digging to find the spot she wanted, and ripping the blade out—with what looked far too much like a silver piece of liver. The bot, having lost something terribly critical, whimpered and collapsed to the ground.

Rashida blinked, staring at the bundle of scrap on the floor. "Was that your husband?"

"Don't even start," Adelaide snapped like she hadn't just excised a robot organ in brutally Spartan fashion. She made her way through the sticky floors and scattered flesh over to the console by Diego's tube, grimacing when she got close enough to identify its contents. "Oh, *lovely*. This place is gross in all corners."

Osyen crouched down to Zatia, cupping her face in his hands. "You are the most beautiful little psychopath to ever have my back. You don't get to die today. We've still got to burn your dad's house down, you hear me?"

And Lord, if that girl didn't nod back to him.

Osyen stood up and gave a look at his ragtag crew. "Let's show 'em who we are!"

CHAPTER 38

ZATIA

THE WALLS LOOKED RADIOACTIVE, shifting, and glittering. Did things always look like this, behind all the boring, drab nothing? It was like everything was wrapped in a glow, a halo around every light, a blanket of warmth to keep back the cold.

She couldn't move her fingers. She couldn't move her eyes. And she could feel her heart beating out of tune. This wasn't a seizure. She was dying.

They had been running for some time. She'd heard some gunshots, some grunts of pain, but all she saw was those sparkling lights.

"Turn left up ahead," Lily said through Roche.

"Which left?!" Rashida grunted, with Zatia draped over a shoulder.

Zatia wished she could help, but it looked like the hallway had nothing but doors for miles and miles. And the doors were all bricking themselves up, hiding. And the wall at the far end was rushing in to greet them.

Rashida reached for a door.

"Not that one!" Lily and Roche barked in one voice.

"Well, be more specific!"

Roche ambled on ahead, grabbed the handle two doors down with the red cross painted above the frame. But the knob made an obnoxious honking sound at him.

Zatia wanted to giggle. It sounded like an angry goose.

Roche was far graver. "Lily, we're locked out. I need biometric access."

"Stand by."

Zatia could see that wall approaching, like a wave off the ocean ready to crash down on them. And the water always wanted to pull you down, down...

"Ah!" Rashida yelped as her feet sank into the floor, the blocks opening up underneath her.

"You see that too?" Zatia muttered.

Rashida tried to high-step her way out, dancing along a floor that voraciously snapped at her ankles. Roche, meanwhile, just sank further and further as the floor tried to swallow him whole. And it seemed to be choking on its meal.

"Lily," Roche said with some insistence.

And it was like the floor coughed in time with the door chiming a happy welcome. Roche hopped out of the gaping maw, pushing his door open, and let Rashida stumble in after him.

Into a much smaller room with another door. "Oh, come on!"

Zatia looked up at the roof to see a great big vent that tugged on her hair, pulling on her but too weak to take her. Some pipe else-where blew cold gases on her face before the second door chimed its welcome.

Medical Bays. They always had that familiar smell that stings the nose. Some people saw the eggshell white walls and caught that anti-septic scent and they just lost their pretty little minds.

The doctors here seemed very alarmed to see a patient. Some woman walking on the ceiling raced on over to Rashida, who was also standing on the ceiling—oops, no. Zatia was just hanging upside down in Rashida's arms. Easy mistake.

Oh. There was the nausea, as she tasted a bit of bile at the back of her throat like a frog trying to jump out of her mouth.

"She's in toxic shock!" Rashida tried to explain. "She's overdosed on something."

The nurse spoke and Zatia was sure that the words didn't quite sync up with the lip movements. Was she having double-vision or was this nurse a robot? "We're very sorry to hear that. Do you have your company ID card with you today?"

"No," Rashida said.

And the nurse went slack for a second, before extending one hand quite aggressively. Their voice was suddenly deep, deep, like the bottom of the ocean opened its mouth to command them. "Please surrender at this time. There is no further use in struggling."

The Commandant. She knew that voice. She remembered how it pulled the bricks around her like a smothering shroud.

And Roche placed one round tree trunk of a leg into the robo-nurse and shoved it so hard it rocketed across the room. The big guy had a bit of leverage in that frame. Before its servos could counter the high-speed thrust, it slammed into the far wall, shattering its head against the brickwork and popping out a bunch of circuit boards.

"Hey!" a technician shouted, muffled by his full-face respirator. "That's an expensive piece of—who are you?!"

"It spoke like a demon and tried to grab us," Rashida admonished the tech. ' What would any reasonable person do?"

But Roche was just staring at the robot and its pieces, clutching Lily's core to his chest. "People pay for broken things?"

"Not getting into it right now!" Rashida trudged into the heart of the medical bay, plopping Zatia down hard onto a bed. It felt like getting hit with a dense bit of cloud.

The voices were muffled now, arguing, as the plexiglass dome closed over her. She heard the misting of the antiseptic fog as the AutoDoc closed in around her. For a moment, she wondered if the Commandant would seize this too and smother her. Would Lily protect her?

Which is roughly when the machine drove four large-gauge needles into her arm. Two were giving her blood that sailed up her arm and into her heart like a cold mountain stream.

The other two were drawing out. And not slowly. She had felt vacuum suction on her fingers before and lost more than a few small screws down cleaning chutes. But she had never thought to imagine what that would feel like in her *cardiovascular system.*

She was instantly alert. The halos fell away, the warping of the walls. And the worst headache she'd ever felt hit her like a brick. Her skull felt like it shrank two sizes and her brain was not having its new accommodations.

Zatia sat upright with a shout, shoving the AutoDoc dome open and spilling the antiseptic fog out onto the floor. Rashida, Roche, and the technicians all jumped back away from her, not sure what to make of that sudden entrance.

She looked down at the needles in her arm, still cycling her body's entire bloodstream through the AutoDoc's innards at alarming velocity.

And she shivered. "Anybody got a fuzzy sweater?"

"You alright?" Rashida asked, immediately sweeping her shawl off and draping it over her friend.

"I think so. Hell of a cleanse," she said, holding her arm out for the AutoDoc to finish its work. She pointed at the nearby screen. "How much longer does it need?"

Rashida beat the tech to the monitor and read it off. "Another thirty seconds for the dialysis, then a minute for sterilization and bandaging."

They plugged her into a large artificial liver and just scrubbed every drop of blood. Wouldn't help with her withdrawal symptoms none, but it at least purged the stims from her system. "Then I guess I'll just sit here a minute."

The defensive tech gesticulated wildly in his hazmat onesie, breath fogging up his mask as he tried to wave them toward the door. "You have to leave the lab now!"

And Rashida and Roche shouted back in unison. "Oh, shut up!"

But Zatia's eye locked on what was behind them. The white coats in full respirator gear were working on samples of Pilgrim Metal. Drilling and cutting it to be precise, flecks and powder sailing in the air like fairy dust. Ventilation systems overhead were capturing a great deal but...

The tech wasn't for defensive. There were airborne particles. And they were the only ones without respirators.

"Maybe we should listen to the experts on this one." Zatia grabbed some gauze from under the Doc and slapped it over her arm as she deftly tugged the needles out of their place. The machine barked in annoyance, but they were always programmed not to resist too much, as that could cause further damage. And she had plenty of practice.

"You able to walk?" Rashida asked.

Zatia plopped off the table onto her feet, and her world tilted abruptly. She caught herself on the edge, feeling the hot blood trickle down her arm. "I mean, I wouldn't give myself a good rating or nothin'."

"There are foreign contaminants in your air stream," the tech warned. "You have to quarantine now or you'll breathe that out everywhere you go!"

Roche shook his head. "Yeah, mitigating circumstances: we're *not* doing that."

That Commandant spoke again, its voice thrumming so deeply the dust in the air trembled, like it was afraid. "You are commanded to surrender at this time. Resistance will prompt your summary execution."

"They really like to justify shooting somebody in the back, don't they?" Zatia grunted as she drew herself up to her full height.

The lab techs backed away from the trio like they held a bomb, but any vibration might set it off. The nearby technician didn't dare move at all, hands slowly rising up in surrender. He glanced at Rashida. "They're talking to you three, right?"

"Lily?" Rashida asked, leering at Roche. "Lily, you got this?"

Roche's implanted eye flickered blue, straining, weak. And then it flared, and Roche inhaled sharply. "They have achieved complete access."

Zatia jumped back onto the AutoDoc—just before the floor opened up underneath her and the machine. The bed lurched to one side, slipping into the artificial sinkhole. Rashida and Roche leapt forward, tumbling past their technician friend.

He was not so fortunate.

The smart bricks in the floor swirled in a whirlpool, alternating rows in opposing directions like the teeth of a drill bit. And the technician dropped straight down. His feet crushed first, spraying red and drawing a horrible scream. He reached up for Zatia, flailing hands for anything.

She reached back, snagging his wrist. "I got you!"

But the ground was motivated, and it drew him down, crunching and gurgling as it swallowed him up to his waist. Between the gloved hands of his hazmat suit and the sprays of blood, Zatia lost her grip on him, and down he went. The glass of his mask cracked, the plastic of his suit torn to bits, and the blood and bone reduced to a syrup.

The rest of the lab technicians fled to the other side of the lab, even as Rashida helped Roche up onto their tables. The walls, roof, and floor were lava—but the furniture was made of happy, solid steel or plastic. If they stayed on the furniture, they'd be okay.

Zatia heard the smart bricks sliding against one another. She turned to see a tendril of bricks stacking up, building at high speed straight out of the wall at her. For being made of individual blocks, it had a strangely fluid behavior, like an alien goo or a cloud.

And she knew it had no intent of taking her alive, or even in one piece.

Zatia gripped the side of the AutoDoc and leaned away from the tendril, dangling herself over the gnashing, grinding maw. Sensing the opportunity, that whirlpool shot two tentacles up at her like a sea monster. She got her feet against the side of the Doc and pushed off, throwing herself across the lab to another table.

She belly-flopped onto the surface, swiping both equipment and Pilgrim Metal onto the evil floor.

"Zee!" was the only warning she got, Rashida shouting her name.

So she pulled herself tight into a ball—in time to avoid the roof driving a tentacle down right into where her head used to be, punching a foot-wide hole into the table.

Move.

Zatia rolled to one side as the tentacle ripped lengthwise through the table and sheared it clean in half.

Lily! Zatia bounced over their comms. *Lily, help us out here!*

They've locked me out of systems and achieved complete control.

Lily, do something or we're all dead! Rashida screamed.

Attempting access through secondary and tertiary ports. Complete packet loss, no server response.

She looked back to see the AutoDoc had stopped sinking into the floor, the whirlpool itself starting to migrate across the floor toward them. The evil sky-computer might be able to make split-second decisions to kill them, but the bricks still had to take the time to execute the moves.

Zatia scrambled to get her feet under her and jumped again, as her new safe haven began to tip into the deadly circling grinder. *Lily, I'm running out of tables!*

I have no access. You must exit the room.

Sure, yes! Get out. The lab techs had all run out a door. Where did they go?

Oh.

There was a door on the far side of the room, but it was just finishing being bricked up. And a flat wall of hostile was rising up out of the floor like a tidal wave. It picked up tables and tossed material, rolling down the narrow room, ready to sweep them all into their imminent squishy death.

Lily! Rashida begged.

And the wave broke, vanishing into the ground. The gnashing, whirring death behind them went silent. And the tentacles melted back into the walls.

Zatia collapsed onto her table, hugging it to her chest. "Thank you, Lily," she said into the steel surface.

Much as I would like to accept your future worship, I am not responsible for this pleasant turn of events.

You're welcome, Adelaide said. *Cable is severed. The Commandant AI is officially out of the equation.*

Zatia patted the table, the good little safe table. The storm had passed, and Poseidon was silenced. The ground was now a pristine smooth surface again, despite having a fresh pink swirl to its color scheme, fragments of cloth and glass embedded in a few places. Which might be nicely artistic on its own merit, except for the nightmarish explanation of how they got there.

Roche hopped down to the floor with alarming confidence. "Very good. Thank you, Adelaide!"

Rashida just stared, wide-eyed, at Roche as he calmly walked around on the floor—which seemed to be extra tacky under his feet. He was just walking around on what used to be a man, on the very surface that ate him, with not a care in the world.

Roche approached Zatia, leaning over with some concern. "Are you alright?"

"Don't mind me," Zatia gasped face-first into her lifeboat. "I'm just going...just going to lay here a second. Then we can finish with the escaping, same-sa?"

CHAPTER 39
ADELAIDE

IT WAS ACTUALLY KIND OF neat to look at a fiber optic cable this large: a full-foot across, an amalgam of almost a thousand individual optical lines. It was like cracking open a geode and seeing the smooth dark shine of one side and the angry sputtering of lights on the other.

The Commandant was screaming into darkness, and she could see the visual representation of their orders failing to go anywhere.

Of course, behind every smart brick, every wall in the building, there was the original super-structure. They had built a scaffolding skeleton upon which everything was laid, a foundation for everything else.

And in that skeleton lay command nerves. And those nerve clusters could be severed by anybody with a knife and enough back strength. Such a tragic weakness, Adelaide thought with a chuckle. An eldritch nightmare that could be unplugged.

"Alright," Osyen said with some confidence, "that's one hurdle down."

Adelaide stood up, pocketing her knife. *Lily, can you scan the building for Thom?*

Not completely, they said, *but I can confirm that our Thom is not present on this level of Installation Zero One.*

Adelaide looked up at Osyen. He didn't seem entirely surprised by that revelation. And when he caught her staring, he averted his gaze. Lovely.

What about Anze? Rashida asked. *Any sign of him?*

The Godfather is not present at any level of Installation Zero One, Lily confirmed. *Additionally, Godfather forces seem to be disorganized in their threat response, with individual officers issuing contradictory orders.*

Adelaide chuffed at that. Every lord had their own fiefdom, but everyone believed themselves viable candidates for the throne. And with the King's unannounced absence...

Let them pull themselves apart, Osyen said. *Get to the Hangar Bay.*

I'm not leaving without Thomas, Rashida objected.

Me neither, but nobody's leaving without that ship. So get down there and get our new ride ready. I'll find him.

You better.

Adelaide looked up at Osyen again. "Want to try for your mother?"

And his face went sour. It hadn't entered his head until she'd said it. He could, but...

Lily? he asked. *Where is Yellow Eyes? Commander Isaac?*

His Entiglas came to life, and Osyen let it project up to the wall. There was a visual representation of the curved tower of Installation Zero One reaching out over Sunnyside. On one of the wider upper levels, there were two green dots. No explanation needed—that was the two teams.

One red dot, on the move.

He has detected the loss of the Commandant AI, Lily explained, *and the significant loss of the tactical advantage that allowed him. He had strictly been observing behavior, but he is now in high-speed intercept for the hangar bay.*

"He's going to the *Aurum*," Osyen said. "We've got to stop him."

Osyen was already running. He was always running everywhere. Adelaide grimaced as she took off after him. "With what? Harsh language?"

"I'm open to suggestions!"

They ran, boots beating on the metal grating. Adelaide couldn't help but glance at the backside of the smart-brick walls on either side of them. The thought of those same walls reaching out, choking, swallowing, rending flesh.

She hoped Zatia was okay. Because if she wasn't...

Adelaide would raze this whole building to the ground.

A voice from behind. "Stop right there!"

Adelaide just dropped to the ground, covering her head. Because Osyen turned, producing his stolen guard pistol. Not the fanciest thing, but still a gauss-powered system. He snapped two clean shots down the corridor back the way they came, the supersonic crack going over her head. At least one bullet sang off steel instead of sinking into muted tissue.

One body clanged against the floor behind her, the impact shaking Adelaide's boots. But his lucky friend shot back with something a helluva lot louder, rattling the steel grate under Adelaide's face even worse. And it fired fast, repeated gas-blowback that chambered shot after shot.

Combustion?! Black powder? That goon was shooting a cartridge-based weapon system? What was this, 2076?

The shots came ripping overhead, sparking off of the world around her and screaming in her ears. Osyen leaned against the wall, no cover to speak of—and she saw a shot whip through his right sleeve, passing through what would have been his arm, had there been anything there.

He didn't even notice as he tried shots three and four, with the fourth finally silencing the shooter. The extremely loud gunfire stopped with the man's fall.

Adelaide looked up at Osyen, and the smoking hole in his sleeve.

He stared back the way they came, hawkish, making sure the man stayed down. His gun hand trembled in the air, the barrel strafing side to side. "You alright?"

Adelaide grabbed her wrist, rubbing away the ache. "The last time I fell down that fast, I didn't get up so good."

"You could always lay there for a while," he said, "wait for someone who feels sorry for ya."

"Asshole." But she smiled.

———

They popped out of the wall near the top of the hangar bay, their skeletal walkway continuing out of the maintenance space and into the open air, suspended a full thirty feet from the ground. The automated cranes were busy below, whining and grinding as they churned through, unloading their cargo ships like nothing was going on. Automated processes which had not been modified.

But the crews, well, they were in full-blown panic. Some were running about like ants with a kicked nest. Others were in stand-offs, multiple ones, across the entire bay. Some rogue groups had tried to abscond with various valuable crates, while loyalists held them at gunpoint. Proper shouting and cursing was happening on all sides.

Rogues vs. Loyalists. God left the room for less than an hour, and they were at each other's throats.

With all of that going on, there was the *Aurum* itself. A crew of Rogues were mid-gunfight with some Loyalists, as the Rogues tried to fuel up and leave and the Loyalists were trying to stop the theft of a valuable asset of their Master.

Lily? Osyen bounced, *I don't see Isaac.*

He's here, Lily assured them, *but may be keeping a low profile with all of this chaos.*

"There!" Adelaide hissed pointing down below.

"You see him?" Osyen asked, raising his pistol.

"No, jackass, look!"

It was Zatia. The other team had casually made their way across the open battlefield. The Godfather's men were so preoccupied with each other that the threesome just walked right across the deck and had taken shelter behind some crates near the new *Aurum*.

Having deposited the two noncombatants in that relative safety, the reckless Zatia just calmly walked up behind the Loyalists' firing line.

The first guy to see her turned, trying to bring his rifle to bear— but she popped a knife from up her sleeve and took a knee right under his gun barrel to let him fire harmlessly overhead while she sliced up his gut with a quick one-two-three cycle that gave Adelaide heartburn The man crumpled, and if he made a sound, it wasn't loud enough to break through all of the existing shouting and gunfire.

As Zatia made her way down the line, Rashida and Roche moved up, getting closer to the *Aurum*.

Which is when Commander Isaac melted out of thin air, ground floor, a curious large rifle tucked to his shoulder, with three distinct barrels. And tracking right on Roche's exposed back.

Of course. Take a jockey, take the AI—take away escape.

Osyen saw it, raising his pistol, but he'd never have time to make the shot. And from this range? At an Oskie?

Lily! Adelaide called out. *Lock him down!*

The Oskie squeezed the trigger—but the red light that spat from the center barrel went awry as the ground swallowed his ankle. It tipped him backwards, sweeping his shot far too high, scoring the first of many new carbon scars on the *Aurum*'s hull.

Isaac looked down at his ankle with irritation. And he kicked, shattering the bricks in one move.

"Oh shit," Adelaide muttered, shifting to the radio. *Everybody, you gotta go-go-go!*

Osyen took a knee and braced himself against the railing, popping off shots at the Oskie. Isaac sneered up at him, not even dodging the bullets that rained around him. Osyen wasn't placing them on target anyhow. Isaac would know if one ever was.

Instead, Isaac turned back to the *Aurum*. And in the blink of an eye, the rifle was up on his shoulder—to find a wall punching up under the barrel, ripping the gun from his hands.

A face pressed out of the brickwork, with a stylish mustache and pigtails and a threatening thunder. "You shall not touch them!"

Isaac cocked his head at that curiosity, and simply rolled to the right, snagging the rifle off of the ground before Lily could consume it. He tumbled along to avoid Lily's attacks and mid tumble, he fired.

But bricks rose up around Roche, forming a kind of bunker tunnel to shield him from fire all the way up to the *Aurum*'s dock.

Frustrated, Isaac toggled something on his rifle—trading from laser to the two-high caliber Gauss chambers. He fired one then the other on either side, punching holes through the bricks big enough to crawl through.

"An anti-tank rifle?!" Osyen shouted. "That's just cheating!"

Adelaide watched as Isaac broke open the breach of his rifle, palming two more metallic slugs into place, each bigger around than her thumb!

If he was reloading, he had to think he'd need them. Roche and the others had to be okay. But their cover meant nothing with that rifle in play.

Lily, what do you need me to do? Adelaide asked.

Look after Osyen, Lily said, *before he does something foolish.*

Understood. Adelaide looked over to see...Osyen was already at a full sprint, all of his broken pieces running all the catwalk to get closer to Isaac. "Of course," Adelaide cursed under her breath, rushing off after him.

Isaac heard them coming easily, turning over to take aim. But Lily lashed out with multiple tendrils of smart bricks. Isaac flipped up to his feet, sliding away like a dancer.

This was an old Oskie, a master of his craft, even if he had gotten a step slower in age and never quite the competitor with kids and their new implants. Each step left that telltale trail of yellow haze, the glow of his implants tracing through the air as he moved faster than the eye could follow.

Bringing that rifle up again, he deftly sniped away three of Lily's tendrils—before toggling over and blasting a slug up to the catwalk. The thick metal seared past Osyen's head and clean through the catwalk support, like it was made of suggestions. The ground quaked underneath Adelaide's feet, and she slid to a stop. Any undue stress and the whole thing might collapse.

Osyen wasn't as observant. "Hah!" He cackled at the old Oskie.

But Isaac didn't even give him a second look. Osyen took the step —and the catwalk ripped free of the roof. It was thirty feet to the ground, with nothing but steel grating to cushion their landing.

Lily raised the floor in a kind of ramp, meeting them halfway. They hit hard, tumbling and sliding down to the safety of the stillness.

And Adelaide felt something in her left hip snap, pain searing up her back and side.

The other half of the catwalk slammed hard into Roche's bunker-tunnel, shattering it—and blocking his access to the *Aurum*, locking him out with rubble.

Osyen and Adelaide hadn't been the intended target. He was trying to keep Roche out of the ship.

A weapon leveled down at her head, the shuffle of a hand reseating itself nicely on the grip. Isaac? No, just some enterprising Godfather goon trying to be a hero. Just one of many Loyalists and Rogues swarming that crumpled bit of catwalk, happy to work together against their common enemy. They had circled up, two factions on either side, unwilling to get too close to Osyen or Adelaide.

Adelaide looked up at her executioner with an exasperated sigh. If the cigarettes didn't kill her, she always figured one of the Godfather's triggers would. She lifted her head up, best she could muster, pressing her temple against the barrel, and closed her eyes.

Finger squeezed. Trigger clicked. And the hum of batteries—

Rashida sailed in, leading with her knee into his jaw. The gun went skittering away, and the man fell with a very disturbing stiffness to him, like his body had seized up before the power had been cut. He might very well have been dead, but he was at the very least not getting up.

He hadn't even hit the ground when the entire circle opened fire on Rashida. But a dome of bricks shot up around her, shielding her from all directions. Lily's horrid little face popped out of the cardinal corners, roaring back at the firing line.

And the gunfire stopped for a perplexed second, with one goon muttering aloud: "What the fuck?"

Which was all Zatia needed, drenched in blood and knives in both hands. She slipped between the next nearest two, slashing the back of their knees. As they went down, she turned and threw both blades into their throats.

And the firestorm began. Rashida leapt from her cover like she was rocket-propelled—Lily literally threw her out with a springboard! And Rashida used the momentum to hurtle into her next target.

The duo of Zatia and Rashida worked their way around the periphery, taking turns bashing in kneecaps and skulls in a demented ballet. Adelaide could swear she heard music as Rashida would cup her arm around Zatia's waist to hurl the young girl at the next goon in line, and Zatia would kneel to clear the way for Rashida to come in swinging. And every shot that rained in was soaked by the moving wall of bricks that walked around with the Valkyrie duo, Lily roaring back in unsettling fashion every so often.

And when the gunfire stopped and that acrid stench of ozone had finally saturated the air, the duo stood tall, scuffed and bloody and bruised. Rashida wiped her mouth, only smearing more muck on her perfect face.

Zatia laughed, giving her friend a good-hearted punch to the shoulder, to a muted "ow" from Rashida.

One last goon stumbled up, gun raised. "*Fra tow ni laska,* bitches!"

He reared back like he was going to punch the bullets out of his gun—only to be sucked into the ground under his feet with a vicious grinding sound, wet and frothy. But his cries were silenced by a single shot.

Adelaide looked over to see Osyen, still laying on his back on the catwalk, smoking gun. He'd spared the goon any more of the horrific end Lily had selected.

He looked at Adelaide, chuckling and collapsing backwards against the metal grating like it was a couch. "My back really hurts."

"Your back?" Adelaide shook her head with a smile. "Lily told me to take care of you, they did."

"Oh yeah," he asked. "How's that going?"

"I'm too old to be following you around, that's what."

CHAPTER 40
ROCHE

THE OSKIE HAD DROPPED a cage of twisted metal in front of the only hatch to board the *Aurum*. Clever bastard.

A patter of thumps rolled overhead. Too quiet to be gunshots but too loud to be far off. Footsteps? He clutched Lily's fragile, dented core close.

The ship is hooked up for refueling, right?

That is correct, they confirmed.

So you have access?

Only tertiary systems. Navigation has not yet been activated, but the reactor is in power idle.

Right, Roche said, *those open hard points? Would those accept a payload right now?*

The core vibrated in his hand, almost pleased. *Why Roche, you most devious of folk.*

The very thought of it felt immoral, to arm a civilian vessel. But it's not like the Empire was going to give them a ticket or seize the ship if they were ever spotted again.

Do it.

Which is when Isaac leapt into view, feet planted into the other side of the catwalk that gated him off. And the Oskie jammed his rifle into place, aimed right for Roche's head.

But Roche found his head jerked aside, the blast cutting through the air right by his ear. It felt like someone had clocked him with a bat, yanking him against his will.

Lily.

A free wall of bricks leapt up, blocking that point of access. And he heard the feet clop along the roof above him.

Apologies, Lily said, *but you were going to get us both killed.*

He wasn't going to complain about anything but the whiplash. They needed to get inside the *Aurum* and lock this bastard outside, or Isaac was going to pick them apart. *The shuttle dock! Lily, is there anything docked to the shuttle port?*

Not at this time, Lily said. *Bare hatch is twenty meters aft.*

Get me there!

The wall to his left pressed out at the command, greeting him with more tunnel that curved around some unseen blockage, before bending upward to the meet the hull. He had cover all the way to his destination now.

But he didn't dare move. The Oskie had demonstrated quite effectively that these bricks were more akin to leaves than cinder blocks.

The Oskie was above, listening, waiting. With all the noise outside, it was probably hard to pin down a heartbeat or breathing, but a footstep? Running? Isaac would blow a hole clean through whatever stood in his way, perhaps using the bricks themselves to kill Roche.

No choice. No other choice. He took a deep breath—

—far too deep. The Oskie punched a hand clean through the roof of the tunnel, snagging Roche by the collar. And with the impossible strength of an Oskie, he yanked upward, slamming Roche into the bricks headfirst.

The first hit dazed him, pounding him against the polymer bricks like a hammer to a nail. His hand twitched open, and he felt the cool metal of Lily's core slip from his fingers. That friendly steel ball hung in the air for a second before falling out of reach and clattering against the hangar deck.

The second hit shut down his eye implant, knocking some connector loose. And the tunnel itself seemed to quiver, stumble, shake. Lily was losing their own focus with each subsequent hit to the rental space they occupied in Roche's head.

The bricks tightened in around the Oskie's hand, squeezing, pinching. Roche could hear the Oskie groaning against the pain as he yanked up, slamming Roche into the roof a third time—and the bricks shaved something off of the Oskie's wrist as payment, showering Roche in an unpleasant confetti.

Pop-pop-pop! Gunshots came sailing in. The Oskie dropped Roche, and he fell flat forward onto his face. The ground was so soft now, so kind. Sounds of battle outside, muffled by the tunnel.

Blood pooled into view, sliding in front of his eye.

"Roche, run!" somebody shouted at him.

*I can't...*Roche grunted, *I can't even...*

His hands didn't respond. Everything was so heavy, so dizzying.

Oh, fine! Lily exploded. And Roche's hand snapped up, planting his palm on the deck. His wrist extended, lifting his body up like a jack. And one knee slid under him, then the other. His back straightened up like a lever being thrown. *You're up. Now run!*

Roche snagged Lily's core off the ground, and staggered down the tunnel. It wasn't far. Twenty meters. But twenty meters had never felt so far away. Maybe it was the tunnel that made each step feel like it actually took two or three?

A shot punched in, raining brickwork and filling the space with a momentary flash of light before Lily could patch the hole. Then another. Roche heard something whistle past his ear, bullet or shrapnel. After all, the bullet trajectory was deflecting with the curvature of the tunnel, but it was still sending chunks of polymer in at him like flechette.

He turned right and found himself butting up against the hull of the bare shuttle hatch. As he approached, the door opened for him, and he practically fell inside. He tucked his legs in, getting the rest of him over the threshold, in time for the doors to slam shut behind him —and for a blast of laser red to score the exterior door.

Lily, that door will hold, right?

The Aurum *is rated for up to ten atmospheres of pressure per square inch, but that rifle is outputting quite a bit more than that.*

Right. So he had to get away from the door, even as Lily proceeded to brick up the entrance behind him.

Stepping on to this ugly chrome photocopy of his old home was almost insulting. There was no artistic offense greater than the phrase 'resale value.' Blank canvas appealed to no one, and to please everyone, the factory tried to ensure that any living thing felt at ease inside—assuring that nobody felt at ease. But it made for a very bright interior, that was for certain. Dazzling, in fact, to the point of confusion.

Despite being larger, everything looking quite familiar. An opposing shuttle hatch on the opposite side of the ship, with the impressive cargo bay barren down below him. "Lily," he said aloud, hearing his voice bounce off every surface. "Which way to the Jump Deck?"

Lily's voice murmured from the core in his hands. "This ship is bigger, but ergonomics have not changed. Proceed forward to find the AI socket."

He jogged, up stairs and down hallways, everything so familiar yet stretched and metallic and wrong. But he passed the galley and up beyond the crew quarters—now more than double the number of doors.

Until they came to the Jump Deck. Spacious by comparison, a third seat now added. But while a variant, it was still familiar. He bent over the panel on the floor, center of the deck, and flipped open the AI socket: ready and waiting.

Roche settled Lily's dented and scuffed container into place, quickly placing the necessary cables. And the deck immediately came to life with blue light, swirling pixels and wisps of holographic cloud. Until Lily's head took shape before him.

They yawned and stretched, smiling. "My, oh my, I have missed this."

"Lily, give me exterior cameras!"

The walls melted away as holographic projectors displayed the hangar bay around them. Already patches of the exterior cameras had gone dark with damage or were simply covered by fallen debris. Fire sprinkled throughout the hangar deck, rampant destruction. It looked like a bomb had gone off, with one cargo truck ablaze and another smoldering.

And Roche turned those cameras on just in time to see the Oskie hurling Osyen against the hull of the *Aurum*. The captain was already a broken man going into this moment, and now the Oskie was about to reduce him to a paste.

Zatia swept in with her knives—and the Oskie blink-stepped behind her and backhanded the girl into the ground. Glowing yellow with each careful motion, Isaac moved with purpose as he beat Zatia down for the crime of trying to move again.

"L-Lily!" Roche stammered. "Get those guns loaded!"

"Cranes in operation," Lily said, "but there is an obstruction. Working to clear it."

Roche looked to the far side of the hangar, where two cranes happily worked away at the hull, despite the hellfire that burned around them. A shot had partially slagged one of them, but they diligently turned bolts on a cannon twice the size of a car, affixing it to the *Aurum*.

They weren't going to win a fistfight with this guy. Roche had to give the fight a whole other tenor.

The Oskie looked down at Zatia, who was struggling to get up, wavering like a branch in the wind. And almost dismissively, he roundhouse kicked her back to the ground, the floor bowing to cushion her impact. Tendrils punched up to defend her—and he broke them each with specific blows, shattering the bricks. Each brick was a small computer-controlled block and if there was no computer to receive orders, they simply fell apart.

Zatia spat blood up at Isaac. And Isaac sighed, lifting a foot, ready to slam it down through her chest.

"Leave her alone!" Osyen shouted from the front of the *Aurum*. "I'm the one you want!"

"So bizarre," Isaac tutted, "to think that I have ever given you a second thought."

Osyen peeled himself off of the hull—and the Oskie was immediately on him, planting a rapid-fire set of punches to his head and tossing him in front of the *Aurum*.

"You'll tell me where your friend is! You'll tell me where he took the Master. Or I will pull the answers I want from your bones!"

The ground opened up, gnashing teeth. But Isaac treated that maw like a suggestion. He bounded through its grasp and barreled undeterred into Osyen, hurling him forward like he was throwing out trash. The one-armed punching bag skipped along the pavement, slamming into the back wall of the hangar.

Osyen blinked, focusing, looking up at the *Aurum*. His eyes settling on the work being done on the far side of the ship.

That what I think it is, Roche? Osyen asked.

Ready to blast him to kingdom come, Roche said. Maybe, if the Oskie didn't know that was happening? Get him positioned right and drop a half-ton tungsten shell into his face.

When I get him up here, pull that trigger. No excuses.

Captain! Lily contested.

Just do it!

But—that would…If he hit the Oskie, he'd certainly hit Osyen. With a ship-mounted ballistic cannon capable of blowing apart small starships? The kinetic impact alone would be like setting off a bomb right next to them.

Lily swept in front of Roche, blocking his view. *You can't!*

He blinked, short of breath. "If you think I shouldn't…then stop me."

They weren't ordering him. They were begging him.

Their face glitched and the body broke down into the floor. And their voice was just so beaten and hollow. *I know.*

Roche swallowed hard. *Understood, boss. Give 'em Hell.*

Osyen put his hand into the ground and pushed, giving a shout to will himself into standing. The Oskie heard the battle cry of a beaten man and turned to see what Osyen had left in him. The captain drew himself up as straight as his broken body allowed.

"Look at what your hate has cost you, Brogan." Isaac pointed at all the destruction, at Zatia crumpled on the ground, at Rashida cradling Adelaide. "Look at what it has bought you. You could have been free!"

"I didn't want to be free," Osyen grunted, wiping the blood from his lip. "I wanted my family."

Isaac took a few pointed steps forward, chatting—the yellow glow fading out and cooling, the sizzle crackling at his extremities. He was stalling, letting his implants relax a second.

Before he finished the job.

But his voice was almost respectful, hushed. "What have they ever done for you?"

Osyen looked at them all, and silently said his goodbye, before looking back at Isaac. "They made me proud. Anze? He made you into a pet."

Isaac cocked his head, confused. And Osyen barked softly, two taunting woofs.

The Oskie huffed—and blink-stepped over to Osyen, snagging him around the throat. And he leaned in, whispering something.

Now, Roche! Shoot him!

The bolts weren't seated, but the gun was connected, ammo belted in. A crosshair came up into Roche's heads-up display, and the gun groaned as it canted onto target, clicking and clacking into lock.

The Oskie heard it, looking back at the ship, gripping Osyen in his hands. They wouldn't dare.

A tear trickled down Roche's face. "Dodge this."

// Weapon Group Alpha-1, Chain Fire. Confirm. Guns-Guns-Guns.

The concussive blast of the cannon going off blew out almost every fire in the hangar, and the shock wave blew visible contrails over most every rough surface. Roche immediately lost sight of the Oskie, but the shot sailed right on through to the back wall, blowing out an enormous chunk of the building.

Roche sat back in his chair as the dust cleared. *Osyen? Osyen, can you hear me?*

No response. No Oskie either. But the bricks of the wall crumbled and flaked off, revealing the enormous laboratory beyond...

And at the center of it was a single floating orb of Pilgrim Metal. It was neither suspended nor supported by chain or pillar. It simply hovered in space there. Dozens of scanners and scopes were aimed at it, collecting data from it.

They had built Installation Zero One around this, reaching up to circle this curiosity, to study it and hide it from view. This was the great secret at the heart of Anze's world.

And Roche had just shot it with a gun that could've blown up most modern spacefaring vessels.

There wasn't a mark on it.

CHAPTER 41
OSYEN

ALL THINGS CONSIDERED, waking up was a positive result. Breathing hurt, his head rang, and his legs didn't seem to want to do much of anything. It was like his blood was on fire and made of sludge at the same time, pumping through his head and fingers and chest with a viscous fury. But he was awake.

He turned over, looking up at the ceiling raining powder and brick down on him. A sinister green glow filled the air, uneven and warping, like the light was below some watery surface.

What had happened? He remembered...he remembered the cannon. And then Isaac moved, pulling him...pulling him aside?

He couldn't sit up. And Osyen found that he couldn't roll over, at least not a second time. So he just laid there and listened to the racket of his breathing, the strain and wheeze of it.

Something was near. Calling. Its cold pull, dangling his feet in the ocean depths.

Jump.

Osyen looked up overhead, behind him, where an enormous orb hung in the air. There was some kind of beveling to its surface, an immaculate pattern, like drawing the swirling clouds of nebula in deep space. Green clouds of energy crackling within, swimming from one end to the next. The whole thing was subtly shaking, vibrating to a consistent frequency, like it had been struck with a tuning fork.

It looked like...like the Icon, but on a grand scale. Ten meters wide and hovering without obvious aid. What was this thing?

The collar of Osyen's jacket crumpled, and two hands materialized from the air. The fingers were soaked with fresh blood, smearing the red and black across Osyen's coat. The Oskie's active camouflage had broken once he touched Osyen, but the split lip and the nasty gash to his forehead revealed some of the more intricate augmentation underneath.

"You only ever thought of yourself!" Isaac snarled, swinging Osyen up through the air and down onto a tabletop, smashing glass and instruments underneath him. His gut seized and kicked out whatever air was in his chest.

"He saw to all your needs," Isaac screamed into Osyen's face. "He saw to *all* of *their* needs. And now look what you've done!"

Osyen groaned in pain, feeling the glass shards that stuck through his jacket and into his back.

So Isaac leaned in close. "You will tell me: what have you done with the Master?"

"I know what it's like..." Osyen gasped, "...to lose someone."

Furious at that, Isaac dragged Osyen along the desk, sweeping further tools and instruments off.

"Do you know what we were doing here? The facility, this work?" Isaac asked, gesturing to all the materials and tools, and up to the giant orb. "We were investigating something beautiful. Something incredible. Something challenged everything we thought we knew about the Pilgrim, about ourselves!"

"We?" Osyen choked out. "Teach a lot of quantum physics at Holkstad, do they?"

"We were doing wonders. *He* was doing wonders! What have you done with him?"

"Wherever he is," Osyen sputtered, "I hope he's dead."

And the rage on Isaac's face drew to a kind of still, like the white-water rapids of the river had finally flowed into a place of calm reflection. And he reached across Osyen's front, snagging a shard of Pilgrim Metal off the table. "We found this—and thousands like it—in that dig site beneath Sunset. We don't know what it is. What it's for."

Isaac lowered the shard of obsidian void over Osyen's neck, the tip of it kissing his skin—and Osyen instantly felt cold sap from his fingers to his toes. "You'll break before it does." Osyen tried to speak, but Isaac just shushed him. "It's alright, little one. No need for tears. Your mother would be ashamed."

His mother. Whatever went across Osyen's face, Isaac seemed to relish that reaction. He leaned in. "This place? This was her sanctuary. And in your selfish greed, you have destroyed her world for the second time."

And Rashida came in swinging, a bit of rebar in her hand. Osyen never saw the Oskie move, but his hand was suddenly wrapped around Rashida's wrist, holding her up in the air. And he snapped his other hand to her side. And in doing so, Isaac drove the shard into her gut.

"No," Osyen whimpered.

Rashida's eyes went wide, staring into the Oskie. He didn't say anything, just scoffed at her. Before pulling the shard out, and letting it fall.

Osyen reached for it, but the shard skipped and clicked to the ground, painting imprints of her blood on the floor. Out of reach.

Isaac considered his captive for a moment as blood surged from her open wound. His lip curled in disgust at her before lurching her up into the air, letting her blood drain down her leg and pool on the floor. Rashida's feet kicked and kicked as she clawed at his fingers to no avail. Her voice croaked and scraped, no air to push past it. His fingers clenched on her throat.

And Isaac leered down at Osyen. "Some things take a great deal of effort to break. Iron wills. Or solid bodies." And he looked back at Rashida. "But others? Well, they break like glass, don't they?"

"Let her go," Osyen gasped.

"Tell me where the Master is, and maybe I help her."

Osyen saw his hand on her throat, those burning hot fingers that seared his own. And the voice of a scared little boy came out of his mouth. "I'm sorry."

Isaac blinked, listening to that voice.

So Osyen said it again, tears tumbling down his face. "I'm sorry, please. It's my fault. She wouldn't be here if not—none of them would be here. It's my fault. Don't hurt them."

"But she *is* here," Isaac cooed, a green glow lighting up his face. "And it *is* your fault."

Rashida hung loose in his hand. Was she alive? Had she just passed out? Her skin pallid gray, eyes closed. Isaac watched Osyen as he processed the paleness starting to creep into his friend's face.

"Osyen!"

Whoever was stupid enough to—Professor Charles Ordee. The old professor was crouched nearby, whispering as loudly as he dared, which was far too loud to escape the notice of the Oskie. The old scholar reached out with one hand, batting the Pilgrim shard over into Osyen's grasp.

And just as soon as he had, Isaac came flying in, cracking the professor across the head so hard that his skull simply caved in.

But Osyen's hand closed around the shard—and he thrust it up into Isaac's exposed back, digging it in deep. And on contact, the shard seemed to crack and crunch, the tiniest flash of light releasing, before a force bounced Isaac away from him.

Isaac slid a few feet along the ground, never once losing his balance, carving a small trench in the powder of building materials that had rained around them. He reached backward to feel what Osyen had done, assessing the damage. And he actually laughed, that green light flickering over his face like light through aquarium water.

Ripples on a pond, brighter and faster.

Until that glow flashed, and Commander Isaac stopped with a twitch. A single bead of sweat slipped down his forehead and along his nose. And he reached back at his wound again. First, nothing. But then he started flailing at it, little blurs of hyperspeed motion.

Blackened flesh began to creep up from under Isaac's collar, like all the moisture was freezing up, his flesh withering and crunching. Isaac let loose one raspy cry before his throat was claimed by the black. The skin cracked and snapped—and with a flash of green light —his body splintered, dozens of individual fragments slipping out of his uniform and crashing to the ground.

When the body came to stillness, just a pile of frozen chunky black and red crystals...there sat the Pilgrim shard, everlasting, a happy aquamarine light dancing just under the surface.

Alive.

Awake.

"Osyen?" The voice, a raspy and injured voice. Osyen rolled his head over to see Rashida, hand clutched to her gut. Conscious and in bad shape.

But she was far more worried about him. Her eyes downcast toward his hand. She had a serious puncture to her gut, and she was so anxious about—

The cold. The call. The urge to Jump. Pumping through his veins.

Osyen looked down at the half dozen tiny pricks, individual bits of Metal shards still stuck in his palm. And the blackened haze that began to spread.

CHAPTER 42
ANZE

WHAT A CURIOSITY. It wasn't all that different from zero gravity. Yet without a ground or a down, he still felt like he was on his knees. And when he went to press himself to standing, that sense of vertigo simply vanished. There was nothing he could see or orient himself to that had changed, but the tiny bones in the inner ear told him he was upright.

But what did that even mean here? It wasn't black or dark, per se. It was more akin to nothing. A lack of something, an absence.

Thom stood at his shoulder—no, he was a good ten meters away. But as soon as Anze had laid eyes on the boy, Thom was suddenly lurched closer, but no force imparted, no billowing of hair or cloth.

The boy tilted his head as he studied the band of light that wrapped around the horizon, the technicolor aurora that was painted to the sky in soft strokes of oil to canvas. His hand was curled like he was about to reach out for it, grab that ribbon, and coil it about his wrist.

For indeed, some verdant green light was still tickling the tips of the boy's fingers.

"Where have you taken us?" Anze asked.

Thom whirled about, eyes darting. "Me?"

"Boy, I control electrons. Not astrophysics! You just Jumped us without a ship or a drive! Where are we now?"

"No idea. I only just woke up."

Anze's eyes tracked on to the bit of red trickling down Thom's neck. He drew his handkerchief from his chest pocket, reaching out. "You're bleeding."

And Thom jerked away from him.

"Thomas," Anze scoffed, incredulous, "if we're going to work together—"

"Have you been hit in the head?" Thom snapped. "Like, is some part of your brain just scrambled egg? Do you not remember *why* I'm bleeding?!"

"I'm concerned."

"You weren't that concerned when you ripped an implant out of me, were you?!" And it would have been cute, if Anze hadn't heard that voice echo from all around him, bouncing from and emanating from unseen surfaces, all at once a thunder and a whisper and a curse and a blessing.

This young man spoke and somewhere, monuments were erected to his might.

Thom heard it too, his eyes scanning for wherever that force came from. He couldn't quite believe his own gravity.

"This is the Path," Anze whispered, with holy reverence. "We're standing on the Path, aren't we? The Sojourn? The first steps of the Gnostic afterlife."

"I don't know," Thom said, looking back at the auroras. "To me? It looks like the inside of a black hole."

"Accretion disk from a nearby star." Anze considered the possibility, bobbing his head back and forth. "Well, I hope you didn't destroy the entire planet taking us here!"

"I didn't."

"You're very sure of yourself," Anze said with a smile.

But Thom didn't reflect that mirth. His fist tightened around that verdant sparkling cloud, like he had a grip on the strings of the universe. He squinted at something, waving his hand like to disperse a fine mist. Watching something.

And it was in that moment that a swell came to Thom's chest and a rage infused behind his eyes.

Someone shouted, a distant voice that carried to them like the whispering of a wraith. Anze looked all around, high and low, but it was just more void and more glittering aurora.

"Did you hear that?"

"Yeah," Thom said, lip curled with hate and eyes full of intent. "Sounded like trouble."

The sound grew ever louder, that memory...so rich, he could practically taste the smoke, feel the comfort of the fire, and hear the snap of the wood on the hearth.

Thom waved his hand in front of him again, conjuring a small shard of glass.

"What is that?" Anze demanded.

But Thom didn't answer, studying the reflection in it. He turned it over to study the other side, then turned it over again. He blinked, as if surprised by what he found. Surprised, but gaining confidence.

"Felix?" Thom asked. "Your name is Felix?"

Now how did he know that? What had he seen in that glass? No, perhaps that snake Rashida had told him, dripping poison in the boy's ears over the many months. She'd said the name before, and she likely had retold many an ill-favored tale she herself had heard only from ill-favored folk.

"I've had many names," Anze dismissed, flippant. "But at the moment?"

"No." Thom shut him down. "Your name is Felix Marchand, member of the House of Dunsweir."

Anze smiled, as the smell of the fire grew to fill his nose like it was trying to smother him. "It seems polite in a civilized society to use the name a man gives you, doesn't it?"

"Yes, it does," Thom conceded with a pause, "but you never

stopped carrying Felix with you. Osyen isn't Brogan anymore. But you...you never really put those scars down, did you?"

And like he had summoned it, the veils parted, and a large pane of murky glass slid in front of Anze. But through that glass he saw something...well, it would be a tad off-color to call it 'impossible' given where he was currently standing and how he got here.

But Anze saw a little boy sitting in his father's study. The rascal sat in a high-backed chair far too big for him, leafing through a book. He turned each page with reckless abandon, lost in whatever story was within.

Then Father stormed in, snatching the book from the boy's hands. His only crime had been curiosity, interrogation of his world. But the father knew the value of bound paper and parchment, and the boy could have foolishly damaged something he didn't understand.

The father went to strike the boy—the little boy screamed, peering up at the abuse about to fall.

Violence. That's how Father talked to all of his children.

Make him stop, Anze. Teach him about real violence. Show Father what it means when the boy grows up.

"What are you doing?" Thom asked.

"The right thing," Anze hissed.

And Anze reached out further, digging in...and he found the smallest grip on something there. Thom watched with apprehension as Anze roared, calling to the electricity in the walls of Dunsweir, pulling with every bit of Gnostic mastery he had. Stretched fingers urging those distant electrons to one task: help that child.

All he did was make the lights flicker.

But the blow never fell. Instead, the father looked high and low for what had caused that power surge. Until his eyes settled on the boy. That father looked down at his child—and then he looked up into the glass, directly at Anze, searching for something that he knew to be there.

Of course. Anze remembered what he was looking at. Father had looked up to the mantle where a shard of Pilgrim Metal had sat, one of many such curios. Just a relic of something under glass.

Right now, Thom and he were looking through that Metal. Each one, portals to moments in time.

Thom let out a breath he had been holding in. "That was you. In the Dunsweir manor. The first instance of your power manifesting itself in front of your family."

Anze looked down at his hands. "But I...but *I* did that. Just now, I felt it. Not that boy. The boy didn't do that, I—"

"That boy is you," Thom urged. "Don't talk like you don't recognize the exact time and place."

No. No, it wasn't possible.

"They suspected you were Touched back then, because *you* are Touched. Right here, right now." And Thom sighed, relaxing, as the moment broke for him. He spoke so soft, almost apologetic. "All because I brought you here. Because I showed you that. You have your power because...you looked backward in time. And gave it to yourself."

How could that be possible? Anze had always had this power, but never given it. He had never been allowed to...

Of course. Right there, flexing his power through the Metal into the past and directly at his young self. The Metal had activated, radiated—and a young boy had been cursed. Anze cursed himself, gave himself the strength to fight back, the very strength his family saw as a threat.

"Your power was never given by the Pilgrim," Thom said. "You're a closed loop. You made yourself."

And Anze chuckled, shaking his head. No. No, Thom did this. Did this *to him*. Decades of isolation, and here was the sole person responsible.

Thom wasn't entertaining that thought, lest he have to accept some responsibility for it. Instead, Thom moved right on to the easier target. He started grabbing shards of glass from thin air, like a man perusing news clippings, skimming an entire history for whatever leapt out to him. "Your father was always abusive. But that moment in the study: that was really when it began for you, wasn't it?"

How dare he speak of things he didn't understand. No matter what he was seeing in these shards, he had no idea of the complexity of things.

Anze snarled, stomping away from that memory. He'd rather march into darkness forever than stay another moment in that horrid study.

But Thom threw his arms wide open. "You wanted a partnership! You wanted to see what I could do! Well, *here we are!*"

"We don't have time for this."

"You don't have patience for this," Thom corrected. "Near as I can tell, we have all the time in history. Want to see your first kiss?"

"Could always take a trip back and listen to your father's neck snap," Anze growled.

That sentence seemed to darken the world. Vibrant colors that were once pastel and comforting drew down in contrast until they were rich and heavy. And Thom scowled back at him. "Be careful, Anze."

"Oh, I'm sure you'd have let him live after everything he did," Anze said with a dismissive wave of his hand. "Caught between torment and being ignored. I'm sure you'd do anything for your father's attentions."

Thom was quick. "You did everything for *your* father's affection, but did you get it?"

Anze huffed and turned away—to find Thom staring him in the face. "You can't run from me. Not here, of all places."

Anze turned again, and while Thom did not miraculously appear, that boy's voice dogged his heels. "I've studied every moment of your life, Anze. Watched it three times over."

"We've been here two minutes, boy."

And now Thom emerged in front of him, as if stepping out from behind as curtain. "You think Time means anything here?"

The boy was picking up his powers fast now. Or...or had he

always had this kind of control? Looking through time...was this the same Thom that had brought him here? Or someone much older?

With a flick of his wrist, Thom brought more glass around again —thicker this time, frosted—slinging it between them. Anze turned away from it, and the glass simply rotated with his vision, like it was anchored to his neck. Forcing him to look.

That little boy that Anze one was...had been lashed to a chair. And the boy didn't struggle. The restraints were for him, not to hurt him. With tearful eyes, he silently and dutifully watched as the priests adhered the electrical leads to his chest, shoulders, and face. He looked up at his father, a brave little boy. And his father looked down, with not a small amount of fear.

But not fear for him. Fear of him.

And with the throw of a lever, Anze saw the boy—the teenager—and even the grown man willfully surrender themselves to the torture. His fingers still tingled. Or was it the shock of the batteries dumping through his chest and across his heart again and again?

He had helped strap himself down. He had wanted the curse gone. Maybe, maybe when his father was convinced...

Anze almost laughed, remembering that logic. Whether he was six, thirteen, or thirty-two, it didn't seem to matter. The 'treatments' never provided the results his father wanted, never provided satisfaction.

Sometime around his twenty-sixth birthday, the repeated tortures prematurely grayed him. And after each treatment, he looked up at his father, skin still crackling and blackened...

And his father would turn away.

"You were hurt," Thom solemnly admitted, "tortured, brutalized by cruel and deceitful people."

Oh, he was enjoying this. The sheer irony of it clung to the air. "What do you want me to say?" Anze asked, staring into that glass memory. 'That I haven't come to this very conclusion of my own power sometime in the last decade? 'I have trust issues.' What an epiphany."

"It's not a matter of trust," Thom said. "You trust your officers, your bodyguards, every day."

"Tell me who you trust," Anze said, "that you hide what you can do from them."

And Thom's eyes darkened.

"There are only two of us here," Anze said, gesturing to the nightmarish void. "Only two of us who understand. If they cannot control you, they will destroy you."

Thom huffed, pointing at the mirror. "My father was many things, but he wouldn't have hurt me."

"You think he was so enlightened?" Anze taunted. "Your father was selfish and cold-hearted and—"

"You are *wrong*!" Thom shouted, flexing the full power of his eldritch voice, the full might of it echoing across their void like some distant mountain would shout it back to them. "My father was a foul man! Dismissive, distant. He had very little use for me. And I wanted nothing to do with him. But if he comes to me ready to talk after a year, five, ten—you don't get to decide when I'm ready! You didn't just kill my father—you *took* him from me! Only I get to decide when I'm through with him! Not you!"

Anze scoffed. Thom was still ready to strap himself willfully to the chair, on the off-chance his father might deign to smile or laugh, show some kind of warmth to him. "You cannot comprehend the horror I shielded you from."

The next words that young man said were loud enough to shift entire continents, overturn nations, and splinter mountains. "I didn't ask for your help! I have looked into your entire history, Felix Marchand de Tylmirande—Anze Orchikov, Hephaestus, The Godfather, The Master! You choose a new name whenever the last one exhausts you, but I know them all. And I know your crimes!"

The mirror suddenly flashed through a cacophony of images, so sudden and brief they were, that they dragged up whole new associations. His mother's distance, his siblings' derision. When young Rashida and her flouncing ponytail had been instructed not to associate, when even close family members spoke with pointing and with barely muffled whispers.

"They didn't turn away from you because they feared your Power," Thom said. "You used your Power to make them afraid!"

Anze watched as lights darkened whenever he passed. Locked doors opened at the wave of his hand. Computers would obey him and eventually, even the shocking did nothing. Strapped to his chair and subjected to shocks that dimmed the manor...and Anze just smiled. He looked up at his father with a certain glee in his eye.

Had he done it? Had he finally learned how to harness this power?

But no. Father turned away, more disgusted and horrified than ever.

And the mirror darkened, clearing up to show Thom on the other side. "They shunned you because of you. Not the Power. You've just never been able to distinguish between the two. Your Power has been your entire identity for so long, you don't remember who you were before it."

Felix Marchand was to be shunned, certainly. But only because Thom Hugh brought them here, brought them to the Path, all because...

"You think you're better than me," Anze said, less accusation and more statement of a sad fact. Like Anze pitied him and his foolish assertion. "Like you're *not* using your Power right now—"

"No," Thom said with a shake of his head. "I know what I am, Felix. I know the only thing that separates you and me..."

The mirror flashed again. A seedy little bar on a seedy little world, where Osyen Belt and Jackson Milardi were enjoying a few drinks.

Happier times.

They pointed at a bright young lad, quick on his feet and matted mop of hair, who was bussing tables. The two men were whispering to each other, when some drunken brute of a man threw a mug at the busboy's head, clocking him good. And before the boy hit the ground, Milardi and Belt were on their feet.

They took the lad in.

They tucked him into a bed aboard the *Aurum*. Even had his own room, where he decorated with whatever he could find around the ship.

They fed and clothed him.

And they sat him on the Jump Deck of a starship and showed him the world. Osyen taught him how to palm a coin, and Milardi how to talk smooth.

Then they took on new faces, new adventures. Each an addition in turn. Teaching Thom to drink, dance and sing. Teaching him about love and gossip and craft and life.

The swell of bile in Anze's throat was almost unbearable. What this boy had was privilege, not success. Anze had spared him the pains that Anze had endured. And this boy deigned to assign blame to him?!

"I have built more than you can ever burn," Anze seethed. "I have raised towers and erected cities. I have spurned Evil and cut down the wicked."

"You want a cookie?" Thom asked.

Anze tried to step toward Thomas—but the glass didn't budge. And every time he moved or turned, the glass always blocked his way. Always with something else he didn't wish to see.

A prison.

He was trapped. He pawed at the glass, searching for an edge or seam—but every time he moved in one direction, the glass slid to press him back.

Thom might have spoken with the voice of a young man, but Anze understood the ageless power he was beholding. A boy brought him to this place—but what he spoke to now had seen galaxies forge. "You stand on the Sojourn now, Anze. And here you shall remain. Here you will confront your life's work until I am satisfied."

"I am who I am because you brought me here!"

"You are who you are, Felix," Thom admitted, "and you do have power because of your exposure here." Thom thought for a moment, looking into his side of the glass, at whatever he saw there. Maybe family, or friends, or enormous sums of money. But with a wistful tone, he said, "I am not my power. My friends and family love me because of who I am, not because of what I can do."

"You know what you are!" Anze cursed.

"That's the thing. I have no idea. I don't know who I am or what I'm meant for, if anything at all. I don't think anybody does, Anze! The moment anybody thinks they have it figured out, I guarantee you, they don't! But I know I am something to these people. You only ever saw the Power in me, and assumed we were alike. But I'm nothing like you."

That was it. He was going to do it. Leave Anze here to rot until pity drew him back. Anze pushed on the glass between them, but it didn't budge. "You can't leave me here," Anze whispered.

"I can and I will."

And Anze threw a punch at the glass. It appeared so delicate, like spun sugar. But that sheet of glass took his blow like the hardest steel. Not even a smudge where his knuckles glanced off.

Thom turned away—and Anze's heart broke.

"Don't leave me here!" he shouted, his voice cracking.

"I won't leave for long. Course, the passage of time means...very little here. You will never grow old, you will not hunger, you will not turn ill. But you will spend every coherent moment you have looking at your life. You will watch it, as I did, until you understand."

Anze collapsed in defeat, wilting and drained. "Why don't you just kill me," he demanded through clenched teeth.

The boy could do it, surely. He could do it with a touch of his fingers, drain the life from him, or press Anze through time back to before he ever existed. Or, more simply, drag Anze into the future till even his bones had washed away.

Thom squatted down to his level, hands folded in front of him. "The Thom you met on Farragut...he might have."

"Well, I don't need your mercy!"

"No, Felix," Thom admitted, "you don't. Because you haven't asked for it. When you're ready—and one day, you will be—you will call out from this place, and I will come. And I will listen and judge again. But I cannot give you help unless you ask me for it. And we both know that Anze Orchikov will never ask for help."

CHAPTER 43
THOM

THE WORLD WARPED and boiled around him, the characteristic deep pop. And the emerald glow that blinded him, wrapped his skin in a cold embrace, drifted away. Color returned, delineated outlines of a place tracing themselves in the air that each filled in like oil paints soaking into a canvas.

And he smelt the burning fires and the ozone burn of laser fire.

There had been a battle here.

He stood at the center of a broken laboratory. How had he gotten here? Why not back by the cells? Why here specifically—

"Osyen!"

Thom whirled around to see the captain laid on his back across a table of shattered lab equipment. Rashida hovered over him, panic in her voice. "Osyen, stay with me! Oz!"

Thom rushed over to them, sliding to a stop. Rashida herself was pouring blood on the floor, but she was perched over Osyen—his skin blackening, eyes rolled back.

"What's wrong with him?" Thom asked

"Don't touch him!" Rashida urged. "There's Metal in his hand."

Several shards of Pilgrim Metal had sunk into his flesh, glittering sparks of green light underneath the dark surface. How had Osyen done that? Didn't matter. The Metal was active with Thom nearby, almost singing, little voices to each piece. And each individual shard was connected to the Path—and drawing Osyen there, molecule by molecule.

Thom shouldered Rashida out of the way with enough authority he hoped she'd stay back. Because he had no idea if this was going to work.

He pinched the first shard between his thumb and forefinger. And he pulled, sliding it out of Osyen's hand. "You don't get to go. Not yet, you don't."

So cold, like a burning, but...he remembered that aurora, glowing light that bent around the entirety. How it drew from and gave to itself.

And he pulled the shard out, setting it safely aside, before pulling on another. And as he drew each shard out, one by one, the wound closed behind it.

Rashida watched wordlessly as Thom worked, drawing the jagged pieces from Osyen's hand, until the last one was free. Then Thom swept all six shards up along the surface of the table, into a box and slammed the lid on the container.

"Oz!" Zatia and Adelaide clambered through the wreckage of what had once been a solid concrete wall. "Oz, you okay?!"

Thom watched for any sign of life returning to his captain. Was he okay? Was he too late?

Rashida cupped Osyen's face in her bloody hands, like she was making a wish, laying her own forehead to his.

And he then drew a shallow breath, his chest rising. And he raised his hand up to rub the bridge of his nose. "Rash, you're leaking all over the floor."

And Thom let out a sigh, collapsing with relief across the table. He'd done it. Osyen was safe. They were all safe.

"Thom?" He heard the rasp of Rashida's voice. Her eyebrows twisted in confusion and even a touch of horror. "How did you do that?"

"Which part?" Thom asked with a cough. "'Cause the answer's going to be a shrug to basically all of it."

He had more than a few questions himself. How had he Jumped? How was that possible?! How could he touch the Metal safely and others just...are drained by it?

Rashida slipped her hand into Osyen's, giving it a squeeze, but her eyes never left Thom. "How...did you do that?" she repeated.

There was no denying what she was referring to. Thom hadn't just removed the shards from Osyen's hand, but in doing so, had actually *undone* the injury. The wasting had not consumed him, but had retreated completely, leaving not a trace of it left on his skin. Not even the puncture wounds where they had once sat.

Thom healed him.

"I don't know," Thom muttered, "but I couldn't watch and do nothing."

Osyen's head rolled to one side, looking at the dead doctor nearby with a wistful regret. "You did good," he muttered.

Zatia and Adelaide finally made it closer, running up to Osyen's side. "Thom! Where the Hell have you been?"

Thom chuckled. An apt question. If he had been anywhere, it might've been literal Hell. It might have been a physical place. Who knew?

But that question didn't get an answer, because Zatia immediately moved on to the more urgent and dramatic problem at hand. "Rash! Holy—we need to get you to an AutoDoc!"

"Where's Anze?" Adelaide demanded, grimacing through her own pain.

That part Thom could answer, however cryptically. "Anze won't be a problem anymore."

"Did you kill him?" Osyen asked, slurring his words in exhaustion.

"No," Thom said, quickly adding, "least, I don't think I did. But he won't bother anyone ever again."

Adelaide blinked. "Well, that's vague and unhelpful."

"If you know where he is, let's go pay him a visit," Zatia growled.

Rashida slipped off of the table and staggered over to Thom and then past him. She walked through the lab, and up to where Thom had first appeared. She was looking down...

At a small marble of Pilgrim Metal that laid on the ground. And she looked over at Thom, true horror cementing in her eyes.

"Let's get him to the ship and get out of here," Zatia said, grabbing Osyen roughly.

"No," Thom said, raising a hand. "Get it spooled up and ready to go. But we have one more stop."

———

Rashida got herself cleaned and her wound packed, enough at least to help Osyen to the door. A simple apartment in the Installation. Featureless, nondescript. It was one door of hundreds, but this door... this door was a long time coming.

"We don't have to open it," Thom said. "But I thought you deserved to see it, at least."

His mother's home.

Osyen swallowed hard. "She's in there?"

Confirmed, Lily said, *she is alarmed by the noises, with a heart rate over 150, but otherwise healthy.*

He looked down at Thom, wary and uneasy. "Do you know what's going to happen?"

Thom shook his head. "I know that you have family. No matter what."

Osyen nodded, drawing himself as high as he could to face this moment. "Open the door."

The door hushed aside at his order, Lily bypassing every security check. It was a simple but not inelegant room, with a private kitchenette and plenty of storage—even a genuine bookcase stacked with bound tomes, their spines fresh and strong. Quite an expensive stack there.

And the woman inside rolled away from her bed, where she had clearly been sheltering during the chaos. She put her back to the wall, with a wood chisel in hand.

A wood chisel. Osyen's eyes caught on that and locked there for a moment, sniffling something out of his nose.

She looked so much like him. A strong streak of pearl white striped through her hair in a few places, but it added to her dignity. She was a sturdy build too, like her son, with a square set jaw and solid shoulders. She looked like someone had sculpted her from marble, an example of ancient art and nobility, even in her fear.

And that fear did not paralyze her. "You can take what you want, but you're making a mistake."

"Catharina Batahr?" Thom asked, like he was about to interrogate her.

And she jutted her chin in response. "What does it matter? The Godfather will bury you for this."

Thom looked up—and lo-and-behold, that damn logo was etched into the ceiling. He really wanted everyone to know where they stood in the world.

"Anze Orchikov is gone," Osyen said quietly, like he was trying to soothe a wild animal.

And she withered a bit at that news but kept her stance. Osyen took a step into the room, slowly at first, waiting to see if she'd object. But she didn't say a word.

"You don't sound like..." he paused, clearing his throat. "Sorry. I didn't remember your voice had th-that pitch to it."

"Do I know you?" Catharina asked.

"Yeah," Osyen said, cautious but half-smiling. "I was a bit shorter then, but.. fourteen years, give or take."

It dawned on her, but based on the tone of voice, it wasn't a pleasant discovery. "Brogan?"

"Hi, Mom." Osyen's voice cracked as he tried not to openly cry. "I'm sorry."

"You're sorry?" Catharina whispered, her face twisting into anger. "You're *sorry?*"

Osyen blinked, confused. "Yeah."

"What have you done?" she demanded.

Which almost knocked Osyen clean over. He couldn't even bear the weight of the question, let alone find a suitable answer.

So she pressed. "Fourteen years. I worked my way back into the graces of my colleagues, only to find that they carried on with the research privately! Fourteen years, those bastards took from me. They took my reputation, took my name off of everything. Do you know how much work I put into climbing back up?!"

"You don't have to anymore," Osyen said.

"I *wanted* this!" she shouted back, pointing toward the labs. "This was my life's work, there, in that room!"

Rashida recoiled from the shouting, hands folded across her front. She knew where this was heading, and she bit her lip to keep silent.

"The Empire took us," Osyen said, "separated us."

"We were criminals," Catharina retorted. "There was never any doubt of that. But what could have gone away quiet was suddenly a nightmare!"

Osyen coughed like she'd struck him. "I was ten years old. I was trying to protect you!"

"Well, top marks! You destroyed my career—and looks like, did a good number on yourself!"

Thom glanced around her room. She might have more on her lab desk—if it was still standing. But he saw several digital pictures on the walls. Catharina receiving her doctorate, on digs with Ordee. Not one picture of her son—or spouse, for that matter.

Just her and her work. Oh no. This was about to spiral.

"What was the crime? You-you covering for Ordee's bullshit?" Osyen asked.

That was a soft spot. She actually came off the wall on that one, jabbing a finger in his direction. "Ordee is a good man!"

"He's dead now," Osyen blurted without blinking, "died full of guilt over what he did to you. Blamed himself for everything."

And Catharina shook her head, disgusted. "You killed him?"

"No! No, he died—"

"I cannot believe this!"

"The Imps took us—"

But she cut him off. "The Empire is just. I asked for no considerations and expected none. I performed my service and rejoined society —but clearly, you couldn't. You've ruined everything!"

Thom saw it play out on his friend's face. Osyen couldn't ask the question he wanted to ask. Why hadn't she come looking for him? Why hadn't she done this, why hadn't she come to save him, come to save her son?!

He was starting to blame her.

So instead, he asked something else. "You just...what, you just *worked* for them for the last fourteen years?"

"I did my duty."

"Your duty to *what*? What about your duty to—" He stopped himself, choking back the hatred cutting loose.

"I don't have a son," Catharina spat. "Not for at least fourteen years now. He died, you see."

And Osyen's eyes went dark. "Well then...was that what they told you?"

"Attacking a peace officer is a Capital offense," she said with disdain and a rise to her brow. She said that with no small amount of hatred herself.

"You were charged and convicted of your crime," Rashida confirmed, "but as a *boy*, his crime was worse than yours?"

"Mine was foolish, his was violent," Catharina said. "I'm not sure how else to explain this to you."

"Horrible," Osyen said, "for a son to protect his mother from monsters."

"And they died protecting me from you. Do the math."

That was it, right there. She'd picked her side. And her side was her country, her government. She'd long ago buried whoever Osyen had once been. Maybe too afraid to lose her status, or maybe she'd just plain bought the party line—Brogan Batahr was dead, no matter who Osyen Belt claimed to be. Maybe she'd had a funeral, a memorial service.

This was Anze's ultimate revenge. He'd give Osyen his mother, but she didn't want him. Osyen would have lost everything and gained nothing. Anze knew this—and he'd have twisted the knife before killing Osyen in the darkest moment.

That son of a bitch.

"Leave my home," Catharina demanded in quiet authority, "whoever you are."

Osyen's lips pursed, like he had more to say. But nothing. He simply nodded and turned away. They retreated out her door, and when the lock clicked into place, Osyen drew a ragged breath.

Rashida didn't know what to say. So she just laid a hand on his shoulder. He didn't react. His face screwed, twisted up into a mess of emotions, lips pulled tight and cheeks puffed.

And then finally, he exhaled and looked straight at her. "I'm going to burn it down, Rash. The Empire, the Dunsweir. All of it."

"I know," she whispered, a quiet affirmation.

Osyen snorted, like a bull accepting a challenge. And he looked at Thom. "Find me people who can help me do this."

EPILOGUE

THOM

BREAKING through the blockade of Ilum was a trivial matter. It might've been the same make, but the new *Aurum* had entirely different—and criminally supplied—transponders. They were briefly questioned and set free.

It took two weeks, and more than five Jumps to find what Thom was looking for.

"This is *Tartarus* ATC," the voice on the radio stated with alarming intensity. "Proceed to grid mark Four-Two-Seven-Charlie for inspection by Combat Air Patrol. Confirm?"

"Confirm," Roche said, "Four-Two-Seven-Charlie for inspection."

"I think it's funny that they call it 'air patrol', when we're in outer space," Zaria said.

"You knew what they meant, didn't you?" Osyen grunted.

The *Aurum* was considerably larger than in its past life, but that titan was still the biggest thing in the Imperial sky. It was a floating city—almost literally—with spires that stretched high overhead, and an armored dome underneath. This ship was a fleet unto itself and if it appeared over your skies, leaning its armored belly towards you like an artificial moon, you knew that you had invoked the wrath of God.

Rashida leered up at the enormous dreadnought that loomed over their freighter. "You're sure this is wise, Thom?"

Osyen peered at the holographic display floating in front of his captain's chair. He snagged it from the air, pinching the image to get a better look at it. "Looks like it took torpedo hits?"

"Atmospheric scoring along the keel," Lily noted. "Along with battle damage on the stern. Multiple hull breaches scattered throughout."

"That ship's been through Hell," Adelaide grunted.

"And it's not running Imperial IFF," Roche added.

Zatia leaned over Osyen's chair, squinting. "Did somebody try to take that monster planet-side?"

"Their navigator is trash," Adelaide chided before allotting for the obvious. "Or something really bad happened. A few times."

"That's an Imperial warship," Thom assured them, "but you won't find Imperials up there. You wanted friends to help you take on the Empire? Here they are. Rogues and renegades, the lot of 'em."

"Anze had mentioned somebody attacked Akagi Station a bit ago," Osyen said. "These the same people?"

Thom hemmed and hawed before simply saying, "Yeah, basically. It's more complicated, but yes."

Osyen chucked the hand-held hologram, watching it seesaw back into place over its projector before sighing. "You heard the lad. Take us in."

The *Aurum* presented itself for inspection by a pair of Bearcats. It was a tense moment before they cleared the ship for approach and guided the freighter up to dock in the *Tartarus's* belly.

The inside of the ship didn't look much better than the outside. Crews were skittering about, pushing crates of gear. Ragtag soldiers stood their posts, most of which were still wearing their blood-soaked bandages. One crew of engineers were busily trying to cut a jockey out of their damaged fighter, the woman patiently waiting inside her bubble—if more than a little unnerved by whatever had happened.

The crew of the *Aurum* gingerly walked down the gangway to a welcome committee of armed soldiers, led by a tall officer with a shaved head and the most magnificent beard Thom had ever seen. A groomed and majestic thing. His voice, while stern, lacked the resonance of someone possessing that enchanted facial hair. "Which one of you is the captain?"

Osyen raised his hand and winced in pain. "That'd be me."

"Good to meet you. I'm Trevor Lindell, XO of the *Tartarus*. Apologies, the admiral couldn't be here to meet you in person."

Zatia huffed, taking in the surrounding sight. "Is he still in one piece?"

"Osyen Belt," a voice called out across the hangar deck.

Polished riding boots, heels clicking across the floor. A single green eye like an emerald gem socketed into her head, with radiant red hair draped over her face in a bloody veil. "Thought I recognized that ship, but no. That's a 31-GDT. Gross."

"Fiona?" Osyen asked, breathless.

The pirate queen, Master of the Boolean Edge, smiled wide with charm and pleasure, her fluorescent red hair standing out amongst the drudgery brown and grays of Imperial uniforms that roamed the deck. She still wore her knee-high boots—and had a slick new prosthetic arm: military-issue.

She had been through Hell and high water to get here. But then, so had they.

"In the flesh." Fiona looked Osyen up and down, taking her turn to assess his new outfit, special attention to the absent arm. "You look like shit."

Something in Osyen's eyes came undone, waterworks sparkling. And he marched over, grabbing her hard and pulling her into a hug.

She laughed, clapping him on the back. "I missed you too, Oz."

"We thought you were dead," Osyen said.

Fiona smirked, her eyebrows bouncing around her head with some inside joke. "You wouldn't be the first."

"I'm confused," Roche said with a raised hand. "Last time we saw you, you tried to kill us."

"We left you behind to your turf war with the Navy," Adelaide snarked.

"Didn't go well," Fiona said. "Shoulda figured, right?"

"And yet," Rashida noted, "now you're standing in the belly of an Imperial dreadnaught—however scuffed its appearance—and nobody's even shooting at you."

Fiona looked away, plenty of memories flowing. "Yes, well, the fight's not over. But I am singing a new song."

"No brass quintet?" Thom asked with a smirk.

"Fuck you, by the way," she said, playfully pointing at him. "They were very good."

"Absolutely irreplaceable."

"It's been a struggle without them." Fiona waved some help over. "My friend here needs most of a new torso. Can we help him out?"

Crew members pushed on up to see to each of the newcomers, pressing ration bars into their hands, and a medical team wheeled out their equipment to see to the wounded. The *Tartarus* deck chief was already checking over the new *Aurum* with curiosity, whistling softly to himself. This little ship had broken a blockade, and had only carbon scoring to show for it?

Thom slipped away from all the commotion, tucking himself against one of the pillars that divided the giant bay into its three spaces. He was out of the way here, and less likely to get stepped on while the others were seen to.

A short woman led Osyen to a bench with the firm temperament of a doctor and a soothing voice. She sat the scoundrel down, popping out a small drone from her pack. It chirped happily and began to buzz around the air, scanning him from head to toe—kicking out a dozen or so alarms.

Thom noticed that she wasn't wearing the same slate gray that the rest of the crew was. She wore the most battered brown jumpsuit —one of a Capital Criminal. Now liberated. Interesting.

They were rebels. Fighting battles Thom hadn't even been aware of.

The woman shook her head, reading Osyen's results. "You broke pretty much everything of value."

"And a few things I forgot I had," Osyen grunted.

"It's a miracle you're walking and talking," she said, pressing a few pills into his hands. "Do less of it."

Osyen smirked at that. "Yes, ma'am."

"What did I just say?"

And she turned—revealing the shoulder emblem, where any other uniform would've held the Imperial Orchid. Someone had roughly torn it off. Every single officer on the deck had done the same. Instead, they wore three numbers on the shoulder, a new patch crudely stitched: 626.

Those numbers coincided not with a cause, but with a single man.

"Aaron?" Thom whispered.

"You haven't met him yet."

Thom looked up to see a man that could only be described as narrow, like under-baked bread, or like someone had let the air out of him. He walked with a curious gait, stilted, like one leg was shorter than the other. But his brown hair was full of volume and feathered, hanging low across his gaunt cheeks. An awkward, crooked smile inched part way up his face.

And the voice sounded familiar. "He's a very nice man, if a tad peculiar. I only saw him the once."

The statement came out of Thom's mouth like an accusation. "You're the one from my dreams."

"Well, y'see," the man started, "I-I spent a good long time uh, how to—I was sort of in all places, all at once for...a while?" He pressed his hand to his chest apologetically. "We haven't really met. But also we have...a couple times. It's kind of a loopy back and...forth." He paused, hearing his own awkward phrasing sting his ears. "Let me start over: yes."

Okay, so the dreamwalker he'd been chatting with for six months was super awkward in person. Fun.

369

"You walked me through my visions," Thom said, like he was fishing for confirmation. "Every time I dreamt, we'd get to talk?"

"I mean, not *every* time. But yes, that part. That's complicated. I wouldn't call it talking, really," the man said, running a hand stiffly through his hair. "I'm Hirochi Kaneda, by the way."

"Are you also..." Thom glanced around for anybody listening too closely. "...one of the special people?"

"I'm only very loosely a person," Kaneda said quickly, like he was telling himself a joke. "But I like to think most people are special. To somebody."

"Uh-huh," Thom grunted, "but you know who I am?"

And Kaneda swallowed. "More than most people do, anyway. I'm glad you're actually speaking to me...after the last time. I'm—sorry about your father. I can't say he was a good man, but...he *was* your father."

"Thank you." Thom didn't really know what else to say to that.

"My father died two hundred years ago," Kaneda muttered, "so I don't really remember what it was like."

Sorry, what. Thom's brain had to hard reset after that sentence. "You blew right past the relevant piece of information in that sentence. Did you say 'two hundred years ago?'"

"I did, yes."

Thom blinked at that. "How old are you?"

"I don't know how best to answer that question. Are you asking my age? Or when was my birthday?"

"Those two answers are different?"

"Like I said...it's complicated."

"Are you..." Thom stopped himself short, thinking of that piercing cold call from the Icon, from the Metal, from that cursed void that he left Anze in. What was he even going to ask? What would even be the answer? What would that answer mean? "Are you Touched by the Pilgrim?"

Kaneda's smile slipped, but a great weight came into his eyes, his voice humming low from his chest. "No. I'm something else entirely."

Kaneda pointed back toward the door out of the hangar. "She is Touched."

Thom followed his gaze. A woman seemed to appear where he pointed, and Thom wasn't sure how he could have missed her before. She cleared six feet tall, broad shouldered, her Imperial uniform ragged and torn. Her long black hair fell down only one side of her head, like the other side had been burned off. And her fists seemed perpetually clenched, her eyes tracking the newcomers with suspicion—and yet she had the dumbest, emptiest smile on her face, approachable and a tad goofy.

And the flicker of yellow to her eyes: an Oskie. Fantastic.

But there was also something different about her, elemental. Loose, the way water flowed and fire curled, a spring to her feet but the stability of metal. Most Oskies had a military rigidity. She had... something else.

And he caught the faintest warp in the surrounding air, like a mirage on desert sands. Or like she was faintly smoking.

"I'm only here because of her," Kaneda said. "She saved my life. And she knows my story better than I do, I'm afraid."

"Adrianna Riley," Thom whispered in quiet awe. "Older sister to Marcus Riley. Orbital Strike Command. Lieutenant Commander, Mobile Task Force Artemis."

He could feel her missions play out for him like a gut punch, in the time of a single heartbeat. He felt her friends die, her missions explode, and her loyalties crack. She fought assassins and machines, royalty and criminals. And she could melt the world with enough time and patience, two things she had very little of.

There was no use hiding from the eyes of an Oskie. He knew she'd hear him, no matter how loud he said it. Her eyes tracked on to him, her chin jutting out in recognition.

And she stomped over like he invited her. Thom was instantly hot under the collar, nervous, sweating. But she stopped a respectful distance away, assessing him in silence.

No expression but that doofy smile, no affirmation but a tiny squeeze at the corner of her eyes, the raising of her thick eyebrows. Her voice sounded annoyed, but her face said quite pleased. "Oh, good. More weirdos. We got a full set now."

"You're no friend to the Empire, I take it?" Thom asked.

"Not for a little while," she said with loaded irony. She looked aside, up to the *Aurum*, and the tone of her voice didn't match the gravity of what she said next. "You ready to blow up civilization, kid?"

She said it with enough confidence—he actually believed they could do it. Planet by planet, battle by battle. They were sitting in the belly of one of the most impressive war machines built by human hands, surrounded by people whose stories probably mirrored their own—everyone abused and discarded by an Empire that no longer cared.

"Easier said than done," he countered.

"No," Adrianna said, with a hint of whimsy, "but it *is* going to be that much fun."

THE END

———

Meet the Final Hero of the Capital Adventures
with ***Adrianna Riley***
and see her adventures
in

The Iron Service

AFTERWORD

If you're looking for more thrills, the companion series, *The Blood Service Trilogy*, follows other events in the Capital-verse.

If you're enjoying the Capital Adventures, please leave a review. It really helps small authors like myself.

Signing up for the Newsletter keeps you on top of the latest news around the Capital-verse.

I also have a cat. I will likely be dropping pictures of her there regularly, as she is a consistent part of my office day. She is bad at being a cat, but she is fat and good and adorable. Sign up and see!

https://www.authorivers.com/

ABOUT THE AUTHOR

Allen Ivers started writing original stories at the ripe age of eleven, largely trying to figure out why the Disney villains on the television box were the way they were. Villains, monsters, and politicians have always fascinated him with their behavior. Twenty years later, he's still fascinated by bad people and the bad things they do.

This series began as a whiskey-fueled rant about cabin boys on space pirate ships, and the contrast of sea life to space travel in popular media. And its has blossomed into an examination of faith, religion, and the power of family.

The adventures of Thom, Osyen & the crew of the *Aurum* are obviously far from over.

Allen now lives in beautiful Juneau, AK where he is somewhere at the bottom of the food chain. You can find his thoughts about writing, politics, and the odd cute cat on his Twitter.

ALSO BY ALLEN IVERS

THE CAPITAL ADVENTURES

EACH TRILOGY CAN BE ENJOYED INDEPENDENTLY, OR READ AS PART OF THE LARGER SERIES

Book 1: The Blood Service: Book One of the Military Sci-Fi Adventure

Book 2: The Ranks of the Blood Service: Book Two of the Military Sci-Fi Epic

Book 3: Command of the Blood Service: Book Three of the Military Sci-fi Epic

———

Book 4: The Gold Service: A Space Outlaw Action Adventure

Book 5: The Cost of the Gold Service: The Sci-Fi Action Adventure

Book 6: The Powers of the Gold Service: The Sci-Fi Action Adventure

———

Book 7: The Iron Service: A Super Soldier Sci-Fi Adventure

Other Sci-Fi Adventures

Manifest Destiny: A First Contact Sci-Fi Thriller